Alison Stuart

HEADLINE

First published in 1997 by
HEADLINE BOOK PUBLISHING

First published in paperback in 1997
by HEADLINE BOOK PUBLISHING

10 9 8 7 6 5 4 3 2 1

ISBN 0 7472 5556 3

Typeset by
Letterpart Limited, Reigate, Surrey

Printed and bound in Great Britain by
Caledonian International Book Manufacturing Ltd, Glasgow

HEADLINE BOOK PUBLISHING
A division of Hodder Headline PLC
338 Euston Road
London NW1 3BH

Dedicated to the memory of my mother Edith. She never made a drama out of a crisis and was always there to give a helping hand. Her fortitude and service to others was an example to us all.

A special thank you to my editor, Andi Blackwell, for your advice, enthusiasm and encouragement; you bring out the best in me.

And to Len Thurston for yet another wonderful cover. You always do me proud.

Apologies and love to Colin, my very special step-brother, who is not at all like Giles Warden. And so I don't get struck off my brother Alan's Christmas card list, having just mentioned Colin – love, as always, to him.

And last but never least, special wishes to my readers who make it all worthwhile. May we ever count our blessings and know contentment in our lives.

PART ONE
1935

When lovely woman stoops to folly
And finds too late that men betray,
What charm can soothe her melancholy,
What art can wash her guilt away?
The only art her guilt to cover,
To hide her shame from every eye,
To give repentance to her lover,
And wring his bosom – is to die.

Oliver Goldsmith

Chapter One

'Bad blood will out. You'll rue the day you got involved with Harold Warden, Alice!' The voice of Uncle Clarence bellowed from behind the closed door of the sitting room.

Bethany Masterton dropped her satchel in the hall. Her slender figure bristled with anger. Couldn't Uncle Clarence see that by his bullying he was pushing her mother into this marriage? She suspected it was partly to escape Clarence's dominance that her mother had accepted Harold Warden's proposal.

'Leave Mother alone.' Bethany burst in on them and confronted the arrogant man standing by the black marble fireplace. Her sixteenth birthday might still be a month away in May and she was aware that elders should be treated with respect, but seeing her mother close to tears, she accused, 'You're always interfering, Uncle. Why must you upset my mother?'

He rounded on her, his face flushed and his eyes hostile. His feet were planted firmly apart on the Persian rug and his anger dissipated the cosiness of the cream and red sitting room. He tugged at his greying goatee beard. The prosperity of recent years had thickened his stocky figure. At nearing fifty he no longer dirtied his hands by labouring. Her father, who had been three years his junior, had never been above rolling up his sleeves and teaching the apprentices in their building company new skills.

Clarence Masterton pinned her with his contemptuous glare. 'You're an insolent and ungrateful child. How dare you speak to your betters like that?'

From beneath the sofa her black and white spaniel, Jasper, growled a warning and wriggled out to stand protectively by his young mistress's side. Bethany lifted a black brow and bit her lip to keep silent. Her uncle was a bully. She wasn't afraid to stand up to him. She'd been doing so since she was twelve when her father had died. Edward Masterton had been run down and killed by a drunken driver outside the builder's yard he owned in partnership with Clarence.

Her uncle's thin lips drew back into a sneer. 'I've only your mother's welfare at heart. Alice is a weak fool,' he declared. 'As my dead brother's executor it's my duty to advise her.'

'I think you should leave, Uncle Clarence.' Bethany controlled her temper.

Her mother was dabbing at her eyes and, strengthened by her daughter's presence, rose to face her tormentor. 'You've made your views clear and I find them offensive. Please leave.'

He glowered at both women. 'The day Alice marries Warden I wash my hands of her. I'll have nothing to do with that man or his misbegotten family.' His scowl turned on Alice. 'He's after your money. And foolish woman that you are, you can't see it.'

Clarence thrust his face close to Alice's, his stance bullying. Jasper growled louder. Her face pale, Alice retorted, 'My life is my own to do with as I will.'

'Then on your head be the consequences,' Clarence snapped.

He knocked Bethany off balance as he shouldered past her, and the spaniel darted forward to snarl at his heels. 'Get that damned dog away from me.'

Bethany hooked her fingers in the dog's collar. 'He's only defending his own. He wouldn't hurt anyone unless provoked.' Ordering the dog to stay she followed her uncle into the hallway. Bethany had her own qualms about Mr Warden who was paying court to her mother.

She stifled her irritation at her uncle's bombastic manner. 'Why do you dislike Mr Warden so much, Uncle? Why is his family misbegotten?'

He glared at her. She thought he would ignore her impertinence at questioning him. But she needed to know if her own disquiet was unfounded. Uncle Clarence was capable of disliking Mr Warden purely because her mother had chosen him over the men he had introduced Alice to.

'Bad blood by all accounts,' he proclaimed. 'Warden's mother ran off with a coalman. That's how common they are.'

Bethany had other reasons for disliking Harold Warden but she did not judge him by his background. Uncle Clarence was a snob. He chose to forget that his own father had been a tiler all his life and lived in a rented house. Her grandfather had been a parsimonious man. He never drank. Never smoked. Never spent a penny if he could help it. On his death his savings of a hundred pounds had set Clarence and her father up in business. They worked hard and prospered during the building boom in the late twenties when new houses were built on the outskirts of London.

'Mr Warden is an accountant and he's on the local council. He's hardly common, as you call him,' Bethany placated, still hopeful for reassurance.

Uncle Clarence's attitude remained disdainful. 'My advice is clearly not valued by your mother. She'll regret marrying that man. And she needn't think that she can come running back to me when she realises her error. I'll have nothing to do with anyone associated with that family.'

He marched out of the house leaving Bethany more anxious than ever that her mother had made a serious mistake.

Troubled, she retraced her steps to put her arms around Alice who was holding her head in her hands. At thirty-six her mother was still a beautiful woman, as darkly exotic as a Spanish Condesa for all she was entirely English. Her short black hair softly waved back from her oval face with its high cheekbones. Everyone said how alike mother and daughter were, but Bethany's hair instead of smoothly waving was riotously curly. It cascaded around her shoulders with the abandonment of a gypsy girl's and echoed the wildness in Bethany's spirit. Both women had the same startling violet-tinted eyes.

'Why must Clarence always be so objectionable?' Alice said, composing herself.

Bethany restrained a sigh. It was difficult to accept that another man was about to replace her father in her mother's life. And such a man as Harold Warden . . . He was so prim and correct, so devoid of humour . . .

'I know Uncle Clarence is a bit of a stuffed-shirt . . .'

'Bethany, that is no way to speak of him,' Alice remonstrated though her lips twitched with amusement.

'Well, he is,' she pursued. 'But you're not marrying Mr

Warden just because Uncle Clarence wants to control everything you do, are you?'

Alice widened her eyes and looked flustered. 'I'm marrying Mr Warden because he's a decent and good man.' Seeing the pain in her daughter's eyes, she said more gently, 'Life goes on. Your father has been dead for three years and I mourned him deeply. I'm a woman who needs a husband.'

She touched Bethany's cheek. 'You're more independent than me. You've your father's wisdom and strength.'

'But why Mr Warden?' Bethany persisted. 'There have been other men interested in you. Aunt Enid has introduced you to a half dozen at least.'

Alice stiffened. 'They were nice enough but hand-picked by Enid and Clarence as men they could control. That's why he doesn't like Mr Warden.' She gave a hollow laugh. 'Harold was instrumental in blocking Clarence's latest building development which would have meant knocking down a row of historical almshouses. The almshouses have been saved and turned into a museum.'

That explained her uncle's antagonism towards Harold Warden, but it did not dispel Bethany's unease. After her father's death a bleakness had touched her life. She had adored him. Father was everything that Harold Warden was not: kind, easy going, fun and loving – her hero. A future which contained Harold Warden disturbed her. She didn't know why, she was still too young to trust her intuition.

Alice Masterton pressed a hand to her brow. 'Be happy for me, my dear. The marriage is set for the first Saturday in June. That's six weeks' time. On Sunday you will meet his family. It will be nice for you to have a sister. Louise is only three years older than you. There is also her twin brother Giles.' Her face saddened. 'I always wanted more children. I miscarried twice after you were born.'

Mutiny overrode Bethany's usual compassion. 'Aren't you happy here with me, Mother?'

A frown marred the smooth beauty of her mother's face. 'Of course. It has nothing to do with that. It's not like you to be selfish, Bethany. Mr Warden has been good to you. Look at the presents he has brought you.'

Bribes, Bethany silently judged. Presents to show her mother how caring he was towards the daughter. Presents suitable for the child he thought could be won over by a fluffy toy dog, or a book she had read three years previously. Presents to show her that he regarded her as too young to have any importance. Children should be seen and not heard, Harold had once commented tartly when Bethany voiced an opinion which contradicted his own.

Bethany was no child despite her youthful years. After the death of her father, she had shed her childhood. She had contained her grief, locking it deep inside. She had been aware how inadequately her mother was coping. Alice had no head for finances. Bethany tried to shoulder some of the responsibilities by reminding her mother when the bills were due. She hated the way Uncle Clarence and Aunt Enid had sought to dictate to Alice. Why couldn't her mother see that Harold Warden was just as manipulative? He cloaked it in charm and concern. Bethany resolved not to be domineered by Harold Warden. If her future stepfather saw a girl who could be duped, then he had made a grave error.

Her distrust scrolled around her heart making it pound painfully. It wasn't the inappropriateness of the presents he gave her, it was the coldness in his eyes as he handed them to her. The gift was for the benefit of her mother not herself. Mr Warden did not like Bethany and the feeling was mutual.

Bethany's eyes flashed with ire. She resented the way that he had walked around a room touching the expensive ornaments and silverware. His touch defiled the possessions and home which her father had built for his new bride. Did Harold Warden view her mother as another possession?

Alice Masterton held out her hands and Bethany moved into her arms. Bethany was already two inches taller than her mother. 'I want to do what is right.' There was a plea in Alice's voice. 'Secure our future. In a few years you will be married and I will be alone. Mr Warden is a good man. I miss your father so much. No one can replace him, but . . .' She broke off to gaze into Bethany's violet eyes. 'It's not easy being a widow . . .'

Bethany knew that the years since her father's death had been hard for her mother. Alice was so kindly and gentle, the only child of a widower politician. Grandad had died a year before Bethany's father. Throughout her life Alice had been pampered. First by her father, then her husband. Edward Masterton was twenty-six when he met Alice. She was sixteen. She was his first serious girlfriend. Until then he had been busy working long hours to make a success of his building business, ploughing every penny of profit back to buy more land and build more houses. They had not married until this house in Leytonstone was ready to move in to.

That was the trouble. Until Edward's death Alice had never had to worry about money or make an important decision. She was content in her role of wife and mother and assured of financial security. When she was pitched into dealing with everyday expenditure she was hopelessly out of her depth. Within six months of her husband's death, Alice had been bullied by Uncle Clarence into selling her half share of the building business to him.

Bethany was convinced that her uncle and his grasping wife Enid had cheated her mother by paying her less than the half share was worth. Not that they were poor. Her father had left them financially comfortable. It was when seeking advice how best to invest the money from the business that Alice had gone to the accountant Harold Warden. It was her one act of rebellion against Clarence who had insisted she use a rival company. A year ago Harold Warden's wife had died. Since then he had often visited Alice to discuss business and several times he had taken Alice to the theatre or to dine.

Alice had basked in his attention. At first Bethany was delighted to see her mother happy again, but it was not long before she suspected that Harold's charm was only skin deep.

Sensing Bethany's distress Alice put her hand to her daughter's cheek. 'Harold is a man of position in the community. I don't want to spend the rest of my life alone or worrying about finances.'

'Does Mr Warden make you happy, Mother?'

'Of course. And although we shall move to his home, I have insisted that this house isn't sold. It will be yours when you marry. Until then it will be leased to tenants.'

'But that will mean strangers will live in Daddy's house.' The thought upset her. She loved her home.

'It isn't good for a house to stand empty,' Alice reasoned.

Bethany was being impractical. One day this lovely house would again be her home. Perhaps Mr Warden was not so grasping as she first believed. She conquered her doubts. Her mother's happiness was important. She would withhold her reservations until she met Harold Warden's family.

In her bedroom Bethany took off her green gymslip, white shirt and the hated ankle socks insisted on by the grammar school she attended. She pulled on a maroon skirt and fawn jumper and then ran down the stairs. The moment she lifted the dog's lead from its hook in the kitchen, Jasper barked excitedly.

'Are you going out?' Alice called.

'Just to see Peg and take Jasper on to the common.'

'Be back before it's dark.'

Bethany paused in the garden. The house was secluded, having been built on the site of an old Victorian workhouse. Her father had landscaped the garden with tall trees and shrubs which muffled the sound of the city traffic. A squirrel ran along a cedar branch.

Along the road Bethany saw the willowy figure of Peg Styles waiting by the corner lamppost. Peg was chatting to Frank Hobson. The young man with brown hair looked very dashing in a straw boater, his white coat and navy striped apron starched and spotless. Peg was infatuated with Frank and had been for three years. He was twenty-one and had a reputation for having a different girlfriend each week. He was good looking and quick to tease. He was the eldest of four children and since his father had suffered a severe stroke last year had given up his engineering apprenticeship to help his mother run the corner shop which they owned. As Bethany drew closer she saw the adoring glitter in her friend's eyes as she basked in his attention.

She grinned. Peg would be talking about this meeting for days. She slowed her pace to give her friend more time alone with Frank. He waved to Bethany, then a call from his mother had him hurrying back inside the shop.

'Isn't he gorgeous?' Peg sighed. 'He's going to deliver Mum's order. He said it was too heavy for me to carry. That means I'll see him again this evening.'

Bethany hid a smile as she gazed into her friend's face. Peg was a homely looking girl with mid-brown hair and a peppering of freckles. She had shot up so tall her figure had yet to flesh out into softening curves. They had been best friends since they started primary school. Peg was the funniest and most loving person she knew. It was a shame that in front of Frank Hobson she became shy and tongue-tied and lost all the sparkle which made her so special.

They walked arm in arm to the park with Peg raving about how handsome Frank was and repeating every word he had spoken to her. She ended with a sigh. 'I wish he wouldn't see me as a schoolgirl. What chance do I stand against that Lottie he's going out with who works in the draper's?'

'We know why Frank is going out with Lottie. Why does any man go out with her? She's fast and has a reputation. Let Frank have his fun. Maybe he's just waiting for you to leave school this summer. It won't do his image any good going out with a schoolgirl. By then he'll be ready to settle down.'

She was teasing and regretted it as she saw the longing in Peg's expression. 'Do you think so? I'd wait for ever for him. But who'd go out with a beanpole like me? I wish I had your looks. Loads of boys have asked you out. You never accept.'

Bethany answered, dismissively, 'Only three. I didn't fancy any of them. The last one was Toby the Tuba. He's fat and spotty.'

'Give over. There was Adrian, Frank's mate who was in the shop last week. You must fancy him.'

'Adrian is still crazy about Frank's sister Maureen who just ditched him. He was trying to make her jealous.'

They had reached the open ground and she let Jasper off the lead. As she watched him chase a foraging crow, her voice became weighted. 'Mum's going to marry Mr Warden in June.'

The dreamy look faded from Peg's eyes. 'You don't like him, do you?'

'I want Mum to be happy, but there's something about him which makes me uneasy.'

'The wicked stepfather . . .' Peg provoked.

'It's not a joking matter.'

Peg sobered and slipped her arm through hers. 'I'm sorry, Beth.'

Bethany forced a smile. 'At least old Warden lives close enough for us still to see each other.'

'If he doesn't think that a telephonist is too common to mix with the stepdaughter who has her sights set on becoming a doctor. I got that job. Heard this morning. I start as soon as I've finished my exams.'

'That's great news! And don't think that the difference in our occupations will affect us.'

Peg shrugged, her voice heavy. 'And you'll have a family around you. There's his daughter Louise. She went to the convent school that my cousin Mary attended. Very quiet she was. Unlike her brother . . .' She broke off, remembering what her two older brothers had said about Giles Warden. It was all bad. Giles had been drinking in a pub with friends. He'd been the instigator of a fight starting. The moment it came to blows he had slunk out of a back door. He was a nasty piece of work.

Peg held back from telling Bethany. Her friend was troubled enough. Though Bethany rarely spoke of her father's death, she had taken it hard and was fiercely protective of her mother. If Giles Warden tried to bully Bethany, he would be in for a surprise. Bethany wasn't afraid to stand up for herself or what she believed to be right.

'What have you heard about Giles Warden?' Bethany demanded.

Peg shrugged. Bethany had an uncanny way of reading her mind. Under her friend's piercing stare she was compelled to answer. 'Just that he's a bit of a bully and a troublemaker. He dotes on his twin sister. Bit over-protective though. My brothers said that Giles and his mates gave Clive Roberts a going over one night. They stripped him to his underclothes and tied him to the park railings. That was because Clive had walked Louise home from a dance at the Town Hall.'

Bethany's eyes sparked with a violent fire. 'He needn't think he can bully me.'

'It could be that my brothers exaggerated,' Peg said, seeing the strained look on her friend's face.

There was a defiant set to Bethany's shoulders which squeezed at Peg's heart. According to her cousin, Louise was never allowed to mix with the other girls and since she had left the convent she had become her father's house-keeper. Mr Warden didn't approve of women working. Bethany may be a match for Giles Warden, but there were bound to be problems awaiting her if her mother married Harold Warden.

On Sunday Bethany wore her best navy dress, its skirt cut on the bias to fall in folds around her slender hips. Her mother looked glamorous in a wine-red suit with a matching hat tilted at an angle and a net half-veil falling over her upper face. The Warden house was near to Hollow Pond in Leyton. It was a double-fronted, grey stone Victorian edifice set back from the street with a high brick wall all around it.

'Harold did not tell me his home was so grand,' Alice declared.

Bethany was unimpressed. It looked as welcoming as a prison gatehouse. She swallowed against the unease which churned her stomach. Their own house was smaller and less ornate, but it had been built with loving hands in warm russet bricks. It had an atmosphere of love filling it. This house, with its scrolled plasterwork over its mullioned windows and gables, looked overdressed and superficial. Her sharp eyes saw the rust corroding the wrought-iron balustrade outside the bedroom windows. When she tripped on the marble step and her hand touched the stonework to stop herself falling, it was as cold as a spectre's heart.

She shuddered. You're not wanted here, an inner voice warned. Bethany snatched back her hand, annoyed at the sinister fancy. Her eyes narrowed with resolve. She didn't want to be here, but she wasn't going to be intimidated.

The front door was opened by Harold. His eyes lit with admiration as he regarded her mother's elegant appearance. 'My dear, you are most welcome. You look enchanting.'

He did not acknowledge Bethany's presence as he led them into the overfurnished drawing room. A grand piano filled the bay window and a vast Victorian sideboard was burdened with silverware. The high-backed sofa and chairs looked uncomfortable, as though a person was not expected to sit at ease in them for long.

A woman rose from a chair in the darkest corner and clasped her hands tight to her chest. Her tension and nervousness communicated itself to Bethany who smiled at her.

'This is my daughter Louise,' Mr Warden said. 'Louise, this is Mrs Masterton.'

Again Bethany was ignored. Her pride rebelled. She refused to be treated as though she was invisible or unimportant. She smiled at Louise who was of average height and build and wore a nondescript beige dress. Her short straight red hair with a severe fringe did little to flatter her freckled face, but there was kindness behind the nervousness in her spaniel brown eyes. 'I'm Bethany. I'm very pleased to meet you. I hope we'll become friends.'

Louise cast a nervous glance at her father before replying, 'I-I hope so t-too.'

Bethany could never resist helping an injured animal and her compassion mounted for Louise. Before she could put her further at ease, Harold barked out, 'We're ready for tea now, Louise. See to it.'

The young woman scurried out of the room with her head bent in submission. The sight of her made Bethany's eyes narrow with anger. Harold had spoken to his daughter with less respect than he would address a servant. She stared at him as he led her mother to a sofa and sat down beside her.

'It's a pleasure to have you in my home,' he said softly. 'It's been lacking in feminine refinements since my wife passed away and she had been ill for several years. Anything you wish to change, you have but to ask.'

'It is a lovely house,' Alice replied. 'There are some pieces of furniture I'd like to bring here when we marry.'

Harold took her hand and gazed into her eyes. Bethany

turned away. Why couldn't her mother see through his false charm? Any man who treated his daughter the way he did had no regard for women in general. Outwardly he may fawn upon her mother, his manner adoring, but it made Bethany uneasy.

When Louise reappeared struggling under the weight of a silver tray and tea service, Bethany hurried to help her. She lifted the teapot from its stand. 'That lot must weigh a ton,' she observed, intending the comment as a rebuke to Harold.

He glared at her. 'My daughter is not a weakling and is diligent in her duties.'

Bethany's temper simmered and she bit her lip to curb a retort. Alice was watching Louise with concern and said soothingly, 'The silver tea service is lovely but they are heavy. You have set the tray beautifully.'

Louise kept her eyes lowered and bustled from the room. At a nod from her mother, Bethany followed Louise. She found her returning from the kitchen with a four-tier wooden cake-stand and a plate of sandwiches. Bethany took the sandwich plate. 'You'll do yourself a mischief carrying all that.'

'Papa expects his tea to be served quickly with everything brought in at once.'

Her words confirmed Bethany's fears that Harold Warden was an unfeeling tyrant. She kept her opinion to herself, sensing Louise's underlying need to please. Her father did not even look up at her as she placed the cake-stand by the table. He was deep in conversation with Alice and broke off to gesture to the teapot. 'Would you do me the honour of pouring the tea, Alice.'

Louise had reached out to take up the teapot. Blushing crimson she snatched her hand back and hovered uncertainly.

Alice smiled. 'I'm a guest and have no wish to take Louise's place. The tea looks lovely. Did you make the cakes and scones yourself, dear?'

Louise nodded and backed away to perch on the edge of the seat of an armchair like a frightened wren.

Harold was smiling but his eyes were cold as his gaze moved from Bethany to Louise. 'On our marriage this house will have a new mistress. Louise knows her place.'

'As should we all, Pa,' a male voice drawled. Giles leant against the wall, his peat-brown stare insolent as he regarded the Masterton women. He was a striking-looking man at over six foot. His complexion was milky pale and his auburn hair, sleeked back from his temple with brilliantine, was darker than his twin's. The only imperfection to his handsome countenance was the sneer on his full lips.

Unaffected by his good looks Bethany held his stare. There was a flicker of suspicion in his eyes, then he smiled. It held no warmth or sincerity.

'So this is to be my little stepsister?' he drawled. 'Pa did not tell me you are beautiful as your mother. I can't believe you are three years younger than Louise. You look so much older, more sophisticated.'

Bethany didn't like the way he phrased his compliment so that it ridiculed his twin. Louise made a small sound in the back of her throat. She sat stiffly in her chair, her gaze riveted upon the teapot. Why didn't she retaliate? Give her twin as good as he gave her? Louise's lack of spirit troubled Bethany. It sharpened her stare to accusation as she studied Giles. The tautness of his face muscles showed his annoyance that she had not responded favourably to his praise. There was something sinister in his rigid regard. Was that why Louise didn't retaliate? The lines about his mouth changed subtly. The smile was no longer endearing.

It showed cruelty – a need to manipulate and subjugate to his will.

Although her flesh had risen in goosebumps and the fine hairs on her arms and neck prickled with foreboding, Bethany held his challenging glare. She knew that when her mother married Harold Warden her fate would be sealed. She would never submit to either the father or son's tyranny.

Chapter Two

The deed was done. Bethany's life was irrevocably changed. Her mother was now Mrs Harold Warden. Well-wishers gathered around the couple after the wedding breakfast at the church hall.

Bethany stood apart from the gathering, her unease increasing as she scanned the guests. The local member of parliament was in conversation with the mayor and a group of aldermen. There were several church dignitaries including a bishop and a score of wealthy businessmen. They were all people Harold curried favour with. Yet where were the relatives, the people who really mattered? Apart from herself, Louise and Giles, not a single member of either family was present. It filled her with foreboding.

What kind of man was her stepfather? During the last weeks he had been charming and solicitous whenever he called at the house. He had been jovial as he escorted a retired civil servant, just returned from South Africa, who was willing to pay the high rent Harold was charging for her home. He had walked around rubbing his hands with satisfaction two days ago when the furniture van arrived and the expensive furniture belonging to the Mastertons was taken to his house.

The uncomfortable feeling increased as Bethany watched

her stepfather. He was stiff with pride as he chatted with men of importance in the borough: men who could make him richer, men who empowered him when, as an accountant and financial advisor, he handled and invested their fortunes.

But what of the man beneath the veneer? The man who smiled adoringly at her mother and turned a stare of ice upon herself? Her mother had told her that Harold had fallen out with his father and family years ago.

She stamped down her apprehension. Was she letting her dislike for Harold colour her feelings? Hadn't Uncle Clarence and Aunt Enid returned their wedding invitation announcing that there would be no further communication between their families? Alice, who hated dissension, had been distraught.

'Uncle Clarence is being pig-headed,' Bethany counselled. 'Don't let him upset you. You've done nothing wrong.'

For a long moment Alice held her daughter's stare. She reached up and took her face into her hands. 'Sometimes you speak so wisely, I feel that I am the child and you the mother. You have an old head on your shoulders, my darling.'

Yet all Bethany's pleas to her mother not to marry Harold Warden had gone unheeded. When Bethany realised that her mother was in love with the accountant, she no longer tried to reason with her. Alice needed her support not her censure.

Her concentration returned to the wedding celebrations. Alice was now dancing with Harold. Her mother was smiling but the look of gloating satisfaction on Harold's face turned Bethany's stomach. She looked away, searching for Peg in the press of people. Her friend was seated at a table looking ill at ease as did her mother, Gloria. They were invited as Bethany was going to spend the next week with them while her mother and stepfather honeymooned in Brighton.

As Bethany went to join her friend she passed Giles standing protectively beside Louise. Louise was dressed in an unflattering shade of pink which clashed with her fiery hair. Twice Louise had made to move towards the bride and groom and Giles had prevented her.

Bethany felt compassion for her stepsister. Louise had good bone structure and could be attractive with the right haircut, some discreet make-up and dresses which flattered her instead of making her appear gauche. And if Giles did not stand over her like a sentinel she would make more friends.

'Come and meet Louise,' Bethany said to Peg. 'She's shy.'

'I hadn't expected her brother to be so gorgeous,' Peg observed.

'Better looking than Frank?'

'Oh no.' Peg defended her idol and rose to Bethany's teasing. 'Frank is wonderful. Giles may be handsome but he's an arrogant bugger.'

As they approached Louise and Giles, her stepsister smiled tentatively. Giles raised a brow, his dark eyes glittering. 'Little sister, is this your playmate?'

Bethany's violet stare hardened. 'Don't patronise me, Giles. I'm only three years younger than you. I've brought Peg to meet Louise.' She turned her back on her stepbrother and linking her arm through Louise's drew her away from him. 'Louise, I hope that you and Peg will also be friends.'

Louise held out her hand to Peg, her spaniel eyes

lighting with pleasure. Giles coughed and the light in his sister's eyes faded. She looked nervously at him.

'Pa and Alice have finished their dance,' Giles clipped out. 'We must encourage the other guests to dance. Partner me in the waltz.'

His rude tone angered Bethany. She regarded him frostily. 'Surely Louise can miss one dance and talk to Peg.'

Fingers of iron clamped over her wrist. His lips were drawn back into a sinister caricature of a smile. 'Of course, stepsister, dear. How much better for us to lead the dance and show the unity of our family.'

It was a challenge. Although Bethany resented the way he had manoeuvred her, she wasn't going to let him see it. If she showed any weakness now she would forever be at his mercy. Pain was shooting up her arm from his vicious grip but her smile did not waver as he led her on to the dance floor.

The bonecrushing hold moved to her fingers and his calculating gaze was waiting for her protest. Stoically, she bore his punishment for daring to interfere with his wishes.

'Your friends are not suitable company for my sister,' he hissed.

'Peg is from a decent, hard-working family.'

'A working-class family,' he jeered.

'Don't be such a snob,' she flared. 'They're honest and trustworthy. They may not have a house as grand as your father's, but they're generous and warm-hearted people.'

His eyes narrowed. 'Make the most of your stay with them. You won't be allowed to associate with such riff-raff again.'

'I'll never abandon my friendship with Peg, or be told who is acceptable as my friend.'

The pressure on her fingers increased so that she bit the

side of her mouth to stop crying out. 'You must be guided for your own good. Pa will not allow that girl in our house.'

'Then I shall meet Peg elsewhere.'

'My father does not tolerate disobedience.'

She held his stare unflinchingly. 'My mother likes Peg and is very fond of Gloria Styles.'

'Your mother will do as her husband wishes.'

His tone frightened her. The statement was delivered without emotion and with utter certainty.

'You have been allowed too much freedom,' Giles continued. 'That will change. We will not permit you to bring disrepute to our name.'

How dare he lecture her! Her eyes flashed as she confronted him. 'I was brought up knowing the difference between right and wrong and how to behave correctly. Were you? I've heard how you and your drunken friends tormented an old tramp in the park. And what of the shop window which was smashed? Didn't the shopkeeper refuse to serve you while you were intoxicated and using offensive language?'

A flame of pain shot through her fingers as the bones were ground together. She gasped and needed all her willpower not to cry out. Giles pressed his face close to hers. 'Don't get clever with me. I can make your life very unpleasant.'

Harold Warden waltzed past them with Alice. He grinned at Giles. 'Good to see you two getting along so well. Well done, Giles.' He whirled away and lifted a hand to acknowledge a compliment from the mayor.

Bethany snatched her hand from Giles, her voice low and resolute. 'Don't try and bully me. The Mastertons are not women to be bullied so easily.'

When she returned to Peg and Louise, her stepsister looked anxious. 'Giles is angry. What did you say to him?'

'We exchanged a few home-truths and laid down some ground rules for the future.'

Louise paled. 'Don't antagonise him . . .' She faltered as Giles advanced and propelled her on to the dance floor.

Peg whistled softly. 'Conceited ass. That poor woman is terrified of her brother. I wish you didn't have to live in the same house as him.'

So did Bethany. 'I can handle Giles Warden. And I've got a week's grace before I move into that lair of foxes.'

'The description suits your stepbrother, sly and cunning,' Peg chuckled. 'Take care, Beth.'

It was like a holiday spending a week with Peg. Yesterday had been her friend's sixteenth birthday and after months of nagging Gloria had agreed that Peg's present could be a visit to the hairdresser's. Peg had come back with her hair dyed blonde and fashioned into waves to her shoulders. The style and colour transformed her. In her high-heels she paraded before the family.

'You look terrific, Peg,' said Bethany.

'As long as it makes Frank Hobson take notice.'

'I reckon Frank will be taking his place in a long line of admirers,' Bethany teased. She regarded her own ankle socks and grimaced. 'You're not afraid I'll show you up now you've gone all grown up on me? Especially as I'm staying on at school to get my Higher certificate so that I can enter medical college.'

'Give over. You and me will always be mates. Though now with you living with the nobs they won't like you slumming it with me.'

Bethany shook her head. 'I'll never forget my friends. I

hate false airs and graces. The Wardens and their kind can keep their snooty ways. They aren't for me.'

Mrs Styles came into the kitchen with another pile of dirty dishes. 'Why Peg can't wash and talk at the same time beats me. You'll be all night at this rate. And I could be doing with a couple of slices of ham from the corner shop for your dad's lunch box tomorrow.'

Gloria winked at Bethany as Peg bent her head industriously over the sink. Droplets of water splattered her face as she scrubbed at the saucepans in her eagerness to get to the shop and see Frank. Bethany dried the dishes and smiled at Mrs Styles. She loved being in this house which was always filled with laughter. On several occasions this week she had caught Gloria's troubled stare on her. Her brow was furrowed again now.

'Is anything wrong, Mrs Styles?'

'Course not, luv, why should there be? I'll miss you coming round so often now that you live further away.'

'That won't change anything.' Bethany was adamant.

'You know where we are if you need us.' Mrs Styles left the kitchen apparently satisfied she had said her piece. Her words made Bethany uneasy.

'We'll take Jasper for a walk and get the ham on the way home,' she said to Peg.

'If we're going to the shop I'm going to change my blouse,' Peg announced, before sprinting up the stairs.

Mrs Styles waylaid Bethany in the narrow hall. 'You won't let Peg spend all night hanging round that shop, will you? Much as I like Frank, he's too old for her. He ain't ready to settle down. I wouldn't like our Peg doing anything foolish.'

Upstairs they could hear Peg singing the popular tune 'Anything Goes'.

'Peg isn't flighty, Mrs Styles.'

Gloria squeezed Bethany's arm affectionately. 'She has your steadying influence to thank for that. Most of her friends have their head filled with boys and marriage. Sadly, with the best will in the world, you won't be seeing so much of Peg now. There's a lot of studying to do if you intend to be a doctor. Once Peg gets her weekly wage packet she'll be out enjoying herself. Without your influence she's too ready to let her heart rule her head.'

'You ready then, Bethany?' Peg reappeared and fidgeted with impatience. She was wearing her best red and white print dress and from the smell of her, she had pinched some of her mother's lavender water.

Gloria regarded her suspiciously as she handed Peg some money. 'You've gone to a lot of trouble to walk a dog and buy two slices of ham.'

Fretful for his walk Jasper was whining at the front door and Peg used this as an excuse to avoid answering her mother. Once level with the corner shop Peg stood on tiptoe to crane her neck over the high window display of saucepans and brushes to see if Frank was serving.

'I can't see him,' she groaned. 'I hope he ain't sick. He weren't there last night when I popped in to get some matches. What d'ye reckon he'll think of my new hair? He prefers blondes.'

'Your hair is lovely. Stop worrying. Now let's get Jasper walked and you can linger on the way back.'

Bethany hooked her arm through her friend's and urged her forward. Peg sighed and kept looking back at the shop in case Frank appeared.

'You shouldn't make your interest so obvious,' Bethany warned. 'Men are supposed to like playing the hunter. Play hard to get and you'll rouse his interest more.'

'I ain't clever like you. I go weak at the knees every time I see him and my tongue gets tied in knots. Frank probably thinks I'm a halfwit.'

'Don't be silly. He likes you,' she encouraged. 'You don't want him to go out with you for just one thing, do you?'

Peg's expression became wistful. 'I don't want no one else but Frank. I've waited three years for him to notice me.'

Jasper was exercised on a square of open land and Peg tore back to the corner shop. 'Get a move on, Beth. They shut in half an hour. I'll scream if Frank ain't serving tonight.'

Bethany grinned. Peg was getting worse where Frank was concerned. She hoped her friend wasn't laying herself open to heartbreak. Peg had already entered the shop as Bethany tied Jasper to a lamppost outside. She paused to stroke the dog before following Peg inside. Mrs Hobson was in the shop and Peg was flicking through a display of birthday cards, her gaze riveted on the curtain which divided the shop from the living quarters. Peg was going to hang out buying the ham for as long as possible hoping that Frank would appear.

Resigning herself for a long wait Bethany watched Mrs Hobson serving the steady trickle of customers. Outside Jasper began to whine at being abandoned.

'Was there anything you wanted in particular, Peg?' Mrs Hobson called out.

Peg's shoulders slumped. Then from outside could be heard Frank's voice as he stopped to make a fuss of the spaniel. Peg rammed the sixpence her mother had given her into Bethany's hand and shot outside.

By the time Bethany had purchased the ham she was in time to see Peg running towards her house, her head down and her shoulders shaking.

Frank was staring after her in bewilderment. 'What's got into her?'

'Have you said something to upset her?' Bethany accused.

'Nope. All I said was why did she want to go cheapening herself by dyeing her hair.'

Angered by his insensitivity, she struck him on the arm. 'You're a blockhead, Frank Hobson! You've just broken the heart of the sweetest girl in all London. You must have realised she was keen on you. She dyed her hair because she thought you preferred blondes.'

'Lawd! I never guessed. She's a cute kid.' Frank continued to look puzzled.

'Peg's not a kid any more. She starts work in a couple of weeks. And you haven't got the brains to recognise the treasure you could just have thrown away.'

Untying Jasper she ran down the road after Peg leaving Frank staring after her.

'Beth, you'll never guess what?' The front door of the Styleses' house slammed and footsteps resounded on the stairs before the bedroom door burst open. Peg was grinning inanely.

Bethany was packing her suitcase. Her mother was expected shortly to take her to their new home. She wished she could find more enthusiasm at the move. She had missed her mother while Alice had been away. But now that she had remarried, Bethany had the feeling that they would never again share the closeness of recent years.

'Guess what happened?'

Before Bethany could reply Peg charged on, too excited to wait for her answer. 'Guess who's asked me out?'

She pirouetted around the room and flung herself down

on the bed and hugged the pillow close to her chest.

'There's only one bloke who could get you all dreamy like that and his name isn't Clark Gable.'

'It's Frank. I think I'm in heaven. We're going to the Palais Saturday night.'

'That's wonderful, Peg. But don't go reading more into it than it could be. Frank was disturbed that he'd upset you the other night. He's got a kind heart but you know Frank . . . It's a new girlfriend every week.'

'Not any more. Frank was always meant to be mine.'

Bethany hoped that Peg was not heading for a fall. Frank was a great guy, but he had a reputation. She feared that her friend's romantic illusions would be shattered.

Bethany was clasped tight to her mother's chest and she could feel her tension as they stood in Gloria's front room. 'Did you have a lovely time in Brighton, Mother?'

'We stayed at The Grand. Such an elegant hotel. Now we must hurry home. Harold has gone to check that nothing untoward has happened in the office while he was away. He will wish you to be settled and ready to join us by teatime.'

Why did her words sound like a command not a welcome? Bethany studied her mother and was disconcerted when Alice looked away. Her mother was usually so relaxed and easy going. Why was she so tense?

'I'm all ready to go.' Bethany turned to Mrs Styles. 'Thank you for allowing me to stay.'

'Think nothing of it, luv. It was my pleasure.' She looked over Bethany's shoulder to Alice. 'Any time. My door is always open to the both of you.'

Bethany picked up her suitcase and grinned at Peg. 'I'll see you Sunday afternoon as usual. Have a lovely time with

Frank on Saturday.' She dropped her voice to a whisper. 'Just you make sure he behaves himself.'

There was an embarrassed cough from Alice. 'I believe Harold has made arrangements for the family on Sunday, dear. He'd not approve of you roaming the streets. And we shall also be attending church in the morning.'

'Church!' Bethany said, startled. 'We've never been regular churchgoers except for Easter and Christmas.'

Alice stiffened. 'As an accountant Harold has his position in the community to consider. He says we should lead others by our example.'

In another man Bethany would have considered these sentiments admirable. In Harold Warden his attitude struck her as mercenary rather than one of religious conviction. She deplored such hypocrisy.

'I don't mind going to church Sunday mornings but Sunday afternoon is the only time I can see Peg. She doesn't finish work until late. Harold has already made it clear that if I'm to continue my studies he doesn't want me out after nine of an evening in the week.'

Alice glanced apologetically towards Peg. 'I wish you well in your employment. Bethany will need to study hard to get her Higher certificate.'

Peg's face crumpled. 'Bethany's my best friend. Now you've moved to a posh area you don't want her mixing with the likes of me.' She burst into tears and ran out of the room and up the stairs.

Bethany hurried after her, calling out, 'They won't stop us being friends, Peg. I swear it.'

'Bethany, we have to leave,' Alice stated. She turned to Gloria. 'I'm sorry Peg has taken it so hard. She's a good girl. Of course Bethany and Peg must remain friends.'

'I shall always be Peg's friend,' Bethany proclaimed.

'Yes, dear.' Her mother stroked her cheek but again failed to hold her stare.

Gloria frowned, looking at the mother and daughter. 'Perhaps Bethany could stay over on a Friday night?'

'That's kind of you,' Alice answered, again looking tense and uneasy. Her voice was taut and unnatural. 'I'll have to see what can be arranged.'

Chapter Three

The tram journey to Leyton was strained. Bethany was angered that her mother had not reassured Peg that nothing had changed in their friendship. Alice remained guarded in answering Bethany's questions.

'Why so many questions, my dear? You're making too much of this.' Her irritation was out of character. 'I'm exhausted from travelling all day and ensuring that your room is ready.'

Bethany fell silent. Her resentment simmered. It was not towards her mother but Harold Warden. Within a week of marriage he had formed a barrier between Alice and herself. She halted by the high wall which surrounded the Wardens' house. Her voice cracked with emotion. 'You seem different, Mum. Ill at ease.'

She was enfolded in her mother's arms and her breath soughed through her black curls. 'I'm anxious that you and Harold get on well.' She drew back and stared fixedly at the house, her expression veiled of all emotion.

'I'm afraid Jasper will have to be tied up outside. Harold has purchased a kennel.'

'A kennel! Jasper is a house dog. He's never slept outside or been tied up,' Bethany protested.

'He will have to learn.' Alice's voice was flat. 'Harold

does not like animals. Out of generosity to you he will permit you to keep Jasper. But he must stay outside.'

Horrified, Bethany backed away from her mother. She knelt on the pavement and threw her arms around the spaniel. 'You know how much Jasper means to me. He was the last birthday present Daddy brought me. He isn't just a dog. He's a special part of Daddy.'

There was a tension in Alice which disquieted Bethany. When her gaze held Bethany's, her eyes were shadowed with regret. 'Harold won't allow Jasper in the house.'

'It's your house as well!' The resentment burst forth at this injustice. 'He took our furnishings and rented our home to a stranger. Daddy's lovely house which he built for you as a wedding present. Why did you let him do that?'

'Don't be silly, Bethany. We couldn't have two houses and this is the larger.' Alice began to walk along the gravel drive. When Bethany did not follow she retraced her steps. 'Don't make things difficult, my dear. I loved our home. And I ensured that it would be safeguarded for you. I'll always love your father. But our life has changed. Many things will be for the better.'

'Not for Jasper. I won't allow him to be tied up outside. It's cruel. He's always been with the family and slept on my bed.'

Alice sighed. Her lips which always curved in tenderness when she regarded Bethany were now narrow and grim. A tell-tale flutter of eyelashes showed Bethany that her mother was battling against tears. 'You must accept that things have changed. You can be very stubborn, Bethany. Don't anger Harold over this.'

Bethany's hold tightened around the dog. She hated seeing her mother upset. But this issue was too important to give way upon. 'I'm sorry, Mum. If Mr Warden doesn't allow Jasper into the house I'll never forgive him. He knew that Jasper was part of our family when he asked you to marry him.'

'The question of the dog did not arise then.' Alice crouched beside Bethany, her eyes now pleading. 'Please, my dear, be reasonable.'

Her heart hardened. She would do anything for Alice except betray Jasper. The mother she knew before the wedding had changed. Alice Masterton would never have asked her to make this sacrifice. Clearly Alice Warden was being driven by an uncompromising husband. Hatred burned in her for Harold who had forced this change upon her mother.

Bethany rebelled. 'Dad would never have allowed Jasper to be tied up outside and sleep in a kennel.'

Alice sighed. 'I'll speak with Harold. But you mustn't compare him to your father.'

'I'm not entering the house until this matter is resolved.' Bethany stood her ground. 'I'll take Jasper for a walk until Mr Warden returns.'

'He'd like you to call him Papa.'

Bethany stiffened. 'If he wants me to regard him as a father then he must act like one and not as a dictator. He doesn't like me. Perhaps Mr Warden doesn't realise how important Jasper is to me.'

Anguish twisted her mother's lips. From her expression Bethany knew that she had already tried to change her husband's mind. 'A show of stubbornness will make things more difficult.' Alice stood up and twisted her kid gloves in her hand in growing agitation.

Bethany was disturbed by the way her mother was acting. She appeared frightened of her husband's reaction. It alarmed Bethany. Her loyalty to her mother was torn.

Alice deserved to be happy and her rebellion was upsetting her. Neither did she wish to be the cause of dissension between her mother and her new husband. Yet this was a matter of principle. Life with the Wardens was going to be a bed of roses with the thorns included.

She stared down at the spaniel who was licking her hand. Was she being unreasonable? She didn't think so. Her father had taught her to stand up for her beliefs. She would also be failing him if she backed down over this.

'I'm sorry, Mum. Mr Warden is not being fair on Jasper or me.'

A car turned into the drive and Bethany pulled Jasper to one side as Harold swung his Daimler on to the gravel and proceeded to the back of the house where the car was garaged.

'I'll speak with Harold.' Alice walked towards the house. 'Stay in the garden. Take Jasper into the side orchard.'

Bethany let the spaniel run around the apple trees and began to chase him. Fifteen minutes later she halted their game at seeing Harold striding towards her.

'Good day, sir,' Bethany said politely, though her stomach clenched at seeing the stern set of his face.

'Your mother informs me that this creature is of great importance to you. You wish a special favour from me to allow it into my house.'

He had made it obvious that she was here on his sufferance. Her instinct was to retaliate. Wisdom intervened. Confrontation took many forms. Bethany guessed that to win she had to give some ground.

'Jasper is well behaved and no trouble in the house, sir. He has always slept in my room. He was the last present my father brought me.'

'And it would be hard for you to be parted from this

pet?' his cold voice responded.

'Yes, sir.'

White lines pinched in the side of his long nose and channelled each side of his mouth. 'You have a wilful streak, child. I don't expect my wishes to be questioned. For the sake of your mother I'm prepared to be lenient. Your attitude has distressed her greatly.'

A typical bigot, he could not see that he was the instrument of Alice's distress. 'I regret that, sir.'

He appeared to accept that as an apology, but his tone remained autocratic as he went on, 'There will be conditions to this arrangement.' He paused significantly. 'I will not have the creature running through the house. The dog will be confined to the conservatory during the day. It's unhealthy for a dog to sleep in a bedroom but your mother has previously permitted this. Therefore your bedroom will be moved to the upper floor which is reached by the old servants' stairs. If you cannot control the dog to stay within these confines he will be chained to a kennel in the garden. And lastly . . .'

Again he paused, this time his eyes glittering with triumph. 'If you step out of line; dare to disobey me in anything, the dog stays outside until you learn that I am master in my own home.'

He was using Jasper to control her. Her victory was hollow. She swallowed her ire. She had overcome this first hurdle and she would overcome others. 'I agree with your conditions, sir.'

He nodded, satisfied. 'Go in to the house by the back way. Mrs Binns, the daily, will show you where the old servants' stairs are. Your mother is preparing your new room. Though she could have done without all this upset and extra work. You're a selfish child.'

It said much of him that he had placed her in the wrong. Bethany knew she was being banished to the servants' quarters as punishment for defying him. He wanted to make her feel inferior to his children. He wouldn't succeed. She knew her own worth. She didn't care where she slept as long as Jasper was with her.

'Thank you,' she said with dignified politeness.

His gaze razored over her. 'It would please your mother if you addressed me as Papa. We are a unified family now.'

'Yes, Papa.' Her voice cracked with the effort. No wonder her mother had been so nervous at her rebellion. He was a tyrant. Had he already made other things difficult for Alice? He would never replace her beloved daddy. She would pay him polite lipservice, if that was what it took to placate him, but only to make life less harassing for her mother.

On entering the kitchen Bethany discovered Mrs Binns to be a bespectacled amazon of a woman with greying brown hair tied back in a bun. She smiled as Bethany ordered Jasper to sit. 'Fair set the cat amongst the pigeons you have. Or should I say the dog amongst the lambs. Proper got the master's hackles up.'

'I don't expect you to have to clean up any muddy footprints,' Bethany assured.

'Don't you worry about that. I love animals. I reckon it's a cold-hearted blighter who's got no time for them.' She eyed Bethany with approval. 'Standing up to that old devil takes courage. You're all right, luv. But I wouldn't make a habit of it. He can be a Tartar and will find a way to make you pay.'

She bent down to hold her hand out to Jasper to sniff. He butted it with his head for her to stroke him. 'Nice dogs, spaniels. My own dog is half spaniel, half collie. Daft as a brush it is.'

Bethany groaned at seeing a trail of mud behind them. 'I'll clear that up.'

'Mr Warden is a stickler for cleanliness. It might be best if you hose Jasper's paws down before he comes in. I'll leave an old towel hanging inside the back door just for him.'

Bethany knew she had found a friend. 'Thank you, I appreciate that.'

She ran up the wooden stairs to the top storey of the house. A bare lightbulb illuminated the gloomy landing from which three doors led off. One door was open and Bethany heard her mother moving about inside.

'Looks like I've put you to a lot of work. Sorry, Mum.'

Alice was stooped over the single iron bedstead having just made it up. Bethany saw her wipe her hand surreptitiously across her cheek before she turned to face her. Alice had been crying.

Bethany hugged her. 'I don't mind being up here.'

'It's a horrid room. So small and gloomy. When I think of your lovely room at home . . .' She shook her head. 'But I'll have a carpet brought up and there's curtains from the room which would have been yours that match the bedspread. With a proper wardrobe and dressing table it won't be so bad. We'll get it fixed up properly on Monday when Harold is at work.'

'It's fine. Don't worry.'

There was a discreet cough from the doorway and Mrs Binns carried in Jasper's wicker basket and put it by the side of the bed. 'I'll help you get the room real nice, Mrs Warden. Happen we could also do something with the room across the way. Didn't you say Bethany was staying on at school and would later be going to medical college? She'll need somewhere quiet where she can study. There's an old desk in the attic and a couple of armchairs. We could make it real nice if she has her friends in.'

'It's going to be fine, Mum,' Bethany reassured and smiled her gratitude at Mrs Binns.

When the daily left, Bethany looked searchingly at her mother. 'What's wrong, Mum?'

Alice squared her shoulders, and when she spoke her voice was strained. 'Nothing is wrong. I'm upset that you and Harold have quarrelled. We all have to make adjustments. Our ways are not the ways of the Wardens. We must all give and take.'

And Bethany knew who would be expected to do all the compromising. There were bound to be some stormy days ahead.

The evening meal was another testing ground to overcome. Jasper was whining at being shut in the conservatory and Harold's face was getting redder with anger by the minute. Alice was visibly upset and kept sending warning glances to her daughter to remain in her seat and finish her meal. Giles was looking smug and Louise, having given Bethany a sympathetic glance, kept her head bowed over her food.

A forlorn howl caused Bethany to drop her knife. It clattered on the rim of the plate and fell to the floor.

'That noise is insufferable,' Harold snapped. 'Is it too much to expect peace and quiet in my own home?'

'It will take a while for Jasper to get used to the new house and regime.' Alice tried to defuse the situation. 'He won't be any trouble in a day or two.'

'The dog has been spoilt.' Giles spiked a Brussels sprout and glowered in the direction of the conservatory. 'If it keeps that racket up much longer it will feel my boot.'

Bethany rounded on him. He may be handsome but he had an unattractive personality. 'You hurt my dog and I'll deal the same punishment out to you.'

'That's enough,' Harold ordered. 'I won't have bickering at my dinner table.'

Her appetite deserting her, Bethany picked at her food. Giles smirked, enjoying her discomfort and his father's anger. The tinned peaches and ice cream for dessert stuck in her throat.

Harold studied her plate with a frown. 'I hope Bethany is not one of those silly girls who are fussy eaters. I do not like to see good food wasted.'

'I'm not hungry,' she replied. It was torture waiting until everyone had finished eating and Giles was deliberately being slow.

The meal finished, Harold retired to his study to work on some papers he had brought home from the office. Bethany ran to rescue Jasper from the conservatory. After pacifying the distraught dog she discovered Giles leaning against the conservatory door when she wanted to leave.

'So the old man has put you up in the servants' quarters. Plucky little filly aren't you, standing up to him over a flea-ridden mutt.'

'Jasper does not have fleas. He's always been part of the family.'

Giles laughed unpleasantly. 'Bit of a firebrand, aren't you? Pa won't like that.'

'I've no intention of causing trouble.' She did not like Giles any more than his father.

Unexpectedly, he smiled. 'I like your spirit. The old man can be a stickler for convention. Unlike me. Or you, going by the way you stood up to him.' His stare was insulting as it travelled over her figure. He touched her cheek and it took all her willpower not to jerk away. Such intimacy was unnerving. 'You're a pretty little thing. You'll be a real beauty in a year or two. There's no reason why we can't get on together.'

The words were reasonable enough but unaccountably they disturbed Bethany. She didn't trust Giles. There was a speculation in his eyes she found offensive.

She forced a conciliatory smile. There was no point in antagonising him. 'We are all one family, Giles. I hope that you, Louise and I will become friends.'

'I'm talking about you and me.' His expression changed. If he wasn't her stepbrother she'd have sworn that he was flirting with her. Then a guard slipped over his eyes. 'Louise is another matter. Twins have a special bond formed from the womb. It is inalienable. You'll never come between us.'

It was an unmistakable threat. Bethany swallowed. Giles wanted to control her as he controlled Louise. But he did not want Louise to become close to her. While deriding his sister, Giles was also possessive of her. That troubled Bethany. It was obsessive and unnatural.

Bethany had attended church on Sunday morning with the family. Louise had left a half hour earlier as she sang in the choir. Alice and Harold walked arm in arm to the service and to Bethany's surprise Giles made a great play of escorting her. During the service he solicitously held the hymn and prayer book they shared, his shoulder continually brushing against hers. Afterwards he was enthusiastic at introducing Bethany to any acquaintance and hovered at her side. Harold lingered speaking with the vicar and

Bethany fidgeted impatiently, eager to return home to give Jasper his walk before lunch.

Louise emerged from the church and hurried to their side. Giles scowled. 'If the old man doesn't get a move on the pub will be shut,' he groaned. 'Come on, girls, let's get going.'

Louise shook her head. 'Papa won't like it. He doesn't approve of you drinking on a Sunday.'

'I don't intend to tell him that's where I'm going. You'll cover for me, won't you, Lou?'

Louise looked uncomfortable. 'Then don't come back from the pub reeking of beer. Papa will smell it on your breath. I don't like telling lies. I'm not covering for you all summer while you're down from University.'

Her arm was grabbed and Giles hissed in her ear, 'You'll do as I say. I don't like it when you're disloyal.'

Louise paled. Bethany had suspected that Giles had some hold over his sister. Did he bully her to make her compliant to his wishes?

Giles strode away.

'Where's he off to?' Harold demanded. 'Is he going to visit a public house?'

'He said he'd be back home for lunch,' Louise evaded. 'Giles doesn't tell me where he's going.'

'Not that you'd tell me if he did.' Harold's glare made Louise shrink back and her shoulders hunch. Harold thrust his finger into her shoulder. 'You two always were sly ones. You can stay in your room all afternoon, miss. I won't have you telling lies to save your brother.'

'She isn't.' Bethany broke in, outraged by the way Louise was bearing the brunt of her father's anger because of her twin. 'Giles walked off mumbling he'd be home at lunchtime.'

She felt the tension leave Louise's frame. Harold glowered at her then apparently satisfied turned away. Bethany felt a tentative hand on her arm.

'Thank you, Bethany,' Louise said. 'It's horrid that Papa is making you sleep upstairs in the old servants' rooms.'

'I don't mind. It feels rather grand having a whole floor to myself. I resent it more that he won't let me see Peg today.'

'Papa doesn't like us mixing with others. He's worried we might meet the wrong people.'

'What right has he to stop me seeing my friends?'

Louise sighed. 'It's because grandma ran off with another man. I suppose you've heard the gossip.'

'That was thirty years ago. He'll have us wearing chastity belts next. Or threaten to cast us into a nunnery for our sins.'

Louise blushed and looked horrified. Bethany was startled. She hadn't expected Louise to be a prude. Peg was so open in her comments and curiosity about sex that such speech had become second nature to her.

'Have I embarrassed you? I didn't mean to. I suppose going to a convent school, a comment like that is offensive to you.'

'No. Not at all.' Louise kept her gaze fixed on a trolley bus turning the corner of the High Street and quickened her pace. Despite her denial Bethany felt she had upset Louise. She liked her stepsister and wanted to be friends with her. 'I won't talk about such things if it makes you uncomfortable. I can't see why they make so much secrecy about sex. It's only a man and woman doing what comes naturally. If there was no sex there'd be no babies and then where would the human race be?'

Louise was walking so fast Bethany broke into a trot to

keep up with her. 'Now I *have* offended you. I'm sorry.'

Louise shook her head. 'Let's change the subject. You're determined to go to college, aren't you? What career do you want?'

'I've always wanted to be a doctor. There can't be anything finer than healing the sick. Mum had the most fearful row with your father over it the other evening. He didn't approve. But that won't stop me. I've got another year at grammar school first but I definitely want to tend sick children. I feel it is what I was meant to do. I love writing for children too. I'd really like to get my stories published.'

'I wish I was so certain,' Louise groaned.

'My dad always encouraged me. He rather fancied that I should become a writer. It was something he always wanted to do but was too busy. He made up wonderful stories at bedtime. I suppose I inherited his imagination. I always had my essays read out in class. But you have to experience life before you can write about it. Even if your market is for children.'

'I should think you just need a vivid imagination and to know what children like. What stories did you enjoy most at the age you want to write for?'

'Animal stories and stories of magic.'

'There you are!' Louise laughed. 'My new sister will be the next great children's writer.'

The idea was appealing. 'Somehow I don't think it is as easy as that and I've got masses of studying to do before I qualify as a doctor. I won't have time to write fiction with all those medical notes to take!'

'At least you have some goals in your life. I wish I did. Papa quashes any ideas I have. He insists that a daughter of his has no need to work for a living. With Mama being ill for so long I had to take care of the house and things. But I'm bored stuck at home all day. Now Alice is in charge of everything I've nothing to do.'

Bethany realised that for years Louise had been treated as an unpaid servant. No wonder she had so little confidence. 'You had a good education. It's a shame to waste it. What interests you most?'

She shook her head. 'I was hopeless at most subjects at school. All I know is how to keep house and entertain guests – though some of those have terrified me in the past, they have been so haughty.'

'You'll make some man a fine wife. That's all most women want from life.'

A shadow crossed Louise's face. 'What man will want me?'

There was such heartfelt misery in her voice that Bethany wanted to strike out at Harold and Giles. Their bombastic and domineering attitude had destroyed all the confidence in this sweet-natured young woman.

Chapter Four

A month after the wedding life had fallen into a pattern. It was the summer holidays and Giles was home from University. Bethany noticed that Louise's mood was brighter when her brother was not around. With Peg working Bethany had only managed to meet her once a week. Her friend's world now revolved around Frank Hobson. It was a record that Frank had kept the same girlfriend for so long.

Harold did not like his daughters to go out unescorted in the evening. He frequently gave dinner parties for important clients and expected Louise and Bethany to attend. When Giles was absent Bethany enjoyed Louise's company. They would listen to the wireless or play cards. Louise was fond of chess and since Bethany knew nothing of the game she taught her. Bethany became as enthusiastic as Louise and the nightly games formed a strengthening bond between them.

It worried Bethany that her mother had been looking pale since her marriage. Harold had left for the office ten minutes ago and this morning Alice made no attempt to clear the breakfast table.

'Aren't you well, Mum?' Bethany asked. 'You look pale.'

Alice's teacup clattered into its saucer. 'I've a headache.

Would you massage my neck for me? It always clears the pain.'

Bethany obliged, running her hands gently and soothingly over her mother's scalp and down over her head. As usual when she worked she felt the heat rising in her hands and a feeling of peace and love washing through herself and over her mother. After a few minutes Alice touched her hands. 'The pain has gone, my dear. I swear you have magic in your fingers.'

Bethany laughed. 'The motion of my hands relaxed you. Tension causes headaches. So does lack of sleep,' she added observing the dark circles under her mother's eyes.

'I haven't been sleeping well lately,' Alice confessed.

'Papa does snore loudly.' Louise nodded sympathetically. 'I can hear him from my room sometimes.'

Alice shot her stepdaughter a strained look which Bethany did not understand. Had the idea not been so preposterous she would have interpreted it as fearful.

'What are your plans today, Louise?' Alice deftly changed the subject. She prayed that snoring was the only noise Louise could hear coming from their bedchamber. How could she face the family if they realised the humiliation and pain she was made to suffer every night? Harold had no thought but for his own gratification. He never attempted to arouse her but invaded her dry and unyielding body, bruising and tearing into her until he was satisfied.

After the tender lovemaking of her first marriage, Alice was left feeling used and defiled by the nightly rape. Harold was desperate for another son. He had confided to her his disappointment with Giles and his wild ways. He had raged when he told her he had paid a hundred pounds to silence the family of a young girl whom Giles had made pregnant. The girl was fifteen and from a poor background and Harold would not hear of Giles marrying her. Harold had hinted at other incidents when he had been forced to bail his son out from the police station on charges of disorderly conduct. Harold loathed Giles and was ashamed of him. Only the fear of scandal stopped him disowning his son.

Alice had realised on the first night of her honeymoon that Harold had married her only to give him a son. He had been attracted to her grace and beauty, but he was incapable of love as Alice had been loved by Edward Masterton.

Each night as she cried herself to sleep, she regretted her marriage, yet she was determined never to allow Bethany to suspect how wretched she was.

She dragged her thoughts back to the present, concentrating on her stepdaughter's unhappy expression. Harold refused to allow Louise to take up any kind of employment. The young woman must be bored to distraction.

Louise fidgeted with her napkin. 'I should call on the vicar's wife and see if she needs any help with the church fête. I ran the toy stall last year.' Her lack of enthusiasm was obvious.

'What would you like to be doing with your time?' Bethany enquired. 'Hobbies can be very fulfilling.'

Alice never ceased to be amazed at her daughter's intuition and knack of drawing people out of themselves.

Louise shrugged. 'Something useful. Something with purpose. I hate the futility of just waiting for marriage as Papa believes is right. I haven't even got a boyfriend.'

Bethany studied Louise's weary expression and was saddened by her despondency. Louise would never openly oppose her father's wishes. 'You love flowers and plants.

You showed me the carnation cuttings you had taken and grown on your bedroom windowsill. Bagshott the gardener only comes in twice a week. He only prunes the shrubs, keeps the weeds at bay and mows the lawns. Why not spend more time in the garden? You could propagate your own seeds and plant them.'

'We haven't got a greenhouse and Papa wouldn't like the mess in the conservatory.'

Bethany regarded her gravely. Louise was so easily defeated she wanted to encourage her to do something that was special for herself. 'There's the shed in the orchard and it isn't difficult to build a cold frame. All it takes is a bit of wood surround and some panes of glass over the top.'

'There's nothing like cut flowers in the house from your own garden,' Alice added. 'It must be very satisfying to nourish something from seed and see it grow.'

A light kindled in Louise's eyes. 'I do love the garden and wish Papa made better use of the land. We've no flowers to cut except roses and Michaelmas daisies. I'll speak to Papa tonight to see if Bagshott can build me a cold frame.'

'Why wait?' Bethany urged. 'Why should your father object? We could go into town today and get some seeds and books.'

Louise's eyes shone with excitement and an inner beauty shone from her homely face. 'And you could get yourself some exercise books and start writing your stories.'

Alice nodded. 'Edward was so proud when Bethany won the story competition at school. I don't know why she doesn't send her stories off to magazines.'

'They were child's stuff, but since Louise will be busy in the garden, I might have a go at a new story.' The idea was exciting. 'I'm also meeting Peg for lunch today. Can I stay over with her on Friday night, Mum?'

'I think you should ask Harold first.'

The uncertainty in her mother's voice was another change that disturbed Bethany. Bethany saw that Alice's food had not been touched. Neither had her dinner on the last two evenings. Was she sickening for something? When she sought her gaze, Alice glanced away. Something was wrong. Shouldn't her mother be deliriously happy after only a few weeks of marriage?

An hour later Bethany and Louise caught the tram to the High Street. They went first to Woolworth's to get some exercise books and then trailed around the bookshops looking for gardening books. At lunchtime Louise was excitedly discussing planting seeds with a sales assistant and declined joining Bethany and Peg at the station café. As usual her friend could talk of nothing but Frank.

'When he kisses me goodnight I barely have the strength to stand. He's wonderful. I love him so much. We went to the cinema last night.'

'Any prizes if I guess it was the Jean Harlow film rather than the Douglas Fairbanks?'

Peg giggled. 'Despite it being Jean Harlow, don't ask me what it was about. We sat in the back row and we did a lot more than just holding hands.'

'You know what Frank's like. Don't get too carried away.'

'It's not like that, Beth. He says I'm different from the others. We see each other every night after the shop closes. Usually we climb over the railings of the park so we can have a bit of privacy.'

'Is that wise?' Bethany cautioned.

'I don't care. When he kisses me I love him so much I

don't want it to stop. If I don't let him . . . you know . . . I could lose him, couldn't I?'

'Not if he truly cares for you.' Concern for her friend made her voice sharp. 'Have you gone that far with him? They say men don't respect you afterwards.'

'I've held him off so far. But each night it gets harder.' Peg chuckled, then noting Bethany's frown she glanced at her watch. 'Time for work. You all right for Friday? Frank's going out with his mates that night. We could go up West. Some of the women in work go to one of the clubs. They say it's terrific with lots of handsome blokes.'

'You know I'm not allowed up to the West End. It's hard enough getting away to see you. Let's go to the pictures.'

Peg pouted with disappointment and to tease her into a better mood, Bethany said, 'And why do you want to go where the men are so handsome? Going off Frank, are you?'

'Never. It wouldn't hurt him to wonder what I was getting up to the nights I don't see him.'

Obviously the women in work were giving Peg advice. Bethany wasn't sure it was beneficial to her friend. Peg could be impetuous. She was so in love with Frank she'd do anything to keep him. Quite apart from her dyed hair Peg now wore more make-up. She was changing now she was at work. Inevitably the gap between them would widen whilst she was studying.

Only once in the next month was Bethany allowed to stay at Peg's on a Friday night. This Friday Harold had been in a bad mood since breakfast and on his return from the office insisted that Bethany be home by ten o'clock.

'But it's arranged that I stay the night. Mrs Styles will have made up the bed.'

'You have responsibilities here,' Harold said perversely.

'That dog of yours for one. You can't stay away and expect him to remain in your room. He must sleep in the kennel. If he disturbs the neighbours we'll have to consider whether we can continue to keep such a disruptive creature.'

It was no idle threat. Bethany backed down as Harold knew she would, but it galled her to submit to his petty tyranny. When Bethany arrived at the Styleses' house Gloria answered her knock. She looked flustered at seeing Bethany.

'Didn't you get Peg's message? She left word with your stepbrother when she saw him in the High Street at lunchtime. She's gone up West with three of the women from work.'

'I haven't seen Giles. He didn't come back for tea.'

'I told Peg it weren't right to mess you about.' Gloria looked apologetic and her face was drawn with worry. 'Frank didn't turn up for their date last night. Peg's upset.'

Bethany hid her hurt that Peg didn't want to confide in her. Perhaps it was because she knew Frank so well and had warned her against getting too involved. To put Gloria at ease, she said, 'Mr Warden won't let me stay over. If Peg is upset she's better off going somewhere exciting to enjoy herself.'

She caught the tram and when it passed the Baker's Arms public house she saw Frank and his mates outside talking to four girls. Poor Peg.

On arriving home she was surprised to see the downstairs lights on. Her mother and Harold had gone to the theatre. Louise was at choir practice and Giles was rarely home before midnight. Jasper was barking. She hurried through to the conservatory. Giles was tormenting Jasper by holding his bone out of reach. The spaniel was frantically jumping higher and higher and each time overbalancing so that he landed on his back and yelped.

'Stop that!' she demanded. 'He'll injure himself.'

'The mutt's stupid,' Giles jeered, the slight slurring to his words warning her that he had been drinking heavily.

'Give him the bone.'

He laughed at her. His tie was awry and his hair dishevelled. She could smell the whisky on his breath and his red-rimmed eyes were belligerent. 'You want him to have his bone, then come and get it.'

When she snatched at it, he held it higher out of her reach. Twice she grabbed for it and each time he held it further away.

'Stop being so tiresome,' she returned, her anger mounting. Giles was taunting her as he had the dog. 'Come on, Jasper. Up to my room. I've better things to do than play this inane game.'

He moved to block her exit. 'Not so fast. Isn't it time we got to know each other better?'

'You've had plenty of chances to speak with me.'

He wagged a finger at her. 'We've never had a chance like this. Everyone's out. Even Louise.' He fingered a tress of her curling hair and she pulled back uneasily from his touch. There was a speculative gleam in his eyes which she didn't like, or trust, especially as they were alone.

'I thought you'd rather be down the pub.' She kept her voice level hoping it did not betray her disquiet. He would seize on it and use it against her.

'I'm skint. Have you got ten bob you can lend a chap?'

'I haven't. I spent my two bob pocket money in town with Louise.'

He scowled. 'All pally with Lou are you? What about me? You've got something to keep a chap happy. How about a kiss? Just to show you're willing to be friends.'

Bethany's violet eyes were defiant. 'Get out of my way and grow up, Giles.'

He grabbed her shoulders, his nails digging cruelly into her flesh. 'Me grow up? It's you who's the child. The little innocent. Or so you would have us believe. Girls as pretty as you are never innocent.'

He pushed her up against the wall and his mouth pressed down on hers. It was unpleasantly moist and when his tongue wormed between her teeth she gagged.

'Don't be shy,' he murmured as he held her clamped in his embrace. Forced up against the wall and with his body leaning against hers she could scarcely move.

'No!' Her protest was muffled and goaded him to kiss her harder. She could feel the pressure of his thighs forcing her legs apart and to her horror the jab of his arousal against her stomach. Frightened, she struggled harder; twisting her head aside and pushing against his chest. Tearing her lips away, she snapped, 'You're disgusting!'

He laughed and a hand encircled her wrist dragging her palm down so that it was pressed against his tumescence. When he began to grind himself against it, she screamed and with only her teeth as a weapon bit his cheek.

Jasper growled and snapped at Giles's ankles. He must have struck flesh for there was a grunt from Giles. His foot shot out and the dog yelped and skidded across the room. It was enough to release the weight which held her pinioned. Incensed at his treatment she slapped his cheek.

'You're despicable!' To her relief she heard a key turn in the front door. 'Try that again and I'll tell Harold.'

He chuckled. 'No, you won't. It would upset your mother too much. And Pa's hardly in a position to lecture me on forcing women. Shut away in the servants' quarters you won't have heard your mother's sobs every night after he's finished with her. That pig of a father of mine is snoring his head off uncaring of his bride's misery.'

Bethany sagged against the wall, her eyes wide with horror. 'What do you mean?'

'Just what I say.'

He winked at her. 'Stay up in your virginal attic. Keep your innocence. You'll sleep easier of a night that way.'

There was a footfall in the hallway and Louise called, 'Giles, is that you?'

'Here, sis.'

Louise smiled with pleasure at seeing Bethany. 'I thought you were staying over at your friend's.'

'There was a mix-up. Apparently Giles was supposed to give me a message that she couldn't make it, but he didn't.'

Giles shrugged. 'I'm not a messenger boy. Especially when you can be so unco-operative yourself.'

He pushed past his twin to enter the dining room where they heard the chink of a decanter against a glass.

Louise studied Bethany. 'Are you all right? Has Giles been making demands?'

For a moment Bethany was tempted to confide in her. Something stopped her. He was Louise's twin. Louise couldn't do anything about his behaviour and what was the point of distressing her. She sighed. 'He can be objectionable at times. He was teasing Jasper and we quarrelled.'

Louise's expression was grim as she stared towards the dining room. 'He can be difficult when he's had a few drinks. It's best if you stay out of his way when he's like that.'

'I intend to. Do you fancy a game of chess?'

'Lou, I need another bottle of whisky,' Giles demanded. 'Get it, will you.'

Bethany put out a hand to stop her. 'Don't you think he's had enough?'

Louise flinched. 'It doesn't do to cross Giles. He always makes you pay in the end. If he gets drunk he'll pass out, then Papa can deal with him. You don't know what Giles is like. It's best if we give the chess a miss. I'll sit with Giles. He won't like us being together while he is left out.'

The two rooms given to Bethany had been transformed. Pale green linoleum had been laid in both rooms and this was covered by two large olive rugs. The bedroom had been rewallpapered in cream with a trailing ivy design and the lilac curtains, bedcover and matching ruched eiderdown brightened the room. The second room had been converted into a study. An old oak table had been brought out of the attic, rubbed down and repolished to act as a desk. These walls were papered in white with cheerful yellow daisies. An old pair of dark green velvet curtains were thrown over the cracked leather horsehair armchairs.

Bethany was delighted with the results. The study caught the afternoon and evening sun and Alice had lined the walls with shelves to hold her books, her childhood dolls and her collection of china animals. It was her sanctuary within a house which was beginning to resonate with unsettling and unpleasant vibrations.

What had Giles meant about her mother sobbing at night? Alice certainly wasn't her old carefree self, but Harold's strait-laced attitude was so different from her father's. He could not be an easy man to live with. But they were in love, weren't they? Alice couldn't be as unhappy as Giles implied.

In her innocence Bethany retained an idealised conception of love and happiness. Giles had said those things in retaliation to her reaction to his kiss. She didn't trust Giles after the indecent way he had forced her to touch him. He was trying to frighten her. She'd seen how he controlled Louise by deriding her and destroying her self-confidence. It was the behaviour of a bully to manipulate and nurture fear in others to boost their own inadequacy.

Having so summed Giles up, Bethany resolved not to listen to his perverse insinuations. Even so, the seeds of doubt once sown are not so easily put aside. Hadn't she been filled with foreboding since her mother had announced that she would marry Harold? Nothing had happened to allay that dread.

When Jasper began to whine softly in the night he woke Bethany. He wasn't on the bed but by the closed door. Thinking he needed to go outside, she donned her dressing gown and slippers. As she reached the lower landing she heard the rhythmic creaking of bedsprings coming from the direction of her mother's bedroom. Her cheeks flamed with embarrassment and she ran down the servants' stairs to let the dog out. Jasper ran across the lawn and then she heard him snuffling through the border shrubs having picked up the scent of a neighbour's cat or a hedgehog. It was ten minutes before he came back inside and she was shivering with cold. Once again level with the bedrooms she heard a noise. The hair at the base of her neck prickled and her stomach clenched with anxiety. It was the unmistakable sound of her mother's muffled weeping.

Chapter Five

How could Bethany talk to her mother about what she had heard that night? It was impossible. At least as the days progressed Alice looked less harassed and Bethany hoped that her mother was finding the happiness she deserved. Harold was always insisting that she treated herself to new outfits and visited the hair and beauty salon. Yet Bethany had the uncomfortable feeling Alice's petite beauty was more important to Harold than the feelings of the woman herself.

To ease her mother's distress, Bethany was more attentive. Since the matter was so important to Alice, she was pleasant to Harold, although she loathed him.

Some matters had improved. Giles had gone away to spend a fortnight with University friends in Surrey and the tension in the house eased with his absence. Louise had launched herself into her gardening. It became her passion, helping her to shed her shyness and she had joined the local horticultural club. Unexpectedly, Harold had bought her a greenhouse to work in.

To pass the summer days Bethany spent every morning writing children's stories. Three of her favourites had been sent to magazines but had been rejected although they had asked to see more of her work. It encouraged her to write more and to her delight the next one was accepted.

'I hear you're to be congratulated, Bethany.' Harold peered over the top of his newspaper as a piano concert on the wireless came to an end. 'Writing children's stories is an acceptable occupation for a gently reared young lady.'

Alice paused in her knitting to smile at her. They were the first words of approval Harold had spoken to Bethany. With the concert finished Harold got up and switched off the wireless disregarding that either Alice or herself might wish to listen to the next programme. He scrutinised Bethany with unusual intensity. 'Next week you return to school. What plans have you for your future? You must have talent as a writer. Perhaps you should introduce yourself to some publishing houses and show them your work.'

'That isn't the way to get published, even if I had chosen it as a career. I do it for fun. I intend to become a doctor and work with sick children.'

He laughed derisively. 'Stick to the writing. The only proper doctors are men. It takes years to qualify. You'll be married long before then.'

'I'm serious about this. It's important to me. All I've ever wanted to do is heal the sick, particularly children. Marriage won't stop me. My husband will have to understand that.'

'Balderdash! Stick to the writing.'

His condemning tone caused the colour to drain from her cheeks. A frantic look from her mother pleaded with her not to pursue the subject tonight. Bethany was so angry the only way she could keep silent was to leave the room. Even so at the door she could not hold back. 'I *will* cure the sick. My father would never have stopped me becoming a doctor. He would have been proud of me.'

She walked out accompanied by a furious clacking of her mother's knitting needles. Harold's scathing voice carried to her in the hall. 'Edward Masterton had his head in the clouds. Women doctors. Bah! I wouldn't trust one myself.'

'Bethany has the courage of her convictions,' Alice answered. 'She will succeed. I'm proud that she wants to dedicate her life to healing others.'

'She should leave it to the men,' he snapped. 'And stop clicking those damned needles. They get on my nerves. Clickety-clack-clack every night.'

There was an angry crackle of newspaper and Alice came out of the sitting room wiping her hand across her cheeks. She was crying. She stopped at seeing Bethany.

'I'm sorry, I shouldn't have answered him back, Mum. Don't get upset. He's a pig to talk to you like that.'

'He doesn't like his judgement questioned.'

Bethany's eyes misted. 'He's not like Dad, is he? I miss him so much. But we have each other.' She held her mother close. 'We'll always have each other.'

The following Wednesday Harold was out visiting a client. Bethany caught the tram across town to see Peg, hoping to catch her before she went out that evening.

Mrs Styles was again apologetic. 'She's gone straight up West from work. She shouldn't be neglecting you like this.'

'Perhaps I'm just a kid to her now that she's working.'

'It's not that,' Gloria hastily assured her. 'Peg thinks the world of you. She's real cut up about Frank. She won't talk about what happened.'

Bethany nodded. 'I understand. She needs a bit of fun. Could you tell her that Harold is away next Tuesday evening and Mum said she can come to tea.'

'She'll be there, or I'll want to know the reason why,' Gloria promised.

Walking past the corner shop she was knocked off balance by Frank who came out carrying a large box of groceries and didn't see her approaching.

'You all right, Bethany?' He propped the box on top of a stack of enamel buckets amongst other household goods displayed on the pavement. 'Haven't seen you since you moved. See much of Peg, do you?'

'Not much. It isn't so easy now she's working.'

'She home now?' There was a catch of hope in his voice.

Bethany paused, having intended to walk on as she was angry with Frank for ditching Peg. Perhaps it hadn't been as cut and dried as that. Gloria had said he'd called round the day after standing her up.

'No. She's gone up West with her work friends.'

He didn't look pleased. 'Those mates of hers ain't doing her any favours. Most of them are tarts.'

This wasn't the jovial and charming Frank she was used to. 'Peg isn't like that. She's spreading her wings now she's working.'

'I thought she were different. I reckon women are all the same.'

'Depends what you mean by same.' Her anger sparked. 'Aren't men only supposed to be after one thing? When they get it, they call a woman a tart and dump her. And if they don't get what they want, they dump them anyway.'

He blushed. 'All men ain't like that.'

'And neither are women all the same.'

Frank glowered at her, provoking her to add, 'I thought you'd finished with Peg.'

He looked uncomfortable. 'Peg's a funny kid. She took something I said the wrong way.'

'She isn't a kid, Frank. But neither is she as experienced as many of the women you go out with.'

'Do you think I don't know that? Peg's a great girl.'

'Yes, she is.' Her anger dissipated. Frank had always been a cocky lad, sure of his good looks and charm. Now he appeared uncertain. 'I don't know what happened between you two. Perhaps you don't know what you want from her. Is it that you like her but aren't prepared to court a woman yet?'

'Sort of.' He rubbed the back of his neck as though reluctant to admit the truth.

'You can't play with people's emotions that way, Frank. Don't mess Peg about. If she's acting wild it's because her feelings have been hurt. You were her first boyfriend.'

'You reckon she might still be interested in seeing me?'

'That's for the two of you to sort out.'

He tipped back his straw boater and gave her a roguish grin. 'I thought you and her were thick as thieves.'

She guessed that Frank had never had a girlfriend who didn't fall over herself to please him. Peg had been mad about him. She would have done anything to keep Frank. Perhaps that was it. She had done whatever Frank wanted and when he didn't turn up for a date had felt used and cheapened. For all Peg's infatuation she wasn't flighty. If she had given herself to Frank it was because she loved him. No wonder she was hurting so bad: hurting so deeply her pride and shame were making her stubborn.

'If you care for Peg, then you must prove it to her. If not, then leave her alone.'

'How am I going to prove it, if she won't speak to me? I tried to give her some flowers and the little madam threw them on the ground and stamped on them.'

'You have got our Peg stirred up, haven't you?' Bethany

winked at him. 'I'm sure you'll think of a way.'

Bethany was troubled on the journey home. Since returning from Surrey Giles had monopolised Louise's company. She missed Peg's friendship and, concerned about her mother, she needed someone she could confide in.

When she reached home she was alarmed at recognising Dr Jones's car in the drive. Had there been an accident? No one had appeared ill. Forgetting the rule of taking Jasper through the back of the house, she ran indoors calling out, 'I'm back. Is everything all right?'

No one answered. There was an eerie silence within the house and Bethany's heart clenched with anxiety. Louise appeared at the top of the stairs. She was pale and at seeing Bethany gave a sob and ran down to embrace her. 'It's your mother. She complained of stomach pains and then collapsed. Papa summoned Dr Jones. He's with her now.'

'Did he say what was wrong? I must go to her.' Fear for her mother made her run forward.

Louise called after her, 'They won't let you in the bedroom. Dr Jones is still examining her.'

Anxiety iced Bethany's spine. 'Is it serious?'

Louise shrugged. 'It can't be too serious or Dr Jones would have telephoned for an ambulance.'

There were male voices above them and dropping Jasper's lead Bethany ran up the stairs. Balding and stocky, the doctor was whispering to Harold. 'Yes, she can still have children. But to safeguard a future child you must restrain your attentions throughout the pregnancy. And she'll need to rest during the day. If those precautions are taken she should carry another baby full term.'

He broke off at seeing Bethany.

'How is Mum, Dr Jones?'

Harold glared at the spaniel. Dr Jones, who had been their physician since Bethany was born, studied her gravely. 'Your mother has had a miscarriage. I've more calls to make but I'll return and check on her later. She's naturally distressed. I've given her a sedative.'

'But Mum will be all right?' Bethany asked.

Dr Jones nodded. 'She'll need a few days in bed and lots of love and understanding.'

'Poor Mum.' Bethany turned to Harold. 'It must be very upsetting for you, Papa.'

Harold looked horrified and flushed with embarrassment. 'Quite. Delicate matter. Not something one talks about.' He pointed to Jasper. 'You know the rules, child. That dog shouldn't be in this part of the house.'

The man was an insensitive megalomaniac. She bit back a sharp retort and addressed Dr Jones. 'Can I see Mum?'

'Yes, but only for a few minutes.'

Louise stepped forward. 'I'll take Jasper upstairs. Then I'll bring you some hot chocolate.'

'Don't go tiring your mother,' Harold ordered as she opened the door.

As if she would. Alice lay with her head turned into the pillow.

'I'm sorry about the baby, Mum.'

Alice put a hand to her face and her tears flowed through her fingers. Bethany sat on the bed and took her hand. 'You've got to look after yourself more. You haven't been eating or sleeping properly.'

'Harold expects another son from me. I've failed him.'

'Don't talk that way.' Bethany squeezed Alice's hand. 'You've only been married three months. I heard Dr Jones saying there's no reason why you shouldn't have a healthy baby. Tell me as soon as you suspect you're pregnant next time and I'll make sure that you rest properly.'

Alice nodded and clasped her hand more tightly. For several minutes they remained in silence. Alice lay with her eyes closed, clinging to Bethany as though she was a life raft. Bethany willed her mother to get well. She concentrated all her energy, wanting her own vitality to pass to her mother. She prayed for help and guidance to help Alice. When she opened her own eyes, Alice was smiling at her.

'You're such a comfort, my dear. You bring me peace and give me courage.' Her mother's lids again drooped.

'I love you, Mum. Rest now.'

Alice managed a weak smile, but as the door closed behind her daughter another pain gripped her body. The foetus had come away while Dr Jones attended her and the cramps which followed had been severe. The sedative made her muzzy. Dr Jones had given her a lecture with the intention that Harold should overhear, should she fall pregnant again. More the pity the warning had not come earlier. It was the gross indecencies she was subjected to each night which had caused the miscarriage. Last night Harold had tied her wrists and ankles to the bed and then mounted her from behind like an animal. The pain had been excruciating. She had begged for mercy, as she had every night this week, since she had told him that she believed herself pregnant. In the throes of passion he was deaf and blind to her pleas or wretchedness.

The bedroom door opened and Harold approached the bed. There was no compassion in his face, the lines about his mouth were pinched with bitterness. 'You lost our child. Why didn't you tell me you'd had other miscarriages? I thought you were a normal woman. Childbearing shouldn't be difficult. It's your function in life, after all.'

'You know why I lost the baby. I begged you to stop.'

'Don't make excuses for your own inadequacies. I'm sleeping in the next room tonight. Dr Jones said you should be able to perform your wifely duties in six weeks. I shall return to your bed then. Goodnight.'

His coldness swamped her in further misery. What a fool she had been. She had believed that all men were as considerate a lover as Edward. Edward had cradled her in his arms when she had previously miscarried. He had been so gentle, so caring. Living with Harold had become a nightmare. The charm and solicitation he had shown her during their courtship had been a sham. He was self-centred, caring only for his own well-being and needs. And the things he forced her to do made her want to retch at the memory. Despicable, degrading acts, demanded without love. Alice had been treated like a whore because her husband was impotent unless he became excited by inflicting pain on a woman.

She pulled the pillow against her face to muffle her cries. She wept for her lost ideals. She wept for the travesty of her marriage. And she wept for the lost baby for whom she would have suffered any amount of pain to have borne.

'Rotten luck about your mum,' Peg said as they sat upstairs in Bethany's study on Tuesday evening. 'And I'm sorry I've been a bitch lately. I've let you down.'

'Don't be silly.'

Peg shook her head. 'You were right about Frank. I was stupid enough to give in to his persuasion and then he thought he could treat me like dirt and stand me up. I felt a right fool. Cheap too.'

'But you could have got pregnant. Didn't you think of that?'

Peg grinned. 'Not when Frank got me going. I didn't think of anything but the pleasure he was giving me.'

'So what's happening between you and Frank? I saw him when I called last week and he was asking after you.'

'He was hanging round outside the shop when I got off the last bus. We had a long talk. He says he likes me more than any girl he's been out with, but he don't want to be tied to one woman. He's got enough responsibilities with the shop and helping his mum look after his invalid dad and the kids. He don't want to settle down yet.'

'That's understandable. He's given up a lot to help his parents,' Bethany advised. 'But it's not fair on you.'

'Too right. I told him to grow up. I ain't having no bloke two-timing me. I may be daft about him, but I love him too much to share him.'

'I'm sorry. But you've done the right thing.'

Peg pulled a face. 'I just wish being righteous didn't make me feel so bloody awful. So what have you been up to? I've missed you. Work is great and going out with the girls is fun, but it ain't like it was between us.'

Bethany told Peg about Giles.

'I told you he were a wrong 'un. You watch yourself with him. Couple of the girls from the exchange have said he can be a bastard. He got one of them drunk and roughed her up when she refused to let him have his way with her.'

'She should have gone to the police,' Bethany said. 'You can't let men treat you like that.'

'Wouldn't do no good. It would be her word against his.'

To change an unpleasant subject, Bethany spoke of Louise. 'She's really nice. We get on well. She comes out with me when I walk Jasper and we sneak him into the sitting room when Harold and Mum are out. Mrs Binns won't let on about the dog hairs. She's a brick.'

The evening sped by and the two friends vowed they would not lose touch with each other for so long again.

'We'll meet each Wednesday lunchtime at the station café,' Peg insisted. 'There's a fair over Wanstead Flats Friday night. See if you can get Harold to let you stay.'

'He's being difficult about that. Giles goes drinking with his mates on Fridays. I'll be glad when he returns to University. It would do Louise good to come out with us and have a giggle. Do you mind if she comes?'

'Course not. The more the merrier. I'll meet you by the horse carousel straight from work. Just after seven.'

When Friday came Harold had gone out for the evening. It was the second time this week.

'Mum, are you sure you'll be all right, if Louise and I go to the fair?' Bethany enquired. 'I don't like the thought of you being on your own.'

'I'll be fine. I've a book to read and could do with an early night. You and Louise enjoy yourselves. But be back by ten thirty. Harold will be displeased if he returns and you're not here.'

There was no sign of Peg when they reached the fun fair. They had twice been on the carousel while they waited for her. Twenty minutes later, red-faced from running, Peg was waving at them through the crowd.

'Sorry I'm so late. Frank was waiting for me outside the telephone exchange. He gave me a right quizzing about who I was meeting and where I was going. I told him straight it was none of his business that I was meeting you at the fair.'

Bethany grinned. 'So you managed to tell him where you were even though it was none of his business. You wouldn't be expecting to meet him when the shop shuts, would you?'

'Give over.' Peg assumed an air of injured innocence.

They spent an hour going on all the rides, their voices hoarse from their screams of excitement having to shout above the noise of the organs. Peg nudged Bethany in the ribs. 'Those four blokes have been following us for the last ten minutes. Reckon they're gonna ask us to join them?'

'Oh no,' Louise said looking appalled. 'You mustn't encourage them.'

'Why not?' Peg snorted. 'Ain't no harm in it. They're all wearing suits and look decent enough.'

'It isn't done.'

'Poppycock!' Peg snapped. 'How else you gonna meet a bloke? The one in the grey suit has got his eye on you, Louise.'

Bethany glanced over her shoulder and saw the man in question was studying Louise. He was nice looking. It would do Louise good to have a boyfriend. 'They do look respectable,' she encouraged, 'and if we all stayed together there wouldn't be any harm in it.'

'No!' Louise said sharply. 'I thought we were going on the big wheel next.' She headed towards it and Bethany followed with a reluctant Peg in tow.

When they came off the big wheel the four young men were on the rifle range nearby.

'There's a coconut shy across the way,' Louise announced, setting off towards it. Twice Bethany knocked a coconut on to its side but it didn't topple over.

'They're stuck on,' a man commented from behind her. 'You'll never get one.'

The man had broad shoulders and was blond-haired. He aimed three balls in fast succession at the stand, each bouncing off an unmoving coconut. One hit the attendant on the shoulder.

'Watch it, mate!' the stallholder shouted.

'If it hurt you that much,' the man contested, 'it should've knocked that coconut for six. Same as the young lady's here.' He then jumped over the rope which fenced off the coconuts and lifted the one Bethany had aimed at from its stand. He held it out to her. 'Look at that! It's got lead set into its base. This man's been cheating everyone.'

'No I ain't. A bit of weight's necessary or they fall off in a strong wind.'

The blond-haired man tossed a ball to the stallholder, his voice loud and challenging. 'Then you throw a ball and show us how it's done. And mind you aim at this one.'

The stallholder glowered at him but seeing his antagonist's three companions, he licked his lips nervously. 'Happen the lady deserved to win.' He picked up a garishly painted chalk clown and offered it to Bethany.

It was hideous. 'If I'm entitled to a prize I'd rather have the statue of the dog.'

'But that's for two hits.' The attendant scowled.

'Then she can have it for the prize I was entitled to.'

A crowd had gathered and the stallholder was becoming agitated. 'Very well. Just don't go round saying this ain't an honest stall.'

Bethany took her prize and noticed that the line of people waiting to have a go had disappeared. Serve the man right. The chalk figurine wasn't worth more than a couple of bob. She hated dishonesty. She turned to the blond-haired man. 'You shouldn't have given up your prize for me.'

'What do I need with a statue of a dog? And I hate people who cheat.' He held out his hand. 'I'm Bill Lister. This is my brother David.' He pointed to the man who had earlier shown an interest in Louise. 'And the other two are Terry and Ian.'

'We must be going, Bethany,' Louise announced.

'It's only just gone nine,' she protested. 'And the smell of those chestnuts roasting is making me hungry.'

Bill chuckled. 'If you're hungry you want to try the pie and mash stall.'

'That sounds great,' Peg piped up.

'I don't think so.' Louise looked imploringly at Bethany.

Bethany didn't want to leave. Bill seemed nice and David hadn't taken his eyes off Louise. He looked as shy as she was. 'I'm going to have a plate of cockles,' she addressed Louise, 'and then how about going in to the dance tent until ten?'

'Good idea,' Bill chirped. 'Mind if we join you?'

Peg giggled. 'That's fine by me.'

Bethany had been watching Peg and, following her gaze, had seen Frank Hobson weaving through the crowd. The little minx was determined to make him jealous.

'Only if we all pay our own way,' Bethany insisted. 'Is that all right with you, Louise? It's only for half an hour.'

She nodded but didn't look happy. She kept her head bowed as she ate her plate of cockles and did not join in the conversation. David, who was a darker blond and darker skinned than his brother, stood next to her, also not speaking. When Louise had finished her cockles, he took her plate and returned it to the stall counter. Louise blushed and smiled shyly.

Peg was flirting outrageously with Bill's two friends and Bethany wondered if they should abandon the idea of going to the dance tent. Peg was already being steered towards it by Ian. Bill was amusing. It would be pleasant to spend some time with them.

Inside the tent Peg was whirled on to the floor for a waltz and Bill turned to Bethany. She looked hesitantly at

Louise, uncomfortable at leaving her alone.

'Your friend will be fine with David,' Bill said. 'He hasn't had much time for girls. Our dad died three years ago after a long illness. In the last year while David was still at agricultural college he sold off most of the stock and hadn't worked the land. The bank was threatening to foreclose. David blames himself for not realising sooner but Dad would never admit that there was a problem. Big brother has been slaving day and night to get the farm back on its feet. Succeeded as well. It's time he learned to enjoy himself.'

She allowed him to lead her on to the dance floor and asked, 'Have you been helping him with the farm?'

'Lord no. I'm not cut out to be a farmer. I joined the navy. I'm on leave for a couple of weeks. We've just got back from the Med. Quite a stir-up going on out there for all Britain has signed a naval accord with Germany. Wouldn't be surprised if those Nazis didn't get above themselves soon.'

Bethany nodded. 'I've seen some of the Nazi rallies on the Pathe news. All that shouting and saluting. Hitler strikes me as a fanatic and an egotist.'

Bill frowned. 'More like a madman.' He pulled her closer. 'Let's not spoil our dance by talking about politics. You're a real stunner. You gonna let me walk you home?'

'Louise is my stepsister. I won't leave her.' Bethany was intrigued by Bill but his worldliness made her edgy. David was dancing with Louise who held herself stiffly and kept her head bowed. Bethany sighed. David was different from his brasher brother and seemed hardworking and considerate. He was the right type of man for Louise.

Four dances later Peg touched her arm. 'I've got to go, Beth. I'll see you Wednesday for lunch.'

'Why are you leaving so early?'

Peg winked. 'Something's come up.' She dived through the crowd and as the dancers swirled past was momentarily lost to her. Then she saw her leaving the marquee with an all-too-familiar figure. Frank had his arm possessively around her. At the same time she saw that Louise was laughing at something David was saying.

She looked at her watch. 'I have to go, Bill.'

'David and I will walk you and your stepsister home.'

When the subject was broached, Louise looked frightened. She stepped back from David, her gaze fixed upon his shoes. 'Papa wouldn't like it. Better not. Come on, Bethany. We mustn't be late.' She darted out of the tent.

'Louise, stop! What have I done?' David went after her.

When Bethany caught them up, Louise was very distressed. 'Please, you don't understand. I can't see you again, David.' She again ran off and David stared after her, puzzled.

Bethany felt she had to explain. 'It's not you, David. It's her twin brother who doesn't like her seeing anyone. He even resents Louise and myself being friends.'

'Sounds like a bully. I can handle him,' David replied. 'She's a lovely woman. I'd like to see her again.'

Bill took her hand. 'I want to see you again. I've only got two weeks' leave.'

Her hesitation was brief. 'I must go after Louise. Meet us outside Beardman's store tomorrow at two o'clock. I'll have talked some sense into Louise by then.'

Bethany wanted to see Bill again and guessed Louise had liked David. She wasn't going to let Giles spoil things. Her exasperation showed when she caught up with her stepsister. 'What got into you, Louise? David likes you.'

The stricken look in Louise's eyes stabbed at Bethany's heart. 'Whatever is wrong?'

Louise didn't answer and kept silent during the bus ride home. The bus was crowded so Bethany did not pursue the matter until they alighted and turned into their road.

'Tell me why you're so upset. David seemed really nice. I thought you had got on well with him.'

'Nothing is wrong.' There was defence and fear in her quivering voice. 'I don't want a boyfriend. Ever. Giles will make trouble.'

'Does Giles bully you? If he does, you should tell Harold.'

'No!' The fear was stark in her eyes. 'Forget I mentioned it. If Giles thought I'd spoken . . .' She broke into a run with Bethany pursuing her.

'I won't let Giles hurt you in future. There's two of us now. I'm your friend. Let me help you.'

Chapter Six

'Bethany, you planned this,' Louise accused when she saw Bill and David approach them as they came out of Beardman's shop.

'They were keen to see us again. I like Bill. And you like David. He's a nice man. You've got to stop allowing Giles to dictate your life for you.'

The men's arrival stopped Louise's protest. Bill plunged in enthusiastically, 'It's great to meet you two again. How about a coffee?'

After their coffee Louise had begun talking easily to David and she did not object when Bill suggested that they go for a walk over Coronation Park. Bill took Bethany's hand as they walked but Louise and David remained several inches apart although they were now chatting animatedly.

They sat on a seat in the sunshine. Bill kept telling them jokes and soon their eyes were streaming with tears of laughter. The shadows were lengthening when Louise jumped to her feet. 'Look at the time. We'll be late home, Bethany.'

'Can we see you tonight?' Bill asked.

'I'm afraid not,' Bethany replied. 'My stepfather has arranged for the family to dine out with business associates.

It's very boring but we can't get out of it.'

Bill pulled a face. 'Sunday night then? We'll go to the pictures.'

She shook her head. 'Sunday is difficult. Harold was talking about a picnic by the river if my mother is up to it. She's been ill. If the meal tonight hasn't tired her too much the fresh air will do her good. I've no idea what time we'll be back.'

'So give it a miss!'

'Papa would hit the roof,' Louise cut in. 'He's very old fashioned. He'll insist on meeting you before he allows us to see you again.'

'He's living in the dark ages,' Bill grunted.

'I'd be happy to call on him and introduce myself,' David said, taking Louise's hand.

Worry pleated Louise's brow. 'Then he would want to know how we met. He'd be furious if he learned we'd met you at the fair or outside a shop like today.'

'So how do I get to see you again?' David insisted. 'I can't get away from the farm this week until the evening as we've a crop to harvest.'

Louise looked at Bethany for help. Bethany thought rapidly. 'There's a dance at Stratford Town Hall next Saturday. Harold always picks us up afterwards. We could meet you at the dance. You can introduce yourselves to him afterwards.'

Bill gave David a wary look. Obviously, he didn't like the formality of it. Bethany suspected that Bill, being a sailor, usually had casual girlfriends. She studied his handsome face and experienced a stab of regret. He was fun to be with, but she wouldn't be heartbroken if he had other plans for next Saturday. David, however, latched on to her words. 'That's fine by me. Saturday at the Town Hall then.'

'Yeah!' Bill conceded but Bethany sensed that he was not so happy about the arrangement.

'You've only got a short leave, Bill. Enjoy it,' Bethany said, making it clear that he didn't have to turn up if he didn't want to.

He smiled and looked guilty, realising that she had guessed his thoughts. 'You're all right, Beth. Saturday is fine by me.'

When Bethany met Peg the following Wednesday she invited her to the dance. Her friend was evasive. 'I might be seeing Frank.'

'Come if you can.' Bethany knew it was useless to try and force her when her heart was pining to be with Frank.

To her dismay a tear rolled down Peg's cheek and she blurted out, 'I thought it was all settled between us when he took me home from the fair. I saw him Saturday night and we went over the park Sunday afternoon and to a pub in the evening. Then he came on strong, as he does.' She ploughed her fingers through her blonde hair, dishevelling its curls. Her expression became haggard. 'We had a terrible row. I love him so much, Beth. But he admitted he don't want to be tied to just one girl. I told him to sling his hook.'

'You did right,' Bethany reassured her.

'But I feel awful.' She dabbed at her eyes with her handkerchief, battling against her tears. 'I know Frank likes me. You should have heard him going on about the blokes we were with on Friday. I'd swear he was jealous. He don't like me having other boyfriends, but he's not prepared to give up other women for me.'

Bethany covered her friend's hand with her own. 'Frank does like you. That's the trouble. He's fighting against it.

You either have to forget him or be patient and hope that in a few months he'll see what a fool he's being.'

'Men! Who needs them?' Peg grimaced. 'I'm gonna have some fun. The girls in work have asked me to go up West with them this weekend. I ain't hanging round waiting for Frank Hobson to make up his mind. Neither am I gonna make myself available for him. I'll walk around the block rather than past his bloody shop now. That will show him.'

Bethany would have applauded such bravado if it wasn't obvious how much her friend was hurting. If it was meant to be between Peg and Frank, it would work itself out.

Alice had changed since her miscarriage. No longer did she laugh so easily or take pleasure in shopping for the family or home. The grand piano had been placed in the back drawing room and she had taken to playing it every day. As a young woman she had been an accomplished pianist and had taught Bethany to play. Now Alice had engaged a tutor for herself and practised complicated pieces for hours on end.

At first Bethany was delighted at her mother's interest. Then the persistence with which Alice applied herself to the music began to disturb her. It wasn't natural to be so obsessive. Losing the baby had affected her mother profoundly. She supposed it was a harmless enough therapy to divert that pain into her playing. It didn't help that Harold was insensitive to Alice's unhappiness. Her mother was playing now. She repeated the same passage over and over to perfect it. Disgruntled sounds from Harold made Bethany glance at him across the chessboard. His face was growing redder and his knuckles were white upon his newspaper. Beside her Louise groaned softly. Then Harold flung down his paper and stormed out of the sitting room.

'That infernal racket has given me a headache!' he yelled. 'At least play a proper tune if you must play when I'm here. It's time you pulled yourself together, woman. The meal tonight was not of the standard I expect from you.'

Moments later the front door slammed as Harold left the house. Excusing herself to Louise, Bethany hurried to her mother. Alice was slumped over the piano sobbing. 'Mum, don't cry. Your playing was beautiful.'

Bethany hugged Alice and was shocked to feel the harsh protrusion of her bones through her dress. Her mother must have lost over a stone in weight. She murmured comforting words as she gently stroked her hands over her mother's shoulders and arms. The sobs stilled and Alice pulled away. 'I'm all right now. It's silly of me to get upset. My playing must get on your nerves. Harold has had a difficult day at the office.'

Alice wiped her eyes and blew her nose. Seeing the distress in her daughter's face, she knew that for Bethany's sake she must hide her misery. Her marriage was a disaster. Harold did not love her. He was cold and unfeeling. She was beginning to hate him. She was playing tonight to forget an earlier row when she had walked into the bedroom to find him changing his shirt. Since her miscarriage he was away from the house four evenings a week.

'Not more business, my dear. You work too hard. I see so little of you lately.'

His glare was condemning. 'Your company is hardly conducive of a pleasant evening. You shy away from me even if I kiss your cheek.'

'It isn't just kisses you want, is it, Harold? You know what the doctor said. Another two weeks and I can be a proper wife to you again.'

Ignoring her, he adjusted the line of his tie and shrugged into his waistcoat. 'Whatever makes you think you ever were a proper wife to me? There's scant warmth I've had from you in bed.'

'Sometimes you hurt me,' she retaliated.

He thrust his arms through his jacket and eyed her narrowly. 'You've been a disappointment, Alice. Fortunately there are women who are not so frigid as you.'

'You visit such a woman!' Horror widened her eyes.

'Of course. My first wife, Mildred, understood these matters. As you must accept them. There's a woman in Hackney who I've seen for several years. She has given me a daughter.'

Alice backed away from him. The revelation appalled her. She felt sick with disgust. 'Then why didn't you marry *her*?'

'Her background isn't respectable enough for her to be my wife,' he scoffed. 'She has a loving nature but is common. Though I wonder if I wasn't too hasty in so condemning her. At least she's fertile. She never complains. Never denies me.'

Alice sank down on the edge of the bed, her body shaking with humiliation. 'You wrong us both. Or do you pay this whore of yours handsomely to feign her pleasure?'

He struck her hard across the cheek sending her sprawling across the bed. 'I won't have such filthy talk from my wife. Your duty is to give me a son. If you don't and this woman should do so, then you'll have to accept her son as your own.'

Alice pushed herself up on her elbows to glare at him. The evil in his smile unnerved her. He meant it.

He strode out of the bedroom, his threats hanging menacingly in the air. He was capable of such cruelty. He would shame her and find a way to raise his bastard behind a pious mask.

She had gone to her piano and for a time had lost herself in the complicated music. How could she have been so blind not to see the evil in Harold? Pride squared her shoulders and she forced a smile to reassure her daughter. Her marriage had been a mistake but she would suffer it in silence. God willing she would fall for another child soon and then Harold would be forced to leave her alone. If she gave him his son, she need not endure his attentions again. Dear God, let her bear him a son.

'The place is crowded,' Louise groaned as they entered the ballroom in the Town Hall on Saturday night. 'We'll never get a seat. We should have arrived earlier.'

'Only wallflowers sit round the corners,' Bethany teased. The band was playing, the music pulsed through her and soon her foot was tapping. She wore a calf-length lilac dress which emphasised the violet of her eyes. She had kept her hair down preferring the gypsy abandonment of it to having it tortured into a chignon. Louise was in pale primrose, the dress specially chosen for her by Alice. It accentuated the soft curves of her figure and complemented her fiery hair. That afternoon Bethany had persuaded her to visit a hair salon for a cut and marcel-wave which flattered her face. She looked lovely.

Louise was searching the ballroom. 'I can't see David.' Her disappointment was obvious.

'It's early yet. It won't do David any harm if he finds you dancing with another partner. I'm not waiting round for Bill to turn up.'

During the next half hour they were never without partners. Bill and David Lister eventually sauntered into the ballroom with a group of friends.

Louise blushed then her colour drained. She ducked behind a central pillar and dragged Bethany with her. 'I don't think I should see him. Let's leave.'

'Stop being a ninny. David likes you. This is only the third dance I've been allowed to attend on my own. Don't spoil it for me by rushing off.'

Louise hung her head. 'I hated my first dance. Giles was there. He wouldn't let anyone dance with me. I danced half a dozen times with him, the rest of the time I sat on the side feeling miserable and unattractive.' Louise sighed. 'After that I attended few dances and always with Giles. He always spoilt them.'

'Giles isn't here tonight.'

'But he'll find out,' she said, heavily. 'He always finds out. And then something dreadful happens.'

'You mean his friends beat up your partner.'

'How did you know?' Her eyes widened with horror. 'Is it common gossip? I couldn't bear that.'

'Giles is well known as a bully and David knows that. He's prepared to stand up to him. If Giles tries to cause trouble he may find he's met his match.'

Bethany saw David and his friends standing at the back of the dance floor. Bill was dancing with his cheek pressed against that of a generously curved and over made-up blonde.

David lost no time in claiming Louise for the next waltz. Bethany was asked to dance by a debonair man just as Bill had turned in her direction. Bill winked at her and headed across the floor to scoop a redhead into his arms. Bethany's partner fancied himself and didn't stop boasting about his success with women. She couldn't wait to get shot of him. The next number was the Lambeth Walk and David beckoned to her to make up their number. Halfway through the dance as they changed partners she found herself looking into Bill's grinning face.

'If I didn't know you better, I'd think you were avoiding me,' he said as she twirled under his arm.

'You haven't been short of partners.'

'There's only one dance that's important and that's the last one. I'm saving that for you, sweetheart.'

Bethany laughed. It was easy to enjoy Bill's company although she found him rather too worldly for her taste.

The next dance was a waltz and Bethany was whisked away by one of Peg's brothers, Jack, before Bill could claim her. He shrugged and mouthed, 'The next waltz is mine,' and promptly drew a voluptuous brunette into a tight embrace. Bill was incorrigible.

Over Jack's shoulder she saw David and Louise dancing close and her expression became wistful. 'You fancy that bloke?' Jack nodded towards David.

'I was watching my stepsister.'

A broad smile flashed white teeth at her. 'You look terrific, Beth. Always reckoned you'd turn out a beauty. Fancy coming to the pictures with me on Tuesday night?'

'Jack, you're joking. I'm four years younger than you. Do you want to be caught cradle-snatching?'

'I like them young and innocent in my decrepit old age.'

She knew he was teasing her as he had teased her throughout her friendship with Peg. His expression sobered. 'What's up with Peg? Haven't had a civil word out of her all week. Is it that Frank? Does he need a talking to? If he's laid a hand on her, I swear I'll . . .'

Did all brothers act so protectively? First Giles and now Jack, and an easier-going bloke than him she was yet to meet. Could it be that Louise had blown things out of proportion about her brother?

Jack was looking fierce and she hastened to assure him. 'Peg is growing up. Frank isn't going to do anything silly on his own doorstep, is he? Especially with two hulking great brothers like you and Mike to defend their sister's virtue. Leave well alone, Jack. That's my advice.'

'You always were the sensible one. I hope you're right.'

Bethany hoped so too. And not only about Frank and Jack's behaviour, but about how Louise had regarded her twin.

During the evening Louise danced several times with David. Bethany danced twice with Bill who flattered her outrageously and was probably as effusive to his other partners. A quarter of an hour before the dance ended, Louise grabbed her arm. 'Please, let's go now. A couple of Giles's friends have come in. David's gone to get me a drink. I want to leave before he returns. I can't risk any trouble.'

'You can't run out on David like that. It will be the end of anything between you.'

'It's for the best, believe me.' She was already walking towards the cloakroom and by the time Bethany entered she had retrieved her coat and was pulling it on.

Bethany sighed. Louise was clearly agitated. There was no point in telling her that her fears were groundless and that Giles was being no more protective than Jack was over Peg. From her expression Louise would not believe her.

Bethany felt guilty that they had run out on David. She knew that Louise liked him and it was a rotten trick to play on him. It was probably the last they would see of the Lister brothers. Louise wouldn't speak of David. She became withdrawn and spent hours in her greenhouse propagating cuttings. It had taken her all morning to persuade Louise to join her and Peg in town.

Louise wasn't the only one with boyfriend trouble. When Bethany and Louise met Peg in the station café, her friend was in a bleak mood. Her plan to avoid Frank in the hope that he would miss her had failed. They had just seen Frank walk past the station café with Molly Pearce on his arm. She was clinging to him like a barnacle.

Peg's eyes filled with tears and she ran outside and disappeared down a side alley. By the time Bethany and Louise caught up with her, Peg was sobbing.

'I could kill Frank,' she wailed. 'He's a two-timing swine. I saw him and Molly in a doorway last night and from Molly's giggles they were doing more than just kissing. I'll show that cocky sod. I'll get me a new bloke every week and parade past his blasted shop and see how he likes that.'

'That's not the answer,' Bethany advised. 'You'll get yourself a reputation for being flighty, if not worse. Forget Frank. He's not worth it.'

'But I love him so much.' The tears erupted into torrents. Bethany put her arms around her friend and gave her a handkerchief. 'I know you care for him, but he's not worth getting so upset over. You must forget him.'

'Oh God, I'm in such a mess,' Peg wailed. 'Dad will kill me. I don't know what I'm gonna do.'

Bethany held her tight and let her sob on to her shoulder. 'What's wrong? It's more than just Frank, isn't it?'

Peg nodded. 'I've been such a fool. I believed him when he said I was different. Special to him. I thought he cared.' She lifted her tear-drenched face. 'Dad's gonna kill me. I'm so ashamed. I'm gonna have Frank's baby.'

Bethany swallowed hard. 'Oh, Peg. Why didn't you tell me sooner?'

'I couldn't tell you after what you said. I knew you'd say I was a fool. But I thought it was the only way I could keep him, so I kept on doing it.'

'Have you been to the doctor to make certain?'

Peg nodded and burst into fresh tears.

When she was quieter, Louise surprised Bethany by saying, 'You don't need to have the baby. There's people you can go to who can fix things.'

'Oh no, I couldn't do that.' Peg was emphatic.

'How do you know of such places?' Bethany was intrigued. She had thought Louise so prim and modest.

Louise hunched her shoulders and plucked at a loose thread on her navy cardigan. 'I was only trying to help.' She tensed and her features hardened. Normally Bethany would have pursued the issue but for now she was too worried about Peg.

'Have you told Frank about the baby?' Bethany didn't believe that Frank, for all his philandering, would be so callous as to abandon Peg.

She shook her head. 'He won't want to know. He said he hasn't any intention of marrying for at least another five years.'

'He can't shirk this responsibility. And I don't think Frank is the type who would.' She gave Peg a gentle shake. 'You've got to tell him.'

'But I don't want to force him.' Misery made her voice tremble. 'What if he blames me for ruining his life? He'll hate me.'

Bethany controlled the impulse to jolt some sense into Peg as her exasperation mounted. 'It took two of you to get into this mess and it was Frank doing all the persuading, I bet.'

She rummaged in her pocket for a clean hankie and gave it to Peg. 'Now blow your nose, wipe your eyes and put on some fresh lipstick. This is best sorted out between you and Frank before your family guess what's happened. Your brothers are capable of putting Frank in hospital if they suspect he's done wrong by you. I'll meet you for lunch on Friday and you can tell me when you and Frank have set the wedding date.'

Peg did as she was told, looking so forlorn that Bethany was tempted to tear off down the High Street and give Frank Hobson a piece of her mind. She wouldn't, of course. It had to be settled between Frank and Peg.

At her confidence Peg brightened. 'Do you really think Frank will marry me?'

'Yes. He's not a bad man. And you'll make him a smashing wife.'

Peg was more cheerful as she returned to work but throughout the afternoon at home Louise was uncommunicative. Bethany got the impression that she wanted to tell her something but kept holding back. After they had cleared the dinner table and Harold had gone out, Bethany sought out Louise. She was in the back room with her feet drawn up on an armchair and her expression unhappy.

'What's wrong?'

'Nothing.'

Bethany sensed something was troubling her. 'Do you fancy a walk? Jasper has been shut in most of today and could do with a run. Mum doesn't like me going out alone of an evening, even though it's still light.'

Louise agreed but remained quiet as they walked through the streets until Bethany was prompted to ask, 'Do you regret not seeing David? Giles has been away staying with friends a lot this summer.'

'I don't want to talk about David or Giles.'

Bethany decided to change the subject and talk about what troubled her most. She looked up at the evening sky where the thinnest sliver of a crescent moon was visible, although the sun had not yet set.

'They say from the new to full moon is a time for new beginnings and for growing strength. Let's hope that's right. Peg certainly has a new start ahead of her and she'll need strength to face her family. No doubt they'll be angry at first. But they'll support her. Gloria Styles would never abandon her daughter in her time of greatest need.'

'She's fortunate then. Few families are so supportive.'

The bitterness in Louise's voice caused Bethany to frown.

A church clock struck nine. They had come further than Bethany anticipated and it would take them more than an hour to walk home.

'Aren't you shocked at what has happened to your friend?' Louise said dourly. 'Papa will be angry. He won't want you to associate with her.'

'Peg isn't bad. She's been unfortunate. She loves Frank. She needs my support not my censure.'

A long sigh quivered on Louise's breath. Bethany expected her to speak, but she didn't. Each lost to their own thoughts they walked in silence for several yards.

'A girl at the convent got herself into trouble,' Louise said so softly Bethany had to strain to hear. 'She couldn't marry the baby's father and he forced her to have an abortion. She couldn't tell her parents. They would have thrown her out on the street as a slut.'

It was a story Bethany had heard before and usually a young woman from a middle-class family was involved. The callousness of the parents appalled her. They feared the censure of neighbours, putting their status and pride before their child's need. 'That must have been awful for her. Was she a close friend of yours?'

Louise didn't answer and was staring at the paving slabs as they walked. Finally she said, 'It's always the women who have to pay, carrying the burden of guilt. Even if they marry, the guilt remains. And to have taken the life of a child . . . Do women ever come to terms with that?'

'It's not for us to judge them,' Bethany answered. 'They have done what they thought right. How could your friend have coped as an unmarried mother?'

To change the subject and take her mind from Peg's problem, Bethany spoke of inconsequentials. Louise answered abstractedly and then gave a cry as she was pitched forward and nearly fell on the pavement.

'Confound it! I've ripped the heel off my shoe tripping over that manhole cover.' She retrieved the broken shoe and glared at it. Then snatching the other one off, added waspishly, 'Might as well walk barefoot. Mercifully Papa can't see me. He'd lecture me on acting like a hoyden.'

'In that case I bet the hoydens have more fun,' Bethany laughed.

It broke the tension between them. Louise giggled. 'I wish I had your view on life. I take things too seriously.'

'Harold probably condemns me as a bad influence on you. You're all he desires in a daughter, whilst I . . .' Bethany pulled a face, 'lack decorum and have the temerity to question the supreme judgement of his will. In short, I don't believe he's always right.'

Louise laughed. 'You're a tonic, Bethany. I wish I could be more like you.'

'Nonsense, don't put yourself down. You have many qualities which make you special.'

A car slowed down at the kerb beside them and the

window was wound down. 'Can we give you a lift?'

Bethany was about to curtly refuse when she recognised David Lister in the passenger seat.

Louise cut in before she could speak. 'I broke my heel. But we haven't far to go. Thank you, we can manage.'

The door opened and David got out. He was smiling with pleasure. 'You could get a nail in your foot and get lockjaw or something terrible. Am I such an ogre, that you'd face that, rather than accept a lift from me and my friend?' He nodded to the man behind the wheel and continued with mock formality, 'Allow me to introduce Mark Greenwood. A long-standing friend of my family and in his final year of studying to be a doctor. So he's terribly respectable.'

'I don't think we should,' Louise declared, ignoring the irony of his formal introduction. 'And we have the dog.'

'The spaniel isn't a problem. I'm sure he's well trained.' His smile faded. 'The drive would give us a chance to talk. I'd been hoping to see you again.'

Bethany was exasperated by Louise. It was obvious David liked her. To get them together she slid into the passenger seat and ordered Jasper to sit at her feet. Panting he laid his head on her knees. 'If you don't mind the dog in your car, Mr Greenwood, we *would* appreciate a lift. Louise can't walk the mile home barefoot. I'm Bethany Masterton, by the way.'

'Pleased to meet you.' His smile was open and there was an amused twinkle in his eyes which Bethany liked. She turned to Louise who was still being coerced by David to get in to the car. 'C'mon, Louise. You're just being stubborn.'

'Please, Louise.' David spoke softly and put his hand on her arm. 'I've been thinking of you all the time.'

'Have you?' There was a catch of excitement in her voice. 'I didn't like running out on you. But you have to understand . . .'

'We'll talk in the car,' David urged.

To Bethany's relief Louise got in and she gave Mark their address as they pulled away. At the corner she said, 'You should have turned left there, not right.'

Mark winked at Bethany. He was a good-looking man, with angular and rather rugged features which Bethany found attractive. His hair was brown but his eyes were the most piercing grey she had ever seen. He said in a low voice, 'They aren't going to resolve anything if I get you home in five minutes, are they? David is keen on your sister.'

Bethany nodded agreement. 'We must be home by ten or my mother will be frantic with worry.'

'Plenty of time. We can stop off at the common.'

'As long as you don't go getting any ideas, Mr Greenwood. I don't hold with girls who get picked up off the street. The circumstances tonight were exceptional.'

'I shall be the perfect gentleman.'

Bethany smiled. When she gazed into his handsome face an unbidden thought made her speculate that it would be a pity if he was too much of a gentleman. It might have been exciting to be kissed by Mark Greenwood.

They pulled on to the hard-packed earth of the common. Louise's voice rose from the back of the car, 'Why are you stopping? We shouldn't be here. It isn't proper.'

'I only want to talk with you,' David said.

Mark turned to Bethany. 'Shall we go for a short walk? Give them ten minutes alone.'

Trusting that Louise would not feel she had been deserted, Bethany agreed. She let Jasper off the lead and he ran ahead.

'Bethany, where are you going?' Louise said, anxiously.

'I'm not going to hurt you.' David sounded cross. 'I only want to ask you out.'

'But I can't. I thought I'd explained. Papa can be difficult, also my brother.'

'Then I'll call on your father and ask his permission. Just say you're agreeable.'

'Look here,' Mark intervened. 'If your father is going to cut up rough about you seeing David, how about if Bethany and I come along to make it a foursome? No need to tell your father if we just go for a meal together.' He turned a warm smile on Bethany. 'That's if you aren't averse to spending a couple of hours in my company?'

'I'd enjoy that,' she managed evenly, although her heart was pounding in an erratic manner at the thought of seeing Mark again.

'No, not a meal,' Louise announced, her protest no longer strident. 'At least not round here. What if someone saw us and told Papa?'

'Then you choose where we go,' David said. 'The pictures. How about roller skating over Forest Gate on Friday evening?'

'That sounds like fun.' Bethany willed Louise to accept.

'Very well,' Louise agreed, 'we'll meet you outside.'

David chuckled. 'You're a devilish hard woman to ask out on a date. Anyone would think that some disaster was going to happen.'

Chapter Seven

'Don't tell me Frank refused to marry you!' Bethany was shocked at how dejected Peg looked when she met her for lunch on Friday.

'He agreed all right,' Peg replied, bleakly. 'But he wasn't exactly overjoyed.'

'He needs time to accept the idea. It's a big responsibility.'

'But I didn't want to force him. I love him so much. It's a rotten start to a marriage. What if he resents me?'

'Stop thinking that way. Marriage is what you make it. You and Frank are good for each other. Have you set a date?'

'As soon as possible. We're going to tell our parents tonight. I'm hoping Mum will let us have my room at home until we can afford a proper flat. I'm dreading tonight. Dad will go mad.'

Bethany nodded sympathetically. 'It will soon blow over. They like Frank and your dad loves a chance for a party down the pub.'

That made Peg laugh. 'Dad does love his beer. I'll get a couple of pints down him before Frank comes round. That might mellow him.' Her expression became serious. 'You'll be my bridesmaid, won't you? I'd still like a church wedding, although it would have to be a small affair.'

'I'd be honoured. Just think, you'll be Mrs Frank Hobson. It's what you've always dreamed of. Be happy, Peg.'

Peg cheered up and after she had related the plans she and Frank had made for the wedding Bethany told her about going skating that evening with David and Mark.

'So what's this Mark like? Handsome is he?'

'Not bad. I hardly spoke to him. He's only dating me so that Louise will go out with David.'

'Then he's blind.'

'He's at least six years older than me.'

'So what? And what happened about Bill?'

'There was never anything between Bill and me.'

'Then your heart is free to fall for this doctor? He sounds more your type. You've so much in common.'

'Don't go all romantic on me, Peg. You've got your white knight. Mark is going on this date to help out his friend. The same as I am.'

By the time she had spent an hour laughing and joking in Mark Greenwood's company, Bethany's heart was pounding wildly. He was more handsome than she remembered. It was years since she had been on roller skates and her balance was shaky. He came up behind her and pushed her round the rink at great speed, until she was shrieking with a mixture of pleasure and fear. Then his arm had slid around her waist, guiding her in and out of the skaters whilst holding her close against him. His touch made her flesh tingle with excitement and the warmth of his breath on her cheek was intoxicating. He adapted his long stride to match her shorter one, all the time teasing her. Her cheeks were flushed and her eyes were shining. She couldn't remember when she had last enjoyed herself more.

She had always imagined doctors to be serious men. Mark was a born tease. It didn't take long with Mark's arm around her for her confidence to return and it was only the thought of him releasing her which stopped her racing ahead. Then a woman in front of them lost her balance and sprawled directly in their path. Without thinking Bethany pulled away from Mark and agilely avoided the woman and then had to immediately manoeuvre to avoid another beginner.

'Hey, you can skate.' Mark grinned at her. 'C'mon, I'll race you.'

The romantic interlude was over and it became a challenge to out-skate Mark. She sped up to him and, unable to resist impressing him, swivelled round to skate backwards. One moment she was at his side urging him on, the next he gripped her waist and she was lifted bodily from the floor as he swung her round and round in waltz time to the music.

'Put me down,' she managed to force out through her laughter. 'We'll fall.'

'Oh ye of little faith.'

When he pretended to drop her, she screamed and the sound of his rich laughter echoed through to the core of her heart.

The evening sped by and ended too quickly for Bethany. Mark insisted on driving them home. David and Louise were speaking softly in the back of the car. Bethany was fascinated by Mark and was on tenterhooks to hear if he wanted to see her again.

Louise insisted that Mark park in the side-road off their street. 'Father might get home early and see the car.'

'Perhaps I should come in and meet him,' David offered.

'No. Not yet. I know you mean well, but Papa will only

spoil things. He would want to know your intentions and that would embarrass me.'

'My intentions are serious, Louise,' David said softly. 'I want to know you much better.'

'Same here,' Mark said sliding his arm around Bethany's shoulders. 'I'm on duty all next week. The hours are long and I won't be able to get away. How about tomorrow? I don't start at the hospital until six in the evening. We could spend the day together.'

'We could spend the day in the City,' David urged. 'The weather is supposed to be good. We could take a boat trip down the Thames. Go to an exhibition, or just wander around the parks.'

'I love the City and Westminster,' Bethany said. 'I've never been to the Abbey.'

'Then that's what we'll do!' Mark announced. 'What time shall I pick you up?'

'I'd rather meet elsewhere,' Louise timidly suggested. 'And it's silly Mark coming all the way out of the City from his training hospital and David from Loughton. Let's meet at Liverpool Street Station at ten thirty and go on from there.'

It was agreed. Louise opened the door to get out but was pulled back by David. Mark chuckled and drew Bethany closer to him. 'You're not going to send me home without a goodnight kiss are you?'

His hand moved to the side of her face and for a long moment his grey eyes studied her, their lips remaining a finger's breadth apart. Under his compelling stare she had no thought of protest, she had been anticipating this moment all evening. The warmth of his mouth skimmed her lips, gently at first and then with a deliciously sweet ardour. It was a revelation that a kiss could be so beautiful, causing a *frisson* of pleasure to seep through her entire body. Her lips parted and their breaths mingled. Caught up by emotions she had not thought possible, she moaned softly with pleasure. Her fingers curled through his thick hair binding them closer. Mark eased back from her, his stare intense, and he ran a hand along the line of her jaw to the edge of her mouth. 'A pity you have to rush away. The evening is just getting interesting. I've enjoyed tonight. You're good fun to be with. Until tomorrow, Beth.'

She blushed, treasuring his words. When they parted the glow which had been irradiating her all evening began to fade. She already missed him and was eager for tomorrow when they would be together again. Or was she being foolish? The age gap loomed between them. He may think her too young and drop her when he learned her age. After all he was only seeing her to make up a foursome so that Louise would go out with David.

'Louise, what excuse can we use to spend all day with them tomorrow?'

'That's not a problem. I overheard Papa telling Alice that he's leaving after breakfast to play in a charity cricket match at Billericay. He does that from time to time. He won't be home until late as there's some do afterwards.'

'Mum would have liked to meet the other wives.'

'It's men only these occasions. Giles ribs him about them. Says the old man is likely batting away from home.' At Bethany's blank expression, she went on, 'Got a lady friend.'

'Has he got a lady friend?' said Bethany, shocked.

Louise didn't meet her gaze. 'It was only Giles's wicked tongue. So we're free to meet David and Mark. You liked Mark didn't you?'

'Very much, though I suppose he's too old for me.'

Louise's eyes rounded with alarm. 'You will see him again? I don't want Giles to suspect I'm seeing David.'

After Harold left the house in the morning Bethany went to her mother. She was playing one of her interminable piano pieces with more anger than passion. Bethany explained that Louise and she were meeting two men and told her mother all she knew about them.

Alice looked nervous. 'I'm delighted that Louise has a gentleman friend. Although this Mark sounds too old for you, Bethany.' Alice frowned. 'I suppose as a foursome no harm will come of it. Both men seem respectable. But I can't approve of this secrecy. Louise must tell her father. This David must come to tea next Sunday and so should Mark if you're seeing him.'

'Thanks, Mum.' Bethany threw her arms around her. 'Louise is frightened at Giles knowing she has a boyfriend,' she confided. 'Isn't it odd the way he's so protective of her?'

'Giles has a cruel streak in his nature,' Alice returned, her manner becoming guarded. 'If David has Harold's approval to court Louise, Giles can't do anything about it. He's selfish in denying her a chance of happiness.'

Louise wasn't pleased when she learned that Bethany had spoken to her mother. 'It will all be ruined now.'

'I don't like having secrets from my mother. And she's right. If you and David are to continue to see each other then it's best if Harold gives his approval.'

The day was sunny and hot. Perfect summer's weather. Mark and David were waiting at Liverpool Street Station. At seeing how handsome Mark looked in his cream trousers and striped blazer a thrill of pleasure set Bethany's pulse racing.

David said, 'I thought we'd walk round to Tower Pier

and take a pleasure boat along the river to Westminster. Then we can go to the Abbey as Bethany suggested.'

'I'm happy doing what everyone else wants,' she insisted.

'Best if we have some plan or we'll find we've spent the whole day wandering round getting nowhere,' Mark said with a smile. 'So the Abbey it is to start off with. It won't take more than an hour. There's several parks close by. We could sit by the Serpentine in Hyde Park. There's bound to be a band playing.'

'Sounds fun,' Bethany answered. Being with Mark for a whole day was a thrilling prospect. She tried to constrain her attraction to him but when he kept teasing and complimenting her, she found it impossible.

They sat at the prow of the pleasure boat enjoying the sights of the Tower of London, Tower and London Bridges, the majestic dome of St Paul's, the rows of famous warehouses and government offices. The river snaked its way towards the distinctive skyline of the Houses of Parliament with its famous clock tower housing the most familiar chimes in England.

Big Ben was striking midday as they docked. Its clear sound resonated through the plane trees startling a flock of pigeons into flight. They had to wait outside the Abbey for a service to finish. Then in reverent silence they entered the ancient building and paused at the black marble grave of the Unknown Soldier, the unidentified body brought back from the French battlefields in 1920 and reburied to commemorate the multitudes who gave their lives during the Great War. The sight of it brought a lump to Bethany's throat. There was a poignancy in its simple dedication to the men who died in the trenches of France.

'My grandfather died in that war,' she said softly.

Mark took her hand. 'So did my father when I was

three. He was a field surgeon. A mortar hit their ambulance and they never found his body. This grave was a great comfort to my mother to know that men like him were not forgotten. Sadly she also died last year. All she ever wanted was for me to be a doctor and carry on my father's work.'

'I'm sorry, Mark.' The words were inadequate for she sensed his unspoken pain and that he still mourned his mother's passing. 'She must have been very proud of you.'

They moved on and gazed in wonder at the gilded bronze or brightly painted marble effigies on the tombs of the centuries of monarchs. The high-vaulted aisles were laid with flagstones with inscriptions of lesser royal princes, princesses and dignitaries buried in the vaults. All these were overshadowed by the towering shrine of St Edward the Confessor. The Coronation Chair was a disappointment. Somehow Bethany had expected it to be grander instead of battered and carved with irreverent initials from long-dead vandals. She reflected that some things never changed. Man was obsessed with leaving his mark for all to witness, but thereby destroying and making ugly something which had been beautiful.

The Abbey was a history lesson as they slowly traversed the aisles with their side chapels. It was packed with visitors and a young boy who never stopped asking his parents questions was constantly told to be quiet by his mother.

Mark whispered caustically to David after they passed several monarchs' tombs with their stern effigies, 'Dissolute lot, weren't they? Most of them look like they didn't know how to smile.'

When Bethany agreed with a laugh, the young boy piped out crossly, 'Sssh. The men and ladies are all sleeping. You'll wake them.'

Bethany giggled and had to hurry on. The effigies were lifelike and the boy must have thought the figures were asleep as he kept being told to be quiet.

When they emerged into the bright sunlight they were bathed in warmth after the chill of the Abbey. They crossed the busy road and headed towards Parliament Square and the Houses of Parliament, then along Bird Cage Walk to Buckingham Palace. Mark took Bethany's hand. His touch filled her with pleasure, but she fought to keep her emotions detached. Mark was only with her because of David. She mustn't allow herself to become too fond of him. With each hour they were together it was becoming harder to cling to that resolve. Mark fascinated her. His good humour was infectious.

They had lunch in a restaurant before heading for St James's Park which was crowded with people. Later in Hyde Park there was a long queue to take a boat on to the Serpentine so they abandoned that idea. As the afternoon heat escalated they sought the shade and sat on the grass under a tree.

David and Louise volunteered to fetch ices from the ice-cream cart and Bethany gazed wistfully after them. It was obvious that the couple were falling in love. David couldn't take his eyes off Louise and she had lost her shyness and was chatting easily to him, her dark eyes sparkling whenever they held his gaze.

Mark picked up a swan's feather and ran it along Bethany's cheek. He was propped on one elbow and she sat with her back against the tree-trunk. There was a thoughtfulness to his stare which caused her heart to pump wildly.

'I find it hard to accept that you're only sixteen,' he said heavily. 'You're so much wiser and more sophisticated than Louise.'

'She's been sheltered in her upbringing.' Her voice quivered as she feared he wouldn't want to see her again.

His gaze remained reflective. 'I heard Louise inviting David to tea next Sunday. Am I to be abandoned?'

'I wasn't sure you'd wish to meet my family.'

He frowned. 'Why not? It wouldn't be right for me to continue to see you if I didn't have their approval.'

Her heart gambolled, constricting her breathing. 'You want to see me again? I'm not too young for you?'

Mark grinned. 'I've had my share of older more accomplished women. Well-meaning friends are inveterate matchmakers. Such women have little time for an impoverished trainee doctor who intends to go on and study tropical medicine. If a doctor does not set up practice in Harley Street he will bring them no prestige.'

'Tropical medicine? Does that mean you wish to serve abroad?'

'Eventually. If the war hadn't killed my father it was what he would have done. But it's a specialist field. And I've to earn a living while I'm studying. It could take me years. I've little time or money for socialising.'

'For such a cause sacrifices are worthwhile.'

His eyes brightened, their gaze caressing her in a way which made her body glow. 'Not many women are so understanding. My hours are erratic and sometimes I have to break arrangements if there's an urgent case at the hospital.'

She groaned, not sure of his meaning. He smiled, adding, 'What I am trying to say is, I want to see you again. I knew on Wednesday that you were special.'

'I'd like that. More than anything I want to become a doctor but my stepfather is against the idea of a woman tending to the needs of men.'

Mark's eyes crinkled and his gaze became tender. 'Women doctors meet with many prejudices. You've a strong sense of purpose and won't let it stop you. What field do you want to specialise in?'

'Children's health. Especially amongst the poor. So many die through diphtheria, typhus or polio. Let alone common ailments because the family have no money for medicine.'

He smiled deep into her eyes, causing a shiver of anticipation to speed through her. 'That's good. I knew we had a lot in common.' His hand slid behind her neck and as they were hidden by the wide trunk of the tree, he drew her head down to meet his. His kiss was gentle, experienced and coercing. It caused a quiver of longing to shimmy through her veins. Feeling her reaction, he pulled back and smiled. 'So do I come to tea next Sunday or not?'

Bethany nodded, her heart too full to speak. She knew that she was already falling in love with him. She was tempted to pinch herself; it seemed like a fairytale.

When Louise and David returned she was puzzled by the troubled look in Louise's eyes. Her stepsister had been happy in David's company and they were getting along well. That look darkened Bethany's elation. Inexplicable fear washed through her. She couldn't shake a sense of foreboding.

Chapter Eight

'You may see your gentlemen friends twice a week and they may also take tea with us on a Sunday.' Harold puffed at a fat cigar, eyeing Louise and Bethany with approval. He had summoned them both to his study. A sign that something was either wrong or he was about to impart something of great importance. 'A gentleman farmer and a future doctor. Most satisfactory.'

His expression became stern as he turned a fixed stare upon Bethany. 'That does not mean I endorse *your* foolish ideas of becoming a doctor because I have permitted one to call upon you. I told him that.'

Bethany stayed silent. She had already discussed the matter with Mark. They had walked in the garden and sat on a low wall under a wooden pergola covered with roses.

'It will take several years for you to qualify as a doctor,' Mark advised. 'And you can't begin training for another couple of years.'

'I hate having to wait. There must be something I can do?' She looked down at her hands which were tingling with heat. 'I want to heal people now. Or at least ease their suffering. I know I'm capable of it.'

'Little Miss Impatience,' he said with a laugh. 'You

could enrol in a First Aid course. It's something and could save a person's life. With that training a local clinic tending the poor of the East End may let you help out. Take each step at a time.' He kissed her tenderly. 'Don't be so impatient. You've your whole life ahead of you.'

For the time being she had to be content with enrolling in a First Aid course which she attended twice a week. It wasn't much, but it was a start.

Louise was uneasy as the time neared for Giles to return home for the last week of the holiday before he went back to University. Then a curt letter arrived informing Harold that Giles was driving down to southern France with some friends for a month and would not be going back to University.

Harold's face turned puce with fury. He crumpled the letter and banged his fist down on the breakfast table. 'Damned lay-about! We'll see how he manages without his allowance.'

Alice, the family mediator, said softly, 'He said he'd be back home in a month. I'm sure he intends to find employment.'

Harold scowled at her. 'Too right he will. At his age I was out there with my nose to the grindstone. That's why I'm a success today.'

'You worked hard, no one disputes that, Harold,' Alice placated. 'You deserve your success.'

His stare narrowed and Bethany saw her mother pale. 'I'm not working my fingers to the bone for that good-for-nothing to inherit. I want another son. A son I can be proud of.'

Alice's restraint broke and with a sob she ran from the room. Bethany got up to follow.

'Sit down, girl. I won't have my breakfast disturbed by all these histrionics.'

'Mother is upset.'

'And you think I'm not!' he bellowed. 'Dear God, is it too much to expect some gratitude from a wife and children?'

The sounds of the piano being played made his thin lips whiten. 'I've had about all I can stand of this. I'm telegramming Giles. If he's not back here in three days he can leave this house for good. I wash my hands of him.' Flinging down his napkin, he stormed from the dining room.

Louise groaned. 'Now everything will be ruined. Giles will return home furious.'

'Stop worrying about Giles,' Bethany counselled. 'You have David now. He's not going to let your twin hurt you, if that's what you fear.'

Louise was deathly pale and close to tears. Bethany put her arms around her. 'Giles hasn't given a thought to your happiness this summer. He's been selfish and self-indulgent. You can be free of him now. David is the one who's important.'

'I wish that were true.' Louise tore from her hold and ran weeping from the room.

Bethany shook her head. She had never known such a household for creating tension and drama. But she had to admit that she was not looking forward to Giles's return. His presence always darkened the atmosphere in the house.

Deciding not to disturb her mother's playing, Bethany took Jasper out into the garden. She was in the orchard an hour later sitting on the grass and grooming the spaniel when a furniture delivery van pulled up into the drive. A few minutes later she heard her mother's voice rising in anguish. Bethany ran towards the house and was aghast to see two men in brown overalls carrying out the piano.

'You can't take it. You can't!' Alice pleaded.

'Sorry, ma'am. Orders from Mr Warden. This is to go into storage. You'd best take the matter up with him.'

Defeated, Alice slumped against the doorpost, her hands covering her eyes. 'He's doing it to punish me because I haven't given him a son,' she sobbed.

Hatred for her stepfather blazed through Bethany. How could he be so cruel? Playing the piano gave so much pleasure to her mother. She controlled her outrage, Alice needed her reassurance not her anger. 'You'll give Harold a son, Mum. You'll make yourself ill if you carry on like this.'

A shudder passed through the frail body and with a sigh Alice stared into her daughter's face. There was despair in her violet eyes. 'Playing the piano was my salvation. I could lose myself in the music and forget how I've failed him. Without it I fear I shall go mad. He can be so cruel. So petty.' Then realising that she had been indiscreet Alice summoned a watery smile. 'I always get too emotional at this time of the month when it's obvious I'm not pregnant.'

'Don't talk about failing anyone. You're a good wife, a perfect hostess and the best mother a girl could have.'

'I need to give him a son.' Her voice was tortured.

'And you will. Then everything will be all right between you and Harold.'

Bethany wished she could believe her reassuring words. Alice had changed in the last few months. It was obvious that there was something very wrong with her marriage.

At the end of September the wedding of Frank and Peg was, after all, a grand affair. After an initial angry outburst, Stan

Styles had calmed down and now intended to do his only daughter proud. Frank was a good man and he wanted Peg and him to have a good start to their married life. Bethany was chief bridesmaid, with two of Frank's sisters and two cousins of Peg. Peg wore a white satin gown with a long train and her veil of lace had been worn by Frank's grandmother and mother. An enormous bouquet of white roses and trailing fern hid the slight swelling of her stomach. The reception for eighty guests was at the Crooked Billet pub.

Peg was beaming with pride as they cut the wedding cake. Frank looked pale. He hadn't reached his bed after his stag-night with his friends. He had fallen asleep on the shop step too drunk to get his key in the lock. But when his bleary eyes rested on Peg their expression was warm and loving.

Bethany went up to them as they stood chatting with guests after the meal. 'You look lovely, Peg. I wish you both every happiness.'

'I reckon I've got a gem in our Peg,' Frank said proudly. 'I needed a jolt to come to my senses. And with a nipper on the way, I'll be the proudest man in London. Mum and Dad have been great.'

He looked across at his father who had improved so much in recent months that he had managed to attend the wedding and walk with two sticks instead of being in his wheelchair.

'Your dad looks well,' Bethany observed.

'He's starting to work in the shop again. The fruit and veg shop next door is up for sale. We're going to buy it and Peg and I will have the flat above. If that works out well, who knows, you may be seeing Hobson's Stores in several high streets in the future.'

'Becoming a father has gone to his head,' Peg laughed. 'He has such grand plans.'

'I always had the plans, sweetheart.' Frank winked at his wife. 'I ain't never had the motive before.' He put his hand on her stomach. 'This will be the first of a half dozen Hobsons.'

Peg blushed, but her happiness was obvious. Things had worked out well for her friend and Bethany was glad. She glanced across at David and Louise who had their heads close together in conversation. It was obvious that the couple were in love. She expected they would be the next to announce their engagement.

Mark put his arm around her waist. 'Are you avoiding me? The dancing has started and weddings always bring out the beast in me.'

Bethany laughed. She was head over heels in love with Mark and she was certain that he felt the same.

'David and Louise will be next,' he said holding her closer than custom demanded in a waltz. 'If David has his way they'll be married by spring.'

'They're so right for each other. I've never seen Louise so happy.'

'And are we right for each other?' Mark caressed her with his gaze. 'I love you, Bethany. I can't afford to keep us both until I finish my training but we could get engaged on your seventeenth birthday.'

Her violet eyes clouded and he frowned. She spoke passionately, not wanting to break the magic of the moment. 'I love you, Mark. I don't want anyone else, but I don't want a long engagement. I've so much studying ahead of me. I'm not sure I want to marry until I've qualified.'

'Then you had better reconsider.' His voice was light but

insistent. 'In two years I'll have finished training in tropical medicine. I want us to marry then.'

She smiled, unwilling to spoil the wedding by having her first quarrel with Mark. She wanted to marry Mark but intuition warned her if she was going to qualify as a doctor she could not risk marriage. If she became pregnant her studies would come to an end. Nothing must jeopardise them. Easing the suffering of others was too important to her.

Giles stayed away a month and each day he was absent Harold threatened to disown him. When Alice tried to placate him he screamed at her to give him a son.

Bethany had returned to grammar school for her final year. It was Saturday afternoon and she was helping Louise plant out some wallflowers, which she had grown from seed, before they got ready to meet David and Mark that evening. Louise kept bursting into song.

'You're in a good mood,' Bethany teased.

Louise put down her trowel and sat back on her heels, her expression dreamy. 'David proposed last night. He wants us to get engaged in a fortnight, once the last of the summer crops are harvested, and for us to marry in the spring.'

'That's wonderful. I'm so happy for you.' Bethany gave a whoop of joy. 'You accepted I hope.'

'I love him so much. I don't deserve this happiness.'

'Don't talk like that. You'll attract bad luck. Of course you deserve it.'

A jaunty whistle from the driveway drew their attention. Louise's expression became troubled. Giles was disappearing through the back door of the house carrying a suitcase.

'Now he's for it,' Louise groaned.

Ten minutes later the raised voices carried to them.

'I'm not paying your debts.' Harold's voice ricocheted around the house. 'I told you, you'd get no more money from me. You're nothing but a lay-about and a gross disappointment to me. You'll get a job by the end of the week or you can leave here for good.' There was the sound of doors slamming.

'Why must they quarrel all the time?' Louise said, the hand holding the trowel trembling.

A low growl from Jasper, who was chewing a bone on the grass, warned them of Giles's approach. Louise stood up, clutching the trowel between her hands.

'One day that mean bastard will go too far,' Giles ranted. He ignored Bethany and with a curt nod towards the greenhouse, added, 'Get in there, Lou. We have to talk.'

'I'm busy,' Louise replied, a nervous tremor entering her voice. 'I have these plants to put in before tea.'

'Sod the bloody plants!' Giles thundered.

'But Giles . . .'

'I said sod them.' He scooped up a full wooden seed-tray and threw it into the bushes.

Jasper sprang up and began barking. 'And get that bloody dog away from me.' He kicked out. The spaniel avoided his foot and ran behind him snapping at his ankles.

'Stop being a bully, Giles.' Bethany stood by Louise's side and caught hold of the spaniel's collar to haul him away from her stepbrother. 'Who do you think you are, ordering Louise about?'

His spiteful glare turned on her. 'If anyone is getting above themselves it's you,' he retorted. 'Any more cheek and you'll feel the back of my hand.'

'Try it and you'll regret it,' Bethany returned.

He took a step towards her and Jasper growled. Giles backed away and swung round to face his twin. 'I said we have to talk.'

When Louise made to obey him, Bethany said firmly, 'Why give in to his bullying? It only makes him worse. He can talk to you after we've finished the garden. And a little politeness wouldn't go amiss.'

Her arm was grabbed in a pinching hold and Giles's face thrust close to hers. Spittle sprayed her as he spat, 'Don't come between me and Lou, or you'll suffer. Now be a good little girl and piss off.' His nails gouged her, drawing blood which stained the short-sleeve of her floral cotton dress.

Jasper went wild and launched himself into the air, his teeth sinking into Giles's hand. He released Bethany with a howl of rage. 'That dog is dangerous. He should be put down. I've been bitten.' He held out his hand showing the indent of several teethmarks.

'Don't be such a baby,' Bethany reprimanded. 'You're the one who drew blood.'

'Stop it. Stop it!' Louise wailed. 'I'll talk to you, Giles. Don't take your bad humour out on Bethany.'

Her words incensed him further. 'Siding with her now, are you? Forgotten your twin brother while I've been away? Do you think I'm not important any more?'

There was a flicker of fear in Louise's eyes and within seconds the self-confidence and poise she had built over recent months crumbled. Her shoulders slumped and her head hung down as she turned towards the greenhouse.

Giles delivered Bethany a gloating grin. 'I always win in the end. Don't make the mistake of forgetting that. And keep that damned dog out of my sight or I won't be responsible for my actions.'

Bethany rescued the seed tray from the bushes and her

anger towards Giles mounted at finding half of them broken off at the roots. Why did Giles have to spoil everything? He took a sadistic pleasure in crushing Louise's spirit.

She rubbed her arm and pushing up her sleeve saw three livid bruises forming below the dried globules of blood, She despised bullies. His strength was frightening but it did not cower her. It made her all the more determined to fight back.

Remembering how bravely Jasper had tackled Giles, she chuckled. She looked round for the dog to hug and praise him. The spaniel had scampered off to pounce after some frogs which had escaped from a neighbour's fishpond and were leaping across the lawn. He ran round in a circle barking as three jumped in different directions.

When her attention was drawn towards the greenhouse, Giles was standing threateningly close to Louise who appeared to be trapped against one of the benches. At seeing Giles bend his twin's arm up behind her, she ran to the greenhouse. She wasn't standing by and letting him hurt Louise.

'You're a sadistic coward to pick on a woman who can't match your strength!' she shouted lashing out at him. 'Leave Louise alone.'

'Stay out of this,' he warned.

'Your bullying won't work on her any more, Giles. Louise has her own life now. She's getting engaged soon.'

Louise gave a strangled sob.

'Is that true?' Giles scowled at Louise. There was a manic glitter in his eyes and his lips were drawn back over his teeth.

Louise nodded. He slapped her cheek, sending her crashing across the bench. 'Whore! Slut! Treacherous bitch!' He stood over her panting and again wrenched back her arm. Louise screamed in pain.

Bethany threw herself at him. 'That's enough, Giles.'

The expression he turned on her was murderous. 'This is your doing. I told you not to interfere. You'll pay for this. Both of you.'

He stamped out of the greenhouse and Louise collapsed against the bench sobbing and holding her shoulder.

'It hurts. He's broken it. I can't move my arm the pain is so bad.'

'Sit on the potting stool,' Bethany ordered. She thrust her anger at Giles aside in her worry for Louise who was suffering. 'Let me have a look. He can't have broken it. You'll probably need a sling fashioned. My First Aid course seems at last to have come in handy.' She ran her hands gently across Louise's shoulder. 'Hold still. This will hurt. It's dislocated.'

She placed her hands in position and paused to remember all she had been taught. Please help me to do this properly, she silently prayed. A calm certainty settled over her and Bethany pushed on the shoulder and heard it grind into place. Louise grunted and Bethany kept her hand in place on the shoulder. An intense heat irradiated from the shoulder and the image of ice cooling the pain was strong. Gently she massaged the shoulder.

'A cold compress is what you need,' she suggested, 'and I'll make you a sling.'

'It feels fine to me.' Tentatively Louise moved her shoulder then cautiously rolled it. 'The pain has gone. I can't feel a thing. That's marvellous.'

'Good. You're my first proper patient,' replied Bethany.

Louise was studying her seriously. 'You have a gift in those hands of yours. You'll make a terrific doctor.'

★ ★ ★

That night Louise lay awake for hours dreading the sound of Giles returning. He was bound to be drunk. That always made him worse. She was frightened. She knew the power Giles had over her and the havoc he could wreak.

When the handle of her door turned, she froze. She shut her eyes forcing her breathing to sound slow and even. Perhaps if he believed that she was asleep . . .

The covers were snatched from her figure, the cool air and jolt of fear raising her flesh in goosebumps.

'Don't pretend you're asleep,' Giles snarled. 'Get up!'

'No, Giles. Don't make me do this.'

'Get up!' There was the slap of the flat rubber fly swat on the crumpled sheet. Its thwack made her wince. Giles had fashioned this weapon when they were ten and its vicious sting had too often broken her resistance. The pain was excruciating and he'd perfected how to use it so that it never left a bruise or cut the flesh. And Giles knew how to wield it to inflict the greatest pain.

As she cowered on the bed, he swiped it back and forth so that it slapped across her nipples. With a muffled groan she clutched her hands over her breasts and until the pain subsided bit her tongue to stop crying out. She had learnt long ago not to protest or make a sound for that goaded Giles to hurt her more.

The swat was raised again as he rapped out, 'Get up!'

Shaking violently, she did so. He pulled back the curtains to allow the moonlight to illuminate the room. 'Stand over there where I can see you properly.'

Cold perspiration was running down her back. He would make her suffer tonight. It had been months since he had come to her. That would add to his frustration and anger. Worse, she had dared to defy him – allowed another man to take his place in her affection.

'Take it off.' The end of the swat flicked the hem of her pink high-necked cotton nightgown.

'Giles, this is wrong.'

'So you love this David more than me. Is he your lover?'

She saw her error. The light in his eyes was demoniacal, chilling her to the bone. 'I love him in a different way. You are special, Giles. You always will be. You're my twin. Haven't you always said that we shared the same moment of creation? A soul divided. Flesh and bone as one, yet separate.' When he didn't interrupt she became bolder. 'But we're no longer children. We are separate. We must lead separate lives.'

'So you would abandon me?'

'Never that, Giles.' Witnessing the malicious glitter in his eyes, her heartbeat quickened, threatening to stifle her.

'You will always be mine, Lou. What would your precious David say if he learned about us? That we shared not only the same womb but the same bed. What would David say if he learned how you used to come to me after a nightmare and crawl in beside me begging me to cuddle you? How you would do anything for comfort . . .?'

'You tricked me, Giles. You forced me to do those things.'

His laugh was low, hissing through serpent lips. 'You could have cried out. But you didn't. Why? Because you liked it.'

She shook her head backing away. 'I was terrified of you. You knew my worst fears and you used them against me if I defied you.' Tears were streaming down her cheeks and her mind whirled at the hundred memories of his cruelties. Worms and slugs had been pushed down inside the neck of her dress. Even now when gardening she felt nauseous each time she uncovered a slug. Once he'd locked her in the dark shed with a bird he'd been torturing. It had pecked her cheek and shoulders in its pain and terror. Dead mice were put in her bed. There had been huge spiders in her clothes drawers and maggots in her bath salts. These had kept her in a constant state of fear and torment. And then there had been the dozens of ways he could inflict pain . . .

'And you are defying me now, Lou. Do I have to teach you a lesson?' He flicked the swat, bringing it down on the tender flesh behind her knees. 'Take off your nightgown. Prove to me that it's me you love. That David is unimportant. And then he need never know our secret.'

'You won't hurt David?' Her voice cracked with dread. 'Or tell him? Promise me.'

'I'll keep silent only if you obey me.'

She closed her eyes and, as she lifted the nightgown over her head, her body was rigid with self-disgust. She heard his satisfied sigh and the creak of wicker as he sat down in the bedroom chair.

'Open your eyes.' The thickening of his voice grated on her shredded nerves. 'Come over here and kneel at my feet and undress me, slave.'

Her scared brown gaze fixed upon him. His russet brows were drawn together, his expression menacing. 'Please, Giles,' she wept. 'You can't mean to . . .'

'Do as you're told, or you'll pay for your defiance.'

A glazed veil fell over the terror in her eyes. She obeyed with the jerky movements of an automaton. Her mind was blanked focusing deep into herself; to a part of her he could never violate or reach. It was the only protection she had from him. Vaguely, she heard his commands and obeyed them.

When he finally left her in the small hours of the morning she ran into the bathroom and vomited into the toilet. Tonight had been worse than any other. It wasn't just sex Giles wanted. It was total subjugation. And then he expected her to be grateful, to grovel at his feet and thank him for his favours which had humiliated and degraded her.

Not daring to run a bath for fear the noise would wake her father, she dipped the loofah in the sink of hot water and scrubbed every inch of flesh until it stung. If Harold learned the truth, there would be no sympathy for her. He would throw her out of the house as well as Giles. He was as much a hypocrite as her brother was. She knew about his other woman. He often reeked of her cheap perfume, shaming her mother by his infidelity. The same perfume she still smelt on him since his marriage to Alice.

Her sobs were silent and relentless. When she finally crawled back into bed she lay sleepless staring up at the ceiling. 'Please God, don't let me be pregnant,' she repeatedly prayed. The terror of Giles dragging her to the backstreets of Whitechapel for an abortion still haunted her: the dirt and squalor, a cadaverous man with hands like talons inflicting pain, humiliation and shame.

The sooner she was married the better. Only then would she be out of Giles's reach.

Or would she? He would always have the power to blackmail her. She couldn't live with that fear all her life, it would eventually destroy her marriage. Bethany had shown her how to be strong and confident. To know her own worth and that she was worthy of love.

She couldn't let Giles destroy that. But with her newfound confidence, she also knew that she couldn't live a lie. She must tell David. But not the whole truth. That was too shameful. When they married he would discover that she was not a virgin. All her life she had been brought up to believe that men never married immoral women, that brides must be virgins on their wedding day. How would a man regard a woman who had been forced to commit incest?

Pain lanced her heart. What if David rejected her? She would continue to be at Giles's mercy. She wrestled with her dilemma. She loved David too much to trick him. Somehow she must find the courage to tell him.

The opportunity came the next day after Sunday tea. Giles had been sarcastic throughout the meal, lacing his conversation with barbed hints which could be taken innocently enough by all but Louise, whose conscience was troubling her. She'd had enough of Giles's cruel taunting. David had looked at him strangely and even her father had been prompted to enquire whether Giles had been drinking, his remarks were so obtuse.

After tea, Harold had fallen asleep in his chair and Giles had slunk out of the house in search of entertainment. Alice had gone to lie down. Since Mark had been on duty this afternoon and unable to attend, Bethany had taken Jasper for a walk and intended to call on Peg.

'Let's go into the garden,' Louise suggested, needing the familiarity and comfort of the place, which had become her sanctuary, when she told him her story.

They sauntered across the grass and she absently picked off dead flower heads from the dahlias as she summoned the courage to speak. When they reached the garden seat, David pulled her down to sit beside him.

'What's up? You're not plucking up the courage to ditch me, are you?'

His words were so far from the truth that she gave a nervous laugh and shook her head.

'Then you'll agree to our engagement. When the crops are in we always have a party at the farm. The neighbours are invited and there's a duck shoot the next day. What better time to announce it?'

She looked down at her fingers which were interlocked in her lap. 'I love you, David. But I can't agree to marry you until you know that I'm not all you expect of a bride.'

When he opened his mouth to protest she blundered on in a rush, before her courage faltered. 'I'm not a virgin. I was raped by a friend of the family. He was drunk at a dinner party and came upstairs looking for the toilet and wandered into my room.' She didn't dare look up at him as she spilled the lies she had woven to cover her deeper sin. Lies to save both herself and Giles as her silence had protected them in the past.

The confession spilled out, unstoppable, damning. 'I was so ashamed. So frightened. The man said I'd tempted him. That it was my fault. Stupidly I believed him. I was terrified that Papa would blame me, throw me out of the house. I couldn't speak of it. A few weeks later the man died of a heart attack. I buried my secret. But Giles knew me so well, he could see my fear and, having no one else I could trust, I told him. He uses it to stop me defying him.'

She fell silent. David said nothing. She could feel his tension. It took all her courage to continue, expecting his loathing and revilement to burst over her head at any moment, 'Giles can be difficult. Possessive. He says it's because we're twins. That I'm part of him. Sometimes I don't think he wants me to be married. I intended to tell you this anyway, but even if you can forgive me, Giles will try and stop the wedding. He'll use what happened to make up lies so that you'll hate me.'

David still didn't speak. His breathing was harsh. Her fears escalated. He hated her now. Thought she was no good – just as Giles had told her. Unable to bear it any longer she leapt up and blurted out, 'I'm not worthy of you! But I had to tell you. I understand if you don't want to see me any more.'

With her heart splintering with pain she ran towards the orchard.

'Louise, don't run away.' David caught her arm and spun her round to face him. She kept her eyes lowered, unable to face the censure in his eyes. David was a good man, he would understand, but could he forgive her? She couldn't bear his pity. Her face was awash with tears.

'My darling, don't cry. I was shocked but I know you weren't to blame. I love you, Louise. Don't let this ruin our happiness.'

Her eyes misted, this time with tears of joy. She reached up to caress the taut line of his jaw. 'You don't hate me? Or think I'm bad . . . or disgusting?'

'In all the time I've been going out with you, you haven't let me lay a hand on you. Even your kisses are chaste. Of course I don't think you were to blame. It took a lot of courage to tell me. I'm glad you did.'

'Do you forgive me?'

'My darling, you were the innocent corrupted.' He crushed her to him, his voice fragmented. 'Mark has spoken of many cases of traumatised children brought into the hospital after being raped by people they knew and trusted. It isn't spoken about in polite society. But it happens, more than you would believe. Men like that should be gelded.'

She burst into tears and clung to him, sobbing against

his chest. 'I'll be the perfect wife. You'll never regret this. Never. I promise. I love you so much. So very much.'

'Nothing will harm you again,' David vowed against her hair. His own hurt was masked as he visualised her suffering.

Louise allowed herself to believe him. She needed to. How else could she face the future?

Chapter Nine

Following their talk David hovered around Harold for an hour waiting for a moment alone to broach the subject. Finally Harold had gone in to his study and David pursued him there. He came out beaming and, spinning Louise round in his arms, informed Alice and Bethany, 'It's all agreed. The engagement takes place on my farm in two weeks. And we'll be married in February on St Valentine's Day.'

Their voices rose excitedly and Harold joined them carrying a bottle of champagne. 'I'd kept this from our wedding. I'd hoped that I'd have a happy event of my own to celebrate before this.' He shot Alice a condemning glare. 'But since my marriage has yet to be blessed with a child, there's no point in letting this go to waste.'

Bethany fumed at his cruel jibe. Alice had grown pale, the happiness fading from her eyes. Louise cast her stepmother a sympathetic glance, then David had his arm around her, and Harold was shouting for glasses.

The champagne poured, Alice had recovered her composure and they jubilantly toasted Louise and David and the union of the two families.

'I thought I heard a cork pop.' Giles leaned against the doorframe his hands in his trouser pockets. His face was devoid of expression but his eyes glittered with a brittle, unpleasant light. 'Celebrating are we? Don't I get a glass?'

'Louise and David are to be engaged,' Harold proclaimed.

'Really. Perhaps I should have a chat with David and warn him about some of the vices of my dear twin.'

'Giles, don't spoil this for your sister,' Harold warned.

Giles swivelled on his heel to leave. Alice interceded. 'Aren't you going to drink to the happiness of your sister and her fiancé, Giles?'

'Not engaged yet are they,' he called back petulantly.

Seeing how uneasy Louise looked, Bethany suggested, 'Shall I go after him? He's probably put out that we've been celebrating without him.'

'No,' Louise said summoning a smile. 'Let him sulk.'

Bethany had taken Jasper for a last run around the orchard before retiring when she found her way back to the house blocked by Giles. Jasper growled.

'You had a hand in Louise getting engaged, didn't you?' he stormed and grabbed her shoulder.

Jasper growled louder and made a lunge for his ankles. Giles's free hand was behind him and as he brought it forward Bethany saw that he carried a cricket bat. He swung it at the spaniel and it caught him on his hind leg causing him to yelp.

'You vicious brute!' Bethany raged. 'Leave Jasper alone.'

'Then call him off while I talk with you. You've got an important lesson to learn.'

She was suspicious of his intentions. He was up to no good if he'd sought her out armed with a cricket bat. She ordered the dog to sit and stay, but her eyes were bright and challenging. 'Say what you have to.'

'High and mighty, aren't you? You think yourself clever. You're not. I told you to keep out of mine and Lou's affairs.'

'Don't you want Louise to be happy?'

'She gets married when I say so.'

'What right have you . . .?' Her voice was choked by his hand gripping her throat.

'Lou knows it doesn't pay to cross me. Remember that.'

He shoved her roughly aside and took another swipe at Jasper who was crawling forwards on his belly, his teeth bared ready to attack at the command from his mistress. The dog ducked and darted aside to avoid the blow.

The next day when Bethany returned home from her First Aid course Jasper was missing. He hated being tied up which Bethany was forced to do whenever she left the house during the day. The chain which was attached to the kennel had pulled away from its anchor.

'He must have run off,' Alice said. 'I'll phone the police.'

'But he wouldn't leave the garden. He never goes into the road.' Bethany followed her mother to the phone.

'He does bark and strain at the lead when you're not here, my dear,' Alice informed her. 'Perhaps it was a cat which caused him to break loose and he chased it.'

The police told them that no stray dogs had been brought in that afternoon.

'I'm going out on my bike looking for him,' Bethany announced. 'Perhaps he followed the scent of a bitch up to Hollow Pond. That's where we walk most often.'

'I'll cycle in the opposite direction,' Louise offered, 'we'll cover more ground that way.'

Four hours later there was still no sign of the spaniel. Bethany was in tears. 'He wouldn't miss his meal. He must be hurt.' There was no consoling her. 'I'm going out again. He can't have gone far.'

'It's dark. It's not safe on the streets.' Alice was interrupted by the telephone ringing. She went to answer it. Bethany looked at her expectantly when she returned. Jasper wore a name and address tag on his collar. Had someone found him? Alice's expression made her heart plummet.

'That was the police. I'm so sorry, my dear, Jasper has been found a couple of roads away. He's been hit by a car and was killed. No one saw the accident.'

Bethany sat in stunned silence for several moments before finally saying, 'Where's his body? Can he be buried in the orchard which he loved so much?'

'I asked the police to dispose of it. I didn't want you upset by seeing him. They assured me that he would not have suffered but his head was shattered. A wheel must have run over him when the car struck him.'

Or a cricket bat. The image sprang unbidden to her mind. She had no proof it was Giles. But she couldn't shake the feeling that he was responsible. Had he then made it look like an accident?

When she confronted him, he laughed at her and denied it.

She didn't believe him. There had been a smirking twist to his lips.

During the next two weeks Bethany avoided Giles and was barely civil to him at meal times. She missed Jasper desperately and the manner of the faithful spaniel's death lay heavy on her heart. She hated Giles. Several times she heard him and Louise arguing but Louise would never speak about it. At least he wasn't home so much. Through an associate of Harold's, Giles had got himself a job in the civil service. He had discovered a taste for the high life indulged in by his new wealthy friends. He still argued with Harold and last night had threatened to get himself a flat nearer his work. She wished he would. He'd be here less often. Why couldn't he stay out of their lives for good? It would make them all much happier.

On the morning of the engagement Harold drove Bethany, Alice and Louise to Oakwood Farm early in the day to help with preparing the food for the party. Mary Lister was an apple-cheeked, cheery, matter-of-fact woman. From Louise's first meeting with her, she had been made welcome into the family.

'So you finally set a date for the wedding and put our David out of his misery,' Mary ribbed her as they walked in to the kitchen. 'Welcome to the family, my dear. Let's see this ring of yours.'

Louise blushed and held out her hand to display the emerald flanked by two smaller diamonds. 'Very nice. Not showy. David was all set to buy you a solitaire which would have meant making do for another year with the old tractor which breaks down every week. I'm glad you had more sense.'

'Even this was more than I wanted him to pay. I know he needs to reroof the barns.'

Mary threw back her head and laughed with approval. 'Aye, you'll do as a farmer's wife. But don't go sacrificing too many fripperies. It's a hard life but it can be a good one, if you have an empathy with the land. The land is our lifeblood and we honour it. This is an arable farm, the only animals apart from the dogs and cats are chickens, ducks and geese, four pigs and half a dozen goats for their milk. I've got a stall in Romford market in the week where I sell cheese and eggs and home-made pies.'

The large kitchen with its scrubbed oak table smelt of freshly baked bread and the sunlight was shaded by the bunches of dried herbs hanging from the ceiling which added their own special perfume to the room.

Alice removed her coat and took an apron from her bag to cover her green and white polka dot dress. 'Where do we start? Fire away with your orders and we'll get on with the cooking.'

'There's a mound of pastry for pies still to be made. And I've put out flour and ingredients for fruit and ginger cakes. I'll be seeing to the pig which David has set up on a spit in the farmyard. It needs regular basting.'

They worked companionably all morning. Louise was at ease with Mary. 'I'm going to expand the herb garden,' she informed Bethany. 'Mary is amazing. She knows all these herb remedies for curing all manner of ailments. She said she'd teach me how to make salves and balms. And I'll grow cut flowers to take to market each week with Mary. And have a go at fruit and vegetables for our own consumption. Any surplus can be made into preserves or also sold in the market.'

'Looks like you'll have a busy life.'

Louise nodded, her eyes gleaming. 'I think I was born to be a farmer's wife, though I'm not so sure I can handle the slaughter of animals. I'm going to have to get used to it. David shoots rabbits and ducks for us to eat.'

For the rest of the morning they worked steadily producing the pies, cakes and sandwiches for the evening. The trestle tables put up in the barn were laden with food when Mary nodded in satisfaction.

'It always does to celebrate the end of the harvest in style. Shows our appreciation that God and Mother Earth have been bountiful to us. Now you go along and get yourselves prettied up for the dancing tonight.'

Mark stood with his arm around Bethany's shoulders as David put up a hand to stop the music.

'Family, friends and workers, this year's harvest is the best in a decade. Without your help it wouldn't have been possible. Enjoy the bounty of our table on this special night. Not just to celebrate the bringing in of the harvest, but to honour my engagement to Miss Louise Warden.'

He held out a hand to Louise to join him in the centre of the barn. There was rapturous applause and cheering. Harold stepped forward holding up his glass. 'A toast to the happiness of Louise and David.'

Over the rim of her glass Bethany saw Giles tip his drink on to the floor, his expression malignant as he scowled at the couple. He'd arrived in a car he'd borrowed from a friend. He had been drinking heavily all evening and whenever David was occupied with guests monopolised Louise's company. She'd heard him deriding the farm and criticising her future life as a country bumpkin.

Bethany's eyes narrowed. Why couldn't he be happy for his twin?

The fiddler played a waltz and Bethany was drawn on to the dance floor by Mark. In his arms Giles's sullen manner was forgotten. Their meetings were limited by the long hours he worked at the hospital and sometimes an emergency meant he had to cancel a date with her. The homework from the grammar school didn't fill her evenings and she used her spare time to write children's stories, four of which had now been accepted. They gave her great pleasure but she still yearned to begin her studies as a doctor.

Impatiently she pushed her serious thoughts aside.

Tonight was for pleasure. She danced until her legs ached. Although the barn had been well swept the energetic country reels had thrown up dust which cloyed her throat. Mark fetched her some punch and led her outside into the moonlight.

'It's hot in there,' he said loosening his tie. 'And how could I miss a chance for a stroll with my favourite girl?'

'It's been a lovely day,' she sighed contentedly. 'I'm so happy for Louise and David. And this is a wonderful way to celebrate an engagement. Informality and fun.'

They walked to the edge of the farmyard. The fiddler played enthusiastically on, the music mixing with the distant animal scufflings from the sties and pens.

'Your stepbrother didn't look too pleased,' Mark said.

'Then that's his problem,' Bethany said sharply. 'Don't let's talk of Giles and spoil the evening.'

Mark laughed softly and pulled her into his arms. 'You look ravishing. I've missed you.' He kissed her until her senses were pitched into a maelstrom and she clung to him. When his thumbs grazed the crests of her breasts a sigh quivered in her throat. Abruptly he drew back from her.

'Beth. I want you so much. I see you so seldom. When I hold you and feel your response, I think I'll go crazy.'

'I love you, Mark.' Bethany rested her brow on his chest. 'But I'm not ready to go further.'

He sighed. 'I respect that. But it isn't easy, especially on a night like this.'

She looked up at him and saw that he was grinning and she said, provocatively, 'Patience, my love. Everything comes to those who wait . . . eventually.'

He kissed her again and, aware of the restraint he put on his passion, Bethany was both pleased and grieved. She loved him. She wasn't so naive as to believe that they could continue as they were without becoming lovers. She yearned for it to happen and at the same time feared the consequences. Hadn't Peg become pregnant even though Frank assured her he had taken precautions?

At the sound of laughter behind them, they broke apart and Bethany saw Louise and David sauntering arm in arm across the farmyard. The couple were laughing, their heads close together, their love for each other heartwarming.

Louise's voice carried to them. 'I never thought I could be so happy. It's frightening. This much happiness. Sometimes I have to pinch myself, or it will go away.'

Chapter Ten

Next day the men set out for the duck shoot before dawn. Giles had left the engagement party the previous evening and Harold had declined to join David and his friends. He and Alice had driven home to Chingford at midnight.

Bethany stirred in the double bed she was sharing with Louise and heard the muffled voices of the men as they crossed the farmyard. Eager for sight of Mark, she slipped from the covers and looked out the window. It was still dark and she could only see shadows as David whistled to the two farm retrievers and seven men set off across the fields.

Shivering she dived back into bed only to be awoken a half hour later by an insistent cockerel announcing the dawn.

'Oh damn,' murmured Louise sleepily, 'I wanted to get up and see David before he left. I've missed them I suppose.'

'They set off half an hour ago. You'll have to be less of a slug-a-bed when you're a farmer's wife. Up at the crack of dawn milking the goats and all that.'

'Ah, the joys of future married life,' Louise said with a giggle. She rubbed her eyes and sat up to regard Bethany quizzically. 'I don't know why you and Mark don't marry.

It's obvious you're in love. Don't you want to get away from Papa's strict rules? I'd have married at your age if I'd met David then.'

'Sometimes I'm tempted. But Mark has little money even though he's just qualified as a doctor. He's gone on to study tropical medicine. The house I inherited from my father has been leased for another two years so we'd have nowhere to live.'

'You're so practical.' Louise pulled a face. 'It's not very romantic.'

'Look where romance got Peg,' Bethany reminded her.

They both started at the first volley of gunshots from the shooting party. Bethany said, 'That will be the men playing the great white hunters. And the end of us having any chance of more sleep.'

'We'd better get up and help Mary clear the dishes from the barn. There must be a mountain of washing up.'

They dressed and went downstairs to find the fire burning brightly in the kitchen range and a huge kettle steaming. Mary came in from the farmyard with two buckets of milk. 'That's the goats and chickens seen to.' She smiled approval at Louise. 'I didn't think a city girl like yourself would be up and about for another two hours.'

'It does feel like the middle of the night,' Louise admitted and vainly tried to stifle a yawn. 'Tell us what we can do to help you.'

The three women worked together for the next hour clearing dishes from the barn, hunting for eggs in the fowl pens and then attacking the washing up. A constant cannonade of gunfire accompanied their work.

'We'll be eating duck until kingdom come at the rate they're shooting,' Mary joked. 'Just as well the butcher in the village buys them from us, rabbits as well if a field gets overrun and David has to cull them.'

Another burst of gunfire drew Mary's gaze to the window and she frowned. 'Looks like rain is coming on. Be a few more birds who'll live to fly another day if there's a downpour. And the men will be back with hearty appetites.'

The women continued to work but Bethany noticed that Mary kept glancing towards the window where the rain she had predicted had turned to hailstones. There was no longer the sound of gunfire so the men must be returning.

A half hour later they were still absent and Louise hovered by the window. 'They should have been back by now.'

Mary worked in tight-lipped silence.

Bethany reassured, 'They must have taken shelter. The rain is torrential. They'd be soaked if they were walking in this.'

Mary picked up a scrubbing brush and began attacking the oak table with such vigour that Bethany knew she was concerned. That made her anxious.

'They must be sheltering somewhere,' Louise declared.

Bethany looked at Mary and when the older woman raised her eyes she saw they were troubled. She sent Louise out into the scullery to bring in some potatoes from the sack. 'There's no shelter out there.'

'Do you think something has happened?' Bethany asked.

Mary's gaze returned to the window and the scrubbing brush clattered to the floor. She ran to the door and out into the rain.

Alarmed, Bethany followed and her heart jolted with fear. Two of David's friends ran into the barn and came out carrying an old door which they put in the back of the farm truck.

Mary hurried back into the farmhouse, her face ashen. 'There's been an accident. I've got to go into the village and phone for an ambulance. Why didn't I allow David to have the phone installed last year when he wanted it? I said it wasn't a necessity and we'd managed without one in the past. They can't get the truck closer than three fields from the accident. They've taken the door to use as a stretcher.'

'Who's hurt?'

'David.' Her voice cracked. 'He's been shot. Some dreadful accident.'

The blood rushed to Bethany's head like a steam train thundering out of a tunnel. She felt sick and her knees buckled. Inhaling deeply she ran past Mary's stout figure. 'I'll go. I'll get there faster than you. Where is David?'

'They're bringing him here. Mark is doing all he can but he's no medical bag with him. Tell the ambulance brigade he was shot in the side of the head. He's unconscious.'

The rain sleeked Bethany's springy curls to her head and drenched her to the skin. Her sodden shoes squelched with each step. Heedless of discomfort, she ran down the lane. It was a mile to the nearest phone box by the village pub. Her mind was frozen on the catastrophe, her heart hammering as her feet pounded the lane. Let David not be seriously injured. Let him be all right. Dear God, he mustn't die. He had so much to live for. The breath seared in her throat and lungs and a stitch gripped her sides, but still she forced herself on.

The call made, she paused only to catch her breath before hurrying back to the farm. Her mind was spinning at the consequences of the accident. How bad was David? And Louise? She would be distraught. Her legs were trembling with exertion as she arrived at the farm. In the distance could be heard the clang of the ambulance bell.

When she entered the kitchen it was filled with David's friends. Mary was pouring them stiff drinks of whisky. Louise was sobbing in a rocking chair by the range and Mark was bent over his friend. The horror of the accident intensified as she saw the large splashes of blood amongst the muddy footprints on the stone floor.

The steam was rising off her sodden clothes. She hadn't even stopped to put on a coat. Mary pressed a large whisky into her hand. 'Get that down you. Then go upstairs and change or you'll be down with pneumonia.'

'How's David?'

Tears spilled on to Mary's lashes and she gave a fatalistic shrug. 'It's in God's hands. He's still alive but unconscious. Thank God the ambulance is here.'

Bethany moved to the figure on the table and lifted a hand towards him. The sensation of hopelessness swamped her and her hand fell to her side. David was dying. The strident bell was silenced as the ambulance screeched to a halt. Hating to leave David, but knowing there was nothing she could do except console Louise, she put her arms around her stepsister. 'Be strong for his sake, Louise.' She refused to accept what her intuition told her. 'It may not be as bad as it looks.'

'He's going to die,' Louise sobbed. 'I knew my happiness wouldn't last.'

'Don't think like that. Pray for him. Will him to live.' Realising that she was dripping all over Louise, she eased back. 'I have to change.'

Her wet clothes were thrown on the bedroom floor and she was shivering so violently she had trouble pulling on dry underwear. The only other clothes she had with her were her dance dress and stole which were ludicrously inappropriate. She pulled the dress on. There was a bulky handknitted cardigan Mary had lent Louise last night and she borrowed this, buttoning it to her throat. Still she shivered both from cold and shock.

When she returned to the kitchen David had been transferred to the ambulance. Louise and Mary were travelling with him. On seeing Bethany, Mark clasped her hard to his chest. He was too choked to speak for several moments then said gruffly, 'I'll follow the ambulance in the farm truck.'

'I'm coming too. He's not going to make it, is he?'

He didn't answer as he pulled her with him to the truck and slammed the vehicle into gear. They drove in silence through the village until Bethany asked, 'How did such a terrible thing happen?'

'None of us know. We stayed close together because the mist was slow in lifting. I can't believe that any of us could have made such an error.' His knuckles whitened over the steering wheel. 'A flock of mallard flew overhead and we all fired at the same time. Several birds were hit. Then we heard a dog whimpering and there was David lying in the hedgerow. Shotgun pellets are embedded in the side of his head. Some have penetrated his brain.' He thumped the dashboard with his fist. 'Bloody stupid accident. It doesn't make sense. We're all too experienced for it to happen.'

David was in the operating room for three hours. Afterwards they were briefly permitted to see him. His head was swathed in bandages and Bethany had to look away. It was as though his life force had already drained from him. When they filed out of the ward, Mark went to speak with the doctor.

Bethany paced the waiting room until she knew every crack in the wall and ceiling, every scuff on the brown linoleum floor. When Mark returned he looked haggard.

He paused to speak with Mary and Louise, putting a hand on both their shoulders. Louise burst into fresh weeping and ran out of the waiting room. Mary covered her face with her hands and sank down on to a chair. When Bethany began to go after Louise, Mark stopped her and drew her away from Mary who was now staring dry-eyed into the distance.

'They need time to themselves. I'm afraid it doesn't look good. There's a policeman outside who wants a statement from me.'

'But it was an accident – wasn't it?'

'It's just a formality. David didn't have any enemies. Everybody liked him.'

Not everybody. Giles hated him. The thought flashed into her mind. But Giles wasn't there. He had left the previous night. And although she suspected that Giles had somehow been responsible for Jasper's death, she had no proof. The spaniel was found with the chain still attached to his collar, so he could have escaped on his own and chased after a cat. Giles was capable of hurting a dog and even beating a man, but murder . . . She was allowing her dislike and the uncomfortable feelings which her stepbrother always aroused to colour her judgement. Even Giles at his most vindictive was not a murderer.

David was still unconscious at midday. Louise had become hysterical with worry and it had taken all Bethany's strength and reasoning to calm her. Even so, her loud sobs hammered through everyone's anguish as they sat in the waiting room. Bethany had rung home to tell Harold the news. When Giles arrived he rushed over to Louise and comforted her. He drew her head to his chest and murmured encouraging words while ignoring Mary and the others. Harold and Alice looked stunned as they listened to the report of the accident.

'Such a lovely man,' Alice moaned. 'He must get well. He has so much to live for.'

Mark put his arm around Mary. 'They're doing everything they can for him.'

'What are his chances?' Mary said softly and led him away from Louise, but Bethany was close enough to catch her words. 'Tell me straight, Mark. No hogwash.'

'The shot shattered his skull and several pieces were embedded in the brain.' He kept his voice low. 'It's a wonder he's lived this long.'

Mary shuddered and moved to the window. Her stoic manner touched Bethany for inside Mary must be crushed. Mark came to Bethany, his face blurred through her tears.

'Is there no hope?' she asked.

He shook his head.

She glanced at Louise who had calmed down and was sobbing quietly into Giles's shoulder. At least he was giving her the support she needed. 'Poor Louise. It's unjust and cruel.'

A bald, thin doctor entered the waiting room and Louise opened her eyes and sat up. Everyone's attention was focused upon his grim expression. 'I'm sorry. Mr Lister has passed away. There was nothing more we could do.'

The funeral party left the parish church to trudge back to the farm where Mary had prepared a lavish meal. Louise was so overcome she couldn't walk without Giles's arm around her.

Mary had the comfort of her younger son Bill. His destroyer had been docked at Gibraltar when news was sent to him of David's death. He'd been granted compassionate leave. The normally exuberant sailor had hardly spoken a word since his arrival, so profound was his pain at the tragedy.

When Bethany expressed her condolences to him, his voice was full of anger. 'Why him? David was such a great guy. It's such a bloody stupid tragedy.'

'Mark and the other doctors did everything they could.'

'Yeah.' He sighed, looking older and weary, the vital spark extinguished from his eyes. 'You've got yourself a good man in Greenwood. Mum says you're meant for each other.'

Bill was fighting to control his composure and although he flashed his roguish smile, his eyes remained sad.

'How long is your leave?' Bethany asked.

'A month. Mum's taking this on the chin as usual. I want to make sure she's settled before I return to my ship.'

Later when Bethany spoke to Mary, David's mother seemed determined on her future. 'I'm going to sell the farm. My heart's gone out of it. Bill wanted to leave the navy to help out but that wouldn't be right. He loves the sea.'

'Where will you go?' Bethany couldn't visualise Mary anywhere but on this farm.

'The seaside. I've only seen it once. My husband George and I spent two days honeymooning at Westcliff-on-Sea. I thought I'd take a guest house there. Bring a touch of good farmhouse cooking to all them holidaymakers.'

'You'll be a resounding success,' Bethany assured her.

'It will fill my days. I hope you and Louise will come and visit and I won't be charging you for lodging.'

'We'll come. Louise thinks the world of you. She won't want to lose touch.'

★ ★ ★

Louise existed in a world numbed of all sensation. She had erected barriers to close her mind to David's death. Dr Jones had given her sedatives which left her partly stupefied. That was the only way she could cope. The garden was neglected, the weeds strangling the borders, the wallflower plants rescued from dying by Bethany who watered them and also tended the seedlings and cuttings in the greenhouse every evening.

Louise stayed in her room. She had not cried since the funeral and Mark had told Bethany that was a bad sign. She needed to grieve to allow the pain and misery to surface and then she could begin to heal and cope with her loss.

A month later the letter from Mary telling Louise that she had sold the farm and was moving to the guest house at Westcliff was left unanswered. Bethany tried to rouse her to take an interest in her life again. She failed.

If she teased Louise, she encountered a stony silence. Talking about the plants met with apathy. She resorted to mild bullying which prompted only indifference. Now she was at her wits' end as to how to rouse Louise from her grief. If she didn't pull herself together soon, she'd become seriously ill. Louise must have lost two stone in weight, her eyes looked enormous in her thin face and her auburn hair was unwashed and matted. To try and cheer her Alice brought her several new outfits. They were never worn.

Another disturbing factor was that Giles monopolised Louise's company every evening and weekend. Yet he was the only person Louise seemed to respond to. Every evening he took Louise into the back lounge and played records on the gramophone. If Bethany joined them he made it obvious that she was unwelcome.

For all that Louise accepted Giles's presence Bethany was convinced he was a bad influence on her. He was again manipulative and possessive. He never tried to get her to improve her appearance or take an interest in anything.

Bethany joined Louise and Giles one evening and suggested that Louise play chess. She shook her head.

'Backgammon then. Or cards. Something to occupy your mind rather than keep moping.' She was shocked to see that Louise was holding a large glass of brandy. It was unusual for her to drink. Was this Giles's doing? His glass was empty and the bottle was on the floor between them.

'Stop pestering her,' Giles snapped. 'She's all right as she is. I know what's best for her. You're interfering.'

'I care for Louise,' she protested heatedly.

'Can't you see you're a reminder of all she's lost? Every time that boyfriend of yours comes round, it adds to her pain. Leave her alone. It's me she needs, not you.'

'Do you want me to leave, Louise?'

The eyes turned on her were vague. Bethany picked up the brandy bottle and glared at Giles. 'What are you doing? She shouldn't have alcohol with the sedatives she's on.'

'It blots out the pain,' Louise slurred and held out her hand for the bottle. 'Please. It helps.'

'It isn't the answer.'

Giles sneered. 'You're so prim and proper you make me sick. There's no harm in a bit of brandy. Stop interfering.'

Bethany left them and found Alice listening to a play on the wireless and knitting a cardigan. 'I don't know what Giles thinks he's up to,' Bethany said sitting on the arm of her mother's chair. 'He's giving Louise brandy to drink and she's on sedatives. She's tipsy.'

'Harold must talk to him, except he's never here of an

evening. And you can only do so much. Louise is naturally close to her twin.'

Bethany frowned. There were undercurrents in the house and her mother's tension and Harold's nightly absences added to the morbid atmosphere. 'Where is Harold this evening?'

Alice dropped a stitch and made a great play of picking it up. 'Business. If you're at a loose end why don't you visit Peg tonight?'

Bethany realised that Alice had evaded her question. It was obvious that her marriage was not happy but her mother didn't want to talk about it. 'I'm seeing Peg tomorrow. I think I'll go up to my study and do some writing.'

Bethany had just got settled and was frowning over her handwritten manuscript when Alice tapped on the door and entered. 'I've brought you up some Ovaltine.'

'Thanks, Mum. I've hit a problem with this. It's too long for a short story but every time I cut it another adventure for the character comes to mind and it grows.'

'Why not send it to a publishing house as a children's novel?'

Bethany's eyes sparkled. 'I'm not clever enough for that.'

'Have faith in yourself. You're a wonderful storyteller.' Alice smiled. 'I was wondering if this would help.' She went out and returned carrying an Olympia typewriter. 'Harold brought this home from the office, if you would like it.'

Harold's generosity amazed her. Or was this his way of trying to steer her away from her medical training? 'But it will take me ages to master it.'

'You could learn to type at evening classes.'

Suspicion darkened Bethany's pleasure. 'I'm not going

to train as a secretary if that's Harold's motive.'

Alice looked uncomfortable. 'Humour him. Once you can type properly it will be quicker to type your stories or medical notes than handwrite them.' She put a hand on Bethany's shoulder. 'I know you have your heart set on becoming a doctor, but don't neglect your talent as a writer. We must use the gifts we are given. Your father would have been proud of you.'

The next evening Bethany visited Peg. As she stepped off the tram in the High Street she saw Uncle Clarence and Aunt Enid pull up in their car and proceed to enter a large detached house.

'Uncle Clarence,' she called, instinctively. Her aunt and uncle were looking very well and prosperous. 'It's good to see you.'

They turned to look at her and both their faces glazed. Staring straight through her Clarence took his wife's arm and propelled her up the garden path.

Bethany felt as though she had been slapped in the face. She had pushed to the back of her mind that Clarence had sworn to have nothing more to do with her or her mother if Alice married Harold but now she recalled his anger. The rebuff stung her pride. It was so cruel and senseless. Did blood ties mean nothing to them? Didn't they care at all how they were faring? She'd have thought after so many months her uncle would have at least been prepared to acknowledge her in the street. If that's the way they wanted it, then they could stew in their own snobbery.

She was still smarting from the way they had ignored her when she arrived at Peg's flat over the fruit and vegetable shop next to the corner store. Frank gave Bethany a kiss on the cheek and went off for a pint down the local so they could talk in private. Peg was now noticeably pregnant and her movements were ponderous. She was obsessed with the forthcoming baby which was not due until March.

'So how's married life and impending motherhood?' Bethany said.

Peg rolled her eyes ecstatically. 'Wonderful. Frank is incredible. He won't let me do anything. He's so proud he's going to be a dad. Says he wants a girl just like her mum.'

Peg's expression became more serious. 'I don't know why you won't set a date and marry Mark. You're not happy in the Warden household. And life is short . . . look what happened to David. Take what happiness comes your way while you can.'

'I'm not unhappy,' Bethany protested. 'Mark and I have only known each other a few months. There's no rush.'

'Poppycock. You love him and he loves you.'

'We have our studies. Besides it would be selfish so soon after Louise was denied happiness. It would remind her of all she's lost.'

Exasperated, Peg shook her head. 'Count your blessings, Bethany Masterton. Mark's a great guy and you love him. You can't buy that kind of happiness and love.'

'I know that but . . .' Bethany couldn't put her unrest into words. She wanted to marry Mark but she hesitated. Her mother's marriage had become a trap, her happiness controlled by a tyrant. Not that Mark was like Harold. Mark was a liberal man who supported her aspirations, but even so marriage could curtail the career which was so important to her.

To change the subject she voiced another concern. 'I'm worried about Louise. The way she's mourning David is bad for her. She has to take an interest in her life again.'

'Giles can't be a good influence,' Peg replied. 'But he is

her twin. And twins do have strong ties to each other. I'm surprised he's given up so much of his time. I always had him down as a selfish bastard.'

'He hated it when Louise started putting David before him. He's using her grief to regain his old power over her. He's a strange man. I don't understand him.'

'He gives me the creeps,' Peg said. 'It's the way he looks at a person. Seeing through them, cold, calculating. Sinister.'

'And those are his good points.' Bethany tried to make light of it but she couldn't shake off her troubled thoughts.

Chapter Eleven

It was three months since David's death. For Louise time was a blur, Christmas tarnished as tinsel. The feasting was a mocking celebration of life. The New Year held no future, only emptiness.

At first Louise had been grateful that Giles had changed and was considerate towards her. He became again the sympathetic and understanding twin she had always looked up to and followed. She was cocooned by the sedatives.

'I'm the only one who knows how you feel,' Giles soothed. 'We share the same pain. No one else understands. No one else cares for you as I do. Bethany says she cares, but she's wrapped up in her romance with Mark. She doesn't want unpleasant reminders. Alice is next to useless. She shuts herself away in her room when Pa goes philandering. Where are they now? There's only us. We must stick together.'

His words had become a litany he repeated to her hour after hour. They were soothing. She was fortunate to have a twin to support her. No one else understood her pain. Without Giles to sustain her she would be lost.

Harold came into the back room and sniffed with disapproval at seeing Louise with her head on Giles's shoulder and the brandy bottle opened on the table.

'Time you pulled yourself together, my girl. It's gone eleven and decent folks are in their beds. Giles, you have work tomorrow. You were late leaving this morning.' A fragile truce had sprung up between Giles and Harold since he joined the civil service and David had died.

'We won't be long,' Giles returned.

Harold switched off the conservatory and sitting room lights.

'I'll do the lights,' Giles stated.

'I pay the electricity bill and they go off when I go to bed.' He unplugged the wireless and record player.

'Tight-fisted sod,' Giles muttered under his breath. 'We'll go to bed when we're ready.'

His arm tightened around Louise and he kissed her hair. 'Who needs lights anyway? This is better. More private.'

There was a thickening to Giles's voice which penetrated Louise's stupor. In the last week Giles's compassion had changed. When the opportunity arose his embrace altered from brotherly sympathy to a more intimate stroking. The touch of his hand squeezing her breast broke through her lethargy.

'No, Giles! I told you no more. It's wrong. It was always wrong.'

'We are meant for each other.'

'No, Giles. I still love David. I won't do this.'

His breath hissed through his teeth. 'You'll do whatever I want. Or I'll tell Father how wanton you are? How you can't bear to be without a lover and since David died you come to my bed pleading for me to take you.'

'That's a lie. David was never my lover. He loved me enough to wait until we were married.'

'But you're not a virgin. Any doctor can examine you

and then what would Father say? You'd be out on the street.'

'I'd tell him it was you. What have I got to lose now? I shall never marry. My life has no meaning. I don't care what happens to me. But I won't defile David's memory by allowing you to touch me again.'

'That's what you think. Papa doesn't want you living off him the rest of your life. He'd believe you were lying. Once a whore always a whore. He's got his own fancy bit on the side but he won't stomach his daughter dishonouring his name. I'm your only hope, Louise. You can't escape me. You can't escape our destiny. We were always meant to be together.'

'No!' She wrenched herself free of his hold. The future he painted was a nightmare. She couldn't spend the rest of her life consumed by guilt. David had been her love and her salvation. Marriage to David would have saved her from Giles and his perversions.

Giles had risen from the sofa and was breathing erratically, his eyes heavy lidded with lust. 'You will always be mine, Louise. Only mine. Of course you're upset over David's death. What you need is to get away. How about if I book us into a hotel for the weekend in Brighton?'

'One room, I suppose,' she spat.

'What else? No point in extra expense.'

With sickening clarity the truth struck her. Giles had shot David. Giles had murdered the man she loved.

'*You* killed David! Did you pretend to leave after the party and sneak back to the farm before dawn?'

His smile was evil. 'I told you no one but me will ever have you. We're meant to be together – always.'

She sidled away, her flesh marinating in icy fear. 'You murdered him. I hate you. You're mad. Mad!' Her face was ugly as it twisted in horror. 'You won't get away with it. I'm going to the police. I'll see you hang for this.'

He looked taken aback. 'But I'm your twin. I'm you and you are me.'

'No. You're evil. You're all that is dark and torrid. I wanted only to please people and to be good. I wanted to love and be loved. I hate you. You'll pay for this!'

He sprang at her. His hands grasped her throat. Steely thumbs pressed hard against her windpipe. Above her own bulging eyes, his face was demonic. 'I love you. Don't fight me, Louise.'

She struggled for air. The thumbs dug deeper into her throat. She clawed at his face but he jerked it aside. She dug her nails into his hands. But they were bitten to the quick from her weeks of unhappiness and were ineffectual.

'You don't love David. You love me,' he implored. 'Tell me you love me. I'll make everything up to you. I don't want to hurt you. You're mine. Mine!'

She tried to scream her hatred at him, but her throat was clamped tight, choked so that no breath or sound escaped. She kicked at his shin. But her legs had become jelly. Her lungs were bursting. Her head seemed to swell and explode with pain. Then the impassioned, cruel face above her began to blur and fade . . .

When Louise did not appear for breakfast Alice sighed heavily. 'She can't continue like this. I think she should see a psychiatrist.'

'Louise doesn't need a shrink,' Giles scoffed. He was late for breakfast and ignored the plate of eggs and bacon. 'She's depressed that's all. Small wonder in the circumstances. She poured her heart out to me last night. I got her interested in coming away with me for the weekend to Brighton.'

'That's very considerate of you, Giles,' Alice remarked.

'There's nothing I wouldn't do to make Louise happy. Now I'd better dash or I'll be late for work.' He got up from the table and walked into the hall to collect his overcoat and bowler hat. Then sticking his head back round the dining-room door, he spoke to Harold. 'I won't be back tonight. I'm spending the weekend with Oliver Tranter at his home in Bedfordshire.'

'Who is this Oliver Tranter?' Harold asked.

Giles lifted a russet brow. 'That's not your concern. Except he's got a sister who comes into quite a fortune when she marries. Left a hefty legacy by her grandmother. And I'm taking a flat in Chelsea. You're right about Lou, it's time she got a grip on herself. I've got my own life to lead.'

'I'm glad you're considering your future more seriously, Giles.' Harold put down his newspaper to regard his son. 'And not before time.'

Bethany looked at Alice. 'I'll take Louise up some breakfast.'

'You will do no such thing,' Harold bellowed at her. 'Giles is right. Louise has been mollycoddled too long. She stays in her room half the day. She'll come down soon enough when she's hungry. I forbid any food to be taken to her. I've arranged we're to have dinner guests on Saturday. Counsellor Aldwick and his wife. They're new clients and very important and influential. I expect Louise to be present and no more moping around.'

Mrs Binns was given strict instructions by Harold that no food was to be sent up to Louise. Bethany was at school all day and when she returned at three thirty Louise still had not appeared. Alice was looking anxious.

'Twice I've been up to her room and knocked on the

door. She won't answer. And the door is locked. I tried to persuade Louise to come shopping with me. I've only just got back from town. I've spent hours traipsing from shop to shop for a new winter's coat and couldn't settle on one. Louise still didn't answer me when I knocked on her door a few minutes ago. She can't still be sleeping.'

'I'll talk to her,' Bethany suggested. 'So much for Harold's theory of starving her into coming down stairs.'

'He's as worried as I am about Louise. He doesn't know how to deal with her, that's all. Men are never very good at coping with emotional women.'

Bethany knocked on Louise's door three times and spoke encouragingly to her. There was no response. A more urgent fear struck her. She pounded on the door, rattling the handle in panic. 'Louise? For God's sake answer me! Are you all right? Please open the door.'

Again no response. Not even a tear-filled voice telling her to go away.

She threw herself against the door as she had seen done in several gangster movies. The door reverberated but did not budge and there was a clump against the wooden panel on the inside. Bethany scarcely noted it, agony was shooting so fiercely through her shoulder and arm. For a moment she thought she'd dislocated it. As the pain subsided, she shouted in growing panic, 'Louise!'

When there was no reply she tore down the stairs, calling out, 'Mum, help me get the ladder from the shed. She doesn't answer me. What if Louise has done something dreadful?'

'Louise isn't the type.'

'But she's not answering. There's no sound of movement.'

Alice didn't argue further. Both women were white-faced as they dragged out the long ladder and propped it against

Louise's bedroom window. Bethany climbed it and peered inside. For a second she thought Louise was standing by the door. Then the full horror of what she was seeing struck her, the shock making her reel on the ladder.

'Be careful, Bethany,' Alice warned. 'You'll fall.'

She clung to the ladder and turning her head aside vomited onto the flowerbeds below.

'Good God, Bethany. What is it?'

Shaking violently, Bethany descended the ladder and threw herself into her mother's arms. 'It's Louise. She's hanged herself on the iron coat hook behind the door!'

Chapter Twelve

Bethany could not block from her mind the horror of seeing Louise's body. The police were called and they broke into the bedroom shattering the lock on the door with an axe. Alice had taken Bethany into the sitting room and given her a strong cup of tea with three spoonfuls of sugar for the shock. Each time the axe juddered into the bedroom door, Bethany flinched. She saw again the dangling corpse and the sightless, bulging eyes.

'I failed her, Mum. I should have helped her more.'

'Don't blame yourself,' Alice admonished. 'You did everything you could. We all did. She was heartbroken over David's death.'

'I can't believe she'd kill herself.'

'Nor can I. But grief does strange things to the mind. And sometimes I wondered if Giles wasn't quite the saviour he made himself out to be.' She shook her head. 'None of us are to blame for her death, yet also we are all to blame. We all left her today. Was she alone when she needed comfort and it all got too much for her?' She sobbed and pressed her hand to her mouth. 'And there was me shopping for a winter coat of all stupid things.'

'We don't know it happened today. It could have been last night.'

A man in a brown suit and trilby entered the room. 'Mrs Warden. We need you and your daughter to answer a few questions.' At their nod, he went on. 'I'm Detective Inspector Hawfield. At a guess I'd say your stepdaughter has been dead over twelve hours.'

Bethany wiped her tears away with her hands. 'How awful for her to take her life that way and all of us just a few yards away. Why didn't she talk to one of us?'

The inspector took out a notepad and licked the point of his pencil. 'How is it her body has only just been discovered?'

Alice blanched. 'Louise has been upset over the death of her fiancé. She often didn't come out of her room until the afternoon. I never thought she'd do this.'

'Did either of you hear anything in the night?' the inspector pursued.

Alice frowned. 'I did hear something. A floorboard creaking about two in the morning and Giles's door closing. He must have used the lavatory. Giles is my stepson. Louise's twin.'

'Has he been informed?' the inspector enquired. 'And your husband?'

'Yes,' Alice confirmed. 'Both of them. My husband should be here any minute. Giles works in Whitehall. The civil service. He was out of the office. I left a message for him to ring me the moment he returned.'

As if on cue the telephone jangled into life. Alice picked up the receiver and spoke briefly. There was a shouted, 'No. That's not possible. Tell me it's not possible!'

'I'm sorry, Giles,' Alice said, fresh tears streaming down her face. 'She's been dead several hours. Suicide. She hanged herself. I think you'd better come home. The police need to speak with all of us.'

★ ★ ★

Giles broke the telephone connection and stood with his head bowed. He was aware of the other three men watching him. His shoulders heaved and he put a hand over his eyes. 'It's my sister. She's dead. Found hanged in her room. Poor kid. Took her fiancé's death hard. I thought she was getting over it.' He swayed and clutched at the desk for support.

Oliver Tranter's chair went over backwards as he bolted from his desk. 'God, man, that's awful. You'd better get home. I'll clear it with the Minister's secretary when he comes out of his meeting.'

Giles put a hand on his friend's shoulder. 'Thanks. Appreciate it. Bit of a shock.'

'Awful business,' Oliver muttered. He stared after Giles who dragged his feet as he walked from the office. The poor bugger was taking it hard. He worshipped his sister.

Giles burst into the sitting room, his hair dishevelled and his eyes wild. 'Where is she? I won't believe Louise is dead until I see her.'

Harold lifted his head which had been sunk in his hands throughout the inspector's questioning. 'They've taken the body to the morgue. There's to be a coroner's inquest.' He rose and drew deeply on his pipe, his voice bitter. 'To think a suicide in my family. They'll say she was unstable. All the past of my mother's behaviour will be dragged up for gossip. I spent years living that shame down. Now this.'

'Everyone knows she was grieving for David.' Alice tried to placate him.

Giles was scowling. 'Is neighbours' gossip all you can think of? You disgust me. My sister's dead. She must have been in torment.'

The man in a brown suit stood up. 'Mr Warden, I need to ask you the same questions I've asked your family. What state of mind was your sister in last night when she retired?'

His face worked portraying his grief and it was some moments before he spoke. 'I'd been talking to her all evening. She seemed better. Brighter.' He spun round to glare accusingly at Alice. 'Why was she left alone? When was she found? When did it happen?'

Alice broke into tears. 'Last night.'

'Then why wasn't she discovered earlier?' Giles demanded. He began pacing the floor in long erratic strides.

'The door was locked,' Inspector Hawfield explained. 'Mrs Warden says she heard movement about two o'clock this morning. Was that you?'

Giles looked puzzled. 'Louise and I went to bed about midnight. I got up sometime in the night to go to the lavatory. It could have been then, I didn't notice the time.'

'Did you hear your sister crying or any other noise?'

'If I had I would have gone to her. When can I see Louise?' His manner became aggressive.

'After the inquest,' Inspector Hawfield declared.

Giles was helping himself to a whisky and spun round. Fury twisted his face. 'Isn't it obvious how she died? The wretched creature hanged herself.'

Inspector Hawfield sniffed and scribbled in his notebook. 'It's a formality. The room was locked and the key was on the floor by the body. It was probably dislodged when your stepsister threw herself against the door trying to open it.'

'Are you inferring that there may have been foul play?' Giles demanded.

The inspector regarded him in silence. Giles stared back, then all at once the fight ebbed from his figure and his shoulders slumped. 'I hate the thought of some stranger pawing over Louise's body. It seems so indecent. Why can't they let her rest in peace? The poor girl was tormented enough coming to terms with her fiancé's death.'

The inspector stood up to leave. 'I may have some further questions. But the case looks a clear suicide to me.'

And so it was declared by the coroner although his report did state that the bruising around the throat was not consistent with straightforward strangulation. He concluded that her death must have been slow and protracted thus explaining the strange configuration of bruises.

The funeral was a week later on the day the nation was mourning the death of King George V at the age of seventy. It was drizzling with rain as they stood around the grave. Giles hadn't spoken all morning and when the service was over he refused to enter the funeral car to return home.

'I need to walk.' His glare was hostile as he regarded his father. 'I'm not coming back to the house. This funeral is a charade. Half the mourners are businessmen. They weren't Louise's friends. They didn't care about her. You've turned the tragedy of her death into a way of safeguarding your business interests.'

Harold's stare was contemptuous. 'Someone had to recover the good name of our family. Avoid a scandal. You will attend the funeral tea. Today the family will be united. Walk out now and I never want to see you again. I shall disinherit you.'

Giles flushed. Bethany could see the anger sparking in his eyes as he wrestled to control his temper. Avarice was warring with a deeper demonic emotion.

'Very well. You hold the whip hand. As usual. I'll stay by the grave to say my farewell to Lou then I'll walk home.'

Harold nodded. 'See that you're home within the hour.'

Bethany felt a rush of sympathy for Giles. It was obvious he was upset at his twin's death. Harold was being insensitive. She went up to him. 'Louise will be missed by us all. Harold is upset. Don't take what he is saying too much to heart.'

He shot her an accusing glare over his shoulder, then seeing the concern in her eyes, his expression mellowed.

'I don't just miss Lou. It's as though half of me has died. You wouldn't understand unless you were a twin.'

She put her hand on his arm. 'I hadn't known her very long but I loved her as a sister.'

He shoved her roughly away. 'You corrupted her sweetness. You changed her. Tried to turn her against me.'

'Giles, that isn't true.'

His eyes smouldered with resentment and something darker and more dangerous which sent a shiver down her spine. She pulled the collar of her coat up around her ears. The late January drizzle had chilled the air. They were all upset. Giles as her twin was closer to Louise than anyone and his nature was of the type to turn the agony of his grief into anger. She was being foolish to see it as anything more than that.

Mark joined them. 'Time to get in the car. We should be at the house before the others arrive.'

For an hour and a half Bethany helped her mother as hostess. Giles was right about the funeral being a charade. There were few mourners who knew Louise personally. Men were discussing the King's death and how Edward VIII's reign would influence the stock exchange. The talk disgusted Bethany; it was so disrespectful but typical of

Harold and his associates. Only one woman who had been at school with Louise had come. A sign of how Louise had been cut off from forming friends. Mary Lister had attended the service but had left to catch a train back to Westcliff. Peg was also at the church but had declined coming to the house.

'Your stepfather wouldn't want me there especially in my condition,' she insisted and patted her bump. 'I just wanted to pay my respects. Louise was a lovely woman. Come round and visit soon.'

Looking round the room Bethany noted the other mourners. Some older members of the church choir were present and the vicar. Also a representative from the horticultural club Louise had joined. Another two dozen mourners were all business associates of Harold. It sickened her to walk past these men and hear them discussing the latest share prices or how the conflict stirred up in Europe by Adolf Hitler was affecting their exports. When Giles reappeared he poured himself a large whisky and stood in a corner refusing to mix with the others.

'Giles looks wretched,' she said to Mark who mingled easily, making small talk where necessary. 'Can't you speak with him?'

'I tried earlier and got my head snapped off for my trouble. He's a surly oaf. I know he's hurting and grief affects us all differently, but he's a strange chap.' He studied Giles for a moment before dropping his voice to add, 'He's melancholic. Brooding. Out of him and Louise I would have said he was the one capable of topping themselves. I've been watching him. He's so intense. A savage calm – like the eye of a storm. I felt it at the engagement. He had no time for David. Frankly, I'd steer clear of him.'

He took her arm and guided her through the house to

the conservatory. The drizzle had stopped and a watery sun was trying to break through the clouds. He opened the door and stepped into the garden and walked with her to the orchard. 'This has made me certain of one thing. It's foolish for us to wait to marry.'

'We can't afford to marry with both of us studying.'

Mark drew her close. 'Yes we can. Neither of us care for a grand lifestyle. Isn't it better to live simply and be together?'

'Harold would never permit it. He's such an old fusspot when it comes to conventionality. There will have to be a decent interval after Louise's death. Even to announce our engagement seems unfeeling after what happened to David the day after theirs.'

'I don't want to wait. Life's too precious to squander.'

She smiled tenderly at him. 'It's what we feel for each other which is important. Everyone knows we have an understanding. Let's leave the engagement for a few more months. It doesn't change how I feel for you.'

He bent his head and kissed her. When his hand closed over her breast her blood quickened and she moaned softly. His kisses drove her crazy, rousing sensations which made her long for more of his touch, yet always her conscience stopped her from permitting greater intimacy. Her hand covered his. 'No, Mark.'

'I go crazy for wanting you, Bethany.' He tipped her chin up with his forefinger and stared deep into her eyes. The passion she saw in those grey depths made her heart ache with yearning. 'I love you, so much.'

He stroked the line of her jaw and kissed her cheek before easing back to hold her gaze. The desire in his eyes kindled a profound need within her. She rallied her emotions. 'Mark, this is not a fitting time.'

'It is a reminder, my love, of all that can be lost.'

When his lips reclaimed hers the demand in his kiss destroyed her resistance. She mourned Louise but Mark was dousing her grief with passion. Each parting from Mark was harder to bear. The infrequency of their meetings due to his long hours at the hospital and studying were torment. She lived for his kisses.

Now as his mouth moved persuasively over hers, the sensuous flick of his tongue ignited emotions which she could no longer deny. She clung to him basking in the pleasure his lips created. Her body glowed with an ecstatic urgency and a craving only he could appease. Instinctively, her body moved against his as she was crushed against him. The sharp intake of his breath muffled against the jagged sigh rising to her lips. His mouth trailed down her throat and she arched her neck savouring its poignant trail. His hand dipped inside the low neck of her black dress and as his fingers brushed her hardened nipple, she moaned with pleasure. A potent hunger pervaded her body. Her will was enslaved and restraint was abandoned, every sense centred upon the sensual emotions Mark evoked.

Desire dominated her. Passion seared her until finally lack of breath broke them apart. Mark leant his forehead against hers and whispered. 'My darling, I don't want to wait for ever to make you truly mine.'

She was shaken by the powerful force of her longing. 'Neither do I, my love.' Yet the thought of becoming pregnant alarmed her. She put a hand to her hair and drew a shaky breath. 'We are neglecting Harold's guests.'

'Duty calls. But I want a decision from you soon.'

On returning to the house they passed Giles smoking a cigarette outside the conservatory, his stare cold as it settled on her. As they drew level he threw his cigarette into a puddle and stalked away.

Mark left mid-afternoon as he was on duty that evening at the hospital. Several of the businessmen lingered, encouraged by Harold. They had adjourned to the sitting room and were ensconced with brandies and cigars. Alice looked tired.

'Go and lie down, Mother. I'll make some sandwiches for the men and put out some more cake.'

'Harold would not approve. I should be on hand if they want anything.'

Bethany shook her head with impatience. 'You do too much. At least put your feet up on the sofa in the back lounge and I'll make you a cup of tea.'

Satisfied that her mother was resting, Bethany went down to the greenhouse. Louise had taken dozens of cuttings. She had loved the garden and it seemed a betrayal not to tend them. A glorious show of blooms next year would be a memorial to her. It was fast becoming dark and she was only halfway through watering the plants when the can was snatched away.

'What the hell are you doing?' Giles raged. 'Don't you dare interfere with Lou's plants.'

'I was watering them or they'll die. She loved them.'

'This was her greenhouse.'

He hurled the watering can through the glass. Bethany jumped back to avoid the flying shards. With an outraged snarl he swept the cuttings to the floor and began throwing other flowerpots through the panes. A dozen or more were smashed, the splinters falling around them. Giles was impervious to the danger. He cut his cheek and hand as he continued his destruction.

Bethany raised her arms to shield her face. Giles was

between her and the door. The intensity of his rage was frightening and it was impossible to flee as he guarded the doorway wildly tossing anything against the glass which came to hand.

'Giles, stop it! You'll hurt yourself. I didn't mean any harm. I thought it was what she would have wanted.'

'How would you know what she wanted?' He paused breathing heavily. Then two more flowerpots and a trowel were hurled at the panes above Bethany's figure. A shower of glass rained around her and she crouched covering her head with her hands, her blood pumping through her in fear. 'Giles. Stop it, please. Stop it.'

He picked up a hand fork and jabbed it towards her face. 'Get out and stay out. This was Louise's. No one else is to touch it.'

Bethany straightened. Her legs trembled as she attempted to edge past him. He remained an avenging sentinel barring her way. There was an insane glitter in his eyes. He stank of whisky.

'Come back to the house.' She was desperate to reason with him. 'The guests should have gone by now.'

'Pa is having a business meeting. Can you believe it? I heard him making a deal with two of the men.' Giles's face twisted in agony. 'The man's a heartless bastard.'

He still blocked her exit. Remembering the time he had cornered her before and tried to kiss her, she realised that she was alone. She was some distance from the house and at the mercy of his violence.

'He was upset at the grave,' she reasoned. 'Harold isn't the sort to show emotion.'

Her arm was grabbed and she cried out. 'No one cared for her like I did. I loved Lou. Really loved her.' He jerked her backwards so that her body was folded over the bench, the glass shards, soil and broken plants digging into her shoulders and hips.

'Bitch! You always have to interfere. Lou would never have encouraged that farmer if it hadn't been for you. And she'd still be alive now.'

His legs were pressed against her thighs, the whisky fumes gusting into her face. 'Tart! I saw you in the orchard. Like a bitch on heat. Kissing and pawing at each other and Lou not cold in her grave.'

'Giles, you're upset. You've drunk too much.' The glass was hurting her back and she could feel the warmth of blood seeping through her dress. She tried to push him off, but he gripped her wrists, his weight bearing down on her. The pain in her shoulders was making her squirm and each twist to free herself moulded his body closer over hers.

'Like a man touching you, do you?'

He jabbed one hand down between them and yanked up her dress. His nails gouged as they scraped across the naked flesh above her stockings.

'Stop it, Giles! For God's sake, you don't know what you're doing.'

'You're as heartless as Pa. I saw you with that doctor. Tart! He was all over you. You think you're better than me.'

She screamed as his fingers groped for her panties, tearing them as they pulled them aside, and his hand massaged her with cruel fingers. Horror and nausea funnelled the strength into her limbs. She kicked out, raising her knee and ramming it into his groin.

'Bitch!' he groaned, releasing her to collapse on the floor.

She leapt over him, her high heels sliding on the broken glass. Recovering her balance, she reached the door. Her mother was calling her and in the light from the conservatory she saw Alice walking towards the greenhouse. Bethany wiped a shaking hand across her cheeks and found them wet with tears. Taking several breaths to master her trembling, she straightened her dress. There were several holes in her black stockings and her shoulders and hips felt as if they were on fire where the glass had dug into them.

'Bethany, is that you? I heard a scream and smashing glass.' There was worry in her mother's voice.

Behind her Bethany heard Giles groaning and the sound of scrunching glass as he staggered out of the greenhouse.

'What's happened here?' Alice demanded. 'The greenhouse is wrecked.'

Bethany knew she couldn't let her mother know the truth. Giles would have raped her if she had not escaped. It would upset her mother too much. She was unharmed except for a few cuts and bruises. She could even understand how her presence in the greenhouse would have upset Giles. But his conduct had been deranged. His grief for his sister had been terrible to witness. He was going to be in enough trouble with Harold over the greenhouse. What good would it do to speak about the way he had attacked her? It was Alice who suffered most when Harold was angry with his son. It was then he started raving and ranting about Alice failing him as a wife by not providing him with more children.

She would stay silent about the attack and make sure she stayed out of Giles's way in future. Nevertheless, he wasn't going to get away with it. She raised her voice so Giles could hear her. 'Giles was overcome with grief for Louise. He's had a few drinks too many and started smashing up the greenhouse. It was a painful reminder that Louise was dead. I tried to stop him and slipped on the broken glass. That was when I screamed.'

'Are you hurt? Is that blood on your face?'

'A few small cuts that's all. Don't worry, Mum.'

Giles lurched on to the path. Alice shook her head. 'I don't know what your father will say. He'll be angry. That greenhouse cost a lot of money. And look at the state of you, Bethany. Your stockings are full of holes.'

Harold shouted for Alice from the house and as she hurried to answer his summons, her mother called back, 'You'd both better get inside and get cleaned up before someone sees you.'

Giles lumbered past Bethany, brusquely banging her shoulder with his own. He muttered, 'Bitch! Lou would never have told tales on me.'

'I could have said a lot worse and didn't,' she retorted.

'I'll get you for this.'

'Sober up and grow up, Giles,' she flung back at him. But his words left her uneasy. There had been a madness in Giles in the greenhouse.

Chapter Thirteen

'That's some looker,' Giles said leering at the blonde on the tennis court who was playing mixed doubles. Although it was April there wasn't a cloud in the sky and it was as warm as summer.

'Who, the brunette?' Oliver Tranter replied. 'That's Veronica. And you can keep your hands and eyes off her. It's understood between our families that we'll marry.'

'No, the blonde,' Giles added.

'You don't mean Fliss? You can definitely keep your hands off her. Honourable intentions only as far as she's concerned.'

'That's your sister Felicity?' Giles voiced his astonishment. 'When I saw her last year she was spotty and skinny with a pony tail and three inches shorter.'

'A year at finishing school in Switzerland did wonders for her,' Oliver laughed.

Giles knew that Felicity was worth a bit of money. He made it a point of learning how much family or friends of his friends were worth. In the three months since Louise had died he had not seen his father. There'd been an almighty scene when Harold discovered what he'd done to the greenhouse. Giles had stormed out of the house and not been back.

Now he regretted his decision. Pa had threatened to disown him. Told him to get himself a wife and soon. It was time he settled down. He was worried that Harold would carry out his threat. They'd never got on. What if Alice gave him a son? Although there didn't seem too much chance of that. He'd heard that she'd miscarried again. Even so it was a worrying possibility. Harold was worth a mint. When he died that money was his by right. If that bitch Bethany thought she'd get her hands on it, she had another think coming.

The only way he could get back in Harold's favour was to marry someone from a family his father would be proud of. All the better if she had money. And Felicity inherited an eight thousand pound legacy from her grandmother when she married.

He saw Felicity glance his way and discovering him watching her, she fluffed an easy shot. He grinned to himself. She'd had a crush on him last summer. He'd been amused at having Oliver's sister trailing round after him but he'd only regarded her as a schoolgirl. She was sixteen now, had blossomed into a beauty and had a figure any lusty male would relish getting his hands on. Not to mention eight grand.

He'd have to be careful with Oliver. His friend knew what he was like with women. Love 'em and leave 'em had been his way. He'd have to prove that he'd changed. That would be bloody inconvenient since he worked with Oliver, especially as it was unlikely he'd be able to see Felicity regularly. But for eight grand he was prepared to be more circumspect and stay away from other women when Oliver was around.

It was easier winning Felicity than he expected. While Oliver had gone off to be alone with Veronica, Giles made his move on his sister. Her blush and ready acceptance to walk to the lake with him showed she was still infatuated.

When he kissed her as they lay under the willow trees, it was obvious that she was not such an innocent. It made him bolder. There was no resistance when he explored her heavy breasts. She moved enticingly against him, grinding her hips against his arousal. Her legs parted obligingly when his hand slid inside her panties, but he wasn't sure if he was delighted or displeased when she tugged at the buttons of his fly. He'd have preferred his prospective wife to be less worldly. At her touch desire swamped coherent thought. Her hands were competent but when he tried to enter her, she pushed him away.

'No. I don't go all the way. It's too risky.'

'Hell, Felicity! You can't lead a man on and then play the tease.' He could have throttled her at that moment.

She smiled and her hand again closed over him, working furiously. 'I'm going to my marriage a virgin, but there's other ways I can give you pleasure.'

Throughout the spring and summer he learnt that Felicity was the ultimate tease. She badgered Oliver so that Giles was invited to their home every weekend. When the family had retired for the night they'd sneak out of the house to the boat house, throw off their clothes and swim naked in the lake. But she never allowed him to take her virginity.

Tonight the house had been filled with dinner guests and they'd had no time to themselves. They slipped away to the boat house at ten o'clock when it was dark and the guests were playing charades. The late September evening was balmy and ideal for clandestine lovers.

Felicity's kisses were as wild and passionate as usual. Giles was impatient with her reticence. It should be the man who made the running, not the woman, and tonight he was determined to end her teasing.

'No, Giles. You can get off me if you try that again.' She pushed against his weight, her legs clamping shut as he tried to push into her.

'But we're going to be married,' he groaned in frustration when she continued to resist. With any other woman he would have forced her, but the thought of losing eight grand stopped him.

'Are we?'

'You know I adore you. I want you to be my wife.'

She laughed. Not a light and teasing sound but one that was heavy with ridicule. 'Do you really think I'd marry you, Giles? What have you got to offer me? There's not much excitement in being the wife of a civil servant. I've a mind to marry a baronet at the very least. Haven't met one yet that I fancy who's young and single. I thought you were the type of chap who liked a bit of fun with no strings attached.'

'But I love you, Felicity,' he lied. 'I'm not going to be a dogsbody in the civil service all my life. There's a post in India I've been offered. It's a promotion. It's a great social life out there mixing with important diplomats and dignitaries.'

She yawned. 'But I'd still be plain Mrs and not a Lady.'

Somehow he mastered his temper and didn't strike her. The little tart had used him. Last week to get back in Pa's good books he'd gone home and told him he intended to get engaged at Christmas. Harold had been effusive and welcomed him back home with open arms. Now Felicity was making a fool of him. At least he hadn't told his father his intended bride's name. But he'd have to work fast now to meet someone suitable.

'But you've said that you love me.' He tried again to persuade her. 'Aren't we good together?'

'What has love got to do with marriage? It's a business arrangement, a way of bettering yourself. I've got the looks to win myself a title and, thanks to Gramma, enough money to make the match acceptable.' She eyed him provocatively through her lashes. 'But, darling, that doesn't mean we'll have to stop seeing each other. Once I'm married we can continue as lovers. Our relationship will be all pleasure.'

His fingers itched to strike the supercilious expression from her face. His plans were in ruins. He'd show her he wouldn't be toyed with. He'd get the damned bitch pregnant then she'd marry him soon enough. She'd been drinking heavily at the meal and she was tipsy. It had convinced him that he'd be able to take her easily tonight. Unfortunately, the drink had brought out her stubborn streak.

'The thought of another man having you drives me crazy.' He began to kiss her passionately, determined that in the throes of passion she would yield both to him and his entreaty that they marry. She was naked, having worn nothing under her figure-hugging satin evening gown. She lay on his suit jacket and earlier he'd removed his trousers. Now he rolled across her. 'If I just knew that you loved me, Fliss,' he groaned. 'Show me how much you love me.'

She giggled and wriggled down to take him into her mouth. Forestalling her, he clamped his hands around her waist and rolled on top of her. Then jamming his knees between her thighs he manoeuvred himself to enter her.

'No. You bastard. No!' She began to struggle.

His temper snapped. She'd humiliated him. Led him on. She'd used him. And now she thought she could discard him. Just like Lou. A red mist formed before his eyes. She was a whore like his twin. Leading him on and then deserting him. Lou had paid the price for her treachery. So had her fancy man Lister. Bloodlust spurred his desire. It had been so easy to return to the farm and lie in wait in the mist for the moment to fire at Lister. No one got the better of him. No one.

When Felicity began to squirm beneath him, he held her pinioned. The movements of her body made him ejaculate before he could enter her. Again she had thwarted him.

'Bitch! You'll pay. Just like Lou did.'

He was merciless. They were close to the water. He dragged her to the mooring and pushed her into the lake. She thrashed and floundered but he held her head down. Bubbles rose to the surface. Gradually they slowed and stopped. He stared at the pale body bobbing face down in the water. Another death which could be made to look like an accident.

Removing his socks, he waded into the water, and dragged her further into the moonlit lake. Afterwards he dressed, grabbed up Felicity's clothes and shoes, dumped them by the lake and walked towards the house. The garden was dark except for the waning moon which silvered the water. There was a steep bank this side of the lake which obscured its edge from the house and had hidden his movements. The terrace of the house was lit by Chinese lanterns and he saw the silhouette of several figures talking and drinking.

'Come on, Felicity,' he shouted. 'You've had too much to drink. This is no time for a swim.'

He strode purposefully forward acting out a part. He halted and looked back, again raising his voice. 'No. It's freezing in there. Come on . . .' A dramatic hesitation, then, 'Fliss, are you mad? It's too cold to swim.'

Allowing a suitable pause, he yelled, 'Oh God. Felicity! Help! She's gone under. Help!' He ran towards the lake, throwing off his shoes and jacket as he shouted frantically, 'Help! Felicity's in trouble. Help!'

He plunged into the water. By the time Oliver and his father had arrived at the lake, he had managed to pull Felicity on to the grass. Gasping, he slumped down beside her. 'She went under. Couldn't find her at first.'

Oliver knelt down and felt her wrist. 'There's no pulse.' He turned her over and tried to pump the water from her lungs and resuscitate her.

Giles pushed himself to his knees, breathing heavily. 'She's not moving. She can't have drowned. She wasn't under that long. Oh hell, she's had a lot to drink.'

Oliver gave a harsh sob and sank back on his heels. 'She's dead!'

Roger Tranter stared at his daughter and took off his jacket to throw over her naked figure. 'What the devil has been going on here?'

Giles looked suitably shocked. 'She got it into her head to go for a swim. I tried to stop her. Said it was madness in this weather. But she'd been drinking. I thought if I came back to the house she'd follow. Then I heard her splashing in the water and she cried out that she had cramp. When I saw her go under I ran back to the lake calling out for help.'

He broke off and shook his head. 'If I'd stayed with her this would not have happened. But it was a bit awkward when she started pulling off her dress. I thought the cold would stop her. I blame myself. I shouldn't have left her. I never thought she'd go in.'

'Felicity was headstrong,' Roger Tranter said brokenly.

A strident woman's voice demanded to know what had happened. Roger Tranter picked up his daughter and staggered slightly as he walked to the house. 'Devil of a business. My poor baby.'

Giles marvelled at the man's control. He doted on his daughter. There was a scream from Felicity's mother and the sound of weeping. He hung back, keeping to the shadows of the willow trees. 'Oliver, I'm so sorry. Ghastly tragedy – so senseless. I should never have left her. You must have guessed I was crazy about her.'

'Don't blame yourself. I can't believe it.'

'It happened so fast. Nothing I could do.'

'It's OK, old chap.' Oliver's voice was leaden but his natural good manners were unaffected by the shock. 'I know you were keen on her. Fliss didn't exactly make it a secret that she wanted you here.'

Oliver turned away. There was no point in telling Giles that his father had asked him not to invite Giles so often. He didn't approve of Felicity's infatuation and thought she could do better for herself. But Oliver had to hand it to Giles, he had changed in recent months. He was more diligent at the office and had been rewarded by being considered for the post in India. He turned away, saying, 'I'd better go in. Ma's bound to need comforting. It doesn't seem possible that Fliss is dead. She was so full of fun and life.'

'It's the shock. It numbs you.'

Oliver nodded, his expression stunned. Ever the considerate host, he added, 'You should get yourself into dry clothes. You did your best to save her. We're grateful for that. She was always swimming in the lake. Loved it.'

Giles said nothing. The blood had been pounding through his body so fast, it had kept the chill of the night air at bay. He was dripping wet and picked up his suit jacket and slipped it over his shoulders and took a cigarette out of the pocket. Drawing deeply on it, he stated, 'I'll leave your family to your grief. The police will have to be informed and I should be here to answer any questions. I'll leave after that.'

Giles parted from Oliver in the hall. A sombre hush had fallen over the guests and he heard Roger Tranter end a phone call to the doctor and then ask the operator to connect him to the police station. Giles hurried to his bedroom. Once the door was closed behind him he pressed his hand to his head. The family had accepted his story. Just the police to face now. Thank God this was Bedfordshire. This constabulary would not know of Louise's death so no awkward questions would arise. Not that any suspicion had fallen on him. Louise had been declared a suicide.

He changed into another suit and composed himself to face the police. He didn't expect any problems but it didn't do to be too cocky. It was only eight months since Louise had died. His hands shook as he lit a second cigarette and dragged the smoke deep into his lungs. That night still gave him nightmares. He hadn't meant to kill her. But his damned temper had got the better of him. Why had she defied him?

It wasn't until he felt her body go limp beneath his hands that he realised he had strangled Louise. He'd panicked and contemplated fleeing the house. But that would have confirmed his guilt. He had no intention of spending the rest of his life as a fugitive, or in prison awaiting the hangman's noose.

So he decided to make her death look like suicide. It wasn't uncommon for a woman losing her lover so tragically to take her own life. But where to suspend the body?

He'd discarded the orchard as it was overlooked by the houses across the road. He couldn't risk being seen, besides there was the difficulty of moving the body out of the house.

First he considered using the attic where there were some sturdy roof joists. He discounted that idea as he'd have to carry Louise's body upstairs and past Bethany's bedroom. The attic stairs creaked and she'd hear him. At least he'd got rid of her damned dog, dumping its body several streets away so it looked as if he'd been hit by a car. The cur wouldn't be raising the house as he prowled around.

Lou's bedroom was the first one at the top of the stairs and at the far end of the landing to Harold and Alice's room. It was easy to carry her upstairs since she had lost so much weight. He'd doubled the cord from her dressing gown and carefully tied two knots in it which were spaced to coincide with the thumbmark bruising on her neck. He then wound it around her neck and looped it over the sturdy iron hook on the door. It was more difficult getting the body at the right height with the footstool laid on its side so it looked that she had kicked it from under her. He'd locked her door from the outside and pushed the key underneath where it would be found inside. They'd have to break the lock to get in and he banked on the police believing the key had fallen out then.

He stubbed out his cigarette and buttoned up his jacket ready to face the police when they arrived. A drowning had been so much easier to stage.

Bethany and Mark made the most of the sunny weekend in the middle of October. It was rare for Mark to have a complete weekend away from the hospital. In recent months Alice had begun having asthma attacks after any argument with Harold. A fortnight ago she had suffered a nervous breakdown and was now in a convalescent home. Bethany and Mark had visited her this morning and she was looking better but her hands twisted nervously whenever it was mentioned that she return home. Harold had much to answer for. He had spent most evenings away from the house throughout the summer and Bethany suspected that he had a mistress. It was an insult to her beautiful mother.

On leaving Alice they drove to Hampstead for lunch and in the afternoon walked on the heath. Mark was quieter than usual and when he did speak it was of the escalating civil war in Spain.

'This Spanish civil war is stirring up more unrest than there already is in Europe,' Mark observed. 'A doctor at the hospital has a Spanish wife. The last letter she received from her family told of terrorism and persecution. Franco's Fascist army are steadily advancing, thousands are reported killed. Some doctors are going out there to help with the wounded.'

'You're not planning that are you?'

'I did think about it, but I could have the chance to go out to Africa for three months and study at a hospital there.'

'You haven't mentioned this before.' She had the uncomfortable feeling that Mark was keeping something from her.

'I didn't think I stood a chance. There were four of us interested but only one position. I was told on Friday that it was between me and Henry Porter. Porter's old man is with the Red Cross in Africa. It will probably be him.'

'Three months would be a long time for us to be apart.' She took his hand and interlocked their fingers. 'But it's what you've always wanted. I hope you get it, Mark.'

He smiled. 'Probably not. It's a wonderful opportunity, but we see little enough of each other with the long shifts I do at the hospital. It's been a month since we've had any time alone.'

They were near a secluded clump of gorse bushes and Mark sat down on the warm grass and pulled her down beside him. There was no one close by though several walkers were in the distance. He leaned towards her, his fingers a featherlight caress on her face and his voice was husky with longing. 'I've missed you, my darling.'

He kissed her and her arms went around him. Time stood still as they slaked the hunger of their passion. When Mark's hand slid over her thighs to caress her more intimately, she tensed. 'No, Mark. I want to wait until we're married.'

He groaned and rolled on to his back, his forearm across his eyes. 'Then we must get married soon. I'm tired of all our partings. I want to make love to you. I *need* to make love to you. This is crucifying.'

It was becoming an uncomfortable and familiar discord between them. 'Mark, I love you so much, but I'm too young to marry. I'm only seventeen and I've got years of studying ahead.'

'There's a lot I could teach you,' he whispered. He turned to lie with his head propped on his elbow and stared tenderly down at her. The sun was sinking fast in the sky and the air was filled with the song of skylarks. In the distance a dog barked but they were hidden by the long grass from any prying eyes. Their seclusion on the sun-warmed earth was a sanctuary. The days away from Mark were torture for her. Why couldn't she give him the answer he wanted?

There was an unspoken demand in his eyes which caused her heart to ache. It was becoming impossible to stave off his passion as her own young body clamoured for more than the kisses and caresses she had so far permitted. But always at the back of her mind was her fear of becoming pregnant. That a child would ruin her chances of becoming a doctor.

'We're meant for each other,' he coerced, his hands sensually circling her breasts, rousing them to an aching fullness. His eyes were dark with desire. 'For over a year I've been patient and waited until you're ready to be completely mine.'

The denial was on her lips but not in her eyes or heart. When his tongue traced the outline of her mouth, her lips parted. She moaned softly and when his hands worked their magic over her yielding body she knew her surrender was inevitable.

Mark saw the submission in her heavy-lidded eyes and vowed she would never regret this moment. It must be perfect for her and his own impatience curbed. Knowing that they had all evening before them, Mark kissed Bethany with leisurely persuasion. When the moon rose to cast its ethereal light over the heath he slowly undressed her.

She had never been completely naked to Mark's gaze before and to hide her embarrassment she closed her eyes.

'Look at me, Beth. This is nothing to be ashamed of. It's the natural blessing and affirmation of our love.'

She forced her eyes open and the love which shone from his face stole her breath. She lifted her arms to draw him down to her, the heat of his naked flesh setting her blood aflame. Her palms slid over his body savouring each movement of the flesh conquering hers. For her it was a time of discovery and intoxicating initiation. Of pleasure unbounded, given and received. There was the briefest hesitation as he moved above her, the sharp stab of pain and barriers breached. Then the heavenly ascent to the stars as they enshrined their love and passion enslaved them.

The descent to the earthly plane was of shuddering intensity. They lay entwined until their breathing slowed. Mark raised himself to stare at her and his face creased into smiles. 'I want an answer from you soon for our wedding date.'

She should be elated by his passion. Why then did a stubborn part of her hold back from total commitment? Marriage was irrevocably linked with the bearing of children. Mark had assured her that the precautions he had taken tonight would safeguard her. If only she could convince herself that would always be so.

Throughout the autumn Mark worked longer hours at the hospital which was now short-staffed as colleagues left to tend the wounded in Spain. Bethany saw little of him and he was becoming persistent that they married next year. Still she hesitated from setting a date.

Alice was back home and Harold was less antagonistic towards her. He had even reinstated the piano which her mother again played daily. Bethany had left grammar school after getting her Higher certificate but she had to wait another year before she was old enough to go to medical college. Having taken the course in typing to aid her story writing, Bethany took an interim job as a secretary at a small children's infirmary. She enjoyed the work and typing up the doctor's case notes gave her an invaluable insight into children's ailments and their treatments.

November brought several surprises. Giles was back in his father's favour after a whirlwind romance had sprung up between him and Rosemary, the daughter of Sir Jerome Crispin, MP. His engagement was set for New Year's Eve. Rosemary was shy and not at all the wife Bethany thought he would have chosen. She was several years older than Giles, rather plain, buxom with heavy hips and thighs and very horsey. She was fanatical about her three mares and her father had set her up running a riding stables near Epping. She dedicated her life to her horses and hated parties or socialising.

When they met at Sunday tea Bethany liked her. Rosemary had promised to teach her to ride. So far Giles had put obstacles in the way of her getting to know Rosemary better. He never wanted anyone to get close to someone he cared for.

The news of their engagement spurred Mark to demand they set a date for their own. They quarrelled when Bethany would not commit herself. She loved Mark but still felt she was too young for marriage.

Giles was to spend Christmas and Boxing Day at the Crispins' house in Epping. On Christmas Eve he came into the sitting room where the tree was being decorated by Bethany and Alice carrying his wrapped presents.

'The tree looks lovely. You two have worked hard.' He hesitated before adding, 'I know I've been difficult and I'm sorry.'

Alice smiled, won over by his sincere tone. Bethany wasn't so sure that Giles had turned over a new leaf. If he was being pleasant, he was probably after something.

Even so, this new Giles was certainly an improvement. Rosemary was a good influence on him. He hadn't argued with Harold for weeks. He had just emerged from a talk with his father in the study and was looking smug.

'I've just told Pa that Sir Jerome Crispin is giving a fancy dress ball to celebrate my engagement on New Year's Eve to his daughter.'

'That's wonderful,' Alice said merrily, 'Harold must be pleased.'

'Pa's been very generous. He's offered a tidy lump sum to help furnish the large house Rosemary's father will settle on her as a wedding present.'

Alice offered her cheek for Giles to kiss. 'Congratulations. There's so much to celebrate. I suppose now is the time to tell you my news if Harold has not already mentioned it. I'm expecting again.'

Giles felt his smile freeze on his face. He had hoped her childbearing days were past. He didn't want to share his inheritance with anyone. If she bore Harold a son that would be intolerable. He knew Harold was disgruntled with his conduct. Another son would be a rival. He kept his emotions guarded and forced a jovial laugh.

'Great news! No wonder Pa has been looking so pleased this visit. Nineteen thirty-seven is going to be a momentous year one way or the other. I suppose Bethany will be getting herself engaged at last. Or is her doctor fighting shy of marriage?'

'I don't want a long engagement, but Mark is becoming persistent,' Bethany retaliated. 'You may yet find you are not alone in becoming engaged.'

Her flushed cheeks and sparkling eyes were those of a woman deeply in love. Jealousy ground through him. He felt nothing like that for Rosie. She was a means to an end.

It rankled that Bethany was finding a happiness which only Louise could have given to him.

Again he kept his own counsel and drew his lips back into a caricature of a smile. 'I insist you open my presents while I'm here. I'm off to Rosie's and won't be back until the New Year. Pa has already opened his.'

He held out a slim parcel to both Alice and Bethany. Alice gasped in pleasure at her double row of pearls. When Bethany opened hers an opal and pearl bracelet gleamed on a satin background.

'The bracelet is lovely, Giles.' Bethany tried to gauge his expression but he was lighting a cigarette and guarding his emotions from her. She had an uncomfortable feeling that the expensive gifts were not a peace offering but a warning.

'Aren't you going to put the bracelet on?' Giles took her wrist. His touch made her flesh cringe and she steeled herself not to flinch away. His gaze was piercing as he studied her before bending over the clasp and adding softly, 'Think of me whenever you wear it.'

Her throat dried. Opals and pearls were gems superstitiously associated with misfortune and tears.

Giles noted the widening flare of Bethany's eyes and savoured her reaction. She was uneasy. Good. That would give her something to dwell upon. She was too spirited to be frightened of him, but she was aware of the power he could exert over her. That pleased him. He hadn't forgotten that she was responsible for Louise rebelling against him. And one day he would crush her as Louise's betrayal had crushed him.

Women deserved all they got. They were liars, cheats and tarts. Louise and Felicity had proved that. He still became angry when he remembered how Felicity had used him. Meeting Rosemary had soothed some of that rage. She adored him. That meant more to him than beauty. Compliance and devotion were more abiding than the fickleness of lust. A pity she was such a lump. But then in the dark all cats were grey. Fortunately Sir Jerome Crispin could deny his daughter nothing and he was immensely wealthy. The old boy had intimated to Giles that Rosemary's husband would get a seat on the board of his paper mills and his wedding present would be a house set in several hundred acres of land. Giles knew where his future bread would be buttered. Harold was delighted with the prospect of a marriage between the two families. Apart from his generous wedding present he had given Giles a substantial amount to invest in a business project with Sir Jerome Crispin.

Life did have its moments and while things were going well for him, Giles was prepared to play the role of loving son and devoted boyfriend. Though everything had a price, and apart from Rosie's lack of looks and horse-orientated interests, he'd had to give up the promotion offered to him in India. Rosie had refused point blank to leave her blasted horses. India had been more than a promotion. The situation in Europe was hotting up with Hitler's soldiers having occupied the Rheinland in defiance of the Treaty of Versailles. He had the unpleasant feeling a war could be brewing. In India he'd have been safely out of it.

Still, the fortune Rosie would bring him on their wedding day was worth a few risks, and it didn't mean he had to stay married to her for ever. After all, riding accidents weren't uncommon . . .

The Christmas decorations completed, Bethany took Peg,

Frank and their baby son Michael their presents. A publishing house had accepted her first children's novel about the antics of Jester, an accident-prone puppy, and she was giving the first copy to Michael. The publishers wanted a children's novel every six months. She loved writing the stories and with Mark working such long hours it was enjoyable to spend an evening composing another adventure for Jester. As always her thoughts returned to Mark. She loved him so much. They wouldn't even have Christmas together this year as he was on duty. But he was free over the New Year and they would be attending Giles's engagement party together.

The long absences in recent weeks had shown her how much she missed Mark. Her love consumed her. She believed in destiny. If she was meant to be a doctor or work in any form of healing and helping others, it would happen in some way or another. With that faith she had decided that when next Mark asked her to marry him she would agree. Now the idea was in her head she was excited about the prospect of spending her life at Mark's side as they healed the sick.

It was bursting on her tongue to tell Peg her decision, but she stopped herself. It wouldn't be right to tell anyone until she and Mark had set the date. Until then it would remain an exciting secret.

Chapter Fourteen

The first sight of the Crispins' house astounded Bethany. She had expected it to be large but not palatial. There was a tennis court, croquet lawn and a swimming pool and the neo-Georgian structure had over twenty rooms. They arrived at seven and were met by a footman and a maid took their coats.

'Sir Jerome and Lady Crispin are greeting their guests in the ballroom at the head of the stairs,' the butler announced.

Crystal chandeliers and a row of family portraits dating back three generations lined their passage. A butler stood imperiously by the door and held out his hand for their card and announced them in haughty tones. Everything was far grander than Bethany expected and though at ease with such opulence she found it too ostentatious for her taste. Harold would adore it. No wonder he had been so pleasant to Giles since his son had announced his intentions to marry Rosemary.

While Bethany and Mark waited for their host to welcome Harold and Alice, she gazed into the ballroom. There were already over a hundred guests present, all in elaborate costumes. Bethany had chosen a fun costume and with her black hair thought it appropriate to come in a bright full skirt and white peasant blouse of a gypsy. Harold had not been pleased. When he saw Mark's pirate's costume of a full-sleeved shirt and black leather jerkin, with his head covered by a red bandana and his eye by a roguish patch, he had voiced his displeasure.

'A gypsy and a pirate create quite the wrong impression. Now if you had dressed as Nelson and Lady Hamilton that would be another matter.'

'But Emma Hamilton was Nelson's mistress,' Bethany responded with devilment. 'I didn't think you'd approve of us advertising such a scandalous union.'

Harold paled and blustered. 'No, indeed not. Lady Hamilton was not a suitable choice. But you know what I mean.'

Bethany knew only too well. They should at all times appear respectable and she had thought a fancy dress ball meant having fun.

Harold had donned a frock coat and high-winged collar of the Edwardian era. He nodded to Alice in a primrose Regency dress. 'Your mother has impeccable taste. You should have consulted her before hiring the costumes.'

Alice looked distressed but Bethany winked at her. Her mother had thought the gypsy and pirate costumes a romantic combination.

A glance at the guests and Bethany knew her costume had been a practical choice. Many were already red-faced and perspiring in heavy medieval robes. There was a handful of monks, several red devils, two gorillas and one grotesque Punch character. Three large chandeliers hung from the ceiling and half a dozen casement windows were draped with red velvet hangings: for nothing as grand as the elaborately draped and ruched material over the windows could be described as mere pelmets and curtains.

Lady Crispin, who was dressed as Cleopatra, smiled thinly at her. Her hand was taken in a butterfly hold and quickly released. 'Delighted to meet you, Bethany, isn't it? Rosemary has spoken of you. Such a novel costume. Very rustic.' Her tone was conciliatory. She was as bad a snob as Harold. They should get on well.

The ceramic smile changed to one of pleasure when Lady Crispin's gaze shifted to Mark. Her haughty expression was transformed, her eyelashes fluttered and she clasped Mark's hand, pulling it against her so that his fingertips rested between the cleavage of her gown. 'Dr Greenwood, such a pleasure to meet you. I shall be most vexed if you don't ask me to dance later.'

If Mark was surprised at her behaviour, he didn't show it and lifted her hand to his lips then released it. 'My pleasure, Lady Crispin.'

'Call me Ann. We're practically family, I believe.'

Bethany couldn't believe the blatant way Lady Crispin was flirting with Mark. She was in her forties and there was no mistaking the hunger in her eyes as she watched Mark move on to be greeted by her husband. Sir Jerome Crispin wore Roman robes and a wreath of laurel on his head. He took Bethany's hand and welcomed her, his manner as remote as his wife's.

Next in line was Rosemary who had rather disastrously chosen to wear a pink crinoline which emphasised the plumpness of her figure. Beside her Giles was in evening dress and a red-lined cloak and at Bethany's approach drew back his lips to reveal two long fangs.

'Count Dracula is an odd choice for an engagement party,' Bethany observed.

Rosemary giggled and stared up at him adoringly. 'One bite of those fangs and a woman is his for all eternity. In this life and the next, my darling. I am completely yours.'

Giles leered at Bethany. 'Dracula always gets his woman – none can escape him. Beware the dark when he will materialise and claim his victim to enslave them to his will.'

His words sent a shiver through her. Giles did have an obsessive need to possess and manipulate a person. He had done that to Louise and had tried the same with her, but she had resisted. Was he warning her to remember the vow he had made to her in the greenhouse after Louise's funeral?

She dismissed the notion as fanciful. That was nearly a year ago. Giles was playing the part his costume demanded. She was perfectly safe. Mark was with her. Nothing would happen at Giles's engagement party. He wanted to frighten her.

'That stepbrother of yours is certainly odd,' Mark said as he led her through the press of guests.

Bethany agreed with him. Memories were being resurrected and it was impossible to stop the comparison surfacing at how different Louise's engagement had been. There was none of this pomp but more warmth and family unity. She preferred the unpretentiousness of the barn to this ostentatious display of Sir Jerome Crispin's wealth and position. She could see that Harold was impressed and had joined a group of MPs and was no doubt hoping to win some business for his company.

Mark stared round and whistled under his breath. 'Strewth, it's like Buckingham Palace here. Bit over done, isn't it? There must be a dozen waiters carrying drinks and silver platters of food?'

'They've probably hired caterers.' Bethany couldn't help making further comparisons. 'I can't help thinking of the fun Louise and I had with Mary when we prepared the food and decorated the barn. So much love went into the labour of that day. All this is produced by opening a wallet.'

'A wallet Giles will be very happy to dip in to given half a chance,' Mark declared. 'And that was a thinly veiled pass he made at you when we arrived, if ever I heard one. Does he fancy you? He hasn't ever tried anything, has he?'

What good to tell him that Giles had tried to rape her? Giles had been drunk in the greenhouse and grieving. He had Rosemary now who adored him. Even so she couldn't lie to Mark. 'He'd been drinking one night and got a bit fresh. But it was nothing I couldn't handle. And talking of being fancied . . . You were a hit with Lady Crispin,' Bethany teased, deflecting the anger which had tightened Mark's face. 'She couldn't take her eyes off you.'

'A man-eater and old enough to be my mother. I hate obvious women. I'm an old-fashioned guy who believes the man should be the hunter. Talking of which, you and I have been courting long enough without making it official.'

She had already decided to give him his answer tonight but was forestalled from answering by a cousin of Rosemary's asking her to dance. Several more partners claimed her in quick succession. The only sight she had of Mark was as he waltzed past: once with Rosemary, then Alice and finally Lady Crispin. Her Ladyship was doing her utmost to press her body against his and Mark was stoutly keeping her at arm's length. As Mark's gaze met Bethany's he nodded towards the terrace and mouthed, 'After this dance.'

She nodded. Her partner who was dressed inappropriately as Harlequin, for he had too large a stomach and skinny legs for such a revealing costume, was Lady Crispin's nephew, a conceited actor. He chuckled lecherously, 'An assignation. I'll meet you on the terrace any time, sweetie.'

'He's my boyfriend.'

'Variety is the spice of life, dearheart.' His hand slid down her back to pinch her bottom.

Her heel ground on to his foot. 'Keep your hands to yourself if you want your toes to survive this dance.'

'Frigid are you?' His tone became nasty.

'No. Just choosy.' She walked away from him in the middle of the dance. As she made her way to the terrace she had to pass Giles who was lounging by the window with a drink in his hand.

'Barney up to his tricks, was he?' He laughed maliciously. He stepped forward and caught her elbow. 'I'll finish this dance with you.'

'I'm tired, Giles. We can dance later.'

His eyes narrowed dangerously. 'Don't act high and mighty with me.'

'You exaggerate. This tune is almost over. I'll dance with you later. I'm sitting the next dance out with Mark on the terrace.'

'And if I won't permit it?'

She laughed. 'Don't be ridiculous, Giles.'

He scowled and bared his theatrical fangs. 'But I am Count Dracula and you are my chosen one.'

'Then choose someone else, preferably your fiancée,' she said, refusing to be frightened by his histrionics.

'I won't be made a fool of.' The old rancour was back in his voice.

She shook her head. 'Why must you make such a drama out of this? We can dance later.'

'Indeed we shall. But the dance will be of my choosing and there will be no escape.'

She tried to laugh aside the overlying menace, but there

was something about his expression which disturbed her. He always reacted badly when she clashed wills with him. Reminding herself that this was his engagement party, she decided against provoking him further. 'You're a lucky man to be marrying Rosemary. I shall enjoy our dance later.'

Giles glowered after her as she moved out to the terrace. Sir Jerome had announced the engagement at the beginning of the evening. Now the deed was done it had lost its allure. He was impatient to get his hands on Rosemary's money. Fortunately, since Rosie was twenty-eight, her parents had been eager for an early wedding. It was set for April.

His discontent mounted as he saw Greenwood join Bethany. Her love for the doctor shone like a beacon from her eyes. It angered him. Due to her interference he had been denied the woman he loved. Rosemary was no substitute for Louise. Rosemary may adore him and her wealth would give him a future lifestyle he had dreamed of, but he didn't love her. Bethany had driven a wedge between Louise and himself. Her death left a void no one could fill. It was time that bitch, who thought herself so superior to him, was taught a lesson.

Taking another glass of champagne from a passing waiter, he sipped it reflectively. By leaning back against the curtains he could eavesdrop on the conversation between Bethany and her boyfriend.

Bethany was pulled into the shadows by Mark and he kissed her passionately. She responded with equal ardour but the pleasure roused was brief for other revellers strolled on to the terrace.

As they broke apart, Mark groaned, 'I've hardly seen you all evening. And I want so much to hold you in my arms and kiss you. Is there nowhere private?'

'You have a one-track mind,' Bethany murmured although the message in her eyes echoed his thoughts. 'At midnight. Let's sneak away from the revellers.'

'Not an easy task. Several couples have disappeared down the stone steps to the gardens below.'

'We'll meet by that large cedar the other side of the knot garden. All the guests are supposed to assemble in the dining room to hear Big Ben chime midnight on the radio. There's to be fireworks on the other side of the house. We will have our privacy.'

It was quarter to midnight and Giles was dancing with Lady Crispin. The woman as usual was pawing him like a bitch on heat. She had no morals or scruples. From the first time Rosemary had brought him home for a weekend Ann had been unable to keep her hands off him. She had come to his bedroom and stripped off her dressing gown to reveal that she was naked, which had almost proved a disaster when moments later Rosemary tapped on the door and giggled as she demanded he open it. Her mother had scowled. 'I suppose my daughter has first claim on you. But tomorrow morning while she's out riding I'll come to you.' She kissed him and left by the balcony. No doubt to find a more available house guest.

The weekends had become physically shattering. He returned to work on a Monday sexually exhausted. Both Rosemary and her mother were demanding lovers.

'I want you tonight, Giles,' Ann whispered. 'Can't we sneak out now? Everyone will be watching the fireworks.'

'Rosemary has eyes like a hawk. It's too risky. She'll be gone for hours during the hunt tomorrow. You like variety. Dr Greenwood keeps looking your way,' he lied. 'He's supposed to be seeing my stepsister but they often have tiffs. He told me he'd rather see in the New Year with you than her. I'd go over and snare him now.'

'And you won't be jealous?'

'We've plenty of time for fun together. Tonight is too risky. We don't want any speculation before the wedding?'

She placed a cigarette in a long holder and waited for him to light it before answering, 'You're right. Rosemary is such a prissy miss. The foolish girl could call the whole thing off if she suspected that we had a fondness for each other. And it's high time she got married and moved away. It's so damned difficult to meet a lover when she's around.'

Giles surreptitiously gave her bottom a squeeze as he pushed her gently towards Mark. 'Best to get him away while my stepsister is dancing with your husband.'

Lady Crispin arrowed in on Mark who groaned as he saw her approaching. He could hardly be rude to his hostess and he had just seen Bethany excuse herself to Sir Jerome and slip out of the ballroom to get her coat before meeting him outside.

Giles saw Bethany leave and watched as she returned with her coat. Instead of entering the ballroom she went through an anteroom which also led out to the terrace and grounds. A glance towards Lady Crispin revealed that she had backed Mark up against a wall and they were hemmed in by revellers. He chuckled. That would keep the doctor occupied.

A hasty scan of the room showed him that Rosemary was talking intently to the Master of the hunt. From her enrapt expression the conversation was about horses. Which was usual. God, she could be so boring. A distant cousin of hers caught his eye and raised his drink in salute to him and mouthed, 'Congratulations.'

Giles acknowledged it and when the cousin's attention was diverted he slipped through the curtains to the terrace. Whistling softly he followed Bethany. She was already on the lawn below heading towards the cedar.

'Phew! That was a narrow escape,' Mark murmured as he ran across the lawn towards the cedar tree. From the proposition Lady Crispin had made him she was no lady in the true sense of the word. The language of her invitation had been as graphic as a streetwalker's. He had politely declined.

Ahead he could see a dark silhouette of a man walking along the edge of the knot garden. Bethany was to the right of the man, her camel coat lighter in the moonlight against the dark expanse of lawn. 'Bethany!' he called and she turned to wave at him.

Vaguely he noted that the man by the knot garden had disappeared as he approached. No doubt another assignation and the man didn't want his presence known.

Catching up with Bethany he put his arm around her and they hurried to the seclusion of the overhanging branches of the ancient cedar. Drawing her into his arms, he kissed her ardently. His passion flared. He wanted to crush her, consume her, mould with her body and soul.

The kiss inflamed Bethany's senses. Her body quivered, aching for his touch. Yet despite the romance of the setting, frost was chilling the air. She clung to Mark, her coat opened so that their bodies were warmed by each other's heat. His hand squeezed her breast and she sighed ecstatically. 'I've missed you over Christmas. You're right. Let's get married soon – in the summer when I'm eighteen.'

'I've waited so long to hear that,' Mark said between kisses, triggering bolts of desire to fire through her body.

He drew back to study her face. Desire darkened his eyes and tensed the muscles of his jaw. 'You insisted on qualifying first.'

'I was an idiot.' She smiled up at him. 'I love you so much. I keep thinking of Louise and David. I'm scared I'm going to lose you.'

He let out his breath sharply and she frowned trying to fathom his mood. Though he held her against him, she could feel that he had mentally withdrawn from her.

'What's wrong? Don't you want to get married? Have you changed your mind?'

'My darling, you were so adamant that you wanted to wait when I asked you again to marry me a few weeks ago.' He sighed. 'I've been chosen to go to Kenya next month, not just for three months but to spend a year treating patients in a mission hospital.'

His words shattered her dreams but she put on a brave face for his sake. 'You must go, of course. It's too important for you not to.'

'Then we'll get married before I leave, and you'll come with me as my wife. Our honeymoon will be the boat trip over there.'

Panic gripped her at the suddenness with which her life would change. She had never really thought that Mark would get the Kenya post. Events were moving too fast. And she didn't want to be so far from her mother for so long, especially now Alice was pregnant. What if Alice had another miscarriage? Harold was always so cruel to her. Could she desert her mother at such a time?

Her expression showed a wary reluctance. Mark had hoped that Bethany would come round to his way of thinking. Briefly he had glimpsed a vision of their life together fulfilling his aspirations to do research in Africa.

At her rapid change of mood the disappointment was crushing. 'This is a wonderful chance for us to live and work abroad.' His eyes glittered in the moonlight and his tone was accusing.

'I know, but . . .'

The strain of months of overwork made him see her hesitation as outright refusal. Frustration sharpened his voice. 'If it's your studies you're worried about, you can come back to England when you're due to start college.'

Bethany knew that wouldn't happen. She saw her dreams sliding away. She had believed her plan to marry this summer would solve their problems. And now he was demanding more from her. Did he expect her to abandon her career? Seeking a conciliatory path, she ventured, 'What would I do in Africa?'

'They'll no doubt find you some work in the hospital.'

Clearly he had not considered all she would be giving up. Hurt by his attitude she was scathing. 'They'll allow me to scrub the floors I suppose, and wash out bedpans. And if I'm lucky, a bit of first aid since I achieved a certificate in that. No thank you. I've more to offer people than that.'

He plunged his fingers through his hair, his tension palpable. 'I do understand the sacrifice you'll be making. I wouldn't ask you if I didn't know what hell my life will be without you. This post is for a year, it could be longer.'

Reason told her she could still go to medical college, but hurt pride that Mark was disregarding her ambition to further his own made her stubborn. 'You're being selfish to expect me to give up so much.'

He reached for her but she backed away. His eyes blazed and his face was taut as he flared, 'No. You're the one who's being selfish. There's so much research that needs to be done to cure the diseases in the tropics. We can't always put ourselves first.'

His condemnation sent her own anger spiralling. He was putting her in the wrong. She had made such wonderful plans and had thought tonight would be filled with joy. Instead it had all turned sour. She had drunk enough champagne to make her obstinate. 'You must do whatever you think best. We could have got engaged now and married in the summer. You want it all your own way. Go to Africa. We'll get married when you return to England.'

Frustrated and angry, he swung away and slapped the trunk of the tree with his hand. 'If you loved me . . .'

'Don't use emotional blackmail, Mark!' The last threads of reason deserted her. 'Love is give and take on both sides. If you loved me . . .'

She cut off. They were bickering like children and getting nowhere. To achieve their goals in life they were at a stalemate. 'I don't want to quarrel, Mark.'

He remained stiff and unyielding. If he had held out his arms she would have gone into them. Instead he kept his back to her. Her anger simmered to boiling point. Why must she make all the sacrifices?

Still she sought a compromise. 'It's only for a year. Isn't our love strong enough to survive that?'

'Are you coming with me, or not?'

He sounded as autocratic as Harold. Heartache choked her. Speech was impossible. She could feel tears welling. Unable to stop them and too proud to let him see them, she whirled away and headed for the shadows of the nearby shrubbery.

Mark swore roundly before running after her. 'Bethany, we have to talk this out.'

She had disappeared into the bushes. This part of the

garden was pitch black and he could see nothing but the vague outline of shrubs. 'Bethany!'

She didn't answer and he struggled to control his temper. 'Bethany! I love you. We'll work this out.'

Again silence.

Damn her. How could she be so childish? Had he misjudged her? He had always thought her mature for her age. Was she too young to face the responsibilities of a doctor's wife in Africa? Until this quarrel he would not have thought so. He called her name several times and still she did not answer. 'If that's the way you want it,' he fumed. 'It's over between us. You know where to contact me if you change your mind before I leave next month.'

Bethany's eyes bulged with terror. The man's hand clamped around her waist and over her mouth stopped her answering Mark's calls. The grip was like iron. She couldn't move no matter how she tried to wriggle free. She had been dragged further into the shrubs. The smell of a familiar cologne filled her nostrils. Panic gave her a surge of energy. She could hear Mark walking away.

Her foot impacted against an ankle eliciting a groan from the owner. The kick was returned, the impact on her ankle shooting fire through the bone and her foot gave way. Another kick to her shin would have felled her, had her captor not held her so tightly. She was dragged backwards several more yards. A shoe came off and the rough earth gave way to a grass clearing. Twisting her head to try and bite her assailant's fingers, she saw a tall stone figure of Bacchus. The shrubs must border a secluded garden.

Bacchus grinned at her. Her hands wheeled searching for her attacker's face. They contacted only air. Fear pumped the adrenaline into her limbs giving her the strength to thrash with her legs and try to squirm free from his crushing hold. The vicelike grip tightened. She was thrown to the ground and a knee pressed into her stomach before she could roll away. Winded and stunned, she couldn't move.

'Bitch! *Now* you'll dance to my tune.'

The voice was Giles's as she knew it would be. Fear tunnelled through her. It made her gag. He was tearing at her coat and blouse. Her scream was choked by the tongue invading her mouth. The nip of frosty air on her bare skin dispersed her stupor and she fought like a cornered vixen.

She scratched, bit, kicked and bucked. A fist struck her jaw and red and gold flashes exploded in her head. Even dazed, instinct drove her to fight. He stuck to her writhing body like a giant limpet. Immovable. Mauling. Violating.

Material ripped. Her skin was scraped by probing nails. Then the pain of penetration razored into dry, unwilling flesh. Thrusts hammered her bruised body until he collapsed over her.

'Bastard!' she sobbed as he withdrew and stood up. 'Filthy, evil bastard!'

'You had that coming. You had a lesson to learn. You thought yourself better than me.'

Her hands covered her eyes. 'You're evil. Mark will make you pay for this.'

'But you won't be telling him, will you?' He chuckled sadistically. 'Everyone would have to know the details. I'd tell them you argued with Mark and threw yourself at me to get back at him. It would destroy your mother. Harold would be convinced you'd egged me on. He'd never tolerate a whore in his house. He'd throw you out. And as for the saintly Dr Greenwood . . . Does he want second-hand goods?'

He looked down at her with triumph and lack of compassion. 'No, you won't speak of this. The shame is too great and you have too much pride.'

A jaunty whistle accompanied his departure. Hatred burned in her breast as she curled into a foetal ball. She wanted justice against him. Yet even in her traumatised state she knew that Giles had been right. How could she ever hold her head up if it became gossip that she had been raped by him? Many would regard the crime as incestuous and revile her further. There was dignity in silence. Her shame would be forever hidden.

Chapter Fifteen

Misery engulfed Bethany. How could she look Mark in the eyes again? She felt tarnished: unclean and unworthy.

Bitter tears were wrenched from her. Her life was ruined. She remained secreted in the shrubs, her trauma mocked by the cheers, whistles and shouts of joy which heralded the New Year. Flashes of coloured lights lit up the sky as the fireworks decorated the heavens. She gazed up at them through blurred vision. The birth of 1937 held no joy for her. It brought with it corruption and degradation.

Eventually the cold penetrated and realigned her senses. How could Giles have done this to her? How *dare* he have done this to her? Fury blasted through her misery. If there had been a knife to hand she would have struck or gelded him. He wouldn't get away with it. She burned for justice.

As quickly as the anger flared it was doused. This was Giles's engagement party. He didn't deserve Rosemary. But if one thing had been obvious tonight, it was that Rosemary doted on Giles. Rosemary would be heartbroken if she exposed Giles for the base lecher that he was. And the scandal would make headlines in the papers. What good would that do anyone? Except make herself notorious and she didn't want that. Pride surfaced. To denounce Giles would be to expose her shame.

She couldn't subject her family or Mark to that. Looking down at the ragged state of her blouse she concentrated on getting away from the celebrations without anyone remarking on her appearance.

The horror of the rape again threatened to overwhelm her. It took all her willpower to batten down her revulsion. Her pride sustained her, providing her with reserves of strength. Her concentration fixed upon retaining her dignity and getting away with her shame undetected. Giles had meant to humiliate her. He had degraded only her body not her mind. She would not let his attack destroy her.

Always a fighter, her spirits rallied. She would get through tonight and face each day as it came. Her head tilted. It was a new year and a new beginning. She had been raped as the last minutes of the old year died, not the new one commencing. That detail was important. It funnelled her mind towards the future not the past. Only by giving in to despair and weakness could Giles triumph over her. And she would never submit to that.

Inconsequentials became important. The blouse was ripped to the waist but her skirt was only crumpled. There were tears and ladders in her stockings. She tore these off and stuffed them in her coat pocket. Mercifully, when her coat was fastened no one could see her dishevelment.

A shoe had come off in her struggle and as she hunted for it, she could feel the cold trickle of semen down her thighs. Its slimy trail pitched her back into the horror of her violation. Nausea overwhelmed her and she vomited. When she straightened she could not control her shaking. It seemed to take forever to find the lost shoe. The search focused her. If she found it all would be well. She would get away from here without awkward questions being asked.

Determination not to become Giles's victim hardened her eyes and face. She scraped her fingers through her hair and pulled a handkerchief from her pocket, spat on it and cleaned the dirt she could feel on her cheek. Each movement was done with the jerkiness of a puppet.

The fireworks had ended when she finally located her shoe and walked dazedly towards the drive to find Harold's car. Some guests were leaving. One of Rosemary's female friends called out, 'Great party, wasn't it? And Rosemary and Giles are so in love. Did you see how they were all over each other at midnight? So romantic.'

Giles had covered his tracks well. No one would believe her if she accused him of rape. He had been too attentive to Rosemary all evening.

Rosemary's friend giggled as she studied Bethany's pale face and unsteady stance. 'Had a bit too much champers? You look ghastly.'

'I feel awful.' Bethany played along with that excuse. 'You couldn't find my mother, could you?'

'Is it that bad?' The woman made sympathetic noises. 'Makes you feel like death, doesn't it? I'll see if I can find Mrs Warden.'

The woman tottered away calling out to others asking if they had seen Bethany's mother.

Bethany clung to the car for support and prayed that her mother would accept her explanation of having drunk too much. Even in her own wretchedness she wanted to spare her mother further pain. A shock like that could cause Alice to miscarry.

Harold eyed Bethany accusingly. 'It's a disgrace a young girl like you drinking. And to make a spectacle of yourself in public . . . I'm ashamed of you. Do you know how many of my clients are here? Your conduct is disgraceful and you shall be punished. And I'll have words with that young man of yours. I thought him more responsible.'

Bethany kept her head lowered. If Harold was reacting like this at thinking her drunk, he would be apoplectic at discovering the truth.

Alice put her hand under Bethany's chin but Bethany did not lift it. The misery would be stark in her eyes.

'Is it the drink, my dear? Or are you upset over something else?' Alice asked anxiously. 'I saw Mark looking furious and he left the party abruptly before the fireworks. Did you two quarrel?'

Bethany nodded. That at least was a truth her mother could sympathise with.

'I'm sure it's no more than a lovers' tiff. Mark adores you. He loves you too much . . .'

Alice meant well but each word increased her desolation. Would Mark still love her when he learned the truth? Or would he, as Giles had jeered, see her as second-hand goods?

Bethany pulled open the back door of the car and slid inside turning her face away from her mother to stare out of the window. It was a half hour journey home and it took all her control not to break down and sob out her despair.

Harold glanced at her slumped figure in the rear mirror. 'It's no good sulking, my girl. I won't have waywardness or unladylike behaviour. Though I doubt Mark was all to blame for the disgraceful state you've got yourself in. You've always been too wilful for your own good.'

Harold still only tolerated her in his household because she was Alice's daughter. He was quick to judge and accuse her. There would be no sympathy or understanding from him if he learned the truth of tonight. He would condemn her as having provoked Giles. It was even likely that in his dislike of her, he would refuse to believe that Giles was capable of such an act, and that instead she was covering up for Mark. That would be intolerable.

His manner changed as he smiled at Alice. 'I pray daily for the safe delivery of our child, my dear. He will be nurtured and strictly reared and will not be a disappointment to us as others have been before.'

On arrival home, Bethany muttered her goodnights and fled to her room. She longed to bathe and wash the defilement from her body, but it was impossible. The plumbing in the house was noisy and the hot water rattled through the pipes. To run a bath at such a time would cause comment and questioning which she dare not risk.

She tore off her clothes and made do with the bathroom sink. The vigorous scrubbing to which she subjected her body caused her flesh to smart. Still she felt dirty.

'Bethany, are you all right?' Her mother tapped on the door and spoke quietly. 'You've been in there a long time. Are you still upset over Mark?'

Wrapping her dressing gown around her she opened the door. 'I'm fine, Mum.'

'You look awful. Harold's asleep. Do you want to talk about your quarrel with Mark?'

She shook her head and returned to her bedroom. To have confided in her mother would have been a relief but Alice would be devastated by her revelations. It would put more strain on her marriage. Besides, the deed couldn't be undone. And she was determined that Giles would not ruin her life.

The most difficult challenge would be telling Mark. It wasn't something she could keep from him. But how to tell

Mark? Agony seared her heart. Alone in the dark hours of the night it felt as though her shame was branded across her forehead.

By the morning her strength of will had conquered the debasement Giles had subjected her to. She had not been responsible for what had happened to her.

She could do nothing until Mark came off duty in the evening and she would telephone him. Until then she must fill in the long anxious hours without going out of her mind with worry at how Mark would take her confession. Her glance fell on the typewriter. Here was the solace she needed.

Bethany fed a sheet of paper into the machine and conjured images of Jester. She absorbed herself in the world of the puppy and his antics.

Mark didn't sleep after leaving the party. Why had he lost his temper? He should never have walked out on Bethany. It was guilt. He admitted that the thought of not seeing her for a year had made him brush aside the importance of her vocation to heal. Was it any wonder that she was hurt and angry? He would have felt the same.

He cursed himself for an idiot. He couldn't give up this chance to go to Africa and Bethany had not expected him to. Why had he expected her to sacrifice so much? He phoned her the next afternoon from the hospital. She sounded subdued and he cursed being unable to see her during the next five days as he had no time off.

During the next three weeks as he made his preparations to leave for Kenya, Bethany lost her sparkle. His guilt at leaving her troubled him. On their last night together there were circles under her eyes and she looked pale and ill. Harold had been abusive to her since the New Year party and last week Alice had suffered a severe asthma attack and had spent five days in hospital. Such attacks were often brought on by stress and life in the Warden household was always full of tension. Bethany had been distraught at her mother's illness. Tonight she was making the effort to put on a brave face for his sake and he loved her all the more.

'I'm an idiot for taking this post,' he groaned. They were in his flat and in an hour he had to leave to take her home.

She smiled wanly. 'No. I would never forgive myself if I stopped you doing this.' She looked about to say something and her eyes filled with tears. Then in a passionate voice she burst out, 'Hold me, Mark. Love me. I need you to love me so much.'

There was at first hesitancy in her response to his lovemaking, then an abandonment which was all-consuming. When they finally pulled apart there were tears in her eyes and he swallowed against the pain over his heart, saying, 'I love you, Bethany. This year will go quickly. I'll write every week. I'll always love you.'

Bethany nodded and closed her eyes, holding him close. She knew she should tell him about Giles. She was too ashamed and frightened. The unspoken words choked her. Even as he drove her home she could not speak the words which could forever destroy his love. How could she allow him to go and carry the pain of her degradation? He'd want to fight Giles and that could destroy his career. It wasn't until she watched him drive away from the house that her fears returned a hundredfold. A sense of overwhelming dread filled her. She felt that she had missed her moment to make everything right between them. That by not speaking she had sealed her fate.

PART TWO
1953

For winter's rains and ruins are over,
And all the season of snows and sins;
The days of dividing lover and lover,
The light that loses, the night that wins.

Swinburne

Chapter Sixteen

Bethany watched the rain running down the window pane of the children's ward of the hospital with a sinking heart. The red, white and blue bunting strung across the street dripped forlornly. Where was the glorious June sunshine everyone had hoped for to mark the Coronation of Queen Elizabeth? Hundreds of street parties were being held all over London and, for the children's sakes, she hoped they would not be rained off.

As she had driven to the hospital early this morning nearly every house she passed was decorated with bunting, golden crowns, Union Jacks and pictures of her Majesty. The young queen was popular. After the suffering and deprivation of the war and rationing years, her reign was heralded as a time of peace and prosperity.

The parties in the children's ward of this hospital and in a home for mentally handicapped children were being paid for by herself. It had taken weeks of persuasion to coerce the Board of Governors to accept that a party would not be detrimental to the children's health. So much bureaucracy surrounded running the hospitals that she was convinced that the strict rules hampered a patient's recovery instead of assisting it.

Her twenty novels of Jester's adventures and other

stories had made Bethany a very successful children's author and she showed her appreciation of their popularity by helping children. Each child today would receive a white and gold coronation commemoration mug filled with sweets and a copy of her latest Jester novel. There would also be a special meal of jelly and cakes and a magician was appearing at each party to entertain the children with his tricks.

Theresa O'Shea, the ward sister, paused in administering the lunchtime medications to nod with satisfaction as she regarded the decorated ward. 'You've done wonders, so you have. I never thought to see a party within these walls. And the children are overjoyed.'

She smiled at Bethany. Her tall, slight figure was round-shouldered from her years of stooping over patients. All but a narrow line of her brown hair was hidden by the large starched triangle of her nurse's hat. There was warmth and compassion in her face and Bethany had never known her to say a sharp word to anyone. She was five years older than Bethany, widowed in the war with no children. They had been close friends for a dozen years ever since Bethany started her regular visits to the children's ward.

'Today is an event these children will remember all their lives. I'm glad the governors agreed to let them remember it with happiness and not sadness that they were ill and could not join in the celebrations.'

'You bring a touch of sunshine into our lives, so you do. After your visits the children are less restless or homesick and get over their operations much faster. One of nature's healers that's what you are. There was a woman back home in Ireland had the same gift.'

'The doctors do the important work. I do nothing but

ask God's help to heal the child.' Bethany shrugged, she had long ago come to terms with sacrificing her medical career to family duty. Alice had become ill after Maxine was born sixteen years ago. In her desperation to provide Harold with a son she had suffered another miscarriage before giving birth to Tim who was now ten. During those difficult years Bethany had nursed her mother through her attacks and reared Tim and Maxine. Harold had much to answer for his years of mental cruelty which had destroyed Alice's health.

Theresa regarded her thoughtfully. 'You work wonders with the children. I know there's some who are sceptical about the way the children respond after you've spent time with them.'

Bethany shook her head. What she did came naturally to her. Yet it wasn't like being a doctor . . . She curbed those thoughts which always connected with Mark and what might have been. Her destiny had lain elsewhere.

'It's nurses like you who make it possible for me to help in any way I can. You're aware that love is a powerful force and the love of God is supreme.'

Theresa nodded. 'You've so much patience and love for everyone. You've done wonders for Tim. That brother of yours is a credit to you. Most families hide away such children.'

Anger and resentment flashed in Bethany's violet eyes. 'Too many people dismiss a mongol child as retarded. My stepfather was such a one. He was ashamed that his son was not normal. He wanted him shut away in a special home.'

Bethany paused at the surge of painful memories. Alice was over forty when Tim was born and Harold's bullying had been relentless making her mother a semi-invalid. It would have broken her heart if Tim had been sent away. Thwarted of a normal son, Harold had vented his vindictive nature on his wife, Bethany and Maxine. To ease the tension Bethany had moved out to live in the house she had inherited from her father, returning to care for her mother and the children while Harold was at work.

'It's a saint you are, Bethany Masterton,' Theresa said. 'A saint. And I always reckoned that Timmy was God's judgement on Harold Warden.'

'That's all behind us now Harold is dead.' Even now it was hard to think of her stepfather without hatred. He had caused so much suffering; had it been justice that his death had been slow and lingering from a creeping paralysis? He had been bedridden for the last year of his life. The doctors had been mystified by his illness. Bethany wondered if it was caused by his bitterness towards his family and the final shame he had suffered on learning of Giles's cowardice in the war.

Even after so many years his name was enough to make her go cold. Giles had caused so much misery to his wife through his unstable behaviour. It had not surprised Bethany to discover that after his court martial Giles was committed to a mental asylum where he was still locked away.

She pushed those unpleasant thoughts aside, her optimism stronger than resentment. Life in those years had many compensations and even in the darkest days she had counted her blessings.

Theresa locked the medicine trolley and placed a compassionate hand upon Bethany's arm. 'You are an example to us all. Despite all you've had to put up with, I've never once heard you complain.'

A tender smile curved her full lips. 'Maxine is more like

a friend than a sister and Tim is a special joy. Children like him have a great capacity for love and fun. There's much we can learn from them.'

Sister Theresa moved to a patient and Bethany said, 'I have to check that all is ready at the children's home. The presents for the children are in your office.'

'Before you go, could you speak with Millie? She's in a lot of pain after her operation last week. And she won't get up to join in the party this afternoon.'

'She's the one run down by a drunken driver who drove straight off, isn't she?'

'The poor dear. She's been so brave. Her pelvis was broken in two places and that's mended nicely. It's her foot. It was so badly crushed it won't heal. They feared she'd lose it. If this last operation doesn't work and the bones don't set properly . . .' Her worried expression completed the sentence that the doctors would remove the mangled foot.

Bethany nodded. Millie was twelve and a pretty blonde girl. She'd often sat with her but the girl was withdrawn. There was something deeply troubling her that Bethany suspected had nothing to do with the accident.

'How are you today, Millie?'

The girl didn't answer. There was a sadness about her which touched Bethany's heart. She sat on the bed and took her hand. Millie's parents came every evening and bickered the entire time they were here. It wasn't helping their daughter get better.

'Are you in pain?' she asked.

'Yes. They won't make me go home will they?'

'Of course not. You have to stay here until you're better.'

She relaxed, but the urgency which had been in her voice made Bethany question her. 'You want to go home, don't you?'

Millie looked uncertain and before she looked away Bethany saw fear in her eyes. An intuition which rarely failed her prompted Bethany to add, 'Your mummy and daddy love you very much. Why don't you want to go home?'

Millie's lip quivered. 'If I get well Mummy and Daddy won't live together any more. Mummy had left Daddy. She'd gone away to live with Uncle Joe in Dagenham. He's not a proper uncle. He was Mummy's friend. Daddy doesn't like Uncle Joe. He hit him when he came to take Mummy away. When I was hurt Mummy came back home to Daddy so she could visit the hospital every day.'

'Oh my poor love,' Bethany said with feeling. 'You mustn't wish yourself to remain ill so that your mummy and daddy will live together again.'

'I didn't see Mummy when she went away.'

'I'll talk with your mother and father.' Her heart twisted in anguish at the pain this girl was suffering over the break-up of her parents' marriage. She saw her injury as a means to keeping them together. She would never get better and end up a cripple. She had seen children will themselves to be ill to get the attention of an estranged parent.

She looked into Millie's brown eyes. 'You must concentrate on getting well. You're not responsible for how your parents behave. You cannot make them love each other again if that love has died. You're only making it harder for them to see you suffering like this. They love you. And you must love them enough to let one of them go. You will still see your mummy if she lives with Uncle Joe. She will always be your mummy.'

Millie lay in silence, tears spilling on to her cheeks. Bethany gently gathered her into her arms. The girl clung to her and as Bethany whispered words of encouragement she tenderly laid her hand over the girl's plaster. 'You have been so brave. This calls for a different type of bravery. You must use all your energy for getting better. Promise me. You want your mummy and daddy to be happy. They are miserable with worry about you.'

Millie nodded against her shoulder and she managed a weak smile. 'No one understood before. Thank you for talking to me.' She looked down at Bethany's hand still resting on the plaster. 'My foot feels different. Tingly and lighter somehow. I'm not going to lose my foot, am I?'

Bethany smiled. 'You're going to get better. The bones are mending. And you can start by getting up and enjoying yourself at the party this afternoon. Promise me?'

The fear had gone from Millie's eyes as she nodded. 'I promise.'

When Bethany arrived at the children's home, Maxine had just finished putting up the last of the balloons. The young woman's black hair was held back from the sides of her face with an Alice band and a fringe fell over her brow. She was dressed in her usual tom-boy black trousers and a baggy, faded jumper.

Maxine pulled a face at her older sister and teased, 'Trust you to turn up just as all the work is finished.'

'Some of us are the great organisers of this world, others have to do the donkey work,' Bethany returned. 'The dining hall looks lovely. You've worked hard.'

'When's the party gonna start?' A wiry eleven-year-old boy hobbled in. One of his legs dragged and one arm curled in towards his body. His head lolled as he regarded her.

'Hello, Johnnie. The party isn't until teatime. Why don't you go and play with Tim?'

She pointed to her brother who was lying on the floor playing with a fire engine. Johnnie shuffled over but stood staring down at Tim without joining in.

Maxine smiled at Johnnie. 'It's a pity they wouldn't let me bring in some of the pets for the children to play with. The animals help the children to mix better.'

Bethany chuckled. 'There talks a future vet. You've always been potty on animals which is why my house and garden are full of your pets.'

'The kids love the animals. They help them. We've proved that when the children from the home and Timmy's school come to our garden to play with them.'

'That's different. Animals aren't hygienic in a children's home.'

Bethany shook her head in mock exasperation. Maxine was besotted with animals and it hadn't surprised her when the young woman had decided she wanted to be a vet. Ever since Maxine was little she had wanted pets until their back garden had turned into a menagerie. It was then that Bethany had started inviting children from orphanages and Tim's school to visit their home of an afternoon. Unhappy and often traumatised children had delighted in the animals and their laughter and smiles had been her greatest reward. Five years ago she had bought the adjoining bombsite to cater for two ponies and a donkey. She had been amazed how Tim had taken to the animals and shown he could be responsible in feeding and looking after them. Meeting mothers with children at Tim's school had led her to form a support group for women with retarded children who couldn't bear the thought of them being put into homes.

Peg staggered into the room carrying a large cake which she had made in the shape of a crown. In recent years she'd become stout and was puffing with exertion.

'This looks great but aren't you doing too much? You've increased your hospital visits and you're still writing. And there's those blessed animals to look after when Maxine is helping out at the vet's surgery during the summer holidays.'

Bethany waved a hand dismissively. 'Maxine has spent most of the last year at the vet's after school and during her holidays. Once she's got her A levels next year she'll go on to veterinary college. Tim helps with the animals. He takes his responsibilities to them very seriously. He knows what he does is important. That's why he's doing so well.'

Peg shook her head. 'You take on too much.'

'And you don't?' Bethany's eyes sparkled. 'You've five children, help Frank with the management of seven corner shops and have built up your own bakery business specialising in unusual party cakes.'

Peg sent Bethany a blistering look, then giggled. 'We must both be gluttons for punishment. I got into making the cakes by accident. Once rationing finished everyone wanted an elaborate cake for a celebration. It was a terrific idea of yours to put a mock one in each of Frank's shops. They attracted no end of customers.'

'You've made an art form out of it. Especially your children's cakes.'

'That's how I started, wasn't it? Trying to make something special for my kids. A teddy bear or a clown. When they got older they were more demanding. Battleships and aeroplanes for the boys and pony heads or Cinderella's coach for the girls. I've spent some sleepless nights trying to work out how to do it.'

'But it paid off and now you run your own business. How's Frank?'

'The shrapnel wound in his thigh is giving him gip today. Always does when it rains, but he keeps cheerful.' The glow in her eyes told of her love for her husband. Despite Bethany's reservations about Frank, he had been an exemplary husband, working hard, adoring Peg and their children.

Bethany glanced at her watch and looked dismayed. 'I told Mum I'd be home ten minutes ago.'

'How is your mother after her last attack?' Peg asked with concern.

'The asthma seems better and so are her nerves. Her attacks are less frequent and not so debilitating. She's getting stronger now that Harold isn't bullying her all the time. But Mum can be stubborn, she won't rest enough.'

'A family trait,' Peg observed. 'Don't go wearing yourself out so you can't enjoy the dance tonight,' Peg remonstrated. 'I'll see you there. Frank's mum is baby-sitting for us. And it's Maxine's first proper dance, isn't it? That's special in a girl's life. Do you remember your first dances?'

Unfortunately Bethany did. One had been at the fair with Louise when they had met David Lister. Those memories were best crushed. She hoped that Maxine's first dance would not have such far-reaching consequences.

'Are you going with Andrew tonight?' Peg interrupted her thoughts.

'No. I broke off with him a fortnight ago. He was getting too serious.'

'Gawd, isn't that what you want?' Peg shook her head in disbelief. 'You're thirty-four and have never been short of boyfriends but you won't marry any of them.'

'You know why?'

'Because you're an idiot. Forget the past. And forget Mark. You can't still love him after he ran out on you.'

'He didn't run out on me.'

'You never told him all the truth though, did you?'

Bethany stiffened and avoided her friend's gaze. 'Of course not. He couldn't accept . . .' She pulled herself up and glanced towards Maxine who was fixing a bunch of balloons by the door and might overhear. She gave Peg a warning glare. 'It was all so long ago. I've no regrets.'

Peg shook her head. 'You always were one to count your blessings and not dwell on misfortune. So who's the lucky man to accompany you tonight?'

'No man. I'll enjoy myself with Maxine. She's so excited.'

'What it is to be sixteen,' Peg sighed. 'I married Frank at sixteen. Life is so romantic at that age.' She put a hand to her mouth and looked aghast. 'I'm sorry, Bethany. Life wasn't so rosy for you.'

'Sixteen was fine,' she answered grimly. Peg and her mother were the only ones to know the whole truth and Peg, like Alice, would never break an oath of secrecy. 'I was seventeen when I lost all my romantic ideals. Let's hope Maxine is more fortunate.'

Chapter Seventeen

On the drive home Maxine was unusually quiet. 'What's up?' Bethany asked.

She blushed. 'I was thinking about my working this summer with Steve North. Are you sure it's not going to leave you with too much to do?'

'Don't be silly. It's good experience for you.'

'Steve is wonderful with the animals, isn't he?'

'Mr North to you,' Bethany corrected. 'Show some respect to us elders.'

'He's not an elder. Well, only by nine years. And neither are you, Beth. You may be more than twice my age but you've always been more like a friend.'

Bethany's heart swelled with pride. It was true their relationship was special, full of teasing and shared confidences – at least confidences suitable for innocent ears, she mentally amended. While they waited for the traffic lights to change, she studied the younger woman. Sometimes it was like looking at a mirror image of herself at that age. Alice, Bethany and Maxine all had the same black hair and violet eyes. Except that Alice's hair was now turning grey.

Maxine's expression became dreamy. 'Do you think Steve North is rather dishy? A difference of several years in age isn't important, is it?'

'Are you matchmaking for me or yourself?' Bethany teased. Maxine had been infatuated with Steve North ever since she had begun helping out at the evening and Saturday surgeries.

'He's far too young for you, sis. So eyes off him!'

'He's as close to my age as yours,' she couldn't resist taunting. 'He's undoubtedly handsome. And has a wonderful way with animals. As you must know from the times you've found an excuse to call him out to a goat, pony, or taken one of the cats, dogs or your pet magpie to the surgery.'

Maxine pouted. 'Nine years isn't such an age gap.'

Bethany sighed. 'From what I hear several women in Leytonstone are after him and he's too interested in building up his business to have time for any of them.' She changed the subject or Maxine would be daydreaming all morning about the vet. 'Did you think Mum was looking better this morning?'

'She was asleep when I looked in to tell her I was leaving. Bethany, is Mum going to die?'

'Not if we take special care of her. She's been very ill but in the year since Harold died she's got a lot stronger and hasn't had an attack in months.'

Tears sprung to Maxine's eyes. 'It's my fault and Tim's that she's so ill. I heard Papa shouting at her once that it was because of me she had her attacks. If I'd never been born she wouldn't have become so ill afterwards. Her health got worse after having Tim. He nearly killed her.'

Bethany shuddered. Harold always did have a wicked tongue. 'Don't blame yourself. He was wrong to say that.'

'I hated him. And Tim is the son she always wanted to give Papa. He never forgave her that Tim wasn't normal. Papa never had any time for us either. He hated us. I could see it in his eyes. That made Mum miserable.'

'You shouldn't speak ill of the dead.'

'Why not, if it's true? He was horrid to you. It's not as though he didn't have a son. Not that anything has been heard of Giles. Reported missing in action wasn't he? And never turned up when the prisoners of war were released.'

The uncomfortable conversation was rousing too many ghosts. As a child Maxine had been given few details about Giles. But she was old enough to know the truth. It wasn't right to keep it from her.

They had turned into the drive of her home and she switched off the engine. She reached back and opened Timothy's door and gave him some bones wrapped in newspaper she had earlier collected from the butcher's. 'Give these to the dogs. Rusty the setter is in the paddock. The others are probably out the back.'

He scampered off clutching the newspaper and calling to the setter who gambolled to him. Bethany turned to Maxine and said heavily, 'I didn't want Tim hearing this. I think he understands more than we think he's capable of and it could upset him. Giles isn't dead as Harold wanted everyone to believe. Harold disowned him because of the wicked things he had done.' She paused; there were still some things which she could not bring herself to speak of. She concentrated on relating the events which led up to Giles's incarceration. 'During the war Giles deserted his post and half his brigade was wiped out as a consequence. Unable to face a court martial he ran away.'

'No wonder Harold despised him,' Maxine said sharply. 'What a creep!'

'He was the worst kind of coward. Sometimes I think his bullying drove his twin Louise to suicide. He was no good. He was taken prisoner during the war and was later tried for his cowardice in England. Whilst under arrest he grabbed a guard and tried to strangle him and escape. He was declared mentally unstable and locked in a psychiatric hospital for years.'

'But wasn't Giles married? Why didn't we have any contact with his wife?'

'Rosemary was killed in the Blitz. Her marriage wasn't happy. She was in a hotel room with a lover when the bomb fell on them. She didn't have any children.'

Maxine was fiddling with the gold cross around her neck. 'It's not fair that Mum isn't getting better now Papa is dead. He made her life a misery after the war taunting her about her failure to give him a proper son. He never kept secret that he had another woman who he visited in the evenings. She even got a legacy in his will and his two bastard daughters.'

'I didn't know you'd found out about that skeleton in our family closet.'

'Papa enjoyed throwing the knowledge in Mum's face,' Maxine answered, her expression grim. 'I overheard him taunting her.'

'Poor Mum. But it was only right that he provided for his mistress and children.' She took Maxine's hand and squeezed it. 'He can no longer hurt any of us.'

'Why doesn't Mum get better?' Maxine entreated. 'I don't care what you say, Mum became ill because of me. And you've nursed her ever since. You gave up your own studies to be a doctor, even the man you loved, to tend her. You'd have married and had children of your own if she hadn't been ill.'

Caught off guard by Maxine's statement Bethany felt barbed arrows embedding in her heart. She had never stopped loving Mark. Or was it her idealism? No man since had matched up to her first love, but he was forever lost to her. Mark had married after the war and was working in Africa as he had planned.

She rallied her thoughts, the past was the past and to dream of what might have been was foolish. 'How could I allow strangers to look after Mum?' she stated. 'I don't regret looking after her and it didn't stop me working with children. I help them in a different way than as a doctor.'

Maxine was studying her with disconcerting intensity. 'You should have had children, Beth. You would have made a great mother.'

Bethany choked at the unexpected compliment and Maxine thumped her none too gently on the back.

'Well, there's hope for the old spinster yet,' Maxine teased. 'You've still got your looks. I don't know why you don't go out with Terry Browne the butcher. He's been putting an extra sausage or two in our rations for years in a hope of catching your fancy.'

'It would take more than a few extra sausages for me to marry him,' Bethany said getting out of the car. 'That's where nine years *can* make a lot of difference. He's bald, pot-bellied and over forty. I may be old to you but that doesn't mean I don't still prefer my men tall, lithe, handsome and preferably with their own teeth and hair.'

'Beggars can't be choosers,' Maxine said grinning. 'And I bet Aunt Peg has got a bloke lined up for you at the dance.'

'Peg and her matchmaking is the bane of my life. I'm footloose and fancy free and that's fine by me. If we don't get a move on we'll miss the Coronation on the television and Mum's been looking forward to watching it with us all week.'

Bethany sat in front of the small black and white screen

watching the slow procession of the Queen through Westminster Abbey. Her eyes became misty. The last time she had been to the Abbey was with Mark. Long-entombed memories were excavated. She'd had such hopes and dreams when she was Maxine's age. Yet apart from losing Mark she had no regrets.

The years slid back to before the war. She adored her mother and Alice had remained steadfast in her love for her, defending her against Harold's vindictive ploys. At first it had been hard to give up her ideals of becoming a doctor. Her mother's illness and the care she needed stopped her attending college. Alice drew strength from Bethany tending her. Dr Jones had commented that after Tim's birth Bethany's dedicated attendance had pulled Alice through.

Bethany refused to live off Harold's bounty. A publisher had loved her stories of Jester the puppy and her children's novels had sold well enabling her to be financially independent. She immersed herself in her writing.

An image of Mark surfaced in her mind. After all these years she could not forget him or love another. The pain settling over her heart made her clench her fist. She didn't believe in pining for what might have been. Yet the pain lingered and the memories could not be banished.

Mark had returned to England from Africa after a year when war broke out. He had enlisted as a doctor in the army and had only a two-week leave before joining the desert campaign. It had taken all Bethany's courage to tell him of her rape. He had taken the news hard. Who could blame him? He was such an idealist. They had quarrelled frequently when she refused to tell him who had raped her and it tested their love to the limit. When he again left England it was several months before he contacted her by letter saying he had come to terms with what had happened. She had prayed that they could resolve their differences and find happiness.

It was not to be. After the war Mark returned to England and asked her to marry him and join him in Africa where he intended to continue his work. She had been tempted. But by then Alice was ill and needed her. How could she abandon Alice who had always stood by her? She was torn by love and loyalty. Mark who had forgiven her so much now expected more from her than she could give.

The pain around her heart intensified. They should have worked it out between them, but fate had intervened and Mark had only a few weeks before he had to return to Africa to resume his research.

'I've waited this long for you, Beth, but no longer.' Mark's face was dark with passion. He never mentioned her rape but there were times when she sensed the knowledge festered deep within him. 'I've been given a huge grant to continue my work in Kenya. I can't throw all that up because you won't leave your family.'

She had known then that she had to make the ultimate sacrifice. She had stroked his cheek, her eyes brimming with tears. 'I couldn't live with myself if I deserted Mum now. Your destiny is clearly in Africa. It's over between us, Mark. It wasn't meant to be.'

'You don't mean that?'

'We are destroying each other this way.'

Emotions were high after the war and circumstances and time had been against them. She felt that he had misjudged her and Mark was hurt and angry. She could understand that.

A year later Harold took great satisfaction in reading

out to her an announcement in *The Times*. Mark had married a Red Cross nurse in Kenya.

The news had hurt her; she hadn't realised how much she had hoped that somehow they could reconcile their differences. Giles had achieved what he set out to do on the night he raped her: to ruin her chance of happiness with the man she loved.

Her reflections were sombre. Giles had ruined so many lives. He had married Rosemary shortly after his engagement when she was expecting their child. The baby was stillborn. Poor Rosemary had suffered in her misguided love. Six months into the war Giles had been sent home wounded and when Rosemary visited him in hospital he was abusive. On his second leave, eighteen months later, he began to beat Rosemary and accused her of going out with Yanks.

While the Blitz devastated so much of London, Alice's nerves were shredded by the bombing and Harold's cruelty. The day Harold viciously beat Maxine for being naughty and locked her in the cupboard under the stairs, Bethany took her to live with her. Despite all her persuasion Alice refused to leave her husband.

'I married for better or worse. I couldn't face the scandal of a divorce,' she said, and never wavered from her resolve. 'It is easier now that Maxine is not in the house. She's a reminder to Harold of how I failed to give him a son. You can bring her to see me when he's at work.'

Bethany had been delighted with this arrangement. From the moment Maxine was born she had adored her. That they were so physically alike had caused comment. But then there were always vicious tongues to speculate that Maxine was Bethany's child not Alice's.

Each morning after Maxine left for school Bethany

drove to visit her mother and take care of her. During the war Bethany had joined the ATS and learned to drive and when she left home she purchased a Wolseley from the royalties of her children's novels so that she could visit her mother every day. In the evening she wrote her children's novels.

A movement from Alice jolted Bethany back to the present. Her mother was wiping a tear from her eye as she watched the television. The Queen with poise, humility and dignity dedicated herself to the lifelong service of the peoples over whom she had been called to rule. She was solemnly invested with the robes and ancient insignia of sovereignty. When the Archbishop of Canterbury stood back having placed the crown on Queen Elizabeth's head, Alice sighed.

'Doesn't she look beautiful and so dignified? I'm glad you got the television so we could watch it. This is a new reign. George VI was a good man but his short reign after his brother abdicated was blighted by the war. A new reign brings hope of new beginnings – for us all.'

Maxine had been daydreaming throughout most of the Coronation broadcast. The main event of the day as far as she was concerned was the celebration ball at the Town Hall.

'Let Steve North notice me and ask me to dance,' she repeated like a litany under her breath.

Finally it was almost time to leave for the dance. Her heart was doing somersaults with excitement. Maxine fastened the zip of her sapphire taffeta ball gown and pushed her feet into high-heeled silver evening sandals. All trace of the earlier tom-boy had vanished. Her black shoulder-length hair was curled around her bare shoulders. Alice had loaned her a silver and white evening stole and a

Victorian diamanté necklace and earrings. Bethany had shown her how to apply a little rouge and discreet eye make-up and as her older sister's reflection appeared in the mirror beside Maxine, she was startled at how alike they were.

Bethany was wearing a kingfisher full-skirted gown with a tight heart-shaped bodice and a matching bolero. 'You'll knock them dead, tonight,' Maxine teased. 'The men will be queuing up to dance with you.'

It had always amazed her that her sister had not married. She was popular with men and was rarely without a boyfriend.

'Maxine, you look so fresh and lovely. I feel quite old. It's you who won't be short of partners.'

'I hope so.' She sighed theatrically, her expression becoming wistful. Surely, Steve could not fail to notice her tonight. She knew he was going to be there. Oh please, let him ask her to dance. Her body throbbed with yearning to be held in his arms.

Maxine was disappointed that Steve was seated with a group of friends on the far side of the ballroom. From the looks of it his partner for the evening was Marion Cromer. The knowledge destroyed her pleasure in the meal. That woman was always bringing her spoilt and overfed poodle to the surgery. Anyone with half an eye could see she was after Steve. Unfortunately, Marion was a war widow and as beautiful as Rita Hayworth, whom she clearly modelled herself on. Her blonde hair was fashionably styled in an elegant chignon and Maxine felt dowdy with her black hair hanging loose and curling around her shoulders. It made her look young. She should have put her hair up to look more sophisticated. Her heart sank further as she noted

Marion's hour-glass figure, her creamy bosom pushed high above the boned and strapless bodice of her black gown. The dance lost its appeal. Steve would never look at her when he had a woman like Marion Cromer hanging on his arm.

Maxine danced every dance, each partner complimenting her lavishly and two had asked her for dates. She declined. Her popularity buffered her disappointment at seeing Steve dancing with all the women in his party. At least Marion was not monopolising his company. But he had danced with her twice and she was always at his elbow when he returned to the group.

At least Bethany was enjoying herself. Her sister was a wonderful dancer and seemed to glide around the room with a succession of partners. After an energetic polka Bethany graciously declined all further invitations. 'I'm sorry, I need to sit this one out. Perhaps a later number.'

Maxine joined her. Her feet were killing her in the high heels and her last partner had twice crushed her toes. Then she saw Steve North walking across the dance floor. Her heart clattered in her breast. He was making straight for them. Her dreams had come true. He was going to ask her to dance.

Heat rushed into her cheeks. To hide her blush she lowered her head and willed her frantic heart to still. She held her breath when he stopped in front of them.

'May I have the pleasure of this dance?'

A joyous *yes* stuck in her throat. Steve wasn't standing in front of her but Bethany. She looked up through her lashes. Steve was smiling at her sister. The blood drained from her face and misery engulfed her. It wasn't fair.

Bethany laughed softly. 'Mr North, I'm afraid these shoes are crippling me, but I'm sure Maxine will be delighted to dance with you.'

Maxine coloured, her stare fixed on the floor. Why didn't the floor open so she could disappear? She'd never been so mortified. Steve had chosen Bethany first not her. Now Bethany was foisting him in her direction. If he refused to ask her, she'd die of embarrassment. Even so, her heart did a tango in anticipation. The band were playing the opening bars of a waltz. The most romantic of dances and Steve would hold her close.

'I'd be delighted,' Steve said without a pause. She saw the long tapering fingers she admired so often when he worked, come into her line of vision. 'Maxine, will you dance?'

Her hand trembled as she placed it in his and he led her on to the dance floor. He was not the smoothest of dancers but she didn't care. To be held in his arms, held close enough so that she could smell his aftershave and scent of his skin was heaven.

'I hardly recognised you,' he said. 'You're always in slacks and baggy jumpers at the surgery. You look very glamorous. And grown up.'

'Thank you.' Her violet eyes glittered. He was so handsome she could have swooned from the sheer joy of being in his arms. 'I'm looking forward to working at the surgery during the summer. All I've ever wanted to do is work with animals.'

'It could put you off becoming a vet for life,' he joked. 'The hours are long and you get called out in the middle of the night for emergencies. It's not all cuddly pets. The farm animals can be tough work and farmers just as difficult to handle in some instances.'

'I don't care. I sat up all night with Juniper when she was having her kittens.'

'The enthusiasm of youth,' he laughed.

His breath caressed her cheek and sent a thrill of pleasure through her. The shyness which had come over her when they began dancing dissolved. Steve was so easy to talk to. 'I'm not so young. I'm starting college in the autumn to sit my A levels.'

'Watch out for the college wolves after innocent young maids. They can be a menace to pretty young women.'

Did that mean that he thought she was pretty? He did like her. She felt she was floating a foot in the air as they twirled around the room.

'Seeing you with your sister, it's startling how alike you are,' he added.

Again Maxine's heart sank. Was he being kind to her because he fancied Bethany? The music faded and he returned her to her seat. The band struck up the Lambeth Walk and he held out his hands to both of them. 'It will be a pleasure to partner you both if you have sufficiently recovered, Miss Warden.'

'It's Masterton, not Warden,' Maxine corrected. 'Beth's my half sister.'

Maxine was radiant at having a second dance with Steve. Unfortunately partners changed too quickly in the Lambeth Walk and throughout the dance her eyes followed his progress around the room.

'Would you like a drink, Maxine?' Bethany asked her as they returned to their seats. 'I'll get one from the bar.'

'I'm not drinking orange juice, it's so childish.'

Bethany smiled conspiratorially. 'How about a Babycham? Is that grown up enough for you?'

She nodded. Bethany always treated her like an adult. That's what she liked about her. They went everywhere together: the pictures, shopping, up to London to visit museums and Bethany happily complied whenever Maxine wanted to visit the zoo yet again.

Maxine watched Bethany walk to the bar. Her sister didn't look her age and could pass for a woman ten years younger. Steve had also joined the queue by the bar and was talking to Bethany. They appeared to have a heated discussion with much shaking of her sister's head. Then Steve disappeared to the front and soon emerged with a tray loaded with drinks. Bethany was still protesting when he arrived at their table.

'You didn't tell me your sister was so stubborn, Maxine,' he observed. 'And tell her I won't take payment for the drinks unless they are repaid by a dance.'

Maxine pouted. Steve was staring admiringly at Bethany. The pleasure again seeped from the evening. There was a gleam in his eyes which had never brightened his gaze when he looked at her.

Steve moved away with the other drinks. 'I'll be back for that dance, don't forget. Now I'd better get these to the others before they grow weak with thirst.'

'He's such a nice man,' Bethany said handing Maxine her Babycham and sipping her gin and tonic. 'I had a terrible job getting the barman's attention. The old codger clearly didn't approve of a woman buying her own drinks.'

Maxine sat stiffly, miserable in the certainty that Steve fancied Bethany and she wouldn't stand a chance with him. 'When are we leaving?'

'I thought you were enjoying yourself? It's only ten thirty. The dance doesn't end for another hour.'

She shrugged. 'I thought your feet were hurting. Mine are killing me.'

'The price of vanity. It would be rude of me to leave

before I danced with Mr North. We'll leave immediately after if you wish.'

'I'm going to the ladies.' Maxine got up, hating herself for the rush of jealousy she felt towards her sister. She told herself that Steve was only being polite to the elder sister of an employee, but knew she was kidding herself. He really did like Bethany. All he saw when he looked at her was the eager young kid who was mad on animals. That would change, she vowed.

Bethany was worried at the length of time Maxine had been gone. Steve had taken her on to the floor for a waltz and kept her there for a slow jazz number during which he had pulled her close so that their cheeks touched.

Aware that Maxine had an infatuation for the handsome vet, she felt a twinge of guilt. But he had been so charming and insistent on the second dance, it would have been churlish to refuse. They chatted easily about his practice and Maxine's desire to become a vet. It was obvious that the practice was Steve's passion. He even admitted to being a confirmed bachelor because of its importance.

'Until I can take on a partner, no wife would tolerate the unsociable hours I work. Or the number of cancelled engagements because a horse was about to foal, or a cat had been brought in injured from a car accident.'

'They'd put up with it if they understood and loved you. It's no different from the life of a doctor.'

He chuckled. 'Doctors don't return home at four in the morning reeking of the cow byre. I find it hard to believe that a woman as lovely as you hasn't married.'

'Not all women hanker for a knight in shining armour to carry them off into the moonlight. I like the freedom of being my own boss and not having the dubious pleasure of washing and ironing a man's shirts.'

He gave a throaty laugh. 'Are we such a terrible lot?'

'Men have their place.' She discovered she liked teasing him and could discern the faintest of blushes which provoked her to add, 'Much as women have their place in the life of a confirmed bachelor.'

His grey eyes sparkled. 'And what use would that be, Miss Masterton?'

'That would be telling, Mr North. And I've been far too outspoken.' She was surprised that she found it so easy to flirt with him. He made her feel young and carefree. But she must remember that he was several years younger than her; however, what woman of her age would not be flattered at the admiration which shone from the eyes of a younger man.

She realised that she liked Steve North more than any man that she had met for a long time. To spare Maxine's feelings she played down her inclination to flirt with him. No man was worth causing a rift between her and Maxine.

The moment Bethany saw the lights on in her home she knew something was wrong. Alice usually retired at ten and only the hall light was left on until Bethany came in. It saved Alice staying up for her and, if she had dozed and woke, she could tell by whether the light was switched off that Bethany had returned.

Maxine had quizzed Bethany about her dance with Steve all the way home. To cheer her she had told her that he was delighted with her work, which was true. To deflect the vet's interest from her, she had turned the subject back to Maxine and her determination to be a vet.

'I'll need some new clothes to work at the surgery,' Maxine announced. 'Those old baggy jumpers of mine are a fright.'

'I thought they'd become a second skin.'

She pulled a face. 'It's not a crime to want to look nice, is it?'

Bethany wondered how much Steve was influencing her desire to smarten herself up. Probably a great deal. She felt a twinge of guilt at flirting with Steve. Then those thoughts were pushed aside as she saw how white-faced and shaken her mother appeared. Alice was sitting upright in an armchair twisting her handkerchief in agitation.

Despite the illness which had debilitated her, Alice's movements remained graceful. Her hair was cut short and curled naturally into a stylish bob.

'Mum, what's the matter? You should have been in bed hours ago.'

'I couldn't . . . I daren't.' Her voice quivered alarmingly and another tremor shook her body. 'I couldn't have slept. I've been so upset. Why after all this time did he have to come back?'

A frosty claw scraped Bethany's spine. 'Who has come back?'

The stark fear in her mother's eyes told her what she most dreaded to hear.

'He was here.' Her speech was staccato. 'He was rude and abusive. He was demanding money. It was Giles . . .'

Chapter Eighteen

'But he was put into an asylum for the mentally ill!' Bethany protested.

'He's out now. Cured they say.' Alice shook her head. 'He's coming back. He says we stole his inheritance.'

The shock of his reappearance dispersed as Bethany's anger soared. 'That's absurd. Harold disowned him after the way he behaved during the war. Giles knows that.'

Alice raised her tear-reddened eyes. 'You know how vindictive he is?'

Unfortunately, Bethany knew only too well. She had no intention of allowing him to interfere in her life again. 'If he comes here I'll inform the police and have a restraining order placed on him.'

'That won't stop Giles.'

Maxine was shocked at the interchange between her mother and sister. Neither woman was malicious by nature. From what Bethany had told her earlier Giles was a proven coward. Yet had anyone heard his side of the story? Suppose Giles had been made a scapegoat? She didn't like judging someone in their absence. No one was ever all bad, or so she liked to believe. Harold had been an exacting father. He expected so much from his children. Children rebelled under tyranny. Hadn't Bethany done just that by moving back to her father's house when she was twenty?

Her sister's attitude puzzled Maxine. What had Giles done to her to make her hate him so? Bethany never spoke ill of anyone.

She voiced her censure. 'Why are you so mean to Giles? He was wounded in the war. It made him mentally ill. You should be rejoicing that he's well again.'

Bethany paced the room, her violet eyes flashing with anger. 'Giles takes pleasure in destroying people's lives. I have no wish to see him.'

'But he's my half brother. I've a right to meet him.'

'How can you say that after what I told you about him?' Bethany was pale and twisted an amethyst ring on her finger in her agitation. 'You want nothing to do with that man. He was responsible for his twin sister killing herself.'

Maxine had never heard Bethany speak so violently against someone before. She also saw the look of fear in Alice's eyes. When her mother exchanged a look with Bethany she sensed that the two women were keeping something from her. Something sinister.

'Have you any proof of that?'

'No,' Bethany reluctantly acknowledged. 'Just an instinct. Louise wasn't the type to kill herself.'

'How can you be sure? You told me she was depressed after her fiancé was killed. There must be something you're not telling me. There's no point in warning me against Giles if you won't tell me why.'

Bethany poured herself a stiff gin and tonic and walked across to the window to stare into the dark garden. Her body was rigid, her arms hugging the glass close to her chest.

Alice answered. 'He's wicked. He brought shame and suffering to this family.'

'What did he do?' Maxine demanded. She hated her elders when they hinted at secrets but treated her like a child and did not trust her with the knowledge. She glanced at her sister who remained immovable as a standing stone.

'He wants to control people in any way he can,' Bethany announced in a strangled voice. 'He raped a woman who refused to obey him. He has always had a vile temper. Several times I saw his wife with bruises on her face. He was put away in an asylum for his violent outbursts. I don't believe he's cured. He will harm anyone who tries to cross him. Just stay away from Giles.'

Bethany skimmed over the facts, hoping they would satisfy Maxine. She couldn't tell Maxine the truth. The memories resurrected by his return were too painful. She had thought that Giles was out of their life for good. She hated the thought of him being anywhere near Maxine.

The phone rang. Bethany started violently. Only bad news came from a telephone call at midnight. She picked it up and cautiously said the number.

'I was checking you and Maxine got home safely.' Relief flooded her that it was Steve North. 'There was a drunk hanging round outside the Town Hall when we left. He was demanding if anyone had seen you. I was going to offer you a lift but I couldn't find you.'

It must have been Giles. The information frightened her. It was obvious he was out to cause trouble.

'Luckily we left early. It was kind of you to enquire and to offer to drive us home, but I had my own car.'

'An independent woman, I should have guessed,' he said with a laugh. 'I'm glad that man didn't trouble you.'

'My stepbrother has a drink problem.' She thought that she'd better explain. 'I haven't seen him for years. He was probably after a bed for the night.'

She rung off. 'That was Steve North. He was concerned that we may have had trouble. Giles was hanging round the Town Hall when Mr North left.'

'I don't want either of you going out alone at night,' Alice declared. 'I'd be out of my wits with worry.'

'Steve phoned here?' Maxine glared at Bethany. 'Why didn't you put him on to me? He's my boss this summer.'

'It was a general enquiry about us both.'

'Even so, I was the one who should have spoken to him, not you. You've been trying to take him away from me all evening. I saw you flirting with him. How could you?' She burst into tears and ran from the room.

'What was all that about?' Alice looked puzzled.

At least Maxine's teenage tantrum had diverted her mother from Giles's threats.

'She's keen on the vet. He asked me to dance tonight and he was fun. I wasn't deliberately flirting with him.'

Alice sighed. 'For all your spinsterhood you enjoy the company of handsome men and can't help flirting with them. And why not? There's no harm in flirtation. Maxine is too young to realise that. Besides, Mr North is too old for her.' Alice raised her eyebrows at Bethany. 'And by the same token he's rather young for you!'

'Am I such an old fossil? Perhaps if Maxine wasn't so taken with him I might be tempted to see more of him.'

The phone rang again. Both women exchanged anxious glances. Bethany picked up the receiver.

'I know you're back.' Giles's voice was steeped in vitriol. 'You saw to it Harold disinherited me. That money is mine. And I want it. You can start by handing over five hundred as soon as the banks open tomorrow.'

His aggressive tone sparked her anger. 'You got what

you deserved. Nothing. Stay away from us. If you contact me or Mother again I'll call the police.' She put the receiver down then, as a safety measure, took the phone off the hook.

'I'm not having him ringing up all night with his threats. I'll check the windows are shut and the doors locked. But the dogs should keep him away.'

'Nothing will stop him.' Alice began to sob. 'Let's give him some money to get rid of him.'

'And play into his hands? He's not getting a penny from me. Harold disowned him and with just cause. That money is Tim's. Giles inherited money from Rosemary when she died. He can live on that.'

Alice put a trembling hand to her brow, her eyes darkening to deep violet in her fear. 'He won't let the matter rest. He's a dangerous man.'

'And I'm no longer a young defenceless woman.'

Alice shook her head. 'You can't fight his evil.'

Bethany stood tall and her body was stiff with determination. 'I will. His bullying doesn't frighten me.'

'But I haven't your strength. Just knowing he's in Leytonstone . . . that he could come round here at any time . . .'

'I'll deal with him.' Bethany hugged her mother. 'He won't know what hit him if he tries to frighten us again.'

Brave words and Bethany meant them. Yet once her mother was settled in bed with a cup of Ovaltine and a sleeping pill, she did not go to her bedroom. The four dogs were a comfort. The two alsatians Copper and Jet were with Maxine in her room. Rusty the setter was asleep at the top of the stairs and Artemis the lurcher padded round the house with her as she checked every window and door. Twice Artemis whined as they moved through the back of the house. It made Bethany's own hackles prickle. Was Giles out there?

The house was isolated. Fortunately it had escaped any serious damage in the war. Some windows and slates had been broken when the two houses next to theirs received a direct hit. In recent years the land had been cleared of rubble but with so many bombsites over London the property had not been rebuilt. Five years ago she had purchased the land for two ponies and a donkey and turned it into a paddock, but it had made the house more isolated.

With a shiver Bethany realised how vulnerable the house was to anyone wishing to pry on them. The tall chestnut trees surrounding the perimeter which gave them seclusion and privacy could also shield a snooper in their thick canopy.

Giles didn't bother to hide. He sat on the garden bench by the ornamental fishpond in Bethany's garden. He watched a woman he had at first thought was Bethany pace her bedroom. Then he realised that she was too young for Bethany who was now in her thirties. But she was so like her. It must be the girl. She'd turned out quite a looker. His eyes narrowed in contemplation. They wouldn't get away with stealing his inheritance. They'd sold his father's house. The house which should have been his by rights as the elder son. Bethany was the scheming one. Who did she think she was, speaking to him on the phone like he was dirt? She wouldn't get away with it. He thought he'd dealt with her and taught her a lesson not to meddle in his affairs. She had worse coming to her.

As for Alice, that conniving woman his father had married, she must have turned his father against him. She'd given Harold the son he wanted and made sure that he, Giles, was maligned and got nothing. And what a son. The first time he'd seen Tim he'd roared with laughter ridiculing the boy. None of them would escape. They must suffer as he had suffered in recent years.

His hand shook so violently he could hardly light his roll-up cigarette. God, he needed a drink. But he had no money left and the half bottle of whisky he had stolen earlier was gone.

His stomach snarled with hunger. He ignored the discomfort. He was used to hunger since he'd deserted from the army. For two years he had lived a nocturnal existence: hiding in woods, foraging for food like a wild animal. He had survived by killing indiscriminately for food. Scared that his schoolboy French or Italian would give him away it had been too risky for him to venture into villages. He hadn't lived in those years, he had existed. The people he had killed for their food were of no more consequence to him than the faceless Germans he had been ordered to fire upon. Those civilians were the casualties of his private war to emerge alive from the carnage his government had forced him into.

But he hadn't escaped the consequences. He'd eventually been captured and tortured by the Germans and spent the last year of the war in a prison camp. He suppressed those memories for they had been the cause of the madness which had kept him incarcerated in a lunatic asylum for eight years.

Time enough to rage at what he had become. Resentment and his sense of injustice had festered. Paranoia made him see everyone as the enemy. He had learned to curb his violence. He wasn't mad. He wasn't like the other inmates. Harold had paid for him to be locked up. That must have been it. His family were to blame. They were the enemy.

He wiped a shaky hand across his lips. He needed a drink. Lack of food may not trouble him but the craving for drink was another matter. He'd been out of the asylum six months, long enough to drink and gamble Rosemary's money away. And that had been little enough. Sir Jerome Crispin had deceived him about Rosemary's fortune. There'd been only a couple of grand, and the big house he'd promised as a wedding present was on the Crispin estate and only gifted to her during her lifetime. Since she died without an heir, the house reverted to the Crispin estate and Giles didn't get a penny. Now he was broke and homeless. He'd been unable to get work. Office managers turned him away as soon as they learned he'd been in a mental hospital. The Labour Exchange offered him jobs as road sweepers, railway crossing or lavatory attendants. He'd fought a bloody war, for Chrissakes. And they offered him a job as a bog attendant.

His fists balled. Damn them! He scowled at the house. Why should he work when those bitches had what was his? He ground his cigarette under his heel and began to roll another. A second light had come on and he saw Bethany appear at the window as she drew the curtains. He jammed his fist up in an obscene gesture and chuckled. He'd enjoyed raping her. It had given him a taste for it during the war.

Rape, murder or violence were done without conscience and could still get him what he needed now. He'd lost count of the men he'd watched as they staggered drunk out of a pub with half their wages still intact on a Friday night. He'd followed them. Then struck quickly, knocking them down and stealing their pay-packet.

Recently the drink was slowing his reflexes and blurring his judgement. The last man he'd chosen had bested him in the fight and the law had almost caught him last week. Why should he risk his freedom when those bitches in there had so much?

He swayed to his feet and picked up a large stone from the rockery. He hurled it at the dining-room window and there was a satisfactory smash of glass. He was tempted to step inside and steal something but the dogs were barking. It was enough for the women to know that he had been here tonight. His vindictive nature wanted them to suffer: to taste fear as he had tasted it during the war. They would hand over the money soon enough when he began to put the pressure on. All the money would be his. Three women and a ten-year-old, halfwit boy were easy prey.

During the following week Giles made several abusive phone calls. Each time the phone was slammed down but the few words he had uttered had left both Bethany and Alice shaken. To protect Maxine, Alice had forbidden her to answer the phone. After the second call Alice refused to answer herself as Giles had upset her so badly. The last phone call received by Bethany had been obscene. When Giles began to speak of how her body had felt as he invaded her, Bethany rammed the phone back on the cradle. He left it two days before he rang again and then just laughed down the line. That had also unnerved her. But she was determined not to give in to his bullying and threats. Giles was too clever to keep using the same tactics. He didn't have to. Each time the phone rang Alice and Bethany tensed, their heartbeat frantic in case it was him.

'Have the line disconnected,' Alice suggested.

'We need it to ring the police if he comes here to cause trouble,' Bethany insisted.

Most nights a stone would smash a window. Or Bethany would let the dogs out into the garden in the morning and discover cigarette butts or empty drink bottles. It was all evidence that Giles had been spying on them. He wanted them to know that he was watching. The previous two nights he had rattled windows and banged on the door to set the dogs barking then run off into the night.

Bethany went to the police. They were sympathetic, the desk sergeant eyed her kindly. 'I'm afraid there ain't much we can do, ma'am. The constable on the beat will be informed and keep an eye on the house. If we catch your stepbrother destroying property he'll be arrested.'

For such a minor crime Giles would soon be released if not actually given probation. That wasn't the answer. Bethany also made enquiries through a friend who worked at Giles's bank. They discovered that Giles had spent all Rosemary's money since his release. Giles was broke. If he was desperate for money he would carry out his threats to her family.

Bethany hated conceding to him but Alice suffered a relapse and spent three nights in hospital until her condition became stable. She realised that she couldn't fight Giles's tactics of fear which could kill Alice if they continued. She would have to agree in part to his demands but any money she gave him would be on her terms and not his.

Five days went by without a phone call or a window smashed. Alice was cheerful when Bethany took her breakfast up to her bedroom. The doctor had given Alice a course of tranquillisers. 'Giles has stopped his nonsense. He knows you won't give him any money. I think I shall get up at lunchtime. So silly these attacks of mine. You have enough to worry about, without me adding to your problems.'

It was a show of bravado for there were still shadows of fear in her mother's eyes. The lull in calls had not quietened Bethany's anxiety. She had continued to sleep badly. She started awake at the slightest sound, her hands clammy with sweat and her heart pumping. Giles could work his malicious tricks by playing with their minds. He had made them on edge and could choose the time when next to taunt them.

Chapter Nineteen

'I don't like giving in to Giles, but we may have to,' Bethany advised her mother and Maxine. 'Until this is sorted we must be more vigilant.'

Alice nodded agreement. 'Tim must be watched with extra care. We daren't let him wander out of the garden as he has sometimes in the past. We could all do with a break. How about you getting Friday off work, Maxine, and we all go to Chalkwell for a day by the sea?'

'I can't let Steve down.' Maxine wasn't giving up a day working with Steve for anything.

Bethany didn't argue. 'I'll make sure I'm back in time to collect you from work then.'

'I'm not a kid. Giles doesn't frighten me. I can come home on my own.' She shot Bethany a sour look. 'Or are you hanging round for a chance to speak with Steve like all those other women? It's sickening the way they drool over him.'

'I'm not interested in Mr North,' Bethany informed her for the hundredth time.

Maxine was not appeased. Several times Steve had mentioned Bethany to her. Nothing she did seemed to attract his attention, her new more feminine clothes and light make-up went unnoticed. A chance comment from him that he preferred women with long hair made her keep her own flowing about her shoulders in wild gypsy curls.

Steve was outside the surgery when Bethany dropped Maxine off that morning. He was helping a middle-aged woman carry her collie inside for an operation. He paused to wave and smile at Bethany and after greeting Maxine gave her several tasks to complete. She simmered with resentment that Steve virtually ignored her even though she was around him all day. He'd made an effort to notice Bethany. Later when he walked into reception where she was filing and flashed her a winning smile, her antagonism melted under its radiance.

'Have your family had any further trouble with your stepbrother?'

On the Monday following the dance he had quizzed her about Giles. Delighted at his interest, she'd told him all she knew and how Giles was making threatening phone calls. 'He hasn't phoned for a couple of days. Mum is still nervous and upset but he doesn't worry me. I can look after myself. Bethany keeps insisting I get escorted everywhere.'

She pouted, feeling gauche at having admitted that Bethany treated her like a kid over this matter.

'It must give her a lot of extra work. She's clearly worried about you.'

'She can fuss all she wants around Tim, taking him to school and picking him up. I'm not a kid. But try telling her that. I used to think she was my friend, but lately she's like a mother hen fussing over us all.'

He frowned. 'She didn't strike me as a woman to make a fuss over nothing. It doesn't pay not to be careful. From what you've told me of Giles he's got a mean streak. He also has a drink problem. That could make him dangerous.

There's not a man in the house to protect you, is there?'

'Bethany doesn't need a man. She doesn't take any nonsense from anyone.'

'Tough as old boots, is she?' he teased.

'Don't be daft,' she said, rattled that the conversation remained on her sister and sensitive that Steve was criticising her. 'Beth and I stick together. I suppose I've been a bit hard on her. I don't like having my own independence curbed. She used to understand that. Though to be honest it's only since Giles turned up that she's changed.'

He studied her thoughtfully before switching subjects. 'Mrs Meredith's Pekinese Bella was badly mauled by two terriers over in the park. The dog has lost a lot of blood. I'm operating on her and keeping her in overnight for observation. I've got some farm calls this evening. I was hoping you could stay on here to keep an eye on Bella until I get back, then I would run you home. But if your sister is worried about you?'

'I'm not having my life dictated by that creep of a brother of mine,' she said defiantly. 'I won't come to any harm here. And if you run me home . . .' Her heart soared with joy at the thought of being alone with him in the intimacy of the surgery's van. 'I'll be perfectly safe and Mum won't worry. Bella needs to be kept still or she could burst her stitches.'

'Are you sure that in the circumstances it won't make your mother worry? She's just come out of hospital.'

'Mum's had bad nerves ever since I can remember. I'll speak to Bethany after she's finished the afternoon session with the kids from the children's home who are visiting the pets. Since Giles was rude to her on the phone, Mum won't answer it anyway. That creep upset her.'

Steve's sandy brows drew together. 'Something should

be done about that man. It isn't right he can terrorise defenceless women.'

Maxine laughed. 'Hardly defenceless with four dogs in the house. Bethany keeps a poker by the door in case he comes round.'

Steve realised that Giles Warden was probably causing more trouble than Maxine knew. Bethany wouldn't want her younger sister worried..Ever since meeting Bethany he had found himself thinking about her. It was her self-containment, sense of humour and independent spirit, which he had glimpsed in Maxine, but was so much more defined in Bethany, which fascinated him.

He had lived in Leytonstone all his life and knew something of Giles Warden's reputation as a bully before the war. He felt a rush of protection towards the plucky young assistant and her lovely sister.

Bethany felt exactly as Maxine did. Giles was not going to ruin her life. The shock of his return had thrown her into panic. It had made memories surface which she had relentlessly buried. She'd hoped never to see him again. Already the worry was making Alice ill and Bethany was not prepared to allow the situation to continue. She'd had time to think in the long hours of sleeplessness. The next time Giles telephoned she would arrange to meet him. It was time she confronted him. He wasn't going to have any hold over her ever again.

The decision made, Bethany rang the mental institution which had discharged Giles. After a lot of persuasion his doctor agreed to meet with her that afternoon. She wanted to learn about Giles's state of mind whilst he had been shut away and how to deal with him should he turn violent or difficult.

She also rang her solicitor and accountant for meetings tomorrow. She needed to know the legal position regarding Giles being cut out of Harold's will. She may loathe the sight of him, but she wasn't vindictive. If Giles was entitled to a share of his father's estate then he would have it. As to anything else, that depended on Giles's attitude. Giles had wasted the fortune Rosemary had brought him on their marriage. Most of Harold's legacy had gone to his mistress and children by her. Some was in trust for Tim to provide care for him if he should need it. There was also an allowance provided for Alice. Neither Maxine nor herself had received a penny of Harold's money. So Giles wasn't the only one Harold had shown his displeasure towards when he made his will.

In Bethany's opinion Giles had always been unstable. No sane man would have attacked her as he had.

For the sake of family peace it was best to put the bad times behind them. Her life was fulfilled with her work and her family were too important to endanger by refusing to meet Giles. Hadn't she always prided herself on her sense of fair play? She would give him a hearing. Though she had little faith that a leopard could change its spots.

Obviously Alice was in no state to deal with any settlement offered to Giles. If it was put in the hands of solicitors, it could drag on for months. Bethany wanted it over and done with and Giles out of her life for good.

She steeled herself to meet him. He had squandered his wife's money and she wasn't having him begging off her for the rest of his life. Any money would be given on condition that he signed a binding document stating that he had no further claim on the family.

'He's bullying you into paying him,' Alice groaned. 'He doesn't deserve it. Harold made his wishes clear.'

'I don't want the past dragged up,' Bethany protested. 'He's making you ill. I want rid of him. I don't want people saying we swindled him out of his father's money.'

'You know that's not true. We don't owe him anything. He should be behind bars for what he did to you.'

Bethany shook her head. 'Two wrongs don't make a right, Mum. You only destroy yourself if you allow yourself to become bitter over past events. I want my conscience clear.'

'It won't do any good. He'll be like a leech bleeding us dry for the rest of our lives.'

'No he won't. I won't allow it,' Bethany vowed.

By the time Steve arrived back at the surgery Bella had recovered from the anaesthetic and had made no attempt to gnaw at her stitches. Mrs Meredith had rung several times and was anxious to collect her Pekinese, declaring that she would sit up with her all night if necessary.

'I'll drop the dog off while I'm taking you home,' he told Maxine.

She held Bella in her lap as they drove through Leytonstone in the surgery van and daydreamed of being both a vet and a vet's wife. It would be the perfect life as far as she was concerned.

Her reverie was rudely broken when Steve eventually pulled up outside her home. A fire engine was outside and the hoses snaked to the back of the house. The front door was open and the downstairs lights blazing. Steve followed her out of the van as Maxine ran into the house.

'Mum! Bethany! What's happened?' She had to shout above the barking of the dogs.

Fear escalating through her, she ran to the kitchen. The garden door was open and several firemen were moving about in the twilight. Two jets of water were aimed at the shed where the garden tools were stored and two of the chestnut trees behind it had caught fire. Her mother, Bethany and Tim were grouped together. Alice held Tim's hand to stop him getting closer to the dying fire.

Bethany saw Maxine and came to her. 'Someone set fire to the shed. The trees behind it also caught light. The dogs smelt the smoke and started whining, or more damage could have been done before Mum and I realised there was a fire and called the brigade.'

'Was it Giles?'

Bethany looked grim. 'Probably, but some kids could have got into the garden through the paddock. Thank God none of the animals were hurt. If the fire brigade had arrived any later the aviary would have gone up. You'll have to check out the guinea fowl and other birds to see they weren't overcome by smoke.'

'It was Giles,' Alice announced. 'This is just the sort of thing he would do.'

'The man is a maniac,' Steve interrupted.

'He was trying to frighten us that was all,' Bethany said wearily. 'A spiteful prank. He's probably been snooping round all evening, the dogs wouldn't stop barking. We had the doors locked.'

'Have you informed the police?' Steve asked.

Bethany swept back a lock of black hair from her cheek and nodded. 'But there's not much they can do unless he's caught doing damage. There's never been any fingerprints on the stones he used to smash the windows.'

The fire extinguished, the firemen packed up their hoses. The chief officer approached Bethany. 'The fire was deliberately started with some rags soaked in petrol. The police will treat it as arson and they'll want statements.'

Darkness had fallen and Bethany's face was pale in the light from the kitchen window. 'Thank you for dealing with the blaze so promptly.'

Alice had gone inside and was insisting that Tim bathed before he went to bed. Bethany saw her mother sway and ran to her side. 'Sit down and rest. Don't go putting the wrong interpretation on this incident.'

'It was Giles. What if he sets fire to the house next?'

'He won't do that. Because then he will never get any money from us. That's what he's after.'

Steve hovered awkwardly at hearing the interchange. He was angry at the danger these women could be facing. 'Is there anything I can do?'

It would have been a relief to confide in him but Bethany resisted. He was a virtual stranger. 'We'll manage. But thank you for offering.'

'I'm going to check the birds and other animals,' Maxine declared. 'The smoke could have drifted to the rabbit hutches and guinea pigs.'

'That's one job I can help with,' Steve said following Maxine.

'In that case perhaps you would like to stay for supper, Mr North,' Bethany offered.

He was about to decline when Maxine interrupted. 'I'm starving. Steve hasn't eaten either. He's been out all evening on calls.'

'He's welcome to share our macaroni cheese and salad after you've checked the animals.'

Steve nodded and Maxine proudly led him to the aviary and other pens.

'I hadn't realised you had so many pets,' he said, chuckling as he sidestepped two pygmy goats strolling across to nudge his legs. There was a honking of geese.

'I think we'll move their pen nearer to the pony field,' Maxine said. 'They're as good as dogs for alerting you to intruders. Trouble is we have to lock them in at night otherwise the foxes will get them.'

As they checked the animals and penned in the chickens and geese for the night, Steve lingered by the aviary. Apart from the usual finches, canaries and budgerigars, there were separate open compartments for a barn owl and two magpies.

'I rescued Merlin the owl from Epping Forest,' Maxine explained. 'He had a broken wing and is blind in one eye. Willow and Rowan were brought to me by two boys when they were fledglings. The parents had abandoned the nest. All three are quite tame and roost here from choice. I'd never put them in cages.'

He smiled. 'You're lucky to have such a tolerant sister and mother. The children from the homes must love it here.'

'Yes I am. And they do.'

Inside the house the phone rang and Bethany picked up the receiver. Giles's voice grated down the line. 'I want that five hundred for starters. Or it will be more than a shed which goes up in flames.'

'I had already decided to meet you and discuss Harold's will.' The sound of his voice churned her stomach with sickly fear. She swallowed and spoke slowly to control any trembling in her voice. She must never allow him to know that he could still frighten her. 'Tonight's fire had nothing to do with it. Though it has made me resolved to be less generous. I will not be intimidated by your bullying.'

'Bitch! You'll pay what I demand. And don't think you can go whining to the police.'

'I already have.'

'Go to them again and you may find that pretty sister of yours has to learn the same lesson I taught you. Then there's your brother. You can't watch him for twenty-four hours a day. Accidents can be arranged. And you know I don't make idle threats.'

Her knees buckled and cold sweat stung her spine. Then fury rushed in, overriding her fear. She'd kill him before she allowed him to harm Maxine or Tim. Her voice rose. 'Neither do I make idle threats. So much as say boo to them and you won't get a penny. I've reported your threatening behaviour to the police. I'll do so again if you continue. I'll meet you lunchtime the day after tomorrow in the tea rooms in Chingford High Street.'

He gave a malicious laugh. 'I enjoyed teaching you a lesson. You're still an attractive woman. I prefer experienced women to virgins. I look forward to our meeting.'

'Your threats don't frighten me. Try any violence and you won't get a penny. That's a promise,' she raged and slammed down the receiver.

Her knuckles whitened as she gripped the table edge and took a long shuddering breath. Despite her bravado she was shaken by his words. His threats were too real to ignore. Her anger may rise to sustain her to defy him with all the violence of a lioness protecting her cubs, but when it drained away she felt weak and vulnerable.

He didn't deserve even the consideration she had given him. She loathed him. But her conscience decreed that as Harold's eldest son he was entitled to something from the estate. As long as her family were provided for she was prepared at least to consider a payment to Giles. But on certain conditions . . .

She picked up the phone and asked the operator to connect her to the police station. When the desk sergeant answered she told him about the fire and the threatening call from Giles.

'You say you've reported his threats before, Miss Masterton.'

'Yes, but I had no proof. The Fire Officer has agreed to file a report. Is that proof enough?'

'It is proof of arson but not who set the fire. We have only your word that your stepbrother confessed to it. However, we are not unsympathetic to your plight. What's your brother's address? We'll bring him in for questioning.'

'I've no idea. It must be local because of the evidence he's left of being in the garden at night. I've already given a description of him. He seems adept at avoiding the constables on the beat.'

'Without his address we can do little unless we catch him in the vicinity. I'm sorry, Miss Masterton, but we shall keep an eye on your property.'

She contemplated telling him about the meeting at Chingford then decided against it. Giles wouldn't come near if there was any suspicion of police in evidence. Clearly, she needed him to sign something which would incriminate him.

Bethany heard Maxine clattering crockery in the kitchen and was thankful that her mother was upstairs supervising Tim's bath. Neither had overheard Giles's threats. She mustn't let Maxine see that she was upset. A glance in the hall mirror showed her unnatural pallor. She pinched her cheeks and having no lipstick handy bit her lips to restore some redness to them.

Maxine had set the table and rather extravagantly opened a bottle of wine, which they only drank as a treat with their Sunday lunch. No doubt Maxine was also trying to impress Steve, so Bethany didn't comment. Besides she found she was desperate for a drink.

'Would you like a whisky before we eat?' she addressed the vet.

'Thank you.'

She downed her own large gin and tonic and was aware of Steve watching her. When Alice did not appear for supper, Bethany checked on her. She found her sitting in her nightclothes on her bed with two sleeping tablets in her hand. 'I'm tired but my mind won't settle. I can't stop thinking about the fire. Who was on the phone?'

'It was Peg,' Bethany lied not wishing to upset her mother further. 'I'm dining with her and Frank on Saturday. No doubt she's matchmaking again. You know what Peg's like.'

'It's time you met someone and settled down. That vet wouldn't be a bad catch. He kept looking at you I noticed.'

'Are you trying to get rid of me? I'm happy as I am.'

Alice reached out to take her hand and squeezed it. 'I love us all living together, but that's selfish of me. Maxine will be married in a few years but life is barren without love in it. I know Harold could be difficult but I did love him at first. Not with the grand passion I felt for your father, but it wasn't all bad times between us.'

Bethany wasn't convinced of that. In the months since Harold had died, Alice had begun to talk of him as though he was an entirely different man to the one she knew. Harold had certainly made life as difficult as possible for them and had never shown a scrap of affection for Bethany. That didn't mean he had not shown it to Alice. It was usually the case that when someone died you remembered the good about them and not the bad, which was as it should be.

Before going back downstairs she checked that Tim was

in bed and asleep. Maxine was chatting animatedly to Steve in the sitting room and had disregarded the smell of overcooked cheese in the oven. Bethany rescued the macaroni, relieved it was not ruined, and called out for the others to join her. Maxine was looking flushed, more excited about the vet staying for supper than disturbed by the implications of the fire. She would have to warn her to take extra care until this matter with Giles was resolved. They must all be even more vigilant in future.

'Mother has gone to bed,' Bethany explained, then fell silent after serving the food. Giles's threats echoed in her mind and even two glasses of wine could not drown them. At least Maxine had an endless flow of conversation and kept making Steve laugh.

'Is there dessert?' Maxine broke through her troubled thoughts.

'Yes. Some fruit cake or trifle. I'll fetch them.'

She carried out the dirty dishes and brought in the fruit cake which Alice had made that afternoon and the trifle. Steve was again laughing at something Maxine had said. A glance at Maxine made Bethany's throat catch with emotion. She'd never seen her look so beautiful, her violet eyes bright with the special glow of a young woman falling in love.

Bethany put the food on the table. She felt an intruder into their happiness. Trying to appear normal after that phone call had drained her energy. She topped up Steve's wineglass and, filling her own, excused herself to take the dogs out into the garden. The smell of smoke was sharp in the air and she had to call them to keep them away from the blackened timbers of the shed. She sat on the garden seat by the fishpond and drained her wineglass. It was then that the moonlight revealed the half dozen cigarette stubs.

Giles had been here again – watching.

She got up and shook out the folds of her summer dress. The material and seat felt tainted. Memories crowded back overwhelming her. Tears hovered on her lashes as she battled to blink them away. 'Damn him!' She hurled her glass at the charred rubble of the shed. Why had he come back to ruin everything?

Chapter Twenty

The meeting with the doctor at the asylum had not told Bethany much. He had been affronted when she suggested that Giles could revert to violence again.

'Madam, he would not have been released if there was any chance of that.' His ruddy complexion was pitted and his brown hair was shaved high above his ears. As he addressed her he tweaked a waxed handlebar moustache which sprawled across his long ascetic face. 'The mind can be a victim of war as much as the body. Usually more so. The scars cannot be seen. Every man has his nightmares to contend with. Some are more seriously damaged. Mr Warden endured inhuman suffering in the prisoner of war camp.'

She was aware of that and resented his patronising manner. 'Giles was always violent. He had an unstable streak long before the war.'

He flicked open a silver snuff box, tipped some on to the back of his hand and inhaled it up each nostril. Flecks of it clung to the protruding hairs and splattered his moustache. It was a habit Bethany had always considered revolting. He then produced a grubby handkerchief and blew his nose loudly and profusely before answering, 'Mr Warden is capable of leading a normal life. However, any great shock or trauma may cause him to become unsettled; in which case we should be informed.'

'Is it normal to threaten your family? Or to burn down a garden shed? He is a danger to our family.'

He regarded her with a supercilious lift of an eyebrow. She could have hit him, the pompous ass. 'Have you made any attempt to welcome him back to the bosom of his family? Treat him as an outcast and he will behave like one. He is a war veteran and has suffered for his country. He needs understanding. The need to feel accepted.'

The doctor had the audacity to blame her for not welcoming Giles back with open arms. She stood up, her tone cold. 'Have you made yourself aware of his behaviour before the war? He was often in trouble for starting fights. To my knowledge he raped one woman and taunted another so that she committed suicide. Is *that* normal behaviour?'

'Hearsay is not evidence. Was there proof of these crimes? If he was guilty, why was he not charged and tried by law? I've seen families like yours. You're embarrassed to admit that your brother needed psychiatric help. You fear the scandal. Mr Warden is a victim of war. He needs a normal family life. To deny him that is bound to frustrate him and he will act irrationally. Your duty . . .'

She had listened to enough of his sanctimonious pontificating. 'I know what violence he was capable of before the war. You are using the war as an excuse.' She picked up her handbag and gloves and left. She was wasting her time. The doctor was an insufferable egotist.

The meeting with the accountant was more encouraging. Tim had an adequate trust fund set up by Harold which was to pay for any special education and care with Alice and Bethany as trustees. Alice was financially comfortable because of the money invested on Edward Masterton's death.

Bethany would not have accepted Harold's money even if he had made provision for her. She had her father's house and her success as a children's novelist made her financially independent. She could have provided for Maxine's future herself if the need arose, but Alice would not hear of it. Alice was too upset to attend the meeting but she had given Bethany her agreement to pay what she must to stop Giles threatening them. Bethany was determined that the money would be paid, but on their terms not Giles's.

The solicitor, Mr Pritchett, was more cautious. He was a short man in a formal morning suit and black tie. His bald head was bent over the document she had drafted. He looked up, his fleshy cheeks sucked in as he contemplated her before speaking. Unusually for a solicitor he was a jovial man but today his expression was grave. He had been her father's solicitor and she trusted him implicitly.

'The estate can meet the sum of one thousand pounds but it does mean your mother will have less interest and therefore income. Your brother is not entitled to it.'

'My mother's health is more important to me. No price can be put on peace of mind. And I earn enough to ensure that my mother need never go without. If it was just myself I would fight him, but Mother is frail. This worry will kill her. And I couldn't live with myself if anything happened to Maxine or Tim.'

'In the circumstances your family have been more than generous, Miss Masterton.'

'All I want is an end to the unpleasant business. To ensure he stays away from us the sum of seventy-five pounds will be paid into his bank account quarterly. It will give him a chance to get back on his feet and find work. Any future harassment from him and the payments will be stopped.'

'He's blackmailing you,' Mr Pritchett declared. 'And demanding money with menace. The police should deal with it.'

'They can do nothing unless one of us is physically attacked. I'm not waiting for that to happen. That's why I'm insisting on conditions to him receiving any money: most importantly that he never contacts us again. He must sign a document to that effect. I also want a clause added which states that he has no further claim upon the Warden estate.'

Mr Pritchett stroked his chin. 'Even if he signs, you can't be certain that he won't demand more money. He assumed that all Harold's estate should be his. His claim would never hold up in court though.'

'He must know that.' Bethany needed to be optimistic. Giles had already proved that she was no match for him physically. None of the family were. By signing the document as she had worded it, Giles would also be admitting to having intimidated them. It would be evidence against him and the police could use it if he tried to terrorise them again. 'This isn't an admission that he's entitled to any money. It's a gift to a member of the family to help them in a time of need. That's all. If it gets him off our backs, it's worth it.'

'You're in a difficult position. I will consult my partners on the exact wording of this to make it more binding. It will be ready for collection tomorrow morning.'

The next morning was hot and sunny, the clouds spread across the sky like giant ostrich plumes. She had chosen the tea rooms close to the station hoping that a public place would stop Giles making a scene.

There was the usual crowd of shoppers which was reassuring. She went into the tea rooms and ordered a pot of tea and a scone. A half hour later Giles had not shown up. She was fuming. Was this another of his tricks to undermine her? It had taken all her courage to come here and confront him and now she was angry that he hadn't turned up. She paid the bill and walked to her car. As she reached into her handbag for the keys, a voice spoke from behind her.

'You got the money?'

The smell of stale alcohol hit her before she turned round. She would not have recognised Giles. His auburn hair was thinning on top and hanging in lanky strands over his frayed shirt collar. The once handsome face was lined with deep indentations along the side of his mouth. He hadn't shaved in days and the auburn stubble was streaked with grey. There were stains on the lapels of his suit which looked as if he'd slept in it and his shirt was creased and grey with dirt. From the smell of him, he couldn't have bathed in weeks. He used to be so immaculate and fussy about his appearance. Now he looked and smelt like a tramp.

'Give you a thrill to see how the mighty have fallen, does it?'

Her loathing for him brought a rush of bile to her throat. A primitive part of her wanted to strike out at him for what he had done to her, but that would drag her down to his level. A mature calm controlled her instincts. Hatred would destroy her, eat at her with its self-destructive force. But she could not forgive nor forget. She could only act as her conscience dictated.

'I don't get pleasure from witnessing others' misfortune,' she informed him coldly.

'Hand over the money.' He moved towards her and she sidestepped to avoid him.

She conquered a rising fear. There was cruelty in his brown eyes and his fist was clenched. She held out the document Mr Pritchett had drawn up. 'It's not as simple as that, Giles. Before you get a penny you have to sign this.'

He scanned it. 'I'm not signing it. It's as good as a confession of threats and blackmail!'

'I won't use it unless you break the agreement.'

'You think I'd trust you?' His eyes narrowed and his lips pulled back showing gaps from several missing teeth. His handsome looks were gone; raddled by drink and unimaginable crimes of cruelty. He was more dangerous now than before the war. It emanated from him in dense choking waves.

'I don't break my word.' She fought to keep her voice steady. Any sign of weakness and he would crush her with merciless ease. 'Clearly you've fallen on hard times. Harold disowned you. Your own conduct was to blame for that. But you were his son. Out of duty I will make this settlement providing you agree to the terms.'

'Bitch!' He lunged for her, a manic glitter in his eyes. 'I'm not signing that and I'll have my money. By whatever means it takes.'

She evaded his hands but was pushed up against the side of the car. There were several shoppers nearby. When Giles began to shout at her they had turned away, some disappearing into shops. She could see them peering through the window. She had hoped to be safe in a crowded street. Usually there was a policeman on the beat here. Today when she needed him he was nowhere in sight. Fear pumped through her. She hated public scenes and was aware that Giles was capable of violence as well as verbal abuse. He grabbed her wrist.

'Give me what you've got in your purse. I'll be round for more tonight. If I don't get it, you'll regret it!'

'Your threats don't frighten me,' she blustered and kicked out at his shin, holding her handbag tight to her chest. He grabbed for it and they struggled. A punch to her stomach doubled her over. Still she held the bag fast and clawed at his face. 'Stop it, Giles. You'll get nothing now. I told you I won't be bullied or threatened. I tried to be reasonable. You've one last chance to sign this or you won't get a penny.'

'You offer me a pittance of what is rightfully mine.' He yanked at her hair jerking her head back.

'Hey, leave her alone!' a familiar male voice shouted.

'Piss off! This is family business,' Giles snarled.

Giles was dragged several feet away from her and his fingers released her handbag. Steve North had him pinned up against the glass front of a shop. 'I said leave Miss Masterton alone. If I learn you're troubling her again, you'll have me to reckon with.'

Giles swung his fist wildly and Steve agilely ducked the blow. His own fist contacted with Giles's eye and a second rapid punch struck his chin. Her stepbrother staggered backwards and fell to one knee.

'What's going on here?' The policeman on duty finally appeared. He stood between Giles and Steve North. He was a tall, burly man in his late thirties, and didn't look like he would stand for any nonsense.

Steve explained, 'This man was attempting to steal this woman's handbag and he was threatening her.'

The policeman looked towards Bethany. 'Is that right,

madam?' He was holding his handcuffs ready to snap them on to Giles's wrist.

She hesitated. This wasn't what she wanted. It would only make Giles more vindictive and vengeful. Before she could protest, two women bustled out of the shop.

''E was trying to rob 'er, constable,' one shouted.

'We saw 'im threaten 'er. Punched 'er in the stomach. Men like that should be locked up and the key thrown away. A woman ain't safe on the streets.'

'Is that right, madam?' The policeman stared at Bethany. 'Do you wish to press charges? If so, I need statements from those witnesses down at the station.'

'I ain't goin' down the nick for no one.' The first woman sidled away. 'I've got me hubby's meal to prepare. He does shift work on the buses. I ain't got no time for statements.'

The second woman followed her saying, 'I got a tub of washing boiling away in me copper. Can't leave that.'

'This man is my stepbrother, constable,' Bethany intervened. 'I don't want to make trouble for him. I just want him to stop pestering me for money.'

The policeman regarded her sombrely. 'A spell in prison for assault would stop his persecution, madam.'

Bethany shook her head. The prison sentence would be short. He'd be out in a couple of months and then would be set upon greater vengeance. She wanted this settled as amicably as possible. 'I won't press charges this time providing he agrees not to trouble us again.'

Giles glared at her. There was murder in his bloodshot eyes. 'I fought for King and country. No stuck-up bitch is going to tell me what I can and can't do.' He glowered at the policeman but, seeing that the older man was more than a match for him, he slunk a pace backwards. Then he waved his arms erratically and his voice rose. 'They turned my father against me. They stole what was mine. I'll have that money, or else.'

'You're a bully and a liar,' Steve fumed. 'You can't go round threatening women and demanding money by menace.'

'Says who?' Giles swung a punch at Steve. His aim was marred by the drink and when Steve sidestepped caught the constable on the jaw.

'That's it, mate,' the policeman rapped out. 'Attacking an officer of the law. It's down the station for you.'

The constable turned to Steve. 'You want to make that statement?'

Bethany caught Steve's gaze. She shook her head, her violet eyes pleading with him. 'If the lady doesn't wish to, it's not my place to press charges.'

'Then he'll be had up for disturbing the peace and striking an officer of the law. He won't be causing you any trouble for the next week or so. Time enough to come to his senses.' The policeman frog-marched the abusive and struggling Giles away.

Steve looked down at Bethany. 'Are you all right? That man should be locked up for good.'

'I can't thank you enough for helping me. No one else came to my aid. I suppose Giles looked too ferocious. But I doubt he'll come to his senses as the policeman said.' She fought to control the trembling which shook her figure now that the incident was over. 'I was lucky you were here.'

His eyes crinkled with concern. 'I overheard you making the arrangement on the phone. It was obvious you were upset and being threatened in some way. Your sister told me how your stepbrother has been causing problems and that he was probably behind the fire. I was worried about you meeting him alone.'

'I thought I could handle him. He's meaner than ever.'

'I don't think you should drive just yet. You're still shaking. There's a decent restaurant further down the High Street, will you join me for lunch?'

Aware that shoppers were still watching them, she didn't want to hang around, neither did she feel in a fit state to drive. 'Thank you.'

Even as she allowed him to take her arm and they entered the restaurant, she felt a stab of disloyalty to Maxine.

Chapter Twenty-One

Mark Greenwood rubbed the back of his hand against his brow in the fierce heat of the African sun. He leaned against the veranda of the hospital and closed his eyes. Any exertion caused him to sweat profusely and his limbs were weighted. He willed his strength to return. He had another hour's surgery before he could rest. The last bout of malaria had left him weak. Dr Peterson had counselled him to stay in bed another two days. How could he when there were so many casualties brought in from the Mau Mau uprising?

The number of patients and their horrific injuries sickened him. Most were from the Kikuyu tribe, the ones who refused to follow their leaders in the massacre of Europeans to free Kenya from white rule. So many of the victims were hideously hacked to pieces by *pangas*, the bush knife favoured by the terrorists. The extra troops brought in from Britain had arrested most of the ringleaders and back in April over seven hundred Mau Mau faced trial.

But the killings went on. He'd been warned to leave the hospital as it was too dangerous for him on the fringes of the Mau Mau activity. If it hadn't been for his last attack of malaria he would have gone back to Nairobi.

Yet how could he leave the wounded and suffering who

needed him? Apart from the war years when he'd served in the desert, he'd spent ten years in Africa battling against the diseases which decimated the population. Fevers were rampant, caused by insect bites or tiny worms picked up in water burrowing into the skin. The causes of disease were countless and some progress had been made against them from vaccinations. He had come here to research the cause of the fevers and found himself tackling the effects of malnutrition from famine; and more recently performing life-saving surgery on the men, women and children mutilated by the Mau Mau.

In the last year Africa had lost its magic and after the murder of his wife Paula his idealism had faded.

Poor Paula, so brave and worthy. So steadfast in her dedication. Why couldn't he have loved her as she deserved? Why couldn't he have forgotten the violet eyes and gypsy curls and spirit of Bethany Masterton? He'd met Paula on the rebound when Bethany refused to come to Africa. They'd been on the same flight back to Kenya after the war. She was a nurse working with the Red Cross. Their paths crossed frequently and her devotion to her work moved him. After a year of courtship they more or less drifted into marriage.

Professionally they were the perfect couple. He had believed himself to be happy. In many ways Paula was all he wanted in a wife: beautiful, dedicated, passionate and loving. Perhaps too loving. It smothered him sometimes. She insisted on going everywhere with him. He thought she would change after the birth of their son, David. She became worse. She had never been maternal, too often the boy interfered with her work. Mark spent all his free time with his son which increased Paula's jealousy.

It was then he admitted how much of a mistake their

marriage had been. It began to suffocate him. He realised he had never truly loved Paula. He respected her, admired her stamina, her lack of complaint when they worked in appalling conditions. What he found difficult to tolerate was her possessiveness. The passion of her lovemaking could turn so easily into a volatile, jealous rage without reason. The more jealous she became, the more he retreated from her, causing her jealousy to fester. It was a vicious circle.

He stared over the tops of the mud huts of the village and across the heat haze of the plain beyond. The idealism of his youth had long faded. Africa no longer held the enchantment it once had.

The anger at her untimely death still gnawed at him and he blinked away a forming tear. She had given so much to this land and had not deserved that death. Paula had been late returning from a distant village and her truck had broken down. Her body was found two days later. The police reckoned that she had been too close to an ivory poachers' camp and they had murdered her. There had been other such murders by the ruthless men who pursued this hideous trade.

Her death had shocked him. When the Mau Mau attacks started in the area he had sent David back to England to live with Paula's sister Dorothy and her husband Sidney Hubert in Dorset. They had no children of their own and adored their nephew. Mark missed him desperately and strangely he missed rain-soaked, foggy England.

His longing to return to work in England and be with David intensified. With it came memories of Bethany. He had been a fool to let his anger at what had happened cause a rift between them. He should have understood how close she was to her mother and therefore could not leave her when Alice was so ill. Three years ago he'd seen her children's books on sale in Nairobi and had bought a set of them for David. Paula had screamed at him with jealousy. A week later he found the remnants of the books on a bonfire.

He lost his temper and stormed out to spend several days touring villages. During his nights as he lay on the ground in a mud hut, his dreams were haunted by Bethany's smiling face. She beckoned to him. He ached for her. But it was a hopeless dream. He was married to Paula. He believed in fidelity and didn't want David to suffer from his parents divorcing. The cracks were widening in his marriage, his work papered them over. The fragile hold had sustained until Paula's death and he had mourned the passing of a lover and friend, but not the woman he loved.

An outbreak of smallpox had kept him in Kenya and then the Mau Mau killings escalated. Some of the loyal Kikuyu injured had been people he'd known since they were children. There was no replacement doctor available from England. First and foremost he was a doctor and he was needed here. Then just as his replacement Greg Peterson arrived, the malaria had struck. And here he still remained. In a couple of weeks David would be breaking up from school for the summer holidays. He must be in England for him.

Guilt plagued Mark. He had never known his own father who was killed in the First World War and had sworn to be there for any children of his own. England was where he should be.

Tomorrow he'd arrange his return. He wiped the stippled sweat from his brow. Damn this malaria! It left him so weak.

Mwaura, the Kikuyu who supervised the other servants, appeared with a glass of beer. He had been head servant here since Mark first arrived. He was a short wiry man, proud of his status. He ran the team of cleaners, helpers and servants like a sergeant major. Mwaura had been aloof when Mark arrived until Mark had saved his youngest son's life when he was mauled by a leopard. Since then he had been devoted to Mark and his family and despite his position of servant used his age to treat him with fatherly concern.

'Dr Peterson says he need you, bwana.'

'Thank you, Mwaura.' Mark drank down the beer.

The servant's oval face with high defined cheekbones broke into a dazzling smile. There was a dusting of grey in the close-cut hair and the skin of the proud face was leathery. 'You feel better now, bwana. You should rest.'

Mark nodded. 'I've got another two patients to operate on then I can rest. I shall be going back to England at the end of the month.'

'You come back, bwana?'

Mark shook his head. 'I don't think so – not in the foreseeable future.'

'Sad day for us when you leave. Very sad day, bwana.' Mwaura marched back into the coolness of the hospital and shouted orders to a dilatory servant.

Mark walked slowly into the hospital. His body felt like lead. As he turned a glint of sunlight off metal on the plain caught his attention. He turned to stare at it. Was it a truck coming with supplies? He couldn't see any dust stirred up from a vehicle. He shrugged and shook his head. Had he imagined it? He was so tired. After the operations he needed to check the ward patients and then he would call it a day if there were no further emergencies.

He was bent over the unconscious form of a nine-year-old boy on whom he had been forced to operate to cut off his leg below the knee to prevent gangrene from a *panga* wound spreading. It had taken the boy's uncle six days to reach the hospital on foot, carrying the boy on his back after the attack by the Mau Mau on their village. The boy had been severely beaten and left for dead. It was a miracle he had survived the journey.

There was angry shouting from outside the operating room and Mark frowned.

He glanced at Marjorie, the white nurse in her forties who was helping him. There was fear in her eyes. He clamped his down. He had to finish sewing the edges of the skin together over the stump before he could leave the patient.

The doors burst open. Marjorie screamed. Mark looked up in time to see the *panga* slashing through the air towards him. He put up an arm to grab the wrist of his attacker. Four natives rushed into the room yelling, 'Die, all white men!'

The heavy musk of their bodies from days in the bush cloyed his nostrils as he fought. Marjorie's screams were deafening and other screams reached him from the ward. He had no time to think, only to react and fight, a scalpel his only inadequate weapon.

He didn't even see the man who jumped him from behind. Surprisingly there was no pain as the *panga* slashed across his shoulder and an arc of blood spurted from his body. Marjorie was no longer screaming. Her decapitated corpse was slumped across the patient. Instinct made him duck and swerve the oncoming blows. Then fire exploded through his skull and he crashed to the floor. Outside gunfire splattered.

Chapter Twenty-Two

The insistent ringing of the doorbell finally penetrated Bethany's consciousness. It had started the dogs barking. She was working and lost in the world she had created for Jester and his friends. Her publishers were bringing out a bumper edition of Jester stories for Christmas and she was checking the galley proofs for printing errors.

Bethany glanced at her wristwatch; it was one thirty. In an hour a group of children from the special school Tim attended were coming to see the animals. The sandwiches on her desk which her mother had brought her at twelve were curling at the edges. She had forgotten to eat, she had been so absorbed in her work. Alice would be lying down for her afternoon nap. The doorbell rang again and fear spiked her. What if it was Giles? It had been a week since their confrontation in Chingford. If he'd been released from custody after the arrest for hitting the policeman he would be in an ungovernable rage.

She hurried down the stairs, concerned that the doorbell would disturb Alice. She must have taken a sleeping pill. If she had heard the door she would have come to her. Bethany had played down her meeting with Giles but Alice had been nervous and still spoke of buying Giles off so that they could have some peace.

As a precautionary measure Bethany picked up the poker she had placed in readiness. She opened the door a crack and saw Steve North walking away down the drive towards his motorbike.

Pulling the door wide she called to him, 'Mr North! I'm sorry I took so long to answer, I was working in my study upstairs. I don't always hear the doorbell.'

He retraced his steps and grinned at the four dogs clustered around her feet. 'I hadn't meant to disturb you. I hoped to catch you at your lunch break.'

She laughed. 'Lunch is usually when inspiration fails. I forget all sense of time. I set the alarm for two o'clock if there are children coming.' She stood back for him to enter the house and spoke softly to the dogs. 'Friend.' They dropped their guarded stance and edged forward to sniff Steve's outstretched hand.

'I'm about to brew some tea. Come into the kitchen while I make it. After the way you saved me the other day I feel I know you well enough not to stand on ceremony.'

'I'm glad you feel that way. I called to see that you were all right. And that you haven't been troubled by your stepbrother again.'

'No. Though I suspect it's a brief reprieve. He probably got some time in custody for hitting the policeman. He'll be harder to cope with when he comes out.' She suppressed a shiver. Giles wouldn't let the matter drop now.

'I don't like to think of you and Maxine being at risk.' His voice gruffened with concern.

'I know the constables who patrol this beat. They keep a watch on the house day and night. We have the telephone and the dogs.'

'I wish I could help in some way.'

At this unexpected statement, Bethany studied him.

He'd swung the kitchen chair round and straddled it, his elbows resting on the wooden back. It wasn't only concern she noted in his eyes, it was interest. She would have liked to reach out and feel the comfort of his hand on hers. But a nagging voice warned her it wasn't right. She held back and made her tone teasing, 'You take your duties as an employer seriously.'

He frowned. 'Actually it's you I'm concerned for. You've taken on so much protecting your family. I admire that.' His stare gentled as he regarded her. 'More than admire you. You were courageous when your stepbrother attacked you. You were shaken but you didn't weep or get hysterical as many women would have done. Yet you could do with the presence of a man about the place to warn your stepbrother off. I'd be happy to spend more time here at the weekends, the practice permitting.'

She was nonplussed. Maxine would be delighted. She wasn't sure she should encourage Maxine's infatuation or the interest of Steve. To her surprise she was tempted by his offer. She liked the vet. 'I couldn't expect so much from you, Mr North.'

'Steve. I thought we had agreed to forget formality. My motives are purely selfish. I'd like to see more of you. I don't like the thought of your family making virtual prisoners of yourselves, especially at weekends.'

She felt a rush of warmth and affection at his words.

'Your offer is very kind, but I can only accept it, if it is meant in friendship. I don't want a relationship.'

His eyes widened. 'You don't mince words, do you?'

'I don't want any misunderstanding between us, Steve. You're Maxine's employer. I don't want to jeopardise her position.'

'It won't.' He rested his chin on his knuckles as he

watched her. 'You cling to your independence. That's rare in a woman. And I've seen that same stubborn streak in Maxine.'

'We are alike and very close. Working at the surgery means a great deal to her.'

He grinned. 'There'll be no strings attached to our arrangement, I promise. I miss family outings since . . .' His eyes clouded. 'My parents and brother were killed in a direct hit on their Anderson shelter. Any girlfriend I've had finds it hard to accept that the practice is everything to me at the moment. It's just beginning to get on its feet and I don't want any emotional commitments for a year or so. But I'd like us to be friends.'

She nodded and reached out her hand. 'I'd very much like you as a friend, Steve, and so would Maxine. All she talks about is helping animals. I missed my chance to become the doctor I intended.'

'I hadn't thought *you* would be put off from a course of action once your mind was set on it.'

'It wasn't meant to be. I found another rewarding way to help children.'

'Your writing?'

'That and working with the sick and those like Tim. They can teach us so much about courage and accepting life and its pleasures.'

The admiration deepened in his eyes. 'I'd never thought of it that way. But I'm sure it's true. Maxine says you work wonders on the injured pets and the sick children in the hospital. So you don't regret not becoming a doctor?'

'No. I know there are other ways to help others. Listening to their ills can be a wonderful therapy. I seem to have the knack of saying the right things which helps them. I don't believe in regret. Just in making the best of what you have.'

'That's a wonderful philosophy.'

She laughed. 'It works for me.'

'So how about we do something together at the weekend? The rest of your family are included, of course. The weather forecast is supposed to be sunny.'

She was tempted. 'I'll see what Mum and Maxine say. Can I let you know tomorrow?'

He nodded. 'Actually it was Maxine complaining that Giles is stopping you all getting out which gave me the idea. I'll speak to her.'

'Steve, this is difficult.' Bethany hesitated. 'If you talk to Maxine I don't want her jumping to conclusions. Any conclusion. She might think you're asking her out. I don't want her to be upset.'

'I'm aware she's got this kid's thing about being attracted to her employer. I'm flattered. She's a good kid. She knows my life is dedicated to the practice. I like her and wouldn't hurt her feelings for the world.'

Bethany wasn't sure that was possible. But a day out without the worry of Giles hanging over them was just what they needed.

After he left Steve's offer continued to trouble her. There were always consequences to any action. Was it possible they could all remain just friends? She hoped so, but even so the worry that Maxine could be hurt remained.

Unsettled, she picked up the *Daily Chronicle*. The main headlines and pictures were of the Queen's Coronation tour of the country. She flicked through the pages and was halted by a small article. '*British doctors attacked by Mau Mau terrorists.*'

Her heart thudding painfully, Bethany read on. '*Dr Mark Greenwood flew into Heathrow today. He was still weak from the injuries he received when the Mau Mau attacked the hospital. His associate Dr Gregory Peterson and their nurse Marjorie Henderson were murdered. Dr Greenwood said he, "owed [his] life to [his] loyal Kikuyu servant Mwaura who was alerted to danger by the sun shining off a* panga *blade. He radioed the local military base who were camped three miles away."*

'The British Army arrived in time to halt the massacre and ten Mau Mau terrorists were taken prisoner. Six more were killed in the fighting. A dozen hospital patients had been massacred by the Mau Mau before the army arrived.

'Dr Greenwood, looking drawn and ill from a head and shoulder wound, praised the army's intervention which had saved his life. "I am appalled by the killings," Dr Greenwood commented. "But feelings are high in Kenya for independence from British Rule. There is a place in Africa for both whites and blacks. One day I hope they will both live in harmony and mutual respect in a noble land."

'Dr Greenwood was being admitted to hospital for an operation on his shoulder. This is not the first tragedy to strike Dr Greenwood while in Africa. Eighteen months ago his wife was murdered by ivory poachers. Dr Greenwood has no current plans to return to Kenya. He has a young son, David, who was staying with relatives in England at the time of the Mau Mau attack.'

Bethany slumped into an armchair. There was a picture of Mark emerging from the airport. It was not very clear and his tall body was stooped as though he was in pain. He wore a large-brimmed trilby tilted low over his brow and beneath it, just visible, was a dressing over the side of his head. One arm was in a sling.

Her love for him swamped her like a tidal wave. Her whole body trembled with reaction. Oh Mark, my darling, you could have died. She stared at the hazy photograph and traced the line of his beloved face with her finger. Her love for him crushed her. She had borne their parting, even the news of his marriage, knowing how important his work was to him. So often she had been tempted to write to him but how could she when he was married? She would never have come between him and his wife.

Over the years she had tried to convince herself that she could write to him out of friendship but after the first page of a letter she knew it was a lie. She screwed up the paper and threw it away. Every word that poured from her heart was formed from her love.

The need to write to him now was overpowering. She wanted to lay the ghost of their parting. Perhaps it was even naive to hope that they could still be friends. They had parted in anger and recrimination. When they met after the war their passion was undiminished, but the war years had changed them. They needed time to rediscover each other. But time was their enemy. Bethany accepted that only time could solve their differences. Time and circumstances had served only to keep them apart.

'Have you seen this?' Peg bustled into the room waving a newspaper. Maxine, looking intrigued, followed her.

'Didn't you hear the doorbell?' Maxine teased. 'Really, sis, has old age finally overtaken you and your hearing has gone? Peg was on the doorstep for five minutes. She saw your car outside so knew you were in.'

'I'm not fossilised yet,' Bethany returned, automatically answering Maxine's banter, 'and less of your cheek, sibling.'

'Lawd, you two are like a double act when you get going.' Peg was bursting with impatience. 'Haven't you read the paper, Bethany?'

Bethany's emotions were still shaken from the article on

Mark. She could see from the excitement in Peg's eyes that her friend was avid to start matchmaking again. This was too personal. For years Peg had been trying to arrange romances for Bethany.

Knowing how tenacious Peg could be over matters of the heart she conceded gracefully, 'I've read that Mark is back in England.'

'And it says he's a widower.'

'Peg! He was lucky to escape with his life. And his wife was murdered. Don't go getting ideas.'

'I didn't mean that it wasn't awful what happened.' Peg looked contrite. 'I was just thinking . . .'

'I know what you were thinking,' Bethany said. 'You can't resurrect old romances.'

'What is all this about?' Maxine was wide-eyed with curiosity.

Peg handed her the paper. 'That's the man Bethany was going to marry.'

While Maxine read the article in silence, Peg was studying Bethany. 'You can't let this opportunity pass.'

Bethany held up her hands and stepped away to stare out of the window and collect her thoughts. 'Don't go putting the wrong interpretation on this,' she warned. 'I'm going to write to Mark at the hospital where he studied tropical diseases. He must still be in contact with them.'

'What are you going to say?' Peg persisted.

'I don't know. I just feel I should write. I want to wish him well.'

Peg drew her lips into a stern line. 'Is that all?'

'It is enough.' Her look was one which brooked no further questioning.

That evening the letter took over two dozen attempts. She

didn't want to embarrass Mark by putting anything which would make him uncomfortable. She wanted it to be friendly and concerned. Some were too formal. Others too emotional. Too many rambled with inconsequentials. Another sounded reproachful which was her last intention. She compensated in the next with too much humour, which was misplaced in the circumstances. Finally she found the right note of brevity and, she hoped, pertinent understanding.

The letter posted, she decided that it was up to Mark to make the next move.

She didn't want to build false hopes, yet the imagination has its own way of conjuring images and showing the longings of the heart.

Her daydreams were shattered by the phone ringing, the voice on the line sending her reeling back in fear.

'I've been thinking of you all the time I was in the police cell. Thinking how to make you pay.' Giles laughed cruelly. 'You're going to spend the rest of your life regretting not giving me the money I asked for.'

The line was disconnected before Bethany could challenge his threats. She stared at the silent receiver. The nightmare had returned. Giles was again free.

[illegible]

[illegible] would take to [illegible]

[illegible] the scene of [illegible]

[illegible]

Chapter Twenty-Three

There was no reply from Mark to Bethany's letter. She had no idea how long it would take to reach him via the hospital. Not that she dwelt on the problem for long, she was too concerned about the safety of her family.

To avoid worrying Alice she did not confide in her mother. She watched Tim like a hawk and fussed over Maxine until the younger woman taunted her for being neurotic.

The strain was immense. That would be part of Giles's sadistic plan. He wanted to prolong her misery and stretch her nerves to the limit. He was succeeding. Instinct warned her that the danger would come first to either Maxine or Tim. That way Giles could hurt her most. It was how his twisted mind worked.

Her nerves were jagged. The slightest sound made her alert to danger. Artemis barking sent fear gouging through her. Her appetite deserted her. When exhaustion finally made her fall into a fitful doze she would awake with a start having dreamt of seeing Maxine's or Tim's broken body lying at her feet.

On Sunday the whinnying of one of the ponies dragged her to consciousness. It was five thirty and the rising sun was brightening the sky. The whinnying wasn't natural. It contained fear and pain.

Leaping out of bed, Bethany pulled on a pair of slacks and jumper. As she was hunting for her stout shoes she heard running footsteps on the stairs and made a dive for her door. Maxine was disappearing round the curve in the stairs.

'Maxine wait!' She tried not to shout and wake Alice or Tim. Fortunately Alice's bedroom door was shut. 'Don't go outside without me!'

'That's Snowflake. She's hurt. Stop fussing about me.' She continued running to the back door.

Bethany tore after Maxine and stubbed her bare toe in her haste. 'And what if she has been hurt by someone and they're still in the paddock?'

Maxine was already outside having ignored her warning.

'Wait!' Bethany shouted as she rummaged through the assortment of footwear in the porch. She shoved her feet into her wellingtons and ran out after Maxine.

Maxine had reached the pony who was now silent and standing with her head down and shudders passing through her white body. Bethany heard Maxine's sob and increased her pace. The sight of the pony shocked her. Blood was pouring from the three deep cuts on her flanks and rump.

'Get something to staunch the blood!' yelled Maxine.

Bethany ran back to the washing line to snatch a couple of hand towels which had been left out overnight. It wasn't until she got closer that she saw that Snowflake's beautiful mane and tail had been hacked off.

'What bastard did this?' Maxine sobbed. 'Was it Giles? I'll bloody carve him up if it was.'

'How deep are the cuts?'

'They need stitches. I'll ring Steve. Poor Snowflake. Who could be so cruel and evil?'

'Now do you understand why I don't want you to go off alone? This is how Giles acts. When you least expect it and in a way which will bring you greatest pain.'

'I hate him. Yet he's my brother. I feel guilty about that.'

'I know. But Giles doesn't attract sympathy. He uses fear to exact what he wants from others. And it will destroy him as surely as he tries to destroy others.'

Bethany ran her hands over the pony. She could feel its terror and it sickened her. It had taken her years to come to terms with the depths of loathing she felt for her stepbrother. She chose her words with care. 'So much suffering in this world is caused by intolerance and hatred.'

Maxine stared at her in disbelief. 'Are you telling me to love this monster who is my brother?'

'If you're capable of that you are a better woman than I.' Her voice dragged. Then a deeper guilt made her add, 'He was a prisoner of war for a long time and endured torture. He was always greedy for money. He thinks we cheated him.'

'Why are you defending him?' Maxine rounded on her.

Bethany hung her head. She couldn't give an honest answer to that. She just knew that it was important that Maxine did not believe that Giles was all bad. She surveyed the old bombsite which on its purchase had been flattened and grassed over for the animals. The sky was clear and blue and the morning sun warming both flesh and earth. It looked as if it would be a scorcher. There was no red-haired figure lurking in the trees around the field or watching from the wall by the path. To change the subject she said, 'Go and ring Steve to come and tend Snowflake. I'll tether her to the fence nearest the house and you can see to her wounds there.'

Once Snowflake was tethered Bethany spoke soothingly

as she gently ran her hands over the mare's trembling body. The pony nuzzled her chest trusting her to stop the pain. The tremors shaking her body had stopped by the time Maxine came back with a couple of apples as a treat for the pony. 'Steve's on his way.'

Behind Maxine was Constable Albert Higgins who was on duty on the beat. He looked at the pony and made some notes in his book before saying gruffly, 'Nasty business. Did either of you see who did it?'

He asked several more questions before leaving as Steve was walking across the paddock. The vet was wearing faded jeans, a black jumper and his blond hair was dishevelled from his haste to get here. After an initial greeting Bethany left him and Maxine to tend Snowflake and went inside to cook breakfast for them all.

Steve worked in silence as he stitched up the lacerations on the pony's body. Maxine stood by his shoulder. Steve looked incredibly sexy having come straight from his bed. There was a line of stubble on his chin and she was close enough to smell the scent of soap on his skin. She was always enthralled watching him work. He was so gentle with the animals as he touched any injury that she kept imagining how it would feel to have those tender, capable hands caressing her body.

Snowflake fidgeted as the last stitches were being put in. Maxine murmured softly to her and kissed her velvet nose.

'That's it.' Steve straightened and his grey eyes regarded her over the pony's head in a way which made her heart clamour. 'I'd like to get my hands on the nasty piece of work that did this and give them a taste of their own medicine. Do you think it was your stepbrother?'

Maxine nodded. 'Is Snowflake going to be all right?'

'She'll need to take it easy and have only gentle exercise

for a while. You'd better keep her stabled when the children visit.'

He gathered up his bag and swept his hair back from his brow. Again Maxine felt her heart tug with love for him. 'I'm sorry we had to get you up so early. Bethany is cooking breakfast and she's expecting you to stay.'

As he walked with her back to the house, he questioned her about the attack on the pony and as they entered the kitchen, he said, 'This is serious. If it was Giles, it could be one of the family next.'

'The police will get the details,' Maxine replied. 'I hate who did this. They're a monster.'

'It doesn't look good.' Steve looked across at Bethany who hadn't touched the bacon and egg she had served up. 'And the police can't act without proof?'

'We'll have to be more careful,' Bethany replied in a weary voice which showed the strain was telling on her.

'I don't like the thought of three women being unprotected. If you like I can stay over at nights here for a couple of weeks. That may warn Giles off.'

'We couldn't impose on you,' Bethany protested.

'That would be great, Steve,' Maxine burst out and shot a glare at her sister not to turn his offer down. 'It's getting really scary. And Giles has been prowling the garden at night. Bethany found some cigarette ends.'

Steve looked at Bethany. 'A man's presence should warn him off. You look done in. Have you been sleeping?'

Bethany shook her head. 'I appreciate your offer but . . .'

'Don't start with the buts,' Maxine interrupted. 'Think of Mum. It will put her mind at rest to have a man staying here at night. I think it's very generous of Steve to offer.'

Still Bethany hesitated. She was tempted, but she had

been independent so long, she didn't like to think that she couldn't take care of her family herself. And what of Maxine? Would it be such a good idea to have Steve here at night, when she was so obviously besotted by him? 'Let me think about it. It's a generous offer.'

'No strings attached,' Steve answered with a grin. 'Or are you worried what the neighbours will say?'

'I never worry about neighbours' gossip,' Bethany parried. 'Those who gossip most are the ones with most to hide.'

Steve laughed and Maxine joined in; even Bethany found herself grinning as the tension of the morning dissipated. He picked up his bag to leave. 'That's better seeing a smile on your faces than the gloom I was faced with this morning. And talking of smiles. It's going to be hot. How about I pick you all up at eleven and we take a picnic over to Larkswood Pool and spend the day there?'

'That sounds great,' Maxine said flushed with excitement.

'It will be packed.' Bethany grimaced.

'Safety in numbers,' Steve observed. 'A trip out will do you all good. Nothing like sunshine and water. Or do you fancy a drive to Southend?'

'We go wimming,' Tim said with a big smile on his face as he shuffled into the kitchen carrying his favourite wooden aeroplane under his arm. 'Timmy like wimming.'

Steve smiled and ruffled the young boy's reddish-brown hair which was standing up like a hedgehog's spines all over his head. 'The pool it is.'

Bethany nodded agreement. A day out would do them all good. 'I'll have to persuade Mum to come, she shouldn't stay here on her own.'

'I'll be back at eleven. Here's hoping there's no emergencies. It will be fun.'

Alice declined to go to the swimming pool. 'When we saw my old friend Val Murphy in the High Street on Tuesday she invited me over today if I was feeling strong enough. I'd like to see her. She's been a widow for a year and gets very lonely. I'll ring her and see if it's possible to have lunch together.'

Alice made her arrangements. They would drop her off at Val's house on the way to Larkswood Pool and pick her up at seven. Val was arranging for another couple to come in to play bridge. When Bethany mentioned that Steve had offered to stay for a couple of weeks, Alice looked happier.

'That would put my mind at rest. Giles is a bully. He won't trouble us if there is a man around.'

Bethany did not have that faith, but if Steve's presence would put her mother's mind at rest, then it would be no bad thing. She would give the matter serious thought and give him her answer this evening.

At the first sound of Steve's motorbike returning Tim was off like a shot to open the door. He continued to run excitedly around Bethany's car as they loaded up the bags and food hamper singing, 'Going wimming. Going wimming.'

Bethany threw Steve the keys to drive her car and he opened the door and ushered Bethany into the front seat. Seeing Maxine's crestfallen expression, she declined. 'Tim is so excited I'd better sit in the back with him and calm him down. Otherwise he'll be sick.'

As the car pulled away, Giles stepped out from his observation place behind a large shrub in the driveway. So they were going swimming. There were several pools to choose from but Bethany had always favoured Larkswood. He had hung around the house all morning hoping to see signs of distress and fear at what had happened to the pony. And here they were laughing and planning an outing. He scowled. He had spent hours watching this house gauging their movements and following them when he could. Bethany was clever, she didn't leave much to chance. But if he watched and waited opportunity would play into his devious hands.

As Bethany had predicted, the open air swimming pool was packed. They arrived early enough to find a place on the grass and spread out their towels. Tim was impatient to get in to the water and was hopping about with his rubber ring around his waist.

'I'll take him in,' Bethany said. 'Or we'll get no peace.'

'I'm going to sunbathe first,' Maxine announced.

'I fancy a quick swim before the pool gets too crowded to do a length properly,' Steve added.

'Perhaps I'll come in and race you.' Maxine changed her mind. With a burst of energy Bethany envied, the younger woman ran across the grass and flagstones around the pool calling back, 'Last one in is a sissy.' She dived straight in and surfaced taunting, 'It's lovely. Come in. Hurry up.'

Steve dived in beside her. He came up spluttering. 'You little minx, it's freezing.'

They began splashing each other and laughing. Steve ducked Maxine who swam under his legs and from his yelp must have pinched him. Maxine then set off at a fast crawl down the length of the pool with Steve in pursuit.

Bethany grinned. Maxine was enjoying herself. This was just the sort of day they needed to recuperate from the fear which had been hanging over them in recent weeks. Deliberately she checked her thoughts. She would not think of

Giles today. The sun was shining, the air was filled with laughter. She would make the most of it.

Tim was about to leap into the pool having taken off his rubber ring and she scooped him up just in time to stop him. He hadn't yet learnt to swim more than a few strokes.

'Down the steps, young man,' she admonished as she took his hand and led him to the shallow end. 'If you jump in you must keep your ring on.'

'Don't like ring. Want to wim.'

'Then I'll teach you.'

The pool was in the shape of a cross with the deep end in the middle section. Tim had to be watched all the time for he had no fear and would run up to the high diving boards and start to climb the ladder given half a chance. Bethany played with him in the water and continued his swimming lessons. But his attention was too quickly diverted and he preferred to play in the children's pool.

Several times the hairs on the back of her neck prickled and she had the uncomfortable feeling that she was being watched. When she turned to scan the crowds no one was paying them attention. Steve or Maxine would wave to her from the top of the diving boards or slide.

Steve came over to help with Tim's swimming lessons and gave Bethany a chance to have a proper swim herself. The water was too crowded to swim fast and she changed from crawl to breaststroke. Again a quiver of unease made her turn on her back and gaze around. Then she saw two feet inches above her head as some idiot jumped into the water right on top of her. She dived to one side and pain shot through her head dazing her and making her swallow water. Instinctively, she struck out to the surface, her vision blurred by the water streaming into her eyes. A red-haired man was glaring at her. Fear chilled her. The impact of the feet had made her groggy and her vision was momentarily distorted. Was it Giles? Had he deliberately jumped on her? Was he trying to drown her, or just frighten her?

She shook her head to clear her vision. The man was swimming to the far side and pulled himself out of the water. It could be Giles but from the back she couldn't be certain. She swam to Steve.

'I think Giles is here. Someone with red hair jumped in on top of me. He's going towards the changing rooms.'

'I'll go and check them out.' Steve hauled himself out of the water and wove through the sunbathers.

Bethany kept an anxious watch all round. Maxine came up out of the water to lift Tim on her shoulder. 'What's up? You look like you've seen a ghost. And where's Steve?'

'I thought I saw Giles. Steve's gone after the man.'

Maxine paled. 'Can't we even have a day out without him ruining everything?' She surveyed the pool and her scowl changed to a smile. 'There's Steve. He's alone.'

'If that was Giles, he's disappeared,' he informed them.

'Perhaps I was mistaken.' Bethany tried to lighten Maxine's anxiety. 'It happened so fast and the blow to my head did blur my vision. Don't let it spoil our day, but it won't do any harm to remain watchful. It's too easy for accidents to happen in a crowded pool like this.'

Their water games became more boisterous to chase away the cloud of disquiet. Laughter triumphed over fear until an hour later Bethany's skin began to tingle, this time from being out in the sun. Bethany called to Tim who was loathe to leave the water.

'Come and have some oil put on and you must wear a T-shirt now. Then you can go back in the water. I don't want you getting sunburnt.'

Tim protested and Steve swung him out of the water and up and over his shoulders to give him a piggy-back to their towels. Bethany took from her bag a preparation of olive oil and lemon to rub into his body and her own and then handed it to Maxine.

'Do you want some of this, Steve? It's some of Beth's witches brew. It makes you go lovely and brown and you don't get burnt. Do you want some on your back?'

Maxine was making it rather obvious that she was interested in Steve. Bethany studied him through her sunglasses. The vet was laughing as Maxine rubbed the oil in to his shoulders then taking the bottle he began to smooth the oil over her back. He started tickling her so that she screamed with laughter and a mock wrestling match ensued.

Bethany hid her own grin. Their play was boisterous but such frolics often led to a different kind of foreplay. The romantic in her saw them as a perfect couple.

Maxine had a similar idea in mind. She teased Steve throughout the day and was delighted when he responded. Her whole body yearned for a touch from him other than one which was playful. She waited until Bethany returned to the pool with Tim before stating, 'My shoulders are beginning to feel sore. Would you put some more of the lotion on them, Steve?'

As his hands moved over her flesh, she closed her eyes. Their cool competent touch was like the kiss of moonlight. She could feel his warm breath against her hair and languorously rolled her shoulders. In a provocative movement she lifted her black hair for him to circle her neck with his hands. Her face tilted to the sun as he massaged, the excited noise from the bathers blurring. Every part of her longed for him to kiss her. Unconsciously her lips parted and when his hands stopped their sybaritic circling she opened her eyes.

Steve was propped on his side watching her, his expression taut. Maxine trembled, sensing the charged emotion, that their closeness had sparked an answering chord within him. As he continued to gaze at her, her breath stifled in her throat, it stilled, poised as anticipation held her enthralled. Was the darkening in his eyes desire?

Before she could roll towards him he jumped to his feet. Her gaze devoured his long, lean body. It travelled up over his muscular thighs to his slender hips and waist. Across his chest was a smudge of dark gold curling hair and above that there was the glistening of sweat on his neck from the hot sun. A trickle ran down across the firm muscles of his chest and she longed to flick her tongue across it and taste its saltiness which carried the essence of the man. Her mouth parted and for an instant Steve held her stare. The intensity of his gaze dried her mouth and a shiver of pleasure rippled through her heated body. Instinctively, she moved towards him, her youthful body swaying with unspoken invitation.

He swallowed and there was a flicker in his eyes before he jerked back, stopped to pick up his towel and flick her across the arm. 'Let's swim and cool off. It's like a furnace out here. Then I think we'd better sit in the shade, or we'll all be like boiled lobsters tomorrow.'

He laughed and with a second flick of his towel lightly across her leg, he ran to the pool with Maxine in pursuit.

Her disappointment was acute. He was refusing to admit that he was attracted to her. She could almost hear him thinking that he was too old for her. As his body arced in the air in a perfect dive, she was level with him, her mind thrumming with the heat of her passion.

You want me Steve North, I know it. And before long you are going to admit it. You're going to forget the age difference between us and acknowledge that I am the woman you intend to marry.

Chapter Twenty-Four

Later in the week Alice was sitting in the sunny conservatory knitting a red jumper with a footballer on the front for Tim, across her lap a copy of *Good Housekeeping* which she was reading as she knitted. Through the conservatory glass the sun was hot. Bethany had placed two tall rubber plants in the window to provide some shade. Normally on such a lovely day Alice would be sitting on the seat by the fishpond, but she was alone and was too nervous to venture out into the garden even at two o'clock in the afternoon.

She had been feeling tired today and was still upset over the attack upon Snowflake. If she didn't make herself rest she would have a relapse. Bethany hadn't wanted to leave her alone while she took Tim to the dentist, but with all the doors locked Alice was safe. Tim's appointment could not be cancelled as he had been crying with toothache all night.

'Giles has made us prisoners in our own home,' she said as her frustration bubbled up. 'Bethany should have given him the money he wanted. Anything to get rid of that nasty wretch.'

Alice laid down her knitting and poured herself another cup of tea from the pot Bethany had brought her before she had left. A sound from the kitchen made her heart clench in alarm. She clutched up her knitting needles to her breast, their long points outward. They were a feeble weapon but a weapon none the less. Then with a tut of annoyance, she made an effort to dispel her fears. It must be one of the dogs or cats. If there was an intruder in the house or garden the dogs would bark.

To reassure herself, she glanced out of the window. Artemis was lying on her side under a tree. Rusty was also dozing on the grass, his head on his paws. The two alsatians must also be asleep in the garden.

Forcing her thudding heart to be calm she put down her knitting and picked up her tea. Her hand was shaking. Why had Bethany been stubborn and declined Steve North's offer to stay here at night? Was it because Maxine was infatuated with the vet and Bethany feared that Maxine would be hurt? Steve North didn't seem the type of man to trifle with a young girl's affection. Out of the two women Alice had thought that Steve took more interest in Bethany. He now dropped Maxine home from work every evening to save Bethany the task and often stayed for supper or a drink. Did he do that to see more of Bethany? Or was it Maxine, who he teased and chatted to with equal ease, who was stealing his interest?

Stop matchmaking, she chuckled to herself. Maxine has college ahead of her. She didn't want her to miss out as Bethany had done on achieving her dream. Not that Bethany showed any signs of regret. Her daughter had the gift of healing in other ways and she had done so much to help families with children like Timothy.

Alice shook her head. She doubted there would be any future for the vet with Bethany. Fate had been cruel to her daughter with events happening as they did. Guilt assailed her. Even after Bethany and Mark had come to terms with those events, her own ill health had stopped her daughter going to Kenya with Mark.

If only you could put the clock back and with a wave of a magic wand make everything right again. She shook her head, saying aloud, 'My dear Bethany, you gave up so much for me. If only I could repay it.'

'Money is the root of all evil,' a cold voice announced from the shadows of the room behind her.

The bone china cup clattered to the floor and smashed, the spilt hot tea seeping unnoticed through her cream and pink cotton dress. 'How did you get in here? The doors are locked! The dogs didn't bark.'

She struggled out of the chair, her breathing erratic and rasping painfully in her lungs. She was pushed roughly down into the seat and grimy fingers gripped her neck.

Giles sniggered. 'I learnt to pick locks and sneak silently into the houses in France during the war. It was that or starve. As for the dogs . . . Bethany should have taught them not to eat meat left on the grass and path. They'll sleep for hours. This time I chose to drug them not poison them.'

Alice stared at her stepson with horror and loathing. His face was twisted with cruelty the way Harold's could become when he had tormented her. She croaked tremulously, 'What do you want?'

'What's mine by right. Pa's money. For now I'll take whatever is in the house.' Menace dripped from every word.

'There's ten pounds in the Coronation tin on the kitchen dresser.'

'Ten pounds! I want a hundred times that.'

His hands tightened and she smelt the rankness of his

breath and the pungent odour of his body. Nausea was rising to her mouth and she gagged and began to choke. The pressure eased slightly as he rapped out, 'There must be some more money.'

She shook her head. The hold on her neck increased. Her eyes bulged. An iron band was forming around her chest making breathing difficult. Lack of air was beginning to cause faintness. Her asthma attacks had started when Harold began punishing her for not bearing a child. Also two nervous breakdowns had made her a partial invalid for some years. Since Harold's death both the asthma and nervous attacks had decreased until Giles had returned. She'd been warned by doctors that a severe attack could kill her.

'My handbag,' she croaked.

He released her and snatched up the bag from the floor. A roll of ten crisp white five-pound notes was waved under her nose. 'This is more like it. Pa left you all right. This is a pittance compared to what should be coming to me.'

'That's to buy Maxine's books for college. Why don't you leave us alone? Haven't you caused enough harm to this family?'

He pocketed the money and his lips pulled back into a lupine smile, hatred blazing in his pitiless brown eyes. 'I haven't even started yet. Unless I get the money I shall tell people the truth about your precious daughter Bethany.'

Alice spluttered. 'No! Haven't you brought enough shame upon us?'

Giles grinned evilly. 'I'm not a man to harm the hand which feeds me. I know I don't stand a chance of getting any of Pa's money through the courts. It all goes to that halfwit brat while he lives. Accidents can happen.'

Alice trembled violently. 'Tim has never harmed you.'

Giles scowled and went on, his incisive voice lacerating her composure. 'His birth turned Pa against me. Remember rumours can blacken a woman's name and spread like wildfire. No decent person will have anything to do with this family. Your good name means a lot to you.'

Alice began to sob. 'Please, don't say anything. How much do you want?'

'A thousand pounds by next Friday.'

'I don't have that much I can draw upon. My income comes from investments. I've only five hundred in my savings.'

'That will have to do for now,' he snapped, far from pleased. 'You won't trick me out of what is rightfully mine. Leave the five hundred pounds in a paper bag under the ash tree in the paddock on Friday. If you go to the police, there'll be an accident to someone you care for. And I don't make idle promises.'

'I'm not a rich woman.'

Giles slapped her cheek, sending fire through her jaw. He leaned over her, his glare demonic. 'You aren't poor. Your first husband left you a pretty penny and Pa saw you were all right. You've got a few thousand stashed away. All I'm asking is for five hundred – for now. And don't mention this to that bitch of a daughter of yours, or anyone for that matter.'

Alice began to sob. Her chest was tight, threatening the onset of another debilitating attack. She breathed deeply to combat it and by the time it eased Giles had gone as silently as he had come.

She raised a trembling hand to her mouth. She had to get the money for him. Giles had meant what he said. He was even more evil than his father. She couldn't risk one of her children being hurt. She pushed herself out of the chair. Bethany must not find her weak and frightened like this. She had relied on her daughter's strength for so long. This she had to do alone.

She took two sedatives from her bag. She was due to go shopping with Bethany to buy Tim some clothes; she would draw the money out of the bank then. Bethany had been wrong to defy him. What was five hundred pounds if it gave them peace and got Giles out of their lives?

When Bethany returned from the dentist with Tim she found her mother lying down in her bedroom.

'It's the heat, dear,' Alice reassured her. 'I find it difficult to breathe when the air is so close.'

The good weather broke on Friday and it was raining heavily. She looked up from her writing in surprise when Alice came into her study with her hat on.

'It's pouring down, Mum. I know you like to shop but it's silly to go out in this.'

Alice fidgeted with the clasp of her handbag. 'I have to go into town. Tim needs shoes and trousers and I have to call in at the bank.'

Bethany was about to protest when she realised that Alice was looking pale and nervous. When something became fixed in her mind she could make herself ill until she had settled it. She sighed. Alice had been on edge since the attack on Snowflake and the last few days she had looked ill. After Harold's death her mother did not play the piano so often, and when she did it was cheerful light-hearted tunes. Since Tuesday however, she had been playing for two or three hours daily, strident, heavy, repetitive pieces.

'Are you sure that you're up to walking round the shops? You look tired, Mum.'

'Stop fussing, Bethany. I'm not an invalid any longer.' Her irritation was out of character and she immediately looked contrite. 'I know you mean well. I've been a worry to you over the years. I can breathe better after it's been raining and the rain is easing off.'

'I want to finish the end of this chapter first before we go. I'll be about an hour.'

Alice nodded with relief. She had been dismayed to wake up to discover it was raining. She hated deceiving Bethany but she had to get the money from the bank. If she didn't pay Giles off she knew something terrible would happen.

Alice had acted strangely during their shopping trip. When she went into the bank she had sent Bethany off to get a bottle of tonic from the chemist. Since their return home she was jumpy and nervous and had hardly spoken a word. Neither had she touched her food. Halfway through the meal she had left the table. It was ten minutes before she returned and there were spots of rain on her hair.

'Mum, have you been outside? It's drizzling with rain,' Bethany enquired.

'One of the cats wanted to go out and I saw Tim had left his bike out.'

'I put it away before he went to bed.'

Alice flinched and gave a nervous laugh. 'You know what a little devil he is for getting his toys out again.'

Bethany laughed with her, but she was puzzled at how agitated Alice appeared. Her mother retired early and as Bethany was letting the dogs out later in the evening, she noticed that an old pair of Alice's brown shoes had a ring of wet rising from the soles as though she had been walking through long wet grass or had stepped in a puddle. There were no puddles on the paving-stones outside the back door and the only long grass was in the paddock. Why should Alice leave the house? She must have gone out when they were eating. Bethany frowned. She was positive that Tim had gone to bed within ten minutes of her putting his bike away. What had Alice been up to? And she had been ill at ease and nervous.

It was only nine thirty and she went upstairs to question Alice. Her bedroom light was out and she turned away unwilling to disturb her rest. Then she heard a muffled sob.

'Mum, what's wrong?' She stood at the door peering in. 'Why are you upset?'

'It's nothing.'

Bethany wasn't convinced and sat on the edge of her bed. 'Did you see Giles outside? I saw that your shoes were wet. Did he say something to upset you?'

Alice sniffed and wiped a hand across her eyes. 'I didn't want you to worry.' Then the words tumbled out in a torrent as she told her how Giles had broken in to the house and threatened her. She ended by adding tearfully, 'I know you didn't want to give in to his blackmail. But it was the only way to get rid of him. We're free of him now. I saw him take the money as I came in.'

'We'll never be free of him! He's frightened you into paying him once. He'll do it again. Oh, Mum, I know you did it thinking it was for the best, but . . .'

She cut off her recriminations. What was the point of upsetting her mother further? Giles would never give up and they would never know when he would strike. How could they relax in future? He'd broken in to the house once and drugged the dogs. Although she would report it to the police what could they do? They would have to catch Giles red handed. They didn't even know his address to take him in for questioning.

'You must take Steve North up on his offer to stay,' Alice insisted. 'I don't feel safe in my bed any more.'

Bethany hated admitting defeat. She went to her study but found it impossible to concentrate on her novel. Alice was right. It would be comforting to have a man in the house. If only that man could have been Mark and not Steve.

The thought struck her out of the blue and regenerated the agony of her loss and longing. It was more than a month since she had written to Mark. Why hadn't he answered her letter? Didn't he care? Or had he not yet received it?

Mark was in no position to write. After a brief reunion with his son he had been admitted to hospital to undergo surgery on his injured shoulder. By the time he received Bethany's letter his right arm and torso were in plaster. The *panga* which had struck his shoulder had broken the bone and it had not healed properly. The surgeon had reset it. Another blow had damaged the muscles in his left hand and he was undergoing several hours' physiotherapy a week to build up the muscles. The glancing wound to his head which had knocked him unconscious had been operated on in Nairobi. Thankfully he had sustained no brain damage. He had been lucky to escape with his life. Mwaura had saved him by alerting the authorities before the attack. His quick thinking in fashioning a tourniquet to his arm had stopped Mark bleeding to death.

He reread Bethany's letter and stared up at the cracks in the hospital ceiling. It brought back so many memories: so many longings. It was a strange letter with none of the passionate outpourings of her old letters. She had told him nothing about herself. She was probably married with children and had written out of kindness when she had seen the report in the paper.

He turned his head into the pillow. He wanted her love, not her pity. But he had forfeited that right when he had abandoned her to pursue his own selfish ambition. He screwed the letter into a ball and crushed it in his hand.

He'd give so much to see her. But not like this. He didn't need a mirror to know that he looked a wreck. His head had been shaved in the operation and he looked like a convict with the short stubbly growth growing back. The doctors had removed the dressing from his head but the scar was ugly and tapered down to the upper line of his cheek.

And there was David to consider. His son had burst into tears when he saw his injuries. Their conversation had been stilted. In the time David had been in England they had become strangers. The easy camaraderie he craved was lost.

'Why did you send me away, Dad?' David had demanded at their second meeting. 'Why didn't you come back with me?'

The recrimination had cut Mark more agonisingly than the *panga* wounds. David had burst into tears and when Mark held out his arm to him, he had run out of the door. Mark had been admitted to hospital the next day. There were bridges to build with his son before he could consider any other aspect of his life. But at least Bethany deserved a reply, but for the life of him he had no idea what to write. Too many aspirations and emotions had to be battened down. He had to put his son first.

'You've been here two weeks, Steve,' Bethany said as he and Maxine came in to the kitchen after checking all the animals were safely locked in their pens and stables for the night. 'Perhaps Giles did take off after collecting Mum's payment. I feel so guilty that we're stopping you going out with your friends and you're living out of a suitcase here.'

Maxine had been laughing as they came in, now her expression became petulant and she glared at her sister. 'Giles has kept away because Steve is here.'

'Do you want me to leave?'

'Of course she doesn't,' Maxine insisted.

Bethany folded her arms and stared fixedly at the set of copper cooking pans hanging on the wall by the cooker. 'I don't want you feeling you have to stay. We appreciate you've given up so much time to help us and we enjoy your company. Mother is looking better and I'm sleeping at nights. But you have your own life, Steve. Don't remain here out of misplaced duty or kindness. You don't have to stay in every night when I'm sure you would rather be out with friends.'

'I've never been much of a socialiser. I put too many hours into the practice.'

Maxine's mind was racing. She had been thrilled when Steve moved in and had built romantic dreams about him living with them. She'd been aware of the chemistry between them at the pool and had been convinced that it would spark into a romance. Instead Steve's desire had vaporised. He was more circumspect with her now than before when he had treated her like a kid sister. The trouble with Steve was that he was too much of a gentleman. Living here he saw himself as a white knight saving three women from the evil machinations of their cruel and sadistic relative.

Her frustration churned like a bubbling cauldron. Steve could keep his white knight image. She dreamed of him carrying her off on his powerful motorbike out into Epping Forest to make love to her until she swooned with passion.

In a couple of weeks she had to return to her studies and would only be working at the surgery on Saturdays. If he didn't notice her while he was staying here she feared that an older more sophisticated woman would steal his heart. Someone like Bethany. Steve certainly got on well with her sister, too well for Maxine's comfort.

'It's a lovely evening,' she said ingenuously. 'The dogs need walking. It won't be dark for another hour, Steve. Shall we take them up to the fields at Whipps Cross and they can have a good run. Beth won't mind you borrowing her car.'

'Put a blanket in the back or Artemis will go in the pond and the seat will be filthy,' Bethany said.

'Don't you want to come, Bethany?' Steve replied. 'You haven't been out much this week.'

'I prefer not to leave Mum alone. You two go and enjoy yourselves. I'm having lunch with my editor tomorrow and want to read through my proposals for a new series of books. These are about the adventures of a wacky witch and her woodland friends.'

'Is that the one based on Maxine and her menagerie?' Steve said, grinning at the young woman.

Maxine pulled a face and Bethany chuckled. 'They say all fiction has its roots in reality.'

'Thanks very much, I'm sure.' Maxine tossed back her long black curls and picked up the dog leads. The ensuing barking and scampering around their feet ended the conversation.

Maxine threw an old blanket on the back seat of the car. When she looked back to the house Steve was standing close to Bethany. Her sister laughed lightly and flirtatiously flicked his tie with her finger. Jealousy ground through Maxine. What would it take, she wondered, to get Steve interested in her?

They parked the car and walked through the trees. Maxine had always found it hard to restrain her emotions and after ten minutes of walking they were threatening to swamp her.

'Steve, do you fancy Bethany?'

'I admire her tremendously.' His voice was cagey.

'That's not what I meant.' She stopped and hugged her arms about her body, her shoulders hunched. 'Have you fallen for her?'

He didn't answer and looked displeased as he stared at her. 'I like her. It would be hard for a man not to find Bethany attractive. But there's nothing between us except friendship.'

'Do you wish there was?'

He sighed and his eyes squinted against the encroaching twilight to watch the four dogs sniffing through the undergrowth. 'Things are best as they are.'

Her heart beat more lightly. He didn't love Bethany, but he was attracted to her sister. Why couldn't he desire her? Here they were in a favoured lovers' meeting place and he didn't even try to kiss her. Why couldn't she be more sophisticated and elegant like Bethany? She'd just have to try harder if that was the type of woman which interested Steve.

Romantic thoughts fled at seeing the grey lurcher streaking after a duck which had flown up out of the undergrowth. 'Lawd, Artemis is heading for the pond and it's pretty stagnant this time of year. And Rusty is chasing her. Bethany won't be too pleased if they stink her car out.'

Practicality made her run after Artemis, shouting to Steve, 'Head them off if you can!'

She didn't see the broken branch which tripped her. She pitched forward, crashing down on one knee and wrenching her ankle. A stone grazed her cheek and the air whooshed from her lungs. When she levered herself up with her hand, her palm ground into a thistle and she cried out at the unexpected pain. Then humiliation whipped her. So much for sophistication. She'd made an ass of herself. Tears of mortification stung her eyes and her shoulders heaved. She was as clumsy as a setter pup and just as gawky. She flopped down on to the grass with a sob.

Steve knelt beside her. 'Maxine, are you all right? You took quite a tumble.'

She squeezed her eyes shut. She'd made an idiot of herself and couldn't face him.

His hand touched her shoulder, burning through her jumper to sear the flesh. 'Maxine, did you hit your head? There's some blood.'

Gently he rolled her towards him. She kept her eyes screwed shut and her mouth clamped tight in agony as she struggled to master her tears of humiliation.

'Maxine!' His voice was edged with alarm.

He stroked her hair away from the cut on her temple. Through her closed eyelids she could visualise him bending lover-like over her, his handsome face stark with anguish. His touch was mesmerising, she didn't want it to end, which it would if she opened her eyes. She quivered at the thrill of the gently soothing fingers probing the graze.

'Maxine!' His voice sharpened and he put his hand to the pulse at her throat. It was galloping wildly. Her hand moved to clasp his and she drew it down over her breast and held it there before opening her eyes.

When he made to pull back she gripped his hand harder, her voice low and husky. 'What has Bethany got that I haven't? I suppose she's sophisticated and successful. Men have always gravitated to her. But aren't I as pretty as her?' Her hurt broke through.

He removed his hand from her breast and stroked the side of her cheek and gave her an odd smile. 'Don't do this to yourself. You're every bit as lovely as your sister, and special.'

'But not special enough?'

'Very special.' He held up his hands as though he intended to take her face between them, then they fell to his sides. 'I'm nine years older than you.'

'It doesn't bother you that Bethany is that much older than you?'

'I never noticed.' He looked taken aback. 'I thought she was my age. She doesn't look it.'

'Doesn't that prove that age doesn't matter?'

She lifted her arms and entwined them around his neck needing to prove to him that she was as much a woman as her sister. 'Aren't I desirable, Steve?' she whispered, her eyes mirroring her uncertainty.

For a long moment he stared down at her and she could feel the surprise in him at her boldness. There was a poised tension in his lithe body. He hadn't pulled away. Encouraged she smiled and drew him closer, bringing his mouth down to meet hers. She wasn't completely inexperienced. For two months after last Christmas she had gone out with a boy who was three years older than her and learned to drive him wild with her kisses. And before the summer holidays she'd been seeing Ted, the brother of a school friend. He'd gone away for the summer.

Her mouth was supple and inviting, moving over his

with an abandon roused by her months of dreaming of this moment. His response took her by storm: first gentle with surprise, then bruising with a suppressed anger, as though he would teach her a lesson not to play with fire. She matched it with passion. Subtly his searing kisses changed and became cherishing and her body yielded. His kiss deepened. His hands relaxed against her shoulders to slide sensuously down the slender form of her body to the swell of her hips and then tantalisingly up again to her breasts, his fingers circling her nipples through the soft wool of her jumper.

A sensual quiver spiralled through her body and she clung to him.

When he lifted his head, his breathing was harsh and his eyes were shadowed with an indefinable light, part hallowed, part savage. Before she could question it, he wrenched away from her and stood up. He brushed his fingers through his hair, his hand shaking. 'Hell, Maxine, I'm supposed to be protecting you. Don't try a fool move like that again. I'm only human and you're a beautiful young woman.'

'I wanted you to kiss me, Steve. Why are you fighting it? And don't insult me by telling me it's because I'm only sixteen.'

His smile was wry. 'It's more because I'm twenty-five and still not ready to make the kind of commitment a woman like you deserves. Don't go confusing desire with love.'

'I'm not the one who is confused,' she flung back, turning his cynicism against him and masking her own hurt. 'It was only a kiss. From what I've seen of marriage between Mum and Dad, Bethany's independence has a lot to recommend it.'

Maxine whistled to the dogs and they drove back to the house in silence. Fortunately Artemis and Rusty had turned to chasing rabbits and avoided the stagnant water. She could feel a tension in Steve but was too miserable to try and lighten the atmosphere between them. He drew up in front of the garage and Maxine leapt out to release the dogs who went scampering round the back of the house to their water bowls. As she straightened from shaking out the old blanket and folded it over her arm, Steve was beside her. He touched the side of her face.

'I want us to remain friends, Maxine. If things had gone further tonight we couldn't have continued to work together at the surgery. I would regret that. And at your age you should be out having fun. You don't want a serious relationship for quite a few years yet.'

'You think I'm a tramp because of the way I acted.' She glared at him, her cheeks colouring with anger and embarrassment.

'Don't twist my words. Do you really expect me to break your mother's and sister's trust while staying here?'

She hung her head and he tipped her chin up with his finger, his smile tender. 'You're a lovely woman. Don't let's complicate something which is good between us.'

He put his arm around her shoulder as they walked into the house. It gave her hope that he was not as immune to her as he portrayed.

Giles stepped out from his hiding place in the shrubs. The tenderness between the vet and the young woman infuriated him. It reminded him of the closeness between the doctor and Bethany after Louise had died. It was Bethany's fault that Louise was dead. Louise would never have shut him out of the family. These women must pay for all he had suffered. Why should they be happy when he was wretched? Maxine was no different from Bethany. Indeed they looked remarkably alike. At the same age of sixteen they could have passed for twins. And he had lost *his* twin. His darling, devoted Louise. His demented mind focused on the likeness of the two women. In recent weeks Bethany had shown that she couldn't easily be broken. His triumph over Bethany had come when she was Maxine's age. By dominating Maxine he would destroy Bethany. The time had come to teach them all a lesson they would never forget.

Chapter Twenty-Five

During the next two weeks Steve treated Maxine with the same friendliness he had shown before they had kissed. Obviously the kiss which had brought her body alive as a woman had meant nothing to him. She had thought his words when they arrived home that evening held promise. Clearly she was mistaken.

It was hard for Maxine to accept, but, afraid of losing Steve's friendship, she pretended the incident had been part of their teasing. She may have convinced him that her heart was not affected but it was aching for his reciprocation.

Pride sustained her. She stopped seeking him out in the evening when he was in the house, curbed all her impulses to flirt with him and struggled to remain aloof from his handsome looks and charisma. Her friends from school were constantly ringing her up to go out with them. Until now she had declined because Bethany was worried that Giles might cause her harm. Inactivity and being cut off from her friends had added to her misery at being so near to Steve while having to appear indifferent.

Since he had got the money from Alice there had been no phone calls or contact from Giles. On four mornings they had discovered cigarette ends in the garden telling them that Giles was prowling there at night. It was why Bethany and Alice remained wary about Maxine going out in the evening.

'I'm fed up not seeing my friends,' she announced in the surgery to Steve as he was spaying a cat. 'A school friend, Lillian, has a party on Saturday and all my friends are going. Mum won't let me.'

'I'll pick you up. If that will put Alice's mind at rest.' He spoke without looking up as he concentrated on the operation.

Her heart skittered but she calmed it. She shrugged, schooling herself to appear nonchalant. 'Thanks for the offer, but her brother Ted will bring me home. I was seeing a lot of him before Giles turned up. Ted's been away at the family cottage in Dorset all summer. He wanted to take me to the pictures last week but Mum wouldn't let me go.'

'She's naturally worried about you.'

He had shown no reaction to her mentioning a former boyfriend. It made her feel rebellious. 'I'm beginning to feel like a prisoner. It's all right for her and Bethany. Mum only ever went to her bridge evenings and Bethany has her car if she goes to Peg's.' She picked out some instruments from the sterilising unit with tongs and put them on the tray by the operating table. Two clattered to the floor in her mounting agitation. She put them aside to go back in the steriliser before saying with a groan, 'Bethany went to the theatre with a male friend last week. It's not fair I can't go out. Ted's not a kid. He's nineteen and training to become a dentist. I think Mum is making too much of this business with Giles.'

Steve paused in his work and looked over the top of his mask at her. His grey eyes studied her candid stare. 'Does this Ted know what's been happening? Bethany didn't want it to become gossip, but if you're seeing him he should be aware of the dangers.'

'What danger? Giles won't do anything while you're at the house. And you must be getting pretty sick of nurse-maiding three women.'

Steve finished sewing the incision on the cat and lifted her from the table into a cage on the surgery floor before answering. 'That's exactly the point. We know you're safe at home if we're all together. It's away from it that Giles is most likely to strike at one of you. For now he's playing a waiting game.'

'I hate him. Why can't he be arrested?'

'Because there is no proof against him, only your mother's word about the blackmail. No one saw Giles retrieving the money. Alice was foolish not to inform the police. If he'd been caught taking it . . .'

'He won't get caught though, will he?' Her anger and frustration sparked in her eyes as she wiped down the operating table with an antiseptic cloth. 'He's too clever. He wants us to be frightened and ruin our lives.'

Steve regarded her seriously. A lock of dark blond hair had fallen over his brow and she yearned to be taken into his arms and comforted.

'I've been into the garden at all hours of the night and never seen him. If I got my hands on him I'd give him such a beating he'd stay away. Like all bullies he fears confrontation. He knows Bethany won't give in to his threats. He's waiting until we start to relax and think he is no further threat.'

He had lifted a Yorkshire terrier on to the table to sedate while he examined its mouth. Several of its teeth were rotten where the foolish owner had constantly fed it chocolates. Three of them would have to be removed as the dog was in a great deal of pain.

Maxine's chin tilted up with stubborn defiance. 'I won't have that creep manipulating my life. Ted can look after me. I'm going to this party whether Mum likes it or not.'

'I know it's hard on you,' he began.

She cut him short. 'I'm sixteen and I want some fun in my life. As you so aptly told me. It's hardly a lark a minute stuck indoors with you fuddy duddies.'

He grinned. 'Are we as bad as that? And there was me thinking you liked playing dominoes and Ludo.'

Her violet eyes flared with anger. 'Kids' stuff. If Bethany gets that Monopoly board out again this week I swear I'll crown her with it.'

'That's only because you lost last night.'

He was at his most provocative, deliberately goading her so that she rose to his baiting. Usually she couldn't resist it. Sometimes she loved him so much that when he treated her like a kid sister the pain of unrequited love became too much. 'Go on, take the mickey out of me. You're probably still laughing at me behind my back at the way I acted the other week over Wanstead. I'm sick of being treated like a kid.'

The three teeth were extracted and Steve carried the dog to another cage to recover. When he straightened he studied her with a mixture of compassion and tenderness. 'No one is laughing at you, Maxine. I know it's hardest for you to give up going out with your friends.'

'Fat lot you care.'

He sighed. 'We all care. And we all know you're not a kid. Which makes it even more dangerous for you. Bethany has said that Giles has raped a woman. He's extremely dangerous. If you're seeing this young man he has to be aware of the danger. Even so, we don't want you to miss out on having fun.'

He had tried to conceal his fear for her. The vulnerability of Maxine to anything Giles may try to do horrified him. Maxine was beautiful and spirited. If Giles attacked her, it didn't bear thinking about. All that was fresh and innocent about her would be destroyed. And this Ted . . . what did the family know about him? Giles was a skilled soldier. How could Ted at nineteen match up to that?

'If you're interested in this Ted then get him to call round one evening. I'll explain the facts about Giles to him if Bethany or Alice won't. If he cares for you, he won't want you risking any danger.'

'Forget it. He's just a friend. I'll become a recluse. Shut myself away of an evening like some medieval anchorite who shuns the world.'

He grinned. 'You sure you don't want to go to drama school instead of veterinary college?'

When she didn't rise to his teasing, he spread his hands. 'How can I resist those violet eyes? It's hardly a social whirl but I'm judging a dog show at a church fête next Saturday afternoon. Do you fancy coming over for that?'

'You offer me a dog show when I could be dancing the night away?'

'That's all that's on offer from this fuddy duddy I'm afraid. The police are on the lookout for Giles now. He'll be taken into custody and questioned about blackmailing Alice and the fire if he comes to the house again.'

'Providing a policeman is conveniently to hand at the time.' She folded her arms and glared mutinously at him. 'Giles is too sly for that. I hate the way he controls our lives. He obviously gets some perverted thrill out of terrorising us.'

Steve said gravely, 'It's to do with power and manipulation. Bethany said Giles was obsessive about wielding control over another.' Seeing her frown, he said more lightly hoping to cheer her, 'Are you coming to the dog show? It would be good for Tim but I can't keep a proper eye on him while I'm judging.'

Trust him to spoil any romantic illusions which had momentarily flared by also including Tim. 'Put like that how could a girl refuse.'

The church fête turned out to be a full family outing with Alice and Bethany joining them. Early morning rain had cleared but the skies remained overcast.

'Let's hope the rain holds off,' Bethany said as they entered the field by the church where hoopla stands vied with bric-a-brac stalls and refreshments to raise money for the church roof. Part of the field was roped off into an arena for family races, tug of war and the dog show. At the moment the boys' brigade band were playing and marching to the music.

Tim pleaded to go on a roundabout and pulled Alice towards it. Bethany followed them, saying, 'I'll stay with Mum. Tim will want to try everything. We'll get some deckchairs by the front of the arena. It's two o'clock now. What time is the judging, Steve?'

'Three thirty.' He eyed the beer tent appreciatively.

Maxine interrupted, 'You have your beer. I've just seen a couple of school friends including Lillian whose party I'm going to miss. If I stay with them I might avoid Mum insisting I enter the egg and spoon race. It's so childish. The family races start at two thirty. But I'll have to watch Tim when he enters the sack race.'

His eyes crinkled at the corners. 'Pity you think the races childish. I thought I'd better show willing so I'll have to ask Bethany to partner me in the three-legged race.'

'I can outrun Bethany any day.' Excitement rippled through her as she pictured herself tied ankle to ankle with Steve, their arms round each other as they participated in the race. 'And I'm dressed for it in shorts. I was always top at athletics in school. Bethany can partner Tim. But we'll need to practise getting our balance and pace right.'

He chuckled. 'You're very competitive. It's meant to be fun.'

'Oh, I'm very competitive, Steve. When I set myself a goal I don't give up until I achieve it.'

She favoured him with a long assessing look before turning on her heel and swinging her hips provocatively in her tight white shorts. Steve watched her walk away wondering if he was seven kinds of an idiot for encouraging her.

As she joined her friends she was immediately surrounded by them, the girls asking who the dishy man was she had been talking to. It was a pity Ted wasn't there, she could have flirted with him and that might have made Steve take more notice of her.

'Just a friend,' she answered glorying in their envy. 'A rather special friend.'

'Are you going out with him?' Lillian asked. 'Ted will be put out.'

'Ted isn't my boyfriend.'

'So Steve is?' another friend, Hilary, persisted.

Maxine tapped the side of her nose. 'You can't mix business and pleasure. I help out at his vet's surgery. But wait and see how we move together in the three-legged race.'

Hilary sniffed with disbelief. 'I'd have thought he'd be more interested in your sister than you.'

'Shows how little you know, doesn't it.' Maxine bristled

at the challenge. She'd show them. They'd win that race and caught in the throes of their excitement Steve would clasp her to him and kiss her. Oh please, please, let them win.

Fate smiled on her. They won the race and with his arm still tight around her waist Steve leant to kiss her, but the kiss was placed firmly on her cheek not her mouth. He stooped to untie the rope around their ankles and when he straightened she rose on tiptoe to kiss his cheek. 'We make a great team.'

Before he could reply she took his hand as they walked to the prize-giving table and were presented with a wooden plaque. Bethany was untying herself from Tim and taking him back to the start line for the sack race. Maxine and Steve hurried back to the winning line as the race started. Tim bounded forward, his round face reddening from his exertions as he put his heart and soul into each jump. He was in third place and Maxine screamed encouragement, jumping up and down in excitement to spur him on. Tim started to laugh. His eyes were bright stars and his mouth was open with exhilaration. A dozen yards from the winning line he fell over. Undaunted and still laughing, he got up and clutching his sack bounded on only to fall three more times. Everyone had overtaken him and he still had some yards to go. He got up again and in four enormous jumps pitched himself over the line. The crowd cheered his enthusiasm and Bethany ran forward to hug him to her. Some of the children were crying because they had lost. Not so Tim, he was beaming with pleasure. His joy came from taking part and not the winning. He was an example to them all.

'There's one more race and then the dog show,' Steve

remarked. 'I'd better get over to the Stewards' tent and check the entries.' He ruffled Tim's auburn hair as he passed him. 'Well done, old chap.'

Tim was too engrossed to respond, having spotted a man selling balloons on the far side of the arena. 'Timmy want balloon.'

Bethany smiled lovingly. 'Let's get you one for being such a good sport and jumping so hard.' She turned to Maxine. 'Will you stay with Mum?'

She grimaced. 'Stop fussing, Bethany. Nothing is going to happen here.'

Bethany surveyed the crowd before answering. 'It doesn't do to be too careful where Giles is concerned.'

'I'll stay with Mum until you get back, but Lillian and Hilary were supposed to be coming over after the race.'

'I saw them with a couple of boys walking towards the refreshment tent after the three-legged race ended.'

'I'll find them later,' Maxine replied.

Alice was dozing in her deckchair. Despite the overcast sky the afternoon was warm and muggy. There would probably be a storm later. Maxine sat down on the grass beside her mother and watched the first of the dogs led into the arena. There were fifteen, half of which were mongrels and six were led in by children. The prize would go to the best turned-out dog who responded well to its owner's commands. Maxine devoured Steve with her gaze as he moved from contestant to contestant. At becoming aware that her mother was watching her and frowning, she diverted her attention to a Great Dane which was dragging its owner out of the arena. She didn't want her mother guessing how she felt about Steve. Alice may decide that it wasn't wise to allow him to stay on at the house.

Becoming restless, she decided to treat the others to an

ice cream. Whilst fetching them she could watch Steve unobserved by her mother. Alice was admiring Tim's balloon and two bitches in the arena had started to fight which attracted Bethany's attention as Maxine slipped away unnoticed by her family.

Giles pulled his trilby further down over his eyes as he watched Maxine detach herself from her family. In the last few weeks the women were never alone. He knew it would only be a matter of time before one of them became careless. He blended with the crowd keeping pace with Maxine. Not that he reckoned even Bethany would recognise him. He no longer looked the tramp he had become after leaving the hospital. He never thought of that place as an asylum. He hadn't been mad like the other inmates. His behaviour had stemmed from the injustice of being shut away after enduring the horrors of war. He was angry with the world. He'd learned to control that anger for his own purposes. Caged he was powerless. Freedom gave him power over others, the power he craved to right the wrongs done to him.

The money Alice had given him had bought him a decent suit and aware that his red hair was a give-away he had dyed it brown. His lashes and brows had always been darker and although they had a chestnut tinge they didn't look out of place with the new colour of his hair.

He could have wished for a less public place, having followed the family here when they left the house this morning. He'd bought himself a second-hand car out of the old girl's money and a couple of flutters on the horses which had come up trumps had provided him with rooms in the next street to their house. Earlier he had seen Maxine win the three-legged race with that interfering vet chap who had elected himself their guardian. Some guardian the way he had kissed Maxine.

And the little slut kissed him back. Had she no shame? She was just like Bethany. Just like Louise. Whores the lot of them. Saliva dribbled from his mouth and he licked it away. The blood was pumping hard through his body as he saw Maxine join the queue by the ice-cream van.

The small fun fair catering for the younger children was clustered on one side of the field near the hedge. The ice-cream van was beside the caravans and trailers belonging to the fair. The couple ahead of Maxine in the queue were being served. They had four children all demanding different flavoured ice-lollies then changing their minds at the last minute. The father was cross and the mother was trying to pacify one bawling child. No one was behind Maxine and she leaned against the side of the van to count out her money for five large cones.

She looked back across to the arena through a space in the crowd and saw Steve handing over a small silver cup to the winner of the dog show. He looked so handsome, her expression became dreamy with longing.

The blow to the back of the neck which stunned her registered as a brief flaring of pain. Her knees sagged and an arm around her waist dragged her behind the van. Before her wits recovered enough to retaliate, a second blow to the neck keeled her over and blackness descended.

[illegible] who had [illegible] their guardian. Some [illegible] on the way [illegible] Hazards.

And [illegible] Hall [illegible] the Lamas. [illegible]

[illegible]

[illegible]

[illegible]

[illegible]

[illegible]

Chapter Twenty-Six

'A day like this is just what we needed,' Alice declared. 'It has been so enjoyable. Where's Maxine by the way?'

Bethany frowned. She had been here a moment ago. Anxiety gripped her. Her stomach clenched as her gaze searched through the crowds.

'Perhaps she went off with her friends,' Alice added but her voice echoed Bethany's rising fear.

'She would have told us.' Then she spotted Maxine by the ice-cream van. 'It's all right, she's getting an ice cream.'

Bethany made to go after Maxine but Alice put a hand out to stop her. 'She'll be all right. Don't fuss so.'

Bethany relaxed her guard. She couldn't help being over-protective. Perhaps her mother was right. Maxine was sixteen and couldn't be cossetted all the time. It was hard to let go. Harder still to quell the instinct of danger. Was she being melodramatic? Her attentions swerved to Steve who was presenting the cup to the winning owner of an old English sheepdog. When her gaze again swivelled back to Maxine she was gone.

Panic raced through her, clawing at her heart and twisting her stomach into a knot. Her stare raked the crowd. There was no sign of Maxine. 'I can't see her. Mum, get Steve's attention. Tell him to help us look for her.'

She began to run towards the ice-cream van. Fear channelled through her veins and an icy sweat had broken out down her spine. She confronted the couple with the four children, her voice hoarse with dread. 'There was a black-haired young woman here a minute ago. She was in white shorts. Where did she go?'

'Didn't notice no one,' the husband snapped at her. The kids were whining that they now wanted candyfloss. He clipped two of them round the ear. 'Ungrateful buggers. Eat yer bloody lolly. Yer ain't getting nothing else.'

The wife, seeing Bethany's anxiety, gave her a sympathetic smile. 'She was 'ere. I didn't see 'er leave. I 'ad me 'ands full with the kids. She's probably larking around with 'er mates. Ain't nothing but trouble at that age.'

Steve was running towards her calling out, 'Any luck?'

She shook her head. 'I'll try the refreshment tent where her friends went.'

'I passed that on the way over. No sign of her.' His face was pale beneath its summer bronzing. 'I'll check the lane first. Better to split up and search opposite sides of the field.'

He sprinted into the lane. Three cars were parked and unattended. A black Morris was turning right at the crossroads. It didn't slow down and took the corner dangerously fast. It was heading out of town on the main road towards Epping Forest. Had Giles followed them and abducted Maxine? The thought filled him with horror.

Instinct told him Maxine was in that car. He couldn't let it get away. They'd come in Bethany's car which was parked round the front of the church. He'd have given anything at that moment to have his motorbike here.

As he ran back to the arena frantically searching for black dancing curls amongst the crowd, he reasoned he was overreacting. But the instinctive certainty remained. Maxine was in danger.

Alice was holding Tim's hand, looking sick with worry. He shook his head as he ran past her to meet up with Bethany.

'Do you think Giles was here?' Bethany said, her voice quivering with fear.

'A car was speeding off in the lane. Give me your keys. It will be long gone by now, but I've got to try and catch it. Stay with Alice. I could be on a wild goose chase and Maxine turns up in twenty minutes with her friends wondering what all the fuss is about.'

Bethany handed over the car keys. 'Maxine knew we were leaving at five. We'll have to stay until then in case she turns up. I'll give her what for if she's gone off with her friends. We'll take the bus home.'

Their gazes held. Both were bleak with fear.

A violent jolt of her body jerked Maxine to semi-consciousness. Her body was swaying, bumping and vibrating. There was a loud droning in her ears. Her mouth felt as if cotton wool was stuffed in it. She tried to move her tongue. It contacted cloth. A gag had been tied over her mouth. Fear began to swell. Pain throbbed through her entire body as though someone had used it as a football. Her eyes opened to darkness. The smell of petrol cloyed at her nostrils. Cramps seized her legs. She couldn't straighten them.

She struggled to awaken fully and shake off the nightmare images. They remained. The pain and darkness were terrifyingly real. The droning was a car engine. She must be in the boot. How had it happened? Memory flooded back. The fête. Her going off to treat the others to ice cream. Giles?

Dear God help her! Giles had abducted her. Icy dread churned her stomach. Vomit rose to her throat which threatened to choke her. Desperately, she swallowed it down. The acid taste burned her gullet. She mustn't panic. If she did the fear would weaken her. She had to be strong. She had to be ready for Giles.

Tentatively, she moved her arms and legs. They were not bound. From the way her body was being bumped about they were not on a proper road but a rough track. He must be taking her somewhere isolated. For what reason? Rape? Murder? The possibilities were terrifying. She stamped them down. Giving in to her fear would leave her at his mercy.

Her hands moved to snatch off the gag and halted. Better if she looked unconscious when he opened the boot, but her body would be braced and ready for him. To escape she would need to catch him off guard. Her heart was hammering painfully. She struggled to take deep breaths in the stuffy atmosphere. She must stay calm.

To ease the pain in her cramped legs she shifted position and began to massage the muscles. Gradually the pain lessened. The car was slowing. It stopped and the engine was cut.

Steve slammed the car door shut and ran into the house. Bethany, white faced, her violet eyes shadowed with fear, leapt out of her chair. It confirmed his worst fears.

'I'm sorry. There was no sign of the car. I even skirted round part of Epping but it could be anywhere. Even if she was in it.'

'I stopped by at Lillian's house but she left the fête earlier and hadn't seen Maxine after the races.'

'I'll phone the police.' Steve battled against nightmare

images of Maxine being hurt or violated. His rage boiled. He was helpless to save her.

'I did that when we got home, and gave them her description and Giles's. They were issuing it to all their patrols.'

Bethany's haunted eyes went to the mantelpiece clock. 'It's been three hours. Anything could have happened. She could be dead.' Tears streaked her cheeks. 'Why didn't I go to her when I saw her by the ice-cream van? I wanted to. But I thought I was being too protective. She hated being fussed over.'

'I suggested the day out,' Steve groaned. 'Then left her to her own devices. We could go on blaming ourselves all night. Giles outwitted us. Where's Alice and Tim?'

'They're outside feeding the animals. I thought it best if Mum had something to occupy her but one of us had to stay by the phone.' Bethany slumped on the chair and tears streamed down her cheeks. 'I'm to blame. I loved her too much. She'll never know how much I loved her.'

The boot lock creaked as it turned and the grey evening light streaked in. It carried with it chill flecks of rain. Maxine lay still, her eyes closed. A vicious prod in the ribs with a stick brought a moan to her lips.

'Get out of the car. You aren't unconscious.'

Another brutal jab opened her eyes. He'd break a rib if he hit her again. Her ploy had failed. It was the first time she had seen her half brother. The hostility in his eyes shocked and frightened her. He would show her no mercy.

He stepped back giving her enough room to clamber out but not enough so that she could make a run for it. Her legs were reassuringly strong as they took her weight. She feigned a cramp and fell to the ground clutching them in agony. The stick, thick as a man's wrist, descended on her shoulder.

'Get up. You can walk. You're no weakling. I saw you run today and the way you haul hay bales when feeding the ponies.' The stick was raised again.

Maxine held up a hand to fend it off and heaved herself to her feet. She tore off the gag, her violet eyes blazing. 'What do you want with me? I haven't got any of the money you think is yours. Dad never wanted girls around. Mum's income is paying for my education.'

She glanced around. They were in a wood. The trees were thick and there was no sign of human life. A wood pigeon cooed, otherwise all was eerily silent. Giles stared at her belligerently. He kept changing his grip on the stick and running his tongue over his lips. Menace emanated from him.

'It's because you're her daughter,' he sneered. 'I can get at her that way.'

'But I've never harmed you. I didn't understand why Mum wouldn't see you.'

'Guilt. The bitch thought she was better than me. You've got the same look about you. The same wanton streak.'

He was talking gibberish but at least while he was talking he wasn't harming her. Perhaps if she kept him talking, got to learn what he wanted from them . . .

His lunge took her by surprise and he swiped her across the face with the back of his hand. The blow sent her sprawling back against the car. Red and gold stars spiralled behind her eyes. She shook her head to clear it and her fingers were ready to claw at him if he came closer.

'She defied me,' he spat with venom. 'She used to look at me the way you are now. As though I was dirt. She thought she knew it all. She was a whore. Like you. I've seen the way you play up to your lover. Does he service you both now he's moved into the house?'

His eyes were bright with malice and saliva sprayed from his lips. Fear engulfed Maxine. She had thought Bethany had exaggerated the evil of which he was capable – now she knew it was no exaggeration. There was murder in his eyes. Trembling, she edged away from him but was trapped by the car boot pressing into the back of her thighs. He thrust his head forward like a bull terrier, his demonic gaze pitiless.

'Steve is a friend, not a lover.' Her voice cracked as she fought to combat her rising terror. 'And Mum's not a whore. Our father was the one who kept a mistress. Mum was always loyal to him.'

He began to laugh. The malignant cackle raised the hairs on her neck. 'So they've kept you ignorant of the truth, have they? That foolish bitch Alice isn't your mother. The stuck-up cow Bethany is. You're her little bastard. All these years they covered it up. Their secret. Their shame. That must have festered in Pa's gut having to provide a home for a bastard.'

Shock paralysed Maxine and she was incapable of seizing the chance to escape. Giles was insane. He had to be. 'You really are mad. Of course Alice is my mother!'

He shook his head, his grinning mouth evil as a gargoyle. 'They wanted the world to believe that. Alice miscarried when she learned her precious daughter was pregnant. They hid the truth. You're Bethany's daughter. Neither was Harold Warden your father. *I* am.'

She reeled as though a gun shot had thudded into her heart. It wasn't true. It was lies. All lies. Cruel, twisted, malicious lies. Bethany wasn't her mother. They would have told her. And Bethany had been in love with a doctor seventeen years ago. Giles was lying. There was no way he could be her father.

'I don't believe you. This is another trick to get more money out of Mum.'

'They'll pay up all right. I'm the only one besides them who knows the truth. The *News of the World* will pay handsomely to print the story of the famous children's writer and her secret bastard. And Bethany knows what I am capable of . . .' He sniggered.

The woodland canopy above her head revolved crazily. He wasn't lying. Bethany was her mother. So many little things began to make sense. How Bethany always took charge when she was younger. Them living together from the time she was three. But Giles couldn't be her father. Not this monster. She couldn't have his blood in her veins. But hadn't Bethany spoken of a woman Giles had raped. Was that woman Bethany?

The knowledge rocked her. It was all too probable. Bethany wouldn't have shown such loathing to anyone without strong reason. All Maxine had heard of Giles and his cruelties ricocheted through her mind, crippling her motion. She swayed and was close to swooning.

His face darkened. 'You're so like her. It will be a pleasure teaching you I won't be defied – as I taught her.' Lust glazed his eyes.

'That proves you're not my father.' She clung to a final hope. 'It would be incest.' Her outrage at his lies was pumping adrenaline through her giving her strength. She was tense, gauging the moment he would spring at her.

He snorted. 'So what? I had my twin sister whenever I wanted her from the age of thirteen. Bethany was more satisfying though. She had spirit. She resisted. The same spirit you possess. What better way is there to make that bitch Bethany suffer, than by me possessing you as well . . . ?'

Nausea threatened to overwhelm her. Thoughts flashed with lightning intensity through her mind, overriding her will to flee. How Bethany must hate her? She was a constant reminder of her sister's, my God no . . . her mother's defilement.

The chaotic thoughts juddered to a halt. But Bethany had never by a glance or word been anything but loving. She clung to that. It focused her strength and resurrected her need to fight him. Giles had sought to dominate Bethany by terror and had failed. He wouldn't succeed with her. For as long as she could remember she had adored Bethany. She had admired her independence and fortitude. She would not surrender to fate. She would fight this monster.

All at once her brain was crystal clear. A barely perceptible flicker in Giles's eyes was enough to warn her that he was about to pounce. She screamed and darted to one side and round the car. Then she was off in full flight. Momentarily, his fingers grazed her shoulder but she had been too quick for him. Thank God she was wearing shorts and flat pumps.

'You won't get away from me,' he yelled and thudded after her. She wove through the trees confident that she was faster and more agile than him. He may have been a soldier but he had been locked in an institution for several years and could not be as fit as herself.

Even so, Giles remained unnervingly close. She could hear the crashing of his heavy weight through the undergrowth and the rasp of his breathing. Her own lungs and throat began to ache as she pounded forward, leaping over fallen branches. She kept to well-trodden paths praying that her speed and stamina would save her. Still the sounds of pursuit were terrifyingly close. Giles had stopped screaming insults. She ran in silence conserving her breath. The blood crashed like waves on shingle through her head. Her legs were aching and beginning to tremble from the strain. She was slackening, unable to keep up the punishing pace. She dare not look round. A foot in the wrong place could bring her down. Teeth gritted against the pain, she ran on.

The trees were a blur as she laboured forwards. She guessed they were somewhere in Epping Forest. In which direction lay safety, a main road or a pub? It was impossible to tell. The sound of running feet behind her was less distinct. She risked a glance back. Giles was some distance behind her but still in pursuit. She paused to circle, desperate to get some bearing on her location. There was a faint hum of traffic to the right, or was it the thrumming of the blood still pounding in her head? Let it be traffic. The sky was overcast and in another hour it would be dark. In darkness lay safety. Before that hour was up she could be free – or dead.

'I'll get you, bitch!' Giles's threat carried to her. 'You won't escape me. None of you will.'

She bit back a sob and forced her exhausted figure onwards. The trees were thinning. The drone of a car engine was unmistakable. A road must be near by. If she could reach it, she would be safe. She stumbled on a slight incline grazing both knees and ploughed on heedless of the pain in her limbs and lungs. Ahead was the road. It wasn't busy but there were a couple of cars coming into view. Reeling drunkenly she began to wave. They had to stop and help her. Both sped past before she reached the Tarmac.

Another glance behind her showed Giles emerging from the trees. There was no car in sight. He was only a hundred yards from her when a motorbike appeared. Waving and sobbing she ran into the road and she heard the engine growl as it slowed through the gears. 'Help me,' she gasped. 'Please. Get me away from that man.'

Behind the crash helmet and goggles she glimpsed the face of a youngish man and beneath his leather jacket he was heavily built.

'Get up behind me,' he commanded. 'You got the strength to hang on?'

She nodded. From the corner of her eyes she saw Giles running back into the trees. Her rescuer glared after him. 'Tried it on, did he? Lucky I came along. Where d'yer live?'

'Leytonstone,' she said and hauled her trembling limbs over the seat and fell against him in relief as he revved the bike into life and they sped off down the road.

Maxine was still trembling when they pulled up in front of her house and the young man pulled the bike back on to its stand and lifted her off. 'Thank you,' she said, tears threatening to overtake her now that the danger was past. 'He was going to rape me.'

Her legs buckled and he caught her against him. At that moment the front door opened and Steve, Bethany and Alice hurried towards her.

'Thank God you're safe!' Bethany wept.

Steve stood back, stiff and antagonistic, his tone accusing. 'Is this a friend of yours?'

Maxine turned haunted eyes upon him. 'He saved my life. Giles abducted me. He bundled me in the boot of his car and—'

Reaction choked off her words and her sobs turned to a torrent. Bethany and Alice hugged her and led her into the house. 'It's all right. You're safe.' Alice was weeping as she walked. 'Giles didn't harm you, did he?'

Maxine shook her head, too upset to answer. The motorcyclist stood back looking embarrassed and addressed Steve. 'She came running out of the woods at Epping. There was a bloke behind her. He'd been chasing her. She was very cut up. Even so she had the presence of mind to run in the road and get me to stop. I'd have gone after the man. He looked a mean bastard, but the kid was so upset, I thought it best to get her home.'

Steve held out his hand. 'Come inside. We have a great deal to thank you for. Would you be prepared to speak to the police about what you saw?'

'Of course. Maniac like that should be locked up. Did she say he abducted her? Called him by name didn't she?'

'We know who he is,' Steve answered, gruffly. 'It's getting the evidence to have him arrested which we lacked.'

Chapter Twenty-Seven

Why couldn't anything concerning that fiend Giles be simple? He should be behind bars by now. The slippery devil had disappeared without trace.

Bethany was simmering with pent-up anger as she let the dogs out into the garden in the morning. It was five thirty and she had been unable to sleep. A warrant was out for Giles's arrest but he was too sly to be caught. He'd be aware he had gone too far this time. He'd lie low for days or even weeks, choosing his time to strike again.

Too restless to settle Bethany pulled her dressing gown around her and, thrusting her feet into her wellingtons, she decided to water the garden. The soft rush of the water through the spray of the hose was soothing, but not enough to calm her disquiet. So far luck had been with them and Giles had failed to harm any of the family, but he was a vindictive and vengeful enemy. He wouldn't give up.

But Maxine had not escaped unscathed. She had become withdrawn and uncommunicative to the point of avoiding everyone, including Steve. When Bethany tried to talk to her about her abduction the haunted look returned to her eyes.

'I'm fine,' Maxine flared up. 'I want to forget everything

about that day. Just leave me alone.' She ran up the stairs to her bedroom and banged the door shut.

Bethany sighed. Something was wrong but she couldn't force Maxine to talk to her until the younger woman was ready.

She shook herself to force thoughts of Giles from her mind. He was dominating her life. She resented that. To banish the power he insidiously wielded, she must concentrate on her work. She was falling behind with her writing schedule for the new novel. This week she was also heading a deposition to their local MP for better funding for Tim's school, and there was a committee meeting of the parent support group for the mothers coping with handicapped children. She mentally ticked off what had to be covered on the agenda. When unexpectedly she thought of Mark and whether he was out of hospital, she felt the familiar ache over her heart.

'Why can't you forget him?' she chided. 'He doesn't care for you. If he did he would have answered your letter. You can't turn back the clock and revive an old romance.'

She turned off the hose and saw Maxine in trousers and a jumper setting off towards the paddock to tend the animals. What was she doing up so early?

'Want any help?' she called.

She was ignored. Bethany frowned. It was unlike Maxine to be moody. Lifting the hem of her lilac candlewick dressing-gown which was trailing in the dew-covered grass, Bethany hurried to join Maxine. 'Hey, what's up?'

'Nothing,' she said quickening her pace.

'You and Steve had a row?' Bethany could think of nothing else which would make Maxine so surly.

'It's nothing to do with Steve.'

'Then there is something?'

The look Maxine turned on her was wracked with pain. 'Are *you* my mother?' she blurted out. 'Giles said you were. And that *he* was my father.'

It was the moment Bethany had been dreading for sixteen years, her daughter learning the truth from someone else. Why hadn't she told her? She had tried to so many times, but once Maxine learned that Bethany was her mother, she would have to explain who the father was. No child deserved to carry the burden of the brutal manner in which she had been conceived.

Maxine was staring at her accusingly. 'Has my whole life been a lie? A shameful secret to be covered up at all costs?'

'Oh, Maxine, don't ever think that!' Her own pain at her daughter's desolation fractured her voice. 'I'm proud to be your mother. It was to protect *you* from ridicule as much as myself. People have wicked minds and tongues.'

Maxine backed away from her. 'You must have hated me. I ruined your life. That monster raped you, didn't he?'

Bethany stretched out a hand in entreaty towards her daughter but Maxine ignored it. 'Yes, but you didn't ruin my life. You were my greatest joy. From the moment you began to move inside me you were wholly my child. You weren't to blame for what happened. I promised you before you were born that you would never suffer the consequences of your conception.'

Maxine remained tense and hung her head. There were tears streaming down her face prompting Bethany to tell her everything. She deserved that. Did Maxine feel that her real mother had rejected her because she had not been acknowledged?

She began slowly, her voice strangled from words locked deep in her heart. 'Harold wanted to throw me out of his home. I had this house to come to and Mum had put a thousand pounds of my father's money aside for me for when I married. She gave me that. But Mum knew I would be condemned by gossip. So she threatened to leave Harold if he threw me out. He had never given up his mistress after he married Mum. She said she would sue for a divorce on the grounds of adultery. The scandal would have ruined Harold's accountancy business. They had a terrible row and he hit Mum.' Bethany paused, her memories making her voice gruff. 'She miscarried a four-month-old girl the next day.'

'So I was to replace the child Harold's brutality had aborted.' Maxine sounded bitter.

Bethany's heart went out to her. 'Mum was desperate for more children. She'd had several miscarriages. She saw my pregnancy as a mixed blessing. I suppose guilt made Harold agree to the ruse we concocted. I lived with them until you were two. But the atmosphere in the house was unbearable. Harold made sure of that.'

She broke off. Maxine remained guarded against her, her arms wrapped across her chest, her body rigid. It tore at Bethany's heart, making it harder to go on. 'I had begun to sell my stories and two of the Jester novels had been published and were selling well. I was always a thorn in Harold's side. I thought it would make things easier for Mum if I came to live here. Harold refused to allow me to bring you with me. He dreaded the scandal which could ruin his business. I should have stood up to him then, but you were such a comfort to Mum that I continued with the deception.'

Again she had to pause. The anguish of parting from Maxine had been torture. 'I visited you and Mum every day while Harold was at work. I missed you so much, but I wanted to do what was best for you. When you were three

Harold started to hit you. That was when I took you away. I wanted Mum to come too, her nerves were in a terrible state. She wouldn't. I suppose she was too proud to admit that her marriage was a failure.'

'Poor Mum.' Maxine screwed her face up with pain. 'Oh, I suppose I should call her Gran now. And you . . .' Her voice broke. 'Do I call you Mother?'

'I feel I abandoned that privilege when I took the role of your sister.'

Bethany could no longer hold her daughter's stare. It had been the cruellest blow of all not to hear Maxine call her Mother. But it was a price worth paying if Maxine had been protected from gossip. She hadn't cared about her own reputation, although the work she did with children might have been jeopardised had the hospital governors known that she was an unmarried mother. She could have been considered unfit to visit the sick and give what help she could to the suffering.

'How come no one noticed that you were pregnant?' Maxine fired at her.

'Once I began to show I didn't go out. Neither did Mum. No one was told of her miscarriage. When it got near to my time I went to a nursing home outside London. Mum came with me and we returned with you three weeks later.'

'And no one suspected?'

'We took care that they didn't. Harold was insistent that a scandal was avoided.'

'So you lost the man you loved because of me?'

The anguish in her tone made Bethany reassure her. 'Mark's work was as much to blame. Then the war. It took him a long while to accept that you were my child. Once he did Mum had suffered another breakdown and her asthma attacks were worse. I couldn't leave her to live with him in Africa.'

'Did he know that Giles was my father?'

Bethany shook her head. 'I wouldn't tell him who your father was; just that I'd been raped at a New Year's Eve party. It's possible that he suspected from the way he questioned me.'

'It must have been rough for you.' Maxine looked at her through her fringe.

Bethany shrugged attempting to make light of the heartache she had suffered. 'It was difficult at first, but by then I had you. You were the one who was important. I loved you so much. I used to imagine that you were Mark's child but I knew that it was just wishful thinking.'

'There's no chance that I am, is there?' Violet eyes pleaded with her for reassurance.

Pain squeezed Bethany's chest and tears glistened in her eyes as she shook her head. 'I had been sleeping with Mark but not the month Giles raped me. He'd been doing extra duty at the hospital and I hadn't seen him.' Bethany took a deep breath and forced herself to hold her daughter's piercing stare. 'You grew up to be the image of me. There is nothing of Giles in you.'

'Even so, I'm to blame for you and Mark splitting up.' Maxine was pale, her body taut from her inner pain.

'If it was meant to be, it would have happened.'

'But you loved Mark. How could you sacrifice so much?'

'How could I put my happiness before Mum's health?' Bethany sighed. 'Harold used to hit her. I'd gone for him a couple of times when I found her battered. His violence caused her breakdown.'

Maxine was regarding her, her eyes still guarded but the tension in her body was less apparent. 'I'm not sure I could give up the man I loved. I'm not as selfless as you.'

Love for her daughter softened Bethany's voice. 'You would do the right thing. We had just come through the war as well. I was earning enough to be independent. Mark had a special calling for his work. I had family loyalty. I couldn't live with myself if I'd abandoned Mum when she needed me.'

'It must have been hell for you.'

'It had its compensations – my joy in you mainly. And although I missed Mark, I'd built a worthwhile life here in England. And Mum loved you like the daughter she had lost. When you came to live with me I was overjoyed. With Mum being ill the neighbours accepted that I was caring for you to help her get better.'

'Am I like that monster who raped you?' Her deeper torture was wrenched from her.

Bethany vehemently shook her head. 'There's not a mean streak in you, my darling.'

Maxine stared down at the grass. Bethany was wretched, aware of the torment Maxine must be suffering. She held out her arms but Maxine did not move into them and they fell to her sides. 'I love you, Maxine. To me you are the most precious gift I was granted in this life.'

She had hoped to allay her daughter's fear, let her know how special she was to both herself and Alice. Instead Maxine put her hand to her mouth and veered away and ran across the garden to the paddock. It took all Bethany's willpower to let her go. Her daughter had so much to come to terms with and she needed her own time to do it in.

When Bethany returned to the kitchen she found Steve brewing tea. 'What is it this morning?' she declared. 'It's only six and everyone is up.'

'I'm worried about Maxine.'

Bethany guessed that was an understatement. Steve looked haggard from lack of sleep. It was obvious to Bethany that he cared for Maxine, although she doubted he had admitted to himself how much the young woman meant to him.

'She's out feeding the horses. You might be the right person to speak with her.' Bethany searched her heart. Should she tell Steve the truth? He had been a good friend. She was drawn to trust him. But would Maxine see her confession as a betrayal? 'Giles told her some disturbing facts. Go to her.'

He rubbed his hand across the back of his neck. 'What can I say to help her? I'm terribly fond of her.'

'Forget the age difference if that's what is bothering you. Say whatever feels right. She needs someone to confide in. Someone she can trust.'

Steve nodded and wandered out to the paddock. Maxine was standing outside the stable currying Snowflake's coat.

'You look like you've got the weight of the world on your shoulders,' he began. To his dismay Maxine burst into tears.

'Hey, it can't be as bad as all that.' He drew her into his arms and held her against him until her sobs subsided. He could feel the shudders going through her slender figure and the pressure of her breasts through her jumper against his chest. Her eyes were like sparkling amethysts when she looked up at him.

'I don't know who I am any more,' she confessed. 'When I think of him . . . that I am part of his blood . . . part of the evil and brutality . . . I feel tainted. Ashamed. I've caused so much suffering . . . I wish I'd never been born.'

'Don't say that.' He held her tighter. He could smell the

scent of her hair and skin; both of which were intoxicating. The heat of her body burned his hands, rousing emotions far from the friendship he had come out here to offer. 'Nothing can be so bad. Giles didn't harm you, did he?' Fear and anger gruffened his voice and he stroked her hair as he would calm a nervous dog before an examination at the surgery. Her silky black curls had a life of their own and the urge to bury his head in the sweet-smelling tresses was almost more than he could bear. Huskily, he insisted, 'Tell me what's wrong.'

His touch and sympathetic tone broke through her reserve. 'It's awful. You'll hate me when you know the truth.'

'I don't think I could hate you, Maxine. Let's sit down by the fishpond.' He kept his arm around her as they walked and held her close when they were seated.

She had to talk to someone and it seemed so natural to turn to Steve. She prayed he wouldn't turn from her in horror. Keeping her eyes lowered so that she would not see any accusation in his eyes, she related everything Giles and Bethany had told her. As she spoke the blood drained from her features leaving her face pale and strained. Sometimes her voice was a hoarse whisper, at others it rose with her torment. When she finished there was silence.

Maxine sat stiffly. Was it the silence of judgement? Of condemnation? Despair crashed over her. She struggled to maintain her pride, her voice faltering as she added, 'I understand if you don't want me to work at the surgery. Or if you wish to move out. You're here rather under false pretences. Our family has a lurid past.'

'None of which you, Bethany or Alice are responsible for.' Anger made his voice rasp. 'It explains a lot.'

Still she did not lift her head. Steve hadn't moved. His

arm was across her shoulders and she could feel the tension emanating from him, the muscles coiled and tightened. The heat of his body scorched through her clothing where their bodies touched at torso and thigh. She risked a glance up at him through her lashes. She had never seen the lean contours of his face look so fierce and formidable. Or at the same time the lambent radiance in his eyes glow with such tenderness and yearning. It was a trick of the brightening sky where the sun was breaking through the dispersing cloud, she reasoned. How could it be anything else . . . ?

Steve was harnessing a vortex of emotions. Fury at Giles. Sympathy for Bethany and Alice. Turmoil for this haunted and sweetest of women. Maxine had burrowed beneath his guard, her trembling form in his arms innocent and infinitely sultry. Midnight velvety curls rioted over her shoulders in dishevelment. He could feel the hard pounding of her heart and his own responded. When her stare met his gaze, his mouth dried. She was so lovely, so vulnerable. It was that vulnerability which stayed his need to kiss her. Only an unfeeling lecher would use her pain and moment of weakness against her. Her lips parted, inviting. Somehow he resisted.

'I hate him,' she sobbed. 'I hate the man who fathered me. I have that same evil in me.'

His throat worked but he did not speak. He couldn't. Instead he held her closer, his lips moving to her hair. She clung to him, beautiful but forlorn: needing solace, consolation, needing to be loved. 'There is no evil in you, only sweetness – such sweetness.'

With a strangled groan he kissed her hair. In his need to protect and reassure her, he whispered against her ear and along her cheek until her mouth trembled below his. The soft lips parting beneath his own were warm, tremulous as though expecting rebuttal. How could he have rejected her before? He had tried to be noble and to conquer the desire this young woman roused. Giles's attack had shown him how deeply she had inveigled herself into his soul. Her kiss was transfixing. Its sweetness was profound. He had intended reassurance and was unprepared for the passion which careened through him. She was soft and yielding. Their kiss deepened and her back arched, moulding her slender frame against him.

Even as his ardour clamoured to possess her, he knew this was not the time. He would not take her while she was still so vulnerable. Taking her face in his hands, he gently eased back from her.

The spell was broken. Maxine had surrendered to the splendour of his kiss. A cocooning weave of magic encompassed her, healing her heartache, her uncertainty and pain. Steve didn't despise her. He cared. The kiss was her salvation. It restored her confidence and brought her life back into perspective. The trauma of learning the circumstances of her birth was no longer a desolate abyss. She'd had no control over those events in the past. Wasn't the future still hers to shape as she willed?

Though Steve had drawn back, Maxine kept her eyes closed. She could feel him watching her. She needed to savour this moment. Hold on to the promise it held. His fingers light as gossamer traced the line of her cheek and curved along the column of her throat and his voice was soft against her ear. 'Look at me, my darling.'

Leisurely her eyes opened and she saw the love she had dreamed of shining in his eyes. He grinned. 'I think it's time I had a serious chat with your mother and grandmother about your future.'

Chapter Twenty-Eight

'You look done in,' Peg chirped when Bethany called in on her friend.

Bethany explained the events following the church fête. 'I'm almost at the end of my tether. Steve has helped so much by being at the house at nights, but during the day I'm on edge never knowing when Giles will strike next.'

'He isn't daft enough to try anything else for some time. The police are after him for kidnapping Maxine. He'll do time for that.'

'When they catch him. *If* they catch him. Giles is a wily devil.'

Peg studied her with concern. They were in the long cool kitchen of Peg's house. Her baking assistant Mrs Brooks was flat-icing a cake and Peg was fashioning almond paste into a teddy bear to go on a children's cake. She finished the face and put it aside and washed her hands.

'I've come at a bad time,' Bethany said picking up her handbag. 'I dropped in to give you your card. Happy anniversary.'

'You've forgotten that you're coming out with us tonight to celebrate at the River Boat club, haven't you?'

Bethany put her hand to her head. 'It completely slipped my mind with all the worry. I thought we were going on

Saturday. I'll be poor company, I'm afraid.'

Peg shook her head and pulled off her apron. 'I won't hear of you cancelling. I'm going shopping to get myself a new dress and you can treat yourself as well.'

'I can't leave Mum for so long.'

'No excuses. Alice can stay with her friend Val. Tim is at school and Maxine at the surgery. It's time you indulged yourself. The full works. Something stunning and slinky to wear tonight: a shampoo and set, facial and a manicure. You need a bit of spoiling. You've taken on too much.'

'I had no choice.'

Peg lifted a pencilled brow. 'It's all very well being independent, Beth, but a woman can only do so much. Had you married, Giles is too much of a cowardly creep to have shown his face round your door.'

Bethany answered with a strained smile, 'Why won't you accept that I am content enough as I am?'

'Because you'd make a wonderful wife. And you've been a wonderful mother to Maxine. You dote on Tim. And you've still got time to have another child.' Peg grinned. 'I've got another on the way. I hope it's another girl then I'll have three of each.' She looked ruefully at her spreading figure. 'By Christmas I'll be as big as a house. So I'm making the most of being glamorous tonight. And it's time you relaxed and treated yourself by coming up West this morning for a shopping spree. And no backing out of tonight. It would spoil my evening.'

'As long as Frank is at your side, you don't notice anyone else,' Bethany teased.

'Ah, Frank is still a terrific-looking guy and I'm such a dumpling. He's never so much as looked at another woman since we were wed though.'

'He knows when he's well off. You two were meant for each other.'

'So are you coming up West? This is going to be your day as much as mine, I feel it in my bones.'

At nine thirty that evening Bethany was feeling the strains of walking the entire length of Oxford Street before Peg had found the dress she wanted. In the second shop they entered Bethany had chosen a simple off-the-shoulder black number with a pencil-slim skirt and a fitted waist-length amethyst silk jacket which brought out the violet in her eyes. It had been relaxing to sit in the hair salon for an hour and a half being pampered. Yet when their party of six alighted from the two taxis outside the River Boat club, the effects of so many sleepless nights were making her feel heavy and tired.

It was a club she had often meant to visit but never got round to. It was one of the best jazz clubs in London owned by Mike Rivers, a pianist and saxophonist whose band was frequently on the wireless. They had made several records which had become popular hits. It wasn't just a night club. True to its name it was a converted pleasure boat which would sail down the river during the evening while its customers dined in the restaurant and danced to the Mike Rivers Band.

Inside it was grander than she expected. While they were being led to their dining table she recognised two well-known actors, a singer, and a man and woman who she thought were artists and had appeared in an arts programme last month on the television.

'Some place, isn't it?' Peg said gazing round at the thirties-style art decor on the wood panelling of the walls. 'Frank brought me here for our seventh wedding anniversary and we've been back at least once a year for a special occasion ever since.'

They went up a flight of wooden steps to the restaurant. 'It's different than I expected.' Bethany was impressed by the subdued wall lighting behind coloured triangular glass shades. Every dining table was candlelit with a small bowl of fresh flowers giving it a romantic atmosphere. The restaurant was a semicircular half deck which formed a balcony to look down on to the dance floor and stage below.

Beside Peg and Frank, their party was made up of Bethany and Carol, a friend of Peg's who had been widowed in the war, and Jack and Michael, Peg's brothers. Jack had never married and Michael was now divorced after a disastrous wartime marriage. Matchmaking between Bethany and Carol and her two single brothers was one of Peg's passions, although it was destined for failure. Carol fancied Michael but he was too intent on playing the field after his divorce to settle with one woman. Jack and Bethany knew each other too well to be other than good friends.

They ordered drinks and Bethany gazed out of the windows as the restaurant set off from its moorings and began to move upriver past the Houses of Parliament towards Hampton Court. Gradually, the weariness and strain of the last weeks began to ebb. The company was amusing with Frank and Jack telling jokes and anecdotes which made Bethany laugh and temporarily forget her worries.

Halfway through their meal Bethany became aware that Peg kept scanning the tables and ballroom below.

'Looking for someone?' Bethany teased.

Peg coloured. 'Silly. You get a lot of famous people in

here. I'd hate to miss seeing a celebrity.'

At that moment Mike Rivers himself came on to the stage to a round of applause. He was nearing sixty, for his band had been popular for over thirty years, but you would never guess it from his appearance. He looked at least ten years younger. He wore a white dinner jacket and black trousers. He had a debonair presence, his tall figure still slim and he also wore a ruby tie and handkerchief – his special trademark in tribute to his wife the famous singer, Ruby Starr. Bethany wondered if Ruby would be appearing tonight. She often did when not on tour.

As the applause died down Mike Rivers lifted the saxophone to his lips and the soulful blues number sent a *frisson* of pleasure down Bethany's spine. It was pure magic. The lights went down for his fourth number, leaving just a single spotlight on the musician. As the final notes faded a second spotlight focused on a scarlet-sequin-clad woman with long silvery blonde hair perched on a stool by the piano. The applause was deafening. Mike Rivers crossed the stage to sit at the piano and played the opening notes of a sultry number Ruby Starr had made famous a decade ago.

'Wish I could look as good as her when I'm in my forties,' Peg sighed wistfully. 'When she was at the London Palladium a couple of years ago they still billed her as England's sex goddess. Ooh, and look – that famous artist, Faith Tempest, is sitting over there.' Peg tipped her head towards a couple. 'That's her with her husband, the Irish artist Dan Brogan.'

Bethany glanced at the couple watching Ruby. They were the artists she had recognised from the television programme. Ruby looked up at them and winked and blew the handsome Irishman a kiss. The singer may be notorious but there was a charm about her and a sense of irrepressible fun.

Ruby was singing her last number when there was a stirring of interest from the men around the bar at the back of the dance floor. Peg who was again looking around the diners nudged Bethany. 'That's Selena Rivers, Mike and Ruby's daughter. She's a Rank starlet. Wasn't she wonderful in that film with Dirk Bogarde we saw the other month?'

Michael gave a low whistle and both he and Jack couldn't take their eyes off the blonde starlet.

'She's even sexier in the flesh than on the screen,' Michael drooled.

'She's too young for you.' Peg tweaked her brother's ear. 'C'mon, we should be dancing. Mike Rivers and Ruby are taking a break and couples are getting on the floor to dance. C'mon Frank. Get those old bones of yours moving.'

Jack stood up and asked Bethany to dance. 'You look terrific as always,' he said as he placed a hand in the centre of her back and they walked to the dance floor. Years of dancing together had made them accomplished partners. Whether the rhythm was fast or slow they moved around the floor in perfect unison.

After several dances, the last two more energetic than the rest, Bethany pleaded with a laugh, 'Enough. I've got to sit down. Peg dragged me the length of Oxford Street this afternoon.'

'Just one more slow number,' Jack insisted, pulling her close. 'A place like this is real romantic and if I don't dance with you, I'll have to partner Carol and she'll be angling for me to get her a date with Michael.'

They moved into each other's arms, their bodies close as

they swayed in time to the music. Jack squeezed her. 'I don't know why you and I never did get it together,' he said, his mouth against her ear. 'I've always fancied you.'

'And every other passable woman in London as well. You're the biggest flirt I know. You'll never settle down.'

'Will you?' he teased, but his words did not bring her customary smile.

'You know me, footloose and fancy free.'

'But you're not. You try and give everyone that impression. Out of all your male friends, how many of them did you allow to become serious after Mark Greenwood? Three? They all wanted to marry you but you turned them down.'

'Let's go back to the table.' She broke from his arms and walked away. She didn't want to think about her life – her past boyfriends. There had been only one who was important. The other three men she had dated for longest had all been pale replicas of Mark in looks and manner. None had possessed that special something which had been uniquely Mark.

All at once the dance floor and restaurant felt uncomfortably stuffy. She needed some air. The small top deck was open to the elements with seats by the railings. She ignored the couples cuddling together and moved to the railing to watch the scenery go by. The River Boat had reached its farthest point and had already swung about to return to its mooring. She hugged her arms around her as the chill fresh air hit her and lifted her face to the wind. Bethany struggled to blot out the memories of Mark which were so vivid and which often haunted her. It was midnight and the notes of Big Ben struck the hour and carried along the river. The witching hour. The time of bewitchment and illusion. If only Mark were with her here now . . .

Her eyes misted and the image conjured. She closed her eyes to dispel it. What use to dwell upon a lost love? He had not answered her letter. She had been foolish to believe that he would. Too much had happened since they had declared their love so long ago. The image wavered and she opened her eyes. Then blinked rapidly. It had reappeared.

A man, the image of Mark, except that his face was leaner and his hair flecked with grey, was smoking a cigarette and watching her from several feet away in the shadow of an overhead lamp.

She swayed and put her hand to her head to banish the image. When she looked at him again the similarity remained. She clutched on to the railing for support. It couldn't be Mark . . .

'You look as shocked as I was when I saw you on the dance floor.' The man's voice was unmistakable, even though it was huskier than she remembered. 'You haven't changed. You're as beautiful as ever. Is Jack now your husband? He was often hanging round you as I remember?'

'I have no husband.' She somehow found the voice to answer. It was all so dreamlike meeting like this. 'We're here to celebrate Peg and Frank's anniversary. I've never been before.'

'I'm with a couple of doctors and their wives. They're into the social scene and thought it was time I got out more. I only came out of hospital last week.'

Mark had made no move to close the gap between them and Bethany was too shaken to move in case her trembling legs gave way. The coloured lights strung from the rigging illuminated the deck but she could not see Mark's face clearly. He was holding his arm close to his chest and she remembered his wounds. Was it possible that he had not received her letter? 'I saw that you had returned to England from the newspapers.'

'I got your letter.'

Her hopes, which had begun to rise with every surging beat of her heart, turned to dust. He had received it and ignored it. She struggled to recover her composure. They were as awkward as strangers. 'It's been nice seeing you again,' she said, her voice hesitant as she fought to control her pain. 'I hope you're fully recovered. It must have been horrific in Kenya while the Mau Mau were attacking so many Europeans.'

'I was lucky to escape with my life.'

She nodded. 'I'm glad you did. You're too good a doctor to have lost your life in such a way. You have so much still to give.' The chill air made her shiver, she wasn't sure she could trust her legs to carry her away from Mark with the dignity she would have liked. She summoned all her will-power to act naturally. 'I have to rejoin my friends. Good luck, Mark.'

'Is that all you have to say? You can't mean to go.'

'What have we to say? You didn't even reply to my letter.' Her hurt rose up and would not be stemmed.

'Because I was not the man you remembered. If I had written to you, you would have come to the hospital. I didn't want anyone to see me like that. Then there was David, my son. He's found it hard to accept his mother's death. I've so much to make up to him. I'm leaving for the country tomorrow to be with him for a month before I resume my work at the hospital here. But I'd like to see you again.'

'I'd like that.' She felt as breathless as a schoolgirl and silently berated herself for being so foolish.

He moved towards her. The light fell on his features,

leaner, sculptured from experience, but as handsome as she remembered. His hair was cropped short and there was a red jagged scar curling down his temple to the edge of his brow. The newspapers had mentioned a head wound. The scar did not spoil his looks.

'Bethany, you're shivering.' Mark removed his dinner jacket and placed it around her shoulders, adding softly, 'I willed you to come up on deck alone. I wanted to ask you to dance but . . .' A wry smile twisted his lips. 'It was too public and you were with Peg and having a good time with your friends. I didn't feel the circumstances in the club were right for our first meeting after so many years. But for the last hour I've been unable to take my eyes off you. Will you let me drive you home?'

'But your arm? Can you drive so far and back?'

'Exercise strengthens the muscles which were damaged. If you'd gone home tonight without coming up here, I would have called at your house early tomorrow before leaving for Dorset where David is staying with his aunt and uncle.'

Again her emotions swelled, her pulse racing. She struggled for calm. This was foolish. Seventeen years was a long time. They had both changed. 'I'll make my farewell to Peg.' Reluctantly she slipped his jacket from her shoulders. The pleasure of feeling the warmth of his body, which the jacket retained, had stirred memories of their passion.

He lifted a hand to caress the side of her cheek. 'You really are as lovely as I remember.'

But you married another woman. The silent accusation reverberated through her mind as she rejoined Peg's table and whispered in her friend's ear.

'Peg, forgive me for leaving but I've just met Mark Greenwood. I can't believe he was here. He's driving me home when the boat docks.'

There was a twinkle in her friend's eye.

'Peg, did you somehow arrange this?'

'I thought he wasn't going to show up. Then I caught sight of him with a group of men at the bar when we were dancing. They were obviously not here to dine. I thought it was a mean trick not bothering to contact you after you wrote to him. And what with the trouble with Giles, well, I thought you needed cheering up. So I dropped him a line care of the hospital. I sort of mentioned that we would be here tonight. Good luck.' Peg kissed her cheek.

'Why didn't you tell me?'

'Either you would have refused to come, or you'd have built up your hopes and he may not have turned up. When he didn't ask you to dance I could have sloshed him. I suppose it didn't help with our Jack all over you as usual. Anyway, it's all turned out well. I'll be round tomorrow to find out how everything went.'

'Don't go getting ideas. Mark is off to Dorset tomorrow for a month to visit his son.'

As she came down from the restaurant Mark was waiting at the foot of the steps. 'There's a half hour before we dock. Now we've broken the ice shall we dance?'

'I'd love to.' To feel Mark's arms around her again was heavenly. Her heart was beating so wildly she feared he would hear it. The warmth of his cheek pressed against hers made the breath catch in her throat. Her love for him resurfaced, threatening to overwhelm her. A cautious inner voice counselled, *Don't expect too much. He's been married. Just act as though this is a reunion with an old friend.*

By the time the River Boat docked half an hour later, for Bethany it was as though the intervening years had never been. She was a young girl again, her heart filled with love. It was torture to act as though her emotions were uninvolved.

On the drive home Mark questioned her about her novels and work with sick children. She, in turn, wanted to know everything about his work in Africa. Then as they approached her house she asked Mark to park in the road outside and not the drive. The engine might waken Alice who slept in the front.

When the engine died, she sat feeling awkward for a moment. He had made no move to kiss her. She gripped her sequinned evening bag tightly and said softly, 'I read about your wife's death in the papers. Ivory poachers, wasn't it? I'm sorry, Mark.'

He stared at the steering wheel. 'That's Africa for you. Magnificent but savage. She was dedicated to her work. It was a cruel death.'

Compassion overrode her reservations and her hand slid over his. 'It must have been difficult to come to terms with.'

He didn't answer for a long moment and Bethany removed her hand. Finally he said, 'Guilt made it worse. Our marriage was a mistake.' He sank back in the driving seat. 'Peg said in her letter that Giles was causing problems.'

He had deliberately turned the subject and gave her no time to assess his statement about his marriage. She answered automatically. 'Yes. He's made threats and even kidnapped Maxine. Thank God she got away from him. There's a warrant out for his arrest.' Then unable to bear the strain of secrecy any longer she forced out, 'You should know the truth. Giles is Maxine's father. He told her everything when he kidnapped her. She is taking it hard.'

'So it was that bastard. I guessed as much though I hoped I was wrong.' Deep lines of pain indented around his eyes and mouth. 'I left that party because I was angry after our quarrel, if I'd stayed . . .'

'Don't blame yourself. It was a long time ago.'

The silence between them was weighted. Mark rubbed his hand across his brow. 'I do blame myself. That's what I found so hard to accept when I learned Maxine's birth date. I should have been there to protect you.'

'If it hadn't happened that night Giles would have found another chance. It was the only way he could wreak his vengeance upon me for always defying him.'

Mark's fist slammed down on the steering wheel. 'That bastard has always been disturbed. I reckon he was responsible for David Lister's death. None of the shooting party could understand how the accident happened. We were all too careful. I don't like to think of you three women alone.'

'We're not.' Bethany explained about Steve moving in.

'That will set the neighbours' tongues wagging.' He didn't sound too pleased.

'Let them wag. Besides a romance has blossomed from it. Steve has asked Maxine to marry him. They're getting married when she's eighteen.'

'If they love each other I'm not so sure it's wise to wait.'

Their gazes fused. Regret and sadness mirrored the poignancy of their own memories of a blighted romance. Bethany didn't want their reunion to carry any reproaches from the past. She forced lightness into her voice. 'We're having an engagement party for them in the garden here three weeks on Saturday. If you're back from Dorset by then and would like to come?'

'I want to see you again, but not . . .' He broke off at a tapping on the car window.

Bethany started, having seen no one approach. It was

Maxine and behind her the front door was open and the porch light on. Bethany opened the window. 'Is anything wrong?'

Maxine looked radiant. 'I know I shouldn't have come out here like this, but I thought it was Peg with you in the car.' She held out her left hand where a diamond glittered on the third finger. 'We got the ring today and Steve said I could wear it.'

Bethany laughed. 'He spoils you.' She turned to Mark to introduce them. 'This is Maxine. Maxine you've heard me speak of Mark Greenwood.'

Mark wasn't looking at her, he was staring at Maxine. 'She is the image of you,' he said in a cracked voice. 'She's just like you when we first met.'

Maxine was now the one who was flustered. She stepped back from the car. 'I've interrupted your talk. Sorry. I was too excited. I'll let you say goodnight in peace.'

As Maxine walked away Bethany opened the door. 'Thank you for bringing me home, Mark.'

'I'll be at the party if I'm back in London. It's just that . . .' His face was tense and his eyes harrowed with pain.

'You thought Maxine would look like Giles. I shall understand if you don't contact me.' She got out of the car hating herself when she could feel her eyes filling up with tears.

'Bethany, I was wrong all those years ago.' He was looking not at her, but the house where Maxine had disappeared. 'But seeing Maxine and learning the truth . . .' He broke off, his voice rough. 'I still have David to consider.'

She straightened and pasted on a watery smile. 'I understand.'

Chapter Twenty-Nine

The morning of Maxine and Steve's engagement Bethany woke up feeling edgy and nervous. Engagements now left a bitter taste in her mouth. Memories returned of Louise and David's engagement and the tragic aftermath. Giles's engagement had led to his attack on her. She would feel less anxious if Giles was locked up, but he had disappeared without trace. There had been no phone calls, no malicious letters, no signs that he had been prowling around the garden. Why then did she not feel relieved? It had the ominous lull of quiet before a storm, or the peace in the eye of a hurricane before destruction returned with greater devastation.

The police had been alerted and a patrol would be passing the house every half hour during the celebrations. Everyone who knew the circumstances of Giles's return had been cautioned to be vigilant. Any suspicion that Giles was in the vicinity and the police would be called.

Bethany had done all she could to counter any retaliation from Giles. Yet she couldn't relax. Intuition warned her that this was the kind of event that would draw Giles to exact his revenge upon them.

To keep from worrying she had rechecked all the arrangements. A marquee had been erected in the garden in case the weather turned against them. At present it was overcast but dry. Hundreds of tiny white fairy lights had been draped through the trees and around the garden to give it a magical effect. Bethany hadn't wanted any dark shadows for Giles to lurk in. A five-piece band was coming in the evening. Peg had made the cake and helped Bethany, Alice and Maxine to prepare the buffet meal for sixty guests. It had been a week of hard work but it was worth it. Bethany was determined that nothing was going to mar Maxine and Steve's engagement party.

In the last week she had even managed to push aside her sadness and pain that Mark had not contacted her. She had been so sure that the old magnetism of attraction was as strong as ever between them. Had it been wishful thinking?

'Beth, I can't get the cream to whip properly for the cakes,' Maxine shouted up the stairs.

The use of her name by her daughter still had the power to chisel into her heart. For some weeks Maxine had stopped calling either Alice or herself anything. Alice had told Bethany that it would take time to change the habit of a lifetime. It couldn't be easy for her to adjust. Bethany understood that, but it didn't make it easier. For sixteen years she had been denied the title Mother from her daughter's lips. It was hard to be patient when it meant so much – to prove that Maxine had come to terms with the circumstances of her birth.

Bethany hurried down the stairs to tend to the whipping of the cream, determined to focus on everything which had to be ready by the time guests arrived – which included keeping Tim out of mischief. He was excited at the prospect of a party and wanted to help. Already he had dropped a plate of prawn vol-au-vents which had been pounced on and devoured by the dogs.

Keeping Tim occupied proved the hardest task of all. He was into everything, becoming more excited as the day progressed, and the women were trying to dress before the guests arrived. They had got him changed first and he had run off into the garden where Steve had found him rolling about on the grass playing with Artemis. His clean shirt and shorts were covered in grass stains.

'Come on, young man,' Steve said, lifting him over his shoulder. 'Let's check that the animals are safe in their pens. We don't want the geese getting out and giving Aunt Peg a peck on the leg, do we?'

Tim giggled and squirmed out of his hold to run off to round up the fowls. They then discovered that the corner of the guinea pig run had been damaged and four of them had got out. Only three could be found.

'Got to find Treacle,' Tim said pushing through the shrubs. 'She's gonna have her babies soon.'

'She'll be all right,' Steve said. 'She's probably found a nice snug bed for the night. The guests will be arriving in a minute and you've got to get changed again.'

Tim looked troubled. 'Need to find Treacle.'

'She'll be all right,' Steve insisted as he guided the boy back to the house.

The boy kept pulling away to hunt under a bush unconvinced that the guinea pig would be safe. He protested when Alice took him upstairs to change his shirt and shorts, complaining that Treacle was lost.

'I hope Tim's not going to be difficult,' Alice groaned. 'You know what he's like when he gets a thing fixed in his head. Perhaps I should have asked one of the mothers from the support group to have him this evening.'

Bethany reassured her mother. 'It's not good for Tim to be excluded from family celebrations. There will be so much going on once the guests arrive, he'll forget about looking for Treacle. I'll keep an eye on him.'

For the first hour when the guests began arriving Bethany was running all over the garden as Tim persisted in looking for the guinea pig. She tried to distract him by giving him a plate of sandwiches to hand round to the guests, something he usually liked doing. After a few minutes the plate was found abandoned on a chair in the marquee and she caught sight of Tim heading for the paddock. She ran after him.

'I've told you not to go wandering off.' She tried to stop her frustration from showing, but at times like this it was difficult. 'Don't you want to join in the party?'

Tim shook his head. 'Too many people. Too noisy.'

The band was playing and the buzz of voices was rising. 'How about going into the dining room where Steve set up your model railway set?'

'You come.'

Bethany sighed; she'd hardly had a chance to mix with the guests. Alice caught her eye and came across. 'I'll sit with him while he plays with the trains. I find so many people tiring.'

Alice did look strained. She had insisted on spending all yesterday in the kitchen helping with the cooking, and since Maxine's abduction her nerves had been bad again.

The doorbell rang as yet more guests arrived. 'I'll get that,' Alice said. 'Get yourself a gin and tonic and join in the dancing. Tim is my responsibility not yours. It will be his bedtime in another hour. And Maxine wants to show you her presents.'

'Thanks, Mum.' The two women exchanged affectionate glances.

Alice regarded Bethany seriously. 'After the excitement

of the engagement has settled down, you and Maxine need to talk. You haven't discussed things, have you?'

'Maxine avoids the subject. I don't think it's so much that I'm her mother. It's Giles. Poor kid. She hates him. That's not easy to come to terms with.'

Armed with a gin and tonic Bethany sauntered into the marquee. The band were playing a slow number and Steve and Maxine were on the dance floor locked in each other's arms. Her throat worked with emotion. They made a striking couple. Maxine looked sensational in a scarlet gown with a close-fitting bodice and full skirt. Her black hair was swept up high in a neat chignon. Her little girl had disappeared replaced by a lovely woman. She no longer had doubts that sixteen was too young for Maxine to commit herself. They did not plan to marry until she was eighteen and the happiness on their faces was from a deep and profound love shared.

She wiped away a tear of pride. 'Please God, let this work out for them. Don't let their lives be blighted by misfortune.'

The words were spoken beneath her breath as she recalled how Mark and she had danced and kissed at Louise and David's engagement. It had been her last night of pure happiness. Louise's and David's deaths had cast a shadow over her life since then.

'Tears? Isn't this supposed to be a joyful occasion?' The male voice made Bethany's heart leap.

'Mark! You came.'

'I stayed away once before and regretted it. I wasn't going to ruin any chance I may have with you again.'

He took her hand to lead her on to the dance floor. He nodded to Maxine. 'She's a lovely girl. You're very close, aren't you?'

'I used to think so. But as sisters. She never suspected

that I was her mother.' She struggled to go on, her voice shaky. 'It's been hard for her. She was hurt by all the secrecy and hasn't yet come to terms with it. Let's hope tonight is the start and she can forgive me and we can rebuild our love and trust.'

'I'd like that as well.' He gazed into her eyes but his expression was guarded.

'It will only work if you can accept Maxine.'

He nodded. There remained a tension in his limbs and face. 'If we hadn't quarrelled the night of Giles's engagement party . . .'

She put a finger to his lips. 'Don't speak of it now. Tonight is too precious. We'll work it out, Mark. No regrets. No remorse. No bitterness or recrimination. If we are to have a future together, it starts now.'

He drew her close and Bethany's arms entwined around his neck, their bodies touching as they swayed together in the slow dance.

'Come outside so that I can kiss you properly,' he said, huskily. 'It's been so long.'

He took her hand and led her through the dancers to the entrance of the marquee and Bethany suppressed a sigh at seeing her mother hurrying towards her.

'Have you seen Tim? The scamp was supposed to be going to the toilet but he must have gone outside. He'll be looking for that wretched rabbit.'

'Guinea pig,' Bethany amended absently. Worry attacked her. It was dark now. Tim could be anywhere. And so could Giles. 'We'll search outside. Get Peg and Frank to help. There's no point in spoiling Steve or Maxine's fun. He'll probably be close by.'

'Why all the concern?' Mark queried. 'Isn't your brother ten?'

'I've had this awful premonition all day that something was going to happen. If Giles is still in the area and intended to do some harm, it would be today. He's more unstable than before the war. I believe the link with an engagement party will draw him. And Tim isn't like most boys. He was born with Down's Syndrome. He's too trusting. He wouldn't recognise danger.'

Giles fretted as he paced the perimeter of the garden waiting for darkness. The fairy lights cast few shadows. He would have to be careful, but he hadn't waited this long to fail. And tonight he wanted blood. They all thought they were so clever. First Bethany, for flouting his orders to hand over his inheritance. Then Maxine. She had escaped his vengeance: escaped his control as he had controlled Louise and had briefly triumphed over Bethany. Some women could only be dominated by man's superior strength. They all needed teaching a lesson.

He scowled at seeing Maxine walking arm in arm with the man who had insinuated his way into these women's lives. They were engaged. Did Maxine think that would free her from him? There were other ways to make them pay.

He had watched as Alice and Bethany fussed over the idiot child. Bethany had even left the guests to ensure that he was kept amused. The boy was their Achilles' heel. To have taken and dominated Maxine tonight would be the ultimate revenge but the boy . . .

His scowl deepened. That halfwit inherited from Harold's wealth, money which was his by right. And how better to get back at those conniving bitches than through him. He licked his lips, savouring the moment of his approaching revenge.

He bided his time. He had timed the two policemen walking on their beat past the house every twenty-five minutes. Just after ten their shifts changed and for the last four nights there had been a gap of forty minutes in the change over. It would be dark by then and the best time to strike, providing his victim played into his hands.

He mastered his impatience and was finally rewarded. There was the boy. And he was alone. One of the animals had gone missing and the boy had been obsessed with looking for it all evening. Giles pulled the dead guinea pig out of his pocket. He laid it in his hand so that it looked as if it was sleeping and crept around the marquee.

His devious mind played through the scenario of another accident. How convenient there was a fishpond near by. A perfect place for a simple-minded boy to have an accident.

He grinned as he warmed to the notion. Drowning was good. It had worked before with Felicity. The boy's death would devastate the women. He'd let them suffer for a few weeks and then he would return. They would learn that he had the ultimate control over their lives – the power of life and death. And he had chosen death.

Their routine would make it easy for him. Most Sundays they went out for the day. That vet chap went with them. He had it coming to him. The vet had interfered and complicated his plans. They would all go together.

Giles sniggered as he visualised the car spinning off the road out of control and into a bank or tree. He'd fix the brakes on a Saturday night and it would be one Sunday trip none of them would return from. Another tragic accident. The pity of it was that he'd have to sacrifice Harold's money for the law would be suspicious. But they would be dead. And he'd be out of the country. Set up by the money he had blackmailed out of Alice, his gambling winnings and the sale of his car.

He wiped a trickle of saliva from his jaw as his excitement and anticipation mounted. He would triumph, that foolish woman's money enabling him to live free. He intended to set himself up in a bar over in Jersey. The Channel Islands were becoming popular as a holiday resort to the British. They were also only a short hop from France should the police track him down. He didn't believe they would. He would leave too many false trails. They hadn't caught him yet, had they? And they'd had a warrant out for his arrest for weeks. It had been a nuisance keeping his hair dyed brown but his natural red was a give-away. His disguise had fooled the police so far.

The last weeks had made him feel invincible. His confidence had grown. He'd got away with so many murders. Providing they looked like accidents, he could do so again.

Before stepping into a pool of light from the trees, he checked the opening of the marquee. No one was looking his way. It was then he saw the tall, dark-haired man greet Bethany.

An ungovernable rage exploded in him. Greenwood! He'd thought he was long out of the picture. What was he doing here? Even from this distance he could see how each of their bodies moved, drawn inexorably closer in the way of lovers. His eyes narrowed. So they'd been reunited. He'd give them a union to remember.

'Are you sure you're not worrying unnecessarily about Tim?' Mark said. 'He won't have gone far and there's sixty-odd guests here. He's bound to be safe.'

Bethany shot him a blistering glare. 'Like I was safe at Giles's engagement? And Maxine at a crowded church fête? I know the evil Giles is capable of. He strikes when he thinks our guard is down.'

Mark's expression became grim at her accusation. It made her realise how fragile the understanding was between them. Was love enough to overcome the problems life had set against them? The thought was fleeting, her concentration and fear returning to Tim as she called his name. The music and loud conversation and laughter from the marquee drowned any sounds within the garden. Giles wouldn't risk being seen. Thankfully the garden was illuminated by the lights.

But that wasn't so. Fear speared her. Why was it so dark around the fishpond? There were several circuits linking the lights together but if a bulb came loose a section could go out. Or if a bulb had been removed . . .

'The fishpond,' she shouted to Mark. 'The lights round it are out.' The memory of Felicity Tranter drowning in the lake when Giles was staying with them pole-axed her. She had thought for a time that Giles was keen on Felicity . . . but Giles swore he had tried to save her. Or had he?

She ran shouting Tim's name. The darkness around the fishpond was total.

Giles cursed as he heard Bethany's shout. She was close. But was she alone? The boy was stirring beneath his hands as he pushed his head beneath the pond water. The coldness of the water must have revived him. Frustration ground through him. 'Die,' he grunted as he pushed down harder.

Still the boy struggled and somehow his grip on his head slipped and the body bobbed out of reach. He swore profanely. He hadn't expected a lad to put up so much of a fight. Or not fall easily for his bait with the guinea pig. He'd been cautious.

'Let Treacle go,' the kid had ordered.

Giles had beckoned to the boy. 'He needs you to take him. He's sleeping. Curled up under a bush he was.'

He held out the guinea pig so that his hand was over the pond water. Then he let the creature fall.

Tim dived forward. 'Treacle die in there.'

He'd been faster than Giles expected. The boy had jumped into the water up to his thighs and scooped the guinea pig out. His moon-shaped face creased with pain. 'Treacle dead.'

The boy leapt out of the pool and shouted, 'Mum, Treacle dead!'

Giles lunged at him, catching his arm and clamping his hand over his mouth to muffle his cries. The little bleeder wriggled and squirmed, his kicking feet striking Giles's ankle. He slammed his fist into the side of the boy's head and he went limp.

He dropped him in the pond and pushed his head under the water. It should have been over in seconds. Instead the boy had clung tenaciously to life. That was when he heard Bethany call out.

Now Giles saw two figures outlined against the illuminated marquee. He remained stooped as he edged away from the pool. No time to check that the boy was dead. He couldn't hear him moving. He had to save himself. He backed into the shadows. The stillness of the pool must mean the boy was dead. And no one had seen him here. He slunk away as silent as the predator he'd become.

Bethany screamed. She could just discern a darker shade disappearing into the shrubs. 'Someone get the police! Help! Come quickly!'

'There's something in the pool,' Mark declared and waded in. 'It's your brother!' He dragged out Tim's inert form and laid him on the flagstones.

'What's happened?' Steve demanded. 'I heard Bethany's scream as I was heading into the house.'

Bethany pointed to the shrubs, her voice high with fear. 'Search over there. I saw someone. We found Tim in the pool. He's unconscious.'

Steve ran off. Bethany knelt on the ground beside Mark who had turned Tim on his front and was pumping his shoulders and thumping his back. There was a splutter. Tim coughed and heaved, water pouring from his mouth.

'He's going to be all right,' Mark said, taking off his jacket to wrap the boy in. 'Stay with him. I'm going after the intruder.'

There was a crashing noise, grunts, swearing and the unmistakable thud of flesh being pummelled. Giles's voice rose up loud and abusive. It was abruptly cut off. The scuffling continued while Bethany held her young brother close, his sobs shaking his frail figure.

'Come on, Tim, it's all right now. You're safe. The nasty man can't hurt you. Let's get you into a hot bath.' She led him back to the house.

Other guests were gathering, drawn by the shouts. Alice burst into hysterical cries at seeing Tim. 'Timmy! What happened?'

'He's fine, Mum,' Bethany assured.

'Man nasty.' Tim sobbed. 'Treacle dead.'

Steve and Mark reappeared hauling a struggling and swearing Giles between them. All three had battered faces from the fight. 'Get the police,' Steve ordered. 'This bastard is going behind bars for a long time.'

Chapter Thirty

'Thank God that's over.' Bethany shut the front door on the arresting officers who had taken the handcuffed Giles away.

Mark put his arm around Bethany's shoulders. 'Hanging's too good for him. But at least if he spends the rest of his life behind bars your family will be safe.'

'If there is any justice he will be hanged,' Bethany fumed. 'He's inhuman. A monster. I wouldn't be surprised if he was responsible for David Lister's shooting. He could have hidden and shot him during the duck shoot. And what about Louise? I never really believed she would have hanged herself. He could have made her death look like suicide.'

Mark spoke urgently calming her. 'The police will look into all those deaths again.'

Alice came down the stairs with Dr Jones who had been called out on Mark's advice to give Tim some inoculations against tetanus and hepatitis after swallowing so much pond water. 'The lad is fine. Your quick thinking saved him, Dr Greenwood.'

'I'll go and check if any guests remain,' Steve said wearily, 'I asked them to stay but most thought it was best if everyone left.' When he went in to the garden Maxine hung back.

'I'm sorry your party was ruined,' Bethany said. 'We'll have a special meal out somewhere to make up for it.'

Maxine smiled bleakly. 'That would be nice. Tim is all right, that's what matters.' She sighed and then burst into tears. 'That bastard is my father. How can I live with that? I hate him. I hate being part of him. What if a child of mine turns out so evil? I'm tainted with a rapist and murderer's blood.'

'Don't torture yourself.' Bethany embraced her daughter, sensing Maxine's anguish grinding like millstones, crushing and destroying. 'You're nothing like him. Do you think I haven't searched for signs over the years? You are good and sweet.'

Alice said firmly, 'Maxine, you are all your mother's daughter. That is what is important. You're a Masterton. You don't even have his name. Your birth certificate says Masterton. You were only known as Warden to protect you at school. You have Bethany's sweetness. And her strength.'

Maxine was pale and her eyes mirrored disgust and horror. 'I can't forget his evil.'

'Let's find Steve,' Bethany suggested. She prayed that in time Maxine would come to terms with accepting that a murderer was her father. Otherwise Giles's evil would blight her life.

Steve took one look at Maxine and spoke to the pianist who was packing away his music. The guests had all left and the band were loading their instruments in their van. The pianist sat down and began to play 'Moonlight Serenade'. Steve took Maxine into his arms, his voice firm. 'I don't want to see tears tonight. That man will not ruin our engagement. We've a wonderful future ahead of us.'

Maxine swayed against him, holding him tight as he

continued, 'Tim is safe and the danger to your family is over. This is our special night. All that matters to me is that I have a beautiful and special woman in my arms who will one day be my wife. This evening will not end until I see you smiling and laughing.'

He whirled her into the middle of the marquee, holding her close as they danced. Maxine clearly made an effort to relax but her face remained grave.

Alice sighed. 'Poor child. But Steve will bring the happiness back into her eyes. He's a good man.' She began to collect up the plates and glasses.

When Bethany began to help Alice waved her away. 'What are you thinking of, Bethany? You should be dancing with Mark. A fine reunion this has been for you two. I'm doing this to keep my mind occupied. Go to Mark. He's the one who needs you.'

After the chaotic events of the evening, Bethany wondered whether Mark would think himself well shot of her troublesome family. He was smiling as she approached him and put his arms around her and led her into the slow dance. 'Steve isn't alone in dancing with a beautiful and special woman. I'm also honoured.'

'Flatterer,' Bethany said with a smile. 'I hope Maxine will be all right. Why did Giles have to ruin tonight for her?'

He shook his head and a lock of dark hair flopped attractively over his brow. 'Giles takes pleasure in destroying what he can't manipulate. Let's forget him. He's brought enough suffering into our lives. And it's been too long since I held you. I'd like to start over again, Bethany. Is there a chance for me?'

'I never stopped loving you, Mark. But the man I fell in love with must have changed over the years. The ideals I built up were coloured by youthful romanticism. It will be exciting getting to know you again. But can you truly accept Maxine . . .? That is what is most important.'

'She's a lovely girl. A daughter any man would be proud of.'

'I've prayed so often that she could have been yours.'

He held her tightly and they danced in silence. This was the moment she had waited for so many years to come true. Giles was banished from her mind. There was only Mark and the pressure of his arms around her. His face filled her vision. The beloved face of her dreams. Her heart beat a wild tattoo. No other man had ever had this power over her.

The sultry slow rhythm of the music throbbed through her veins as their bodies swayed in unison and perfect harmony. The pianist was happy to keep playing and when Steve came over to ask Bethany to dance, she was pleased that Mark held out his hand to Maxine. A tight ball of emotion clogged Bethany's throat as she watched them. Their dark heads were almost on a level as they danced. Mark was obviously taking pains to put her at ease. As Bethany watched them Maxine smiled. Alice had come back into the marquee to collect some more plates and the pile she was carrying clattered to the floor.

Anxious that something was wrong, Bethany glanced at her mother who was staring at Maxine and Mark, her eyes wide with astonishment. Alice turned to her with an incredulous expression on her face. 'Whatever made you think that Giles was Maxine's father?' Her voice rose above the music. 'With her hair up like that, can't you see her likeness to Mark?'

Mark stopped dancing and Bethany stared at the couple. She couldn't see it. She was too used to seeing her own mirror image in her daughter's face. Then Mark and Maxine looked at each other. Within both faces there was the blossoming of hope as they warily studied each other. The transformation of that look – the same tilt of the head and expression was astonishing. Maxine with her hair up clearly had the lean contours of Mark's angular cheek-bones. In that instant, with the same expression of hope in their eyes, the likeness was unmistakable.

Could it be true?

'Is it possible?' Mark and Maxine spoke together.

Bethany shook her head in puzzlement. 'I was always convinced when I missed my period that Giles was the father. Mark and I had always been so careful.'

She broke off. It was difficult to talk of so intimate a subject in front of her mother, daughter and Steve, but it was too important to be avoided. She forced herself to go on. 'The last time we were together, I was in a terrible emotional state, I was panicking that I was pregnant by Giles and knew that I wouldn't see Mark for months when he left for Africa. But how could I tell him? I was too ashamed. All I knew was that I loved Mark so much. I wanted to blot the horror of Giles's attack from my mind when we made love that night.' She broke off and her voice was ragged when she continued, 'A month later Dr Jones confirmed my pregnancy. I believed the father was Giles. The dates I was given confirmed it.'

'I told you not to believe the worst,' Alice interrupted. 'But things did point to Giles when you missed your period. Perhaps after the shock of Giles's attack your body reacted in that way. I missed a period when your father died and desperately hoped I was pregnant. It was just the shock.'

Wonderment surged through Bethany. This was her

wildest dream come true. 'When Maxine was two weeks late being born I began to hope Mark was the father, but the doctors were insistent that most first babies are late.'

'I never questioned it either,' Alice added. 'Everything pointed to Giles.'

'A blood test will give us the answer,' Mark declared. 'Though for myself I couldn't think of anything more wonderful than discovering that Maxine is my daughter.'

Maxine's eyes shone as she stared at Mark. 'This is the best engagement present I could wish for. Oh please, let it be true!'

Steve grinned. 'You can go ahead with the blood tests, but my money's on Mark. The more I look at you the more I can see the likeness. Though I suppose the moment you put your hair down you will be a replica of your mother again.'

Maxine was transformed, her face radiant with hope. She gave a sob and ran into Bethany's arms. 'Oh, Mum, Mum. I've been so awful to you since Giles—'

The pain was too raw for her to go on, but Bethany nodded in understanding. Maxine kissed her cheek. 'I love you, Mum. It sounds funny calling someone I regarded as my best friend that. But I'm going to enjoy getting used to it.'

Bethany's tears of joy mingled with those of her daughter as she said, 'I am so proud of you, so glad that the secrecy has ended.'

They broke apart with a laugh and Maxine blushed with shyness as she looked at Mark.

'This has been some night,' Mark said slowly. 'I think we are all overwhelmed. I know for one that I feel particularly favoured.' He stooped to kiss Maxine lightly on the cheek. 'Your mother has raised a beautiful and fine woman.' He put her hand into Steve's. 'Both of you be happy together. Count your blessings, they far outweigh the troubles Giles tried to inflict on you.'

He nodded to the pianist to continue playing and taking Bethany into his arms whirled her round and round the floor. Their bodies swayed in perfect unison, their gazes fused: wonder and adoration warmed their eyes.

'How can you forgive me?' he began. 'I should never . . .'

'No regrets, Mark. We both did what we had to do.'

'Will you give me a second chance? From the moment I saw you on the River Boat I began to fall in love with you all over again. I don't think I ever stopped loving you.'

She smiled. 'We aren't the same people we were seventeen years ago. Learning about and rediscovering each other could take a lifetime. And you have David to consider. How will your son accept the news he has a grown-up sister?'

'You will charm him and so will Maxine. The future is before us and together we can overcome anything.'

'The future is what we make of it – together.'

The answering promise in his eyes was of an abiding love, unquenchable and unconquerable, the greatest of all blessings.

Living a Lie

Josephine Cox

Kitty sat tightly huddled on the stairs, head bent and her heart breaking. The row brought back too many memories. Now her mother was gone and nobody wanted her. Not for the first time since that awful day she wished she had died with her mother.

In 1975 Lucinda Marsh throws herself in front of a speeding train leaving her twelve-year-old daughter, Kitty, alone, confused and abandoned – save for a violent father, a selfish aunt and her childhood sweetheart, Harry Jenkins.

When she is sent to an orphanage after the death of her father, Kitty meets Georgie, a lively cockney girl who, through the following difficult years, becomes her loyal friend. Convinced that her feelings for Harry will ruin the brilliant future that lies ahead of him, Kitty decides to turn her back on his love. Together with Georgie, she strives to find fulfilment in other places and other relationships, but when fate throws her back together with Harry, she begins to wonder if true love can ever die . . .

'Pulls at the heartstrings' *Today*

'Hailed quite rightly as a gifted writer in the traditions of Catherine Cookson' *Manchester Evening News*

'Driven and passionate, she stirs a pot spiced with incest, wife beating . . . and murder' *The Sunday Times*

'A born storyteller' *Bedfordshire Times*

0 7472 4832 X

HEADLINE

A Dark Light Shining

Wendy Robertson

'An intense and moving story set against the bitter squalor of the hunger-ridden thirties' *Today*

'A rich fruit cake of well-drawn characters'
Northern Echo

County Durham's New Morven, blighted by pit closures, is not a place where anyone in their right mind would come to live. And many in New Morven would say the strange pair who have just moved into the big house at the end of Mainstreet *are* out of their minds. But from the moment grocer's daughter Finnoula Montague meets eccentric Jenefer Loumis and her oddly childlike husband, she realises that up to now her life has been only half lived.

Jenefer seems to understand the young girl in a way Finn's tyrannical, bed-bound mother has never done. And when Finn meets unemployed miner Michael O'Toole, who opens her eyes to the shocking poverty – and intoxicating emotional riches – on her own doorstep, it is Jenefer who understands, almost better than Finn herself, what the young girl is experiencing. But when Finn is the victim of a vicious attack and Michael is thrown into prison, even Jenefer cannot arrest Finn's decline into a shadow of the vibrant girl she once was. But then Jenefer has a plan – to transport Finn to the world of gloss and glitter Jenefer herself once knew, a world that returns Finn to New Morven a very different young woman . . .

0 7472 4799 4

HEADLINE